CW00631241

To my parents, William and Margaret Kane Woodburn

Ploegsteert, the Western Front, February 1916

The colonel sat alone in his forward command post, known as Laurence Farm, writing at his desk. A whirlwind of positive change had recently hit the battalion. Change to routines, to patrol patterns, food rations, leave. Change to morale. *All at the instigation of the new commanding officer.*

It had been universally welcomed. The men adored him. The officers were at once baffled, bemused and each to a man won over. It was a happy battalion.

In his haste to improve his new interest the colonel had not completely removed from his thought processes those who waited for him back home. He ensured each night to find time to write to his wife.

There was a knock on the door. The adjutant, Lieutenant McDavid entered and tipped his hat.

'Sir, sorry to disturb you but we have a little problem, and I mean "little".' *The colonel laid down his pen, pushed his chair back and stood up.*

'And what is the nature of this conundrum, Lieutenant?'

'He is outside, sir.'

'Then allow this mystery to advance at the double, McDavid.'

The lieutenant went to the door, opened it and signalled; nothing happened for a few seconds, then, to the well-disguised amusement of the colonel of the battalion, a boy in the uniform of the Royal Scots Fusiliers entered the room and presented himself to Winston Churchill.

The youth, his eyes widened in increasing terror, took a step forward but did not salute; his arms remained at his side. He appeared to sway slightly and his legs shook despite his efforts to remain still, as his fingers fastened tighter to the seams of his trousers.

'Who is this young lowland warrior, Mr McDavid?' the colonel enquired.

'This, sir, is our problem: Private James Melville of Edinburgh.'

The colonel settled back in his chair. 'A fine city. But what of its young citizen standing before me? Why does he now appear in such exalted presence?'

The young soldier, unable to comprehend in his misery the by-play of the two officers, was so overwrought that the words spoken barely registered in his addled mind. He heard his name and his home town but their import failed to connect, the irony passing him completely.

'Private Melville was found wandering miles behind our lines by the Military Police. He has no leave warrant and when picked up he told the MP that he had to return home as he had received a letter informing him that his widowed mother had been killed in an accident, leaving his three young sisters alone without a guardian.'

McDavid was twenty years old and a kind young man, highly thought of within the battalion, despite the fact that when rattled he was prone to emitting awesome profanity. He was unsure how his new colonel would react to the matter and believed laying it on a bit thick may aid the boy's cause.

'Oh, and Colonel, there is one more detail,' he added, carefully. 'It transpires that Mr Melville has been less than truthful in regards to his date of birth. Young Montrose here is in fact fifteen, not nineteen years of age.'

The colonel leaned forward, his hands clasped and resting on the desk. 'Lieutenant McDavid, I believe the battalion football team requires a new ball. It appears the last one was kicked a little too far into the opposition half and was not returned. I therefore command you to leave here immediately, remove yourself to battalion office and order another one of these mighty instruments of war. But leave our young friend with me as I investigate further.'

'Of course, Colonel, but can I be sure of your safety left alone with such a felon?'

'Yes, I believe I am equal to the task of attending to him, even if I am not as young and vigorous as this accomplished liar and absconder.'

McDavid saluted and left, smiling at the last comment. He now felt sure there would be an interesting conversation to follow, adding to the likelihood of a satisfactory outcome to this particular challenge in the new colonel's tenure.

The boy had not moved. Colonel Churchill rose from his desk and walked round to stand before the young soldier and stare intently at him.

'Now then, Private James Melville, what do you have to say for yourself? Absconding without informing your platoon commander? That is not the way to proceed; are you aware of the penalties for such behaviour? What are we to do with you?'

Winston was about to turn and walk back to his chair when, from the corner of his eye, he caught sight of the boy beginning to sway more markedly; he lifted one hand from the seam of his trouser and then fell forward, the other arm still at his side. Winston instantly reached around and grabbed the scruff of his collar, jerking the now unconscious youth back just enough to prevent his head clattering off the edge of the desk.

The colonel eased James, who had fainted, down on to the floor.

Winston lifted from a peg his trench jacket, folded it and slipped it under the inert young soldier's head. The boy began to stir; his eyes opened and looked up at the concerned face of his colonel.

'Do not speak, James, lie back and we will get you up on your feet presently.'

The boy lay there, staring up at the ceiling of the command post. He felt thirsty but was too parched and frightened still to speak. He had no understanding of why he suddenly found himself on the floor, having never fainted before in his life. The thoughts running through his head were concentrated now on the man looking down at him and his kind words.

'You are of no use to your sisters if you fall and bang your head, are you? Can you get up?'

James shifted and raised himself stiffly upwards but then, feeling dizzy, eased himself back down. His head felt thick with the stirrings of a headache and his ears were ringing as he settled back onto the rolled-up trench coat.

'No, it is better we get you to a nice comfortable bunk.' Winston lifted the boy and turned to a dark recess in the command post and his made-up bed. He lay James down and grabbed the folded trench coat, spreading it evenly over him.

He hunkered down on his knees. 'Now, as colonel of this battalion, I order you to have a sleep. I also order you not to have any more bad thoughts or dreams. When you wake up I am sure we will sort this little matter out to everyone's satisfaction.'

Introduction – July 1982

Winston and *me*?

We go way back; for I knew him nearly fifty years and can tell tales about him that few men can.

You'll no doubt be thinking, what can this eighty-year-old codger tell us that's not been written elsewhere? James Melville? Never heard of him. He wasn't the butler, the gardener, the secretary, the valet, even the bodyguard.

So, just *who* is this that claims to know what no one else does about Winston Leonard Spencer Churchill?

Along with the rest of the country I found myself engrossed by the recent war in the South Atlantic. Watching the conflict reach its conclusion on television with the lads returning in the aircraft carrier HMS *Hermes* from the Falkland Islands, I noted the commentator announce with great solemnity that our losses for the campaign were around two hundred and fifty dead.

In *my* day we would lose that many in a morning and the rest of us just had to get on with it. But when I look at the faces of those marines and paratroopers, they haven't changed much. Tommy Atkins, Jock, Taff and Paddy still look the same as in my time. They fight and die the same, too.

Another thing I heard as I watched the homecoming was some reporter inferring that Maggie Thatcher was now comparable to Churchill. What a load of rubbish. Alright, as far as I was concerned we were correct to sail down there and take the islands back. Those Argentines were bullies and got what for. It should never have been a difficult decision to make for any British prime minister, but to liken that hatchet-faced old bag to Winston is absolute rot.

So watching all of that started me thinking. My recollections have also been triggered by my daughters starting to sniff around the old fossil that is me, looking for answers. I caught one of them rifling through the drawer where I keep some old papers just the other day. She said she remembered there was a photograph of me with Winston Churchill and wanted to find it.

Maybe they're finally showing interest because they are all getting on themselves, and that's why my girls are paying long overdue, if not too unwelcome, attention to the Old Man. But it's probably *because* I'm such an old man that they want belated closure, now that I'm knocking on God's waiting room door. They are worried about all the secrets dying with me. I don't blame them, of course. It is natural. They should know.

Only, they have waited almost too long because I am nearly past the point of being able to recall it.

Over the years I had mentioned on occasion my wartime service but, having three daughters, if ever I happened to speak of those times I would see the familiar, far-away look of complete indifference in their eyes and turn to another subject.

They managed to lose my medals too. They took them out to play with and they were never seen again. I only found out about this long after it happened because I never bothered about them much and shoved them in a box that lay forgotten. I had to order new ones to replace them because I thought that maybe a grandchild might be interested to see them one day, even if my own were not.

They *are* right about one thing. The secrets do die with us. My mother and father revealed very little about themselves and that reticence to talk meant I never knew my parents at all. They existed in hard times; impervious to any form of introspection other than to brood their days away in drink. Consequently their own children were a burden and spent their young lives paying their parents back. It left me bewildered and angry. Sad, too. But they remain with me always. Those unanswered questions.

I think it's now time to tell it all. Enough years have passed, everyone concerned is just about dead and the departed don't care what is said of them.

I was able to get this old typewriter out of the loft by tricking one of the grandchildren, as I'm no longer able to climb a ladder. Before age and arthritis – which has destroyed the right side of my body – seizes me up completely, I'm going to put it all down.

For *them*; because they deserve it.

For you, too.

Chapter One

I lied about my age in order to enlist. At fifteen, which is how old I was at the time, I was shorter than both my twin brothers, who were a year younger, a particular problem in itself; and looked nearer to twelve years old than to my actual age. We were never a particularly tall lot, the Melvilles. Not midgets, but not giants either, and with my freckles you'll be wondering how any self-respecting recruiting sergeant and examining doctor could allow someone like me to sign his name along the dotted line.

The truth was, the bugger was drunk, I bunged him a ten-shilling note and he had to get his quota filled. But I had not wanted to join the local regiment, the Royal Scots, the reason being that I had five cousins serving within their ranks and if any one of them spotted me I would have had to sling my hook sharpish back to Wardlaw Place, where I lived in Edinburgh. The recruiting sergeant knew that for ten bob he could risk an oversight, as he would expect me to be collared eventually and would still get his fee for signing me, on top of his wee bonus.

I didn't get collared because no one seemed to care. They never asked you to provide any form of identification either. You'll think that strange, but things were different back in 1915. 'Boy' soldiers served throughout the army; there were thousands who slipped under the legal age wire so one more was not going to bother anyone. They were starting to get a lot less fussy also as overall volunteer numbers were dropping off drastically compared to the year before.

The Conscription Act did not come into effect until January 1916, although the groundwork for that was being laid months earlier with the National Register the year before. Anything went, up till then, until things began to be done in a more scientific manner, making it all the more difficult for anyone to lie about things like their date of birth.

The Royal Scots Fusiliers, the regiment I had set my sights on joining, were short on recruits like everyone else, having recently been mauled at Gallipoli, Loos and then in actions around Ypres. They were a South West Scotland regiment so I believed that I would be safe from anyone recognising me. Everyone in Edinburgh wanted the Royal Scots, but I had seen a newspaper article wrapped round a bag of chips that I had for my dinner which said the Fusiliers had spaces for many fine lads, and I would keep that in mind when I went to the recruiting office. The names were similar, I liked the look of their cap badge with the bomb and smoke design, and the white hackle always looked so stylish.

The fact that their barracks was across the country in Ayr also appealed as an additional safeguard from possible detection; I would be able to see another part of the country and get paid for it too. The Royal Scots, the fashionable Edinburgh Regiment strongly associated with Heart of Midlothian Football Club (most of its first team squad joined up, and a few died along the way), were definitely out; though deep down I had wanted to join them.

It was not patriotism and serving the King that drew me to enlist in the army. The truth was a little more prosaic: it was out of necessity. Our father was a violent drunk and we had a poor mother who was becoming more and more unreliable through her own intemperance. Along with three wee sisters and two younger brothers, we lived in a room and kitchen in a tenement in Wardlaw Place in Gorgie. There was no bath, just a sink to wash in and a small box room for all eight people.

The warren of side streets running off the main thoroughfare, of which Wardlaw Place was one, meant the area of the city we lived in was village-like but also claustrophobic and intrusive. Tiny spaces occupied by large families meant that keeping your business to yourself was seen as an eccentricity rather than a virtue. But there was the upside of Tynecastle Park, home of my beloved Heart of Midlothian Football Club, being less than five minutes' walk from my door, as well as numerous small shops abounding alongside pubs and barbers, the local school, library and Dalry baths. Nearby Saughton Park provided greenery and a place to stroll and picnic on a Sunday.

Gorgie Road, being one of the major routes leading from the west into the centre of the capital, teemed with industry. Coal, milk and other goods were delivered daily through the cobbled streets by horse and cart. The odd motor vehicle passing through added to the industrial emissions that gave Edinburgh its famous moniker *Auld Reekie;* its begrimed buildings testimony to the effects of discharge from rubber mills and printing works. Most potent of all, the local breweries in nearby Fountainbridge belched fumes from their smokestacks, leaving visible results on soot-stained walls, creating a cloying but distinctly yeasty aroma, particularly in the early evenings, which always reminded me of the smell of burnt bacon.

It was at the poorer end of the city; nevertheless my mum worked all hours to keep us decent and the Melville kids were known as the best-dressed family in Gorgie Road. My dad, a fitter, worked in a factory building heavy equipment for the paper-manufacturing industry in Sciennes. He was not a bad man, but a serious accident at work left him a changed individual, and he turned in his pain to the dubious consolation of alcohol. Drink transformed him completely from an easy-going, loving family man into a violent lout. I remember him once coming home late from the pub and chasing us round the house with an iron poker in his drink-induced rage. My poor mum was cowering in the bedroom with the rest of the kids whilst my brothers and I tried to subdue the swine.

One day a man from the Corporation came and took the twins, Thomas and Arthur, away. It was years later before I saw them again, as they were fed into the adoption system.

There was not much time to get over this before our family was hit by another blow. Not long after the war began, my dad was found dead in the street one Sunday morning. He had fallen down, drunk from the pub, late the night before, smacked his head on the pavement and bled to death. I was now to all intents the head of the family, with all that entailed, and couldn't allow myself the luxury of grieving over these tragedies too much because Mum immediately started drinking more and someone had to look after the girls.

That's how it was back then. I was fifteen years old and had too much to worry about with the present to be mindful of the past. I mourned my poor father and lost brothers in my own way, in the solitude of my own thoughts; but found within myself the strength not to *brood*.

As the months passed Mum's behaviour grew steadily worse. I was earning a few pence on the carts delivering milk for St Cuthbert's, and handed it all over to her, but I knew I could earn more in the army. I could send it all back home, plus the separation allowance, and she would save on not having me around to eat grub that could be given to the girls. I would be fed in the army, three square without fail, clothed, and I did not smoke or drink. What did I need money for?

My plan envisioned the war lasting only a few more months; then I would be back, because I felt a little guilty about leaving Mum with the three little ones. I eased my conscience somewhat by convincing myself that my departure would act as a spur to my mother to sort herself out and get off the drink.

They say behind every great fortune there is a crime. In my case, I'm still waiting for that fortune but my big start in life did involve theft and the thought of it still haunts me to this and I expect my dying day.

I decided to avoid the main recruitment office in Castle Street for fear of being recognised (I had visions of my mum or someone else walking past and spotting me), and aimed for the smaller office that covered Leith at McDonald Road. I knew that McHenry, the recruiting sergeant in that office, liked a drink. It's a fair walk from Gorgie to McDonald Road, and of course I could not afford the cable car, but I walked there one day nonetheless and watched the goings on. I hung around till lunch-time, when McHenry came out and headed over to the local boozer.

Unfortunately the bugger made for Leith Walk and went into the Volunteer. My dad warned me about Leith pubs so I was a bit jumpy, but kept to the open pavements rather than chance hiding in a side street and risking a stove-in heid from a Leith Ned. I did this for three days and on each occasion McHenry came out stoating drunk. I remember thinking: *what a disgrace to the King's uniform.*

I knew that I would have to try and tempt McHenry into overlooking the minor but unavoidable fact that I was only fifteen years of age, and as drink seemed to be his thing then the demon itself would have to be used in some way. But drink costs money. Where was I going to find enough to buy for a Jakey like him?

I still find it difficult to recount what follows. You may think that strange when you consider what I would later see and do in France and Belgium, but what happened next was the most shameful thing I have ever done, and it pains me every time I think of it. I am an old man now and I know I did it for the best, and I was just a poor wee lad who only had thoughts for his mum and sisters, but that does not remove the hurt.

My mum worked every hour, as I said, but on one Sunday night a month she allowed herself a wee night out with her pals from the printers (she also worked nights as a cleaner in the Royal Infirmary, bless her soul). Mum and her workmates would go to the Station Tavern, have a drink and play housey-housey. She always saved a few pence for this and I never grudged her for it. I stayed in and looked after the girls and would usually get a book from the Gorgie library. I didn't mind; they were good lassies and no real bother.

She returned home absolutely steaming drunk. I had to half-carry her to bed and move the girls along to give them all room. I would lie on the living room floor with my coat over me. She had been really happy in her cups, telling us she had won at the housey-housey and we were all going to have a nice tea the following Saturday to celebrate.

This got me thinking. As soon as she was in bed I took her purse out of her bag. In it there was some change and a ten-shilling note which would have been her winnings at the housey-housey. I took it out and pocketed it. I felt so bad I cried to myself in shame and never slept much, but I was determined to carry out my plan.

Next morning she got up and went to get ready for work. I heard muttering from the bedroom and asked what was wrong. She said that she had left the pub with ten shillings of housey-housey winnings in her purse and it was gone. I said maybe she dropped it in the street. She came into the living room and started crying, saying she was nothing but a drunken, useless cow that was a disgrace and not fit to look after children. She had won enough money to buy a lovely dinner for us all, and had lost it because she was too soused to know what she was doing.

I stood and listened, hiding my shame. I said, *don't worry, Mum, we'll manage,* and told her I would do extra on the carts that week to earn more money. She grabbed and held me and I smelt the drink on her. My mum was a nice person and an attractive woman. Why life dealt her the cards it did I just don't know. She was well-spoken and tried to ensure we did not speak like Edinburgh louts. She should have married someone well-off who would have taken care of her. But at that moment all I wanted to do was run away.

Wasting no time I set off for the recruiting office. I went in, steeled myself and walked up to McHenry's desk.

'Yes, young man?' he asked, whilst pretending to write something.

'I want to join up, sir. I want to join the Royal Scots Fusiliers.'

'And how old are you?'

'Well, sir, the thing is I'm eighteen, but I'm really keen and don't mind the fact that I still have a few months to go till I'm nineteen. It means I can spend more time on... manoeuvres.' I had heard this word bandied around in the papers and it had impressed me. I was also being cunning with regard to my age. No way did I look nineteen.

McHenry now seemed interested. He laced his chubby fingers against his ample gut and leant back in his seat.

'Manoeuvres, eh? There are plenty of them in the army, to be sure, but I really think you should *manoeuvre* yourself out of this office until you're nineteen years of age, then come back and see me.'

I knew what he meant alright. 'Oh well, I thought I'd try. Thanks for your time.'

I left and hung around the Volunteer. I met him there later, he got reeking and we returned together to the office. To make certain my chosen regiment was the Royal Scots Fusiliers I watched him carefully as he scratched it down, to ensure he did not make an error in his state of near-inebriation. I then passed him the ten-bob note. McHenry took it, left the office and returned with the doctor, who 'examined' me. He told me to remove my shirt, stuck a stethoscope on my chest and declared me 'passed fit', and off I went to sign the attestation form to certify that I was nineteen years of age. The fact that I was under the regulation height of five feet three inches was conveniently overlooked.

They probably split the ten bob between them, and my only regret afterwards was how easy it all had been and that it might not have been necessary to grease their palms. But I'll never know. You may be shocked at this, but it was not unusual for the time and there were far worse cases than mine. There were boys of thirteen and fourteen who got through, and I can only imagine what kind of medical examination they received.

My poor mum took the news badly. She was ready to march up to the recruiting office with me, but I told her there was nothing to worry about. I would be able to send her money to look after the girls, and would be fine. At one point, God forgive me, I said I'd had enough of her drinking and that I would report her to the Corporation and they would take the girls away. I also told her I would do it again if she stopped me this time. I then burst into tears and she hugged me.

But she accepted in the end. It was just one more blow. First the twins going, then Dad dying and now this. She must have felt powerless. Resigned, she begged me to be careful and always do what I was told by the officers and to write to her every week.

She was an alcoholic; I know that now, poor soul. She didn't have the strength to stop me.

Chapter Two

I reported for basic training at Ayr Barracks, the first time in my life I had left the city of Edinburgh's boundaries, and got through that part of my military career easily enough – mainly because I was treated like a mascot. I was so small, everyone felt sorry for me. One officer got a bit nosy and asked about my age, but nothing came of it. The corporals were fine to me, though they were severe on others. I discovered I was good at boot polishing ('bulling, as it is known) and ironing. I'd had plenty of practice doing that for my brothers and sisters, and started making a few pence out of it. The blokes who were useless paid me to do their own kit.

The corporals, who were mainly old blokes recalled to the colours, knew of these scams and laid off a bit at inspections as they wanted an easy life. I was able to send the money to Mum, but had a bit spare for myself, and bought chocolate and books. My only complaint was that the food was pretty basic – but it was regular, unlike at home.

Life in the army so far had not been too bad. We were sent down to Fort Matilda near Greenock for some training, which broke up the routine, and the lads helped me with my kit on manoeuvres as I found it a struggle lumping it, being small. I made two good pals, Davie Thom and Jock Paterson, who were hopeless at their kit but were the two hardest bastards in my billet. I helped them out and they me, and we three became close buddies. I liked musketry and always looked forward to going to the ranges. I enjoyed cleaning my rifle and got good marks all round from my corporal, even though he was a Hibs supporter. No one is perfect, anyway – but imagine supporting that shower.

I had leave at Christmas as we were due to set off for France just after the New Year. I saved up some money from my ironing scam and bought nice fish dinners all round for Mum and the girls when I arrived home that night. Also, the lads had chipped in and bought nice wee dolls for the girls to have as Christmas presents. One of the boys made wee uniforms with glengarries for them.

I handed over more money to Mum but she refused it and told me to keep it for France. She advised me to watch out for the French girls as they were notorious for seducing young boys and giving them dreadful diseases. I had heard this talk from the lads but now realised it must be true if Mum also thought this. I told her I was not interested in them and not to worry. I would save myself for a nice girl from Edinburgh when I got back.

At that, Mum started crying. She had held herself together pretty well up till then but that broke the dam. I said goodbye and hugged all the girls; the oldest, Maggie, was eight years of age and starting to understand what was what. I told her that she was now the big girl of the house and had to look after everyone until I got back. Poor wee bairn.

We departed from Fort Matilda railway station and made the long journey south to Southampton to embark on the troopship. I don't remember much about that except we were all sick as dogs, as the channel was really choppy that day, and we lay in the holds crammed together in utter misery. Even Davie and Jock, my two best pals and real tough-nuts, were in a miserable state. It was my first and sadly not my last experience of sea-sickness; and if anything good came out of it, it was that I was bloody glad I joined the army and not the navy.

On arrival at Le Havre we were put on trains which were no better than cattle cars, and forwarded to the large training camp at the town of Etaples, where all new replacements were sent for a week in order to prepare them further for life at the front. This would be the scene of the infamous mutiny in 1917 when men there attacked the NCOs, who were brutalising some of their pals. The 'staff' all wore yellow armbands, which said a lot as it was recognised that none of them had ever been in the front line themselves, but saw fit to act with absolute viciousness and cruelty towards any man they considered not up to scratch.

On de-training we made our way to the self-contained encampment, which appeared as a large, white mass up on its hill, on viewing it from the small railway station. On arrival we were shown to our tents and told to fall out and listen to the camp regulations being read out. We then went to lunch and augmented the meagre fare on offer in some of the small, tented shops, including a YMCA set up for us that sold foodstuffs like jam, marmalade, biscuits and cheese.

On route marches back home at Ayr, the non-coms allowed me to pass items of my equipment to my pals to carry, as they were older blokes with more awareness and knew this fostered teamwork and camaraderie. It always occasioned great hilarity when the corporal would stand before us and enquire, 'whae's carryin' the *bairn's* kit the' day?' But on the morning after we arrived to set out on the march through the town and the surrounding country to the training ground, I made the mistake of assuming that the instructors here were of the same mind.

As we fell in outside the tent, I was carrying my rifle, pouches, water bottle and haversack only, and as usual Jock and Davie loaded up with my bayonet and shovel. This sergeant instructor took one look at me, screamed *where the fuck is all your kit?* and belted me across the face with an open-handed slap that brought tears to my eyes through shock and pain.

Outraged, Jock took a step forward but Davie pulled him

back and I was made to load up fully and marched off, making our way through the dingy streets of Etaples and up around the ridge above the town to the infamous 'Bull Ring' which was originally a soldiers' slang phrase used to describe the various training sites that had been developed in that area, which included shooting ranges, mock-ups of trench lines and drill squares.

I received more bashings during bayonet practice for not showing enough 'aggression' but after I received a punch so hard to the side of my head that I fell down dazed, Jock, who'd had enough of watching me being beaten, immediately stood over me and in no uncertain terms told this swine that he should pick on someone his own size or the next time he would *'batter fuck oot o' ye.'* He was very cold and threatening; and with a bayonet pointed at his belly, the instructor, no doubt thinking he might be taking his life in his hands by stopping to discuss the fusilier's remarks in more detail, sidled away. Jock then helped me back onto my feet.

After that, Davie and Jock stuck to me like glue and I suffered no more blows. Further training included grenade practice with the new Mills bomb, musketry and trench tactics. There were longer route marches over sand dunes which surrounded the Etaples area, and these left me on completion so exhausted that I had to rely on Davie and Jock to remove my kit, undress me and lay me on my bunk, as I was close to physical collapse.

Thankfully I made it to the end of the week but was battered, bruised and dispirited for the first time since joining up. At one point I considered confessing my age in order that I could be sent home, finding the brutality there frightening and arbitrary. The object of the Bull Ring was to prepare men for the horrors of the front but my experience is that there is nothing on earth that can do that. All it achieved was leaving good men, many of whom were highly intelligent and educated, and had volunteered to serve their country, bitter and angry.

Davie and Jock, who had protected me and encouraged me to see it through, cheered me up by giving me some of their sweets and chocolate. The day following the end of the course, we made our way amidst great excitement to our new unit.

Chapter Three

We joined up with the 6th Battalion where it would return to the line just across the Belgian border in Ploegsteert (or 'Plugstreet', as it was better known) in late January 1916. It was a quiet sector back then. The battalion was patching up after heavy losses in earlier actions, beginning at Loos. The commanding officer, Colonel Northey himself, was badly wounded there.

After Loos they were moved to the Ypres Salient. There, a lot of heavy and vicious trench fighting ensued, with no end result other than bitter experience gained at a high cost in dead and wounded. The battalion, which was effectively well below the eight hundred men that was the nominal roll, had been put in a rest area for a few weeks before returning to the line.

The battalion was billeted in the small village of Moolenacker, which was about ten miles or so behind the front line. Living conditions there were pretty rough as the only buildings available were some old and dilapidated farmhouses which were not much better than the trenches we were destined for in the line. There were no roads you could give a name to and everywhere was swimming in mud and the fields surrounding the rest area were nothing more than quagmires. But to men who had just pulled out of the line at Ypres, it was heaven.

I had only been there a week before the new colonel took over, but it had been the talk of the battalion and had caused quite a stir. For days, rumours had been doing the rounds about who it was that was to be the new chief. According to whom you heard it from and their basic level of ignorance, it was either someone called Duke Churchill of Marlborough or Winston Spencer, the Earl of Blenheim. It was believed that our existing colonel was being removed to be replaced unfairly by this famous man; and most of the officers were furious and resentful.

It transpired that the new man was none other than the famous politician, the Right Honourable Winston Leonard Spencer Churchill, formerly Home Secretary, First Lord of the Admiralty and, latterly, Chancellor of the Duchy of Lancaster; and if you are wondering what that is, it is the place they send you in politics when they do not know where else to put you.

He was in the doldrums, having being forced to resign over the Dardanelles catastrophe, him being the convenient scapegoat for a plan that was brilliant on paper but executed disastrously. He stuck being chancellor for a short while before resigning from that post and signing on again as a soldier, which of course, as is well known, is what he was before he entered parliament, achieving great fame.

Mr Churchill had originally requested a brigade and been refused, due to political influence. He was then dumped on the grenadiers, who despised him on sight but had grown to respect him. There was no real mystery as to why he ended up with us; it just boiled down to simple army bureaucracy in the end. When he eventually turned up it was quite a scene.

He rode in that morning on a black horse with Archibald Sinclair, who would be his second in command (and future leader of the Liberal Party), and an entourage of servants from the Grenadier Guards where Mr Churchill had served his 'apprenticeship' before being given the command of our battalion.

The lads were more astonished, even amidst this sight, at seeing the new CO bringing with him a tin bath and a machine for boiling the water, which later became much sought-after by the formerly disapproving officers.

The day became more surreal as the new colonel ordered his officers to attend lunch with him, where he proceeded to inform them that there was a new broom sweeping through the battalion; he had very different ideas from previous commanding officers, and those who were against him he would personally break. Embarrassed, the officers broke up and Mr Churchill then demanded that the battalion be put on parade, where he would inspect them.

The company commanders received orders to be mounted. This was something most of them hated because as infantry officers none of them were steady horsemen. Winston then had the companies marching to and fro and the poor commanders could not keep up as their animals were all over the place, their inexperienced riders unable to control them. The skittish horses dropped shit everywhere and bumped into blokes, knocking a few over; which left the lads in hysterics and the non-coms, in between screaming orders, barely able to contain their mirth.

The colonel then called a halt to proceedings and ordered the entire battalion, whilst at slope arms, to fix bayonets. This resulted in scenes of chaos; there was hooting, sniggering, ridicule and some of the choicest language imaginable as some lads had to put down their rifles to pull out their bayonets. Most did not even bother. He then rolled off cavalry, and not infantry, commands (his former regiments included the 4th Hussars and the South African Light Horse) such as '*Threes Right Trot!*' and '*Sections Right!*' with the result that a lot of lads just clowned around, driving their non-coms daft. Many of the boys were new recruits and thought all this hilarious.

As mentioned, the new colonel arriving had not been popular, as the old CO, Lieutenant Colonel Dutton, was very well liked; but it has to be said he was stuck in his ways and life for ordinary Jocks was grim. Fortunately I had arrived at the right time: because the new chief changed everything.

When I first arrived with a group of replacements, we were led into the courtyard at Moolenacker Farm and Colonel

Churchill walked down the line and looked over each of us.

He had a habit when inspecting the men of staring fixedly into each face as if trying to memorise each one of them in order to store away information; and the lads found that they liked that. One thing soldiers resent is so-called superiors just strolling past them on parade. Some are just plain fearful of being spoken to, of course, and are glad of being bypassed; but most soldiers worth their salt appreciate the Old Man having a chat, especially if they sense he means what he says: and Winston always did that, and more.

When he came to me he had of course to look down, even for a short man himself (he was only about five foot seven). He stared at me intently and I then committed the ultimate *faux pas* by raising a great idiotic grin on my face.

The colonel scowled and crouched even lower; his face came close to mine and I could hear a sort of growl come from him. Though I was only very young, I sensed that he was not being serious, and then he moved onto the next man. I would get to know that scowl (and growl) very well soon enough and was right in my suspicion that he was kidding me on.

He then proceeded to address us:

'Men, I welcome you to your battalion. I can see from my review that each of you is as fine a specimen of manhood as ever walked Scotia's earth! I sense the martial spirit of Bruce and Wallace in you all! I have no doubt that you will do your duty. However, there are two things we must clear up between ourselves from the start. One is that I expect you to obey without question at all times the orders of your superiors. Two, I do not tolerate drunkenness.

'Then again, drink was put on our good Earth for a reason and I would have never got to where I am now without it and every day I thank God for it. So, if you want to get intoxicated,' a few of the lads rolled their eyes at this, 'then you are to do so when in rest areas only when out of the line. I fully expect you to enjoy yourselves and desire that you do therefore imbibe, for I could never entrust my life to a man who is a tee-totalling son of a bitch; for who can trust a man who does not drink? Remember well what I have told you and again, a very warm welcome to you all. Dismissed.'

When the time came to move the men back into the line, Winston discovered that though other battalions were transported up, there was nothing like that laid on for his boys. He somehow commandeered a bus and lots were drawn for the lucky so-and-sos who won a place on it and the rest of us marched up. I had lost out and hoofed it with the rest, but Colonel Churchill joined us all the way and would walk down the line chatting, encouraging and joking.

As usual I was able to get my pals to help me with my kit; I was fair puggled by the end and grateful of the assistance. On arrival at Plugstreet we proceeded to relieve the existing battalion, the Border Regiment, in order to take over a small sector of the front line east of the village. We settled down to make acquaintance of trench life and our new surroundings; which were pretty grim and depressing, to tell the truth.

The village of Ploegsteert, captured later on in 1918 by the Germans, was situated to the south of the infamous Ypres Sector and scattered around its outskirts were numerous farm buildings used as billets and command posts. A small stream, the Warnave, ran from the trench line to one of the main buildings quartering men, Maison 1875, which I got to know well; and the famous Plugstreet Wood was only a few hundred yards away from the forward command centre at Laurence Farm.

I won't bore you with the details of what it was like in the trenches: the filth, the cold, the stench, the rats and lice; these have been well documented elsewhere. The only plus was that food was always hot and plentiful, but the tedium and bone-weariness from standing long periods nearly up to your knees in freezing water, constant fear of snipers and shelling, the disgusting latrines we were forced to use and stink from our own bodies were all a part of the daily grind; and worst of all for me was becoming martyr to terrible sleep deprivation which, as I was not much more than a child, was the most serious problem I faced. After our six-day stretch finally ended, my fuzzy mind craved nothing more than to just lie down and drift off in blessed slumber. The desire to remove the putrid uniform and give myself a complete soaking with hot water and soap came secondary. Again I had to thank my friends Jock and Davie, who saw to it that I was in a suitable state when finally I bunked down before they saw to their own arrangements; for I was in no fit state to help myself. I was completely overwhelmed with exhaustion after the experience.

Colonel Churchill soon set about lifting the spirits of everyone with simple things like arranging pillow fights between platoons, football matches and mule races; and instigated proper leave systems. Food rations improved greatly and each day the great man would come round and visit us and ask if we needed anything.

If you are an old soldier like me, you know that every Old Man does this. But usually, after moaning to the boss, who shakes his head and says it's awful, something must be done, he buggers off and invariably you never hear of it again. Well, with Mr Churchill, things got done alright. One lad was out one day helping with supplies and Mr Churchill saw him and noticed the boots hanging off his feet were tied together with string. He told the colonel he was advised he would have to wait three months for a new pair. Instantly Winston took out a note pad and wrote something and the fellow ran off with it and got his boots immediately.

The colonel was a stickler for strengthening defence works.

He insisted that the parapets were all at least three feet thick as this was proven to stop bullets (actually, four or five feet was a safer bet); and he had a mania for sandbags.

One day he was out touring the forward trenches and saw two blokes working. One was digging in and filling bags but the other was leaning against the trench walls, smoking. He hung back and listened in to a conversation these two were having.

'Stop smokin' and gie us a hand!'

'Whit fur, there are enough as it is, why bother wi' mair?'

The colonel then sprang himself on them.

'You with the fag end in your mouth, what is your name?'

He gave it whilst attempting to put the cigarette out and trying to stand to attention.

'Never mind jumping to attention, finish your fag. Let me ask you a question. How long have you been with this battalion?'

This fellow was part of the group of replacements that I had joined the battalion with. By that time we had been there only about a fortnight.

'Two weeks. Corporal Graham here was at Fosse Alley at Loos. *He is alive.* Does that not tell you something?'

The bloke just looked at him.

'Do *you* wish to stay alive?'

'Yes, sir!'

'Then I suggest you follow this man's example and start filling fucking sandbags as you have been told to!'

He let defaulters away with murder, I can tell you. There was a regulation to the effect that any offence that carried the death sentence could not be dealt with by the battalion commander and had to be passed up the line. The result was the offender standing before a field general court martial, facing down officers who were not from his regiment.

One of our lads, Tommy Reid, got caught sleeping on

watch. Now, you and I know the penalty for that in wartime. Corporal Macleod caught him and, being an old soldier, quietly had a word with Sergeant Douglas, an even *older* old soldier. He knew that if he approached the company commander, Captain Gibb, he would feel compelled to follow regulations and start formal proceedings. Douglas would not take that chance, for Mr Gibb was a civilian in uniform and was not wise to the ways of the world. What the errant Tommy needed was a damned good fright; and Sergeant Douglas knew just the man to give him it.

Boab (Sergeant Douglas) had a quiet meeting with the colonel and, shortly after, Tommy was wheeled in to see the commanding officer. Winston took one look at him (though older, if anything Tommy looked even younger than me) and told him in no uncertain fashion that if he was ever caught sleeping again on sentry duty he would personally write to his parents, telling them how much their son had let down the King, the battalion and worst of all, Winston Spencer Churchill.

To Tommy this was a fate worse than the firing squad and he took fright, almost fell on his knees, begged to be forgiven and swore that it would never be repeated. He was put on shithouses for a week and never fell asleep again until a bullet got him at Arras.

I know that Winston had a few rows with Captain Gibb, who later became adjutant, over this type of leniency. Gibb was a lawyer in peacetime and a bit of a character, but all the officers except one were hostilities only and were learning the trade as they went along. Gibb just felt that Winston's laxity on this score might cause problems. At times he would argue the toss; Mr Churchill remained equable but unwavering in his philosophy. Captain Gibb seemed to forget that few colonels would have put up with any type of criticism and that Mr Churchill was being pretty easy-going with Gibb as well as the men.

He would get his own back on Mr Gibb in his own inimitable way.

Shortly after arriving, Winston had announced to the gathered group of officers that when he asked them a question or gave an order, at all times he expected them to react positively; consequently they were never to reply, 'yes, sir' or heaven forbid 'no, sir' but merely 'sir!' This would cause a lot of confusion at times and a few of the officers were laughing about it behind his back. If asked something they would roar 'SIR!' at the top of their voices for effect, whether they knew the answer or not. This would of course confuse Winston, and Gibb was one of the worst offenders.

Late one night after a mess dinner, Gibb, who had been invited, left with the other officers a little worse for wear, heading back to their billets to sleep off the colonel's as-always generous hospitality.

As he lay snoring off the drink he had consumed, at around 3.30 a.m. Winston sent an orderly to wake him up with an urgent communication. The message stated that the colonel had been advised that information had been received informing him that there was an imminent threat of a gas attack being prepared by the Germans. Captain Gibb was to raise all the company commanders and order stand-to.

After dragging himself up, still in an alcoholic daze, he made his way around the companies and, being heartily abused, was then given a second message from the orderly advising him that the original warning had been a false alarm. He then swore at the poor man, furiously cursed the colonel and stomped off back to his kip.

Next morning he was sent for by Winston.

'Did you feel that last night's warning, though in the end spurious, served a purpose?' Mr Churchill asked him.

'Sir!' the hung over captain replied; meaning, of course, yes, even when he meant no.

'Did you at any time consider the fact that your colonel may well be a complete bastard?'

Gibb was trapped and did not know how to respond.

He then took refuge in answering the way he had been ordered to:

'Sir!'

'Ah! It is good to know that you are, at least, an honest man!'

We were soon a pretty happy bunch. The officers were all good sorts anyway but Winston, as colonel, energised everyone. He improved our drill, bringing guards ideas with him, and had a near-obsession with personal hygiene, insisting that the men wash regularly. He announced he had personally 'declared war on the common louse' and showed a marked degree of concern for every wounded man. He would insist on being at the side of the soldier to talk to him, if he was able to, and ask him if he required anything prior to his being patched up or evacuated.

After spending six days in the line we were rotated and sent back for six days in reserve. Colonel Churchill's command post when in the line was at an old farmhouse that became known simply as 'Laurence Farm', about a thousand yards from the front line. He had an office, a kitchen, a small room to himself and a dugout to dive into when the shelling got a bit close.

During his own reserve time he had his bath and other creature comforts, but I have to stress he was no base wallah when he was there: he shared all he had with everyone and was always either writing or doing something. He spent a lot of his time discussing politics with Archie Sinclair and later I would hear a few things I probably should not have.

Chapter Four

As for my own circumstances, the situation back home in Edinburgh was about to have a major effect on my life at the battalion.

My mum started a better-paid job in a munitions factory in the west of Edinburgh and gave up her night cleaning stint, as there was always plenty of overtime at the works. Mum was a small and slight woman and the thought of her trying to operate lathes and carry big artillery shells brings me out in a sweat even now.

What happened was that one day they got the bloody chemicals mixed up in the explosives, with the result that the factory blew up, killing twelve workers and injuring dozens more. Mum ended up in hospital with blast injuries and burns.

Unfortunately the record office of the factory was totally destroyed, with the result that nobody's next of kin could be contacted; and somehow word got out that my mother was one of the dead. The Corporation turned up at Wardlaw Place and took my wee sisters away as they were now treated as orphans. Someone (a friend of my mum, I suspect), believing the worst, remembered I was in the army and I received a letter from the Corporation, telling me she was dead and my sisters were being taken into care and placed in an orphanage.

When I was young, though I was pretty mature in a lot of ways, when it came to my mum and sisters I had a blind spot when it came to reason. On reading this letter my first thought was to get back home as soon as possible; but I was foolish enough to believe that if I went through official channels then questions would get asked about my real age.

Unfortunately I panicked and did not think it out. I should have gone to my corporal, who was a decent bloke, but didn't want the shame of telling him that my sisters had been put in a home. God, I was stupid; but that's what ties of blood and being young and daft do to you.

Being in the reserve area at the time, after a couple of days considering what to do I reached my decision. I loaded up my pack with as much grub as possible, with the intention of heading for the rear and catching a troopship back to England. I had money saved for a train to Edinburgh and thought as long as I carried my rifle with me I would be safe, because what kind of deserter carries his weapon? I was not a deserter anyway; I would be back right away after sorting things out at home.

I didn't even make the first checkpoint about two miles down the road. This great git of an MP stopped me and asked to see my leave pass. I said I'd lost it but if he contacted my battalion they would sort it out. I was brazen and quaking like a jelly at the same time. He took one look at me and said: 'Son, are you going to tell me what's *really* going on?'

I looked down and burst into tears and told him about my mum. I also told him my real age and handed him the letter I'd received. He looked at it, shook his head and sent me back to the battalion. I was escorted by one MP only, who bought me a cup of tea and a bun on the way and let me keep my rifle. I was absolutely terrified when I got back.

I was left alone whilst the MP went to speak to the adjutant, Lieutenant McDavid; and looked on in increasing alarm as McDavid glanced over at me, the MP appearing quite animated at one point. I was rigid with fear as it dawned on me the implications of what I had done. I also felt bad for letting Mr McDavid down as he was a really decent stick. He then came over to me and said, 'James, I have to put you under arrest. This is very serious.' I was always called James or Jamie by everyone. They could not bring themselves to call me by my surname as I was so young-looking.

I have to say at this point I was near catatonic with fright. It was so intense I could not even cry; and I was so afraid I could not think straight. Many events of that awful day remain just a blur to me even now.

Mr McDavid took me over to the rear echelon command post, which was an old hospice on the road to Armentieres (the nuns who lived there had moved out earlier and it was later evacuated by us, being shelled continually). They put me in the orderly room where they brought me tea and something to eat. I drank the tea but could not face the food. About two hours later he came back and told me I was being taken to see the CO, Mr Churchill.

At this point I could barely stand and Mr McDavid put his hand on my shoulder and told me to try and bear up. He said I was a good soldier and Mr Churchill knew this and I should try and stand up straight when he spoke to me. I mumbled that I was sorry to put them through all this bother.

We made our way forward to Laurence Farm. I have to say those were the longest steps of my life. I was convinced I was going to be shot. I was going to be court-martialled by the colonel and put up against a wall at the Farm, and men from my platoon were going to shoot me. My own pals would have to do this as a warning to others of what happens to deserters. They would have tears in their eyes as they levelled their rifles but they would have no choice and would have to take aim and fire at the wee piece of cloth attached over my heart. I would be buried in a deserter's grave in France. Worst of all, my poor sisters would be taken away to some ghastly orphanage and split up and never see each other again because their older brother was a coward and a disgrace.

All I could think of was their poor wee faces.

These were the happy thoughts going through my mind at this time. I don't know to this day how I made it along with

Mr McDavid to the Farm without running away or collapsing in terror.

I awoke lying on the colonel's bunk to the sound of scribbling and turned my head to see Mr Churchill at his desk. He looked over, laid down his pen, rose from his chair and came over to where I was lying on the bunk.

He crouched down. 'What do we do with you now, eh?'

I looked up at him. Darkness had fallen and the dull electric light inside the farm flickered intermittently. Cigar fumes mixed with those from a coal-burning fireplace, and along with the earthy atmosphere, made the room snug and welcoming on my awakening. But I was unable to wholly recall the circumstances that had led me to this point. I vaguely remember hanging around alone outside the colonel's office door and seeing Mr McDavid look at me, but after that there were only hazy images mingled with the dream of my unconscious state that left me uncertain about placing events in their true perspective.

'You know the penalty for desertion in the face of the enemy? There can be few exceptions. It is a terrible thing to leave your comrades to their fate at the hands of the foe. In your case, however, I believe there may well exist an exception.'

I could only lie back all agog as Mr Churchill spoke. I was beginning to feel more clear-headed and also that somehow, the worst that I had feared would befall me was not going to occur. I started to feel safe but struggled to understand everything.

'Are you able to get up?' he asked.

'Aye, sir, I think so.'

I sat up and got to my feet. I felt light-headed, but determined to start acting like a soldier again, I stood to attention.

Noting this, Mr Churchill placed a steadying hand on my arm. 'Ah, I see the habits of the old soldier die hard, but in your case I feel it is better that you take your ease and come over and have a seat at my desk.'

He pulled a chair over and I sat down. The colonel returned to his seat and stared intently over the desk at me.

'Are you quite sure you can continue?'

'Aye sir, only...'

'Yes?'

'Could I please have some water?'

'Of course, of course.'

Mr Churchill reached round for a metal jug and poured into a cut glass tumbler.

I took the glass and sipped but I found myself involuntarily gagging.

'Oh, I forgot that glass contained brandy and as I sadly at the moment cannot find a servant, fear I may have forgotten to rinse it out,' Mr Churchill explained.

'Sorry, sir.'

'No need. Now tell me everything that has happened since you received your letter from home.'

I told the colonel everything. My mother's death, the fate of my sisters, the MP stopping me.

'And is it true that you are fifteen years of age?' he asked when I had finished.

I looked directly at Mr Churchill. I found I could not speak again, the shame too much, and ever so slightly nodded my head.

'Now listen to me, young man. The army is not a perfect institution, far from it, but at this battalion you have as fine a group of officers as you could ever be fortunate to come across in your military career. Good officers are rare. I say it myself, I have come across the good, the bad and the indifferent and I ask you to trust my judgement in this matter. Mr McDavid,

Mr Hakewill-Smith, Captain Gibb and all the others are very good indeed. If you were to go through the proper chain of command and speak first to your corporal…' Mr Churchill looked down at a note on his desk, 'Corporal McLeod, he would have broached the subject to the relevant officer, who then would have brought the issue to my personal attention and I would have taken immediate action to resolve the matter. Then we would have had a very different and more satisfactory outcome to this whole sorry matter.'

'Aye, sir. I'm so sorry.'

'I have here another letter which has arrived from England. It comes from the War Office by way of the Ministry of Munitions, which is a department run by my own dear friend and colleague Mr David Lloyd George. It states that your mother is in fact not dead, but very much alive and recuperating from her injuries from that most unfortunate blast at the munitions factory.

'It goes on to state that your sisters have been temporarily, I say again, *temporarily*, taken into care until your mother recovers sufficiently to return them home. The letter also goes on to say that a pension will be paid to your mother for the injuries suffered. My friend Mr Lloyd George has also arranged that once your mother is well again, she is to take up employment in the office of the ministry in Edinburgh in a more suitable position, where I believe her long-underused typing skills can be best utilised for the war effort. However, there is a footnote to my friend's letter. Namely that on further investigation it is to be brought to my attention the fact that you are indeed under-age.'

I was almost overwhelmed with joy to hear Mum was alive. There were *two* letters sent to me around the time of my mum's accident. One from the Ministry of Munitions and one from the Corporation; only the Ministry's letter was the more accurate. Owing to a postal cock-up the letter from the ministry arrived later but went straight to Winston, who then contacted Mr Lloyd George in London and personally dealt with the matter on my behalf.

Soon after these events, Mr McDavid resigned the adjutancy and handed over to Captain Gibb. Winston had gently reprimanded 'Jock' (Mr McDavid) over his handling of my case. He told Jock that he should never have mentioned the word 'arrest' to me at any time. This was because an older soldier with more savvy would have immediately requested representation and the matter would have had to be treated formally.

Winston then eased the rebuke by saying that a more experienced officer would have known this and Jock should not be too down on himself, should see it as a valuable lesson learned and had otherwise behaved impeccably.

I believe Winston got a fright when I passed out. He would have loathed the very idea that I had been so terrified of standing before him that it provoked such an extreme reaction as fainting in mortal fear. As far as I was concerned Mr McDavid acted very decently towards me though I understand now how his inexperience could have made matters difficult.

This latest episode may have had a bearing on Jock's decision to quit, as other officers were aware that he was finding it difficult to keep up with the new colonel's demands; and after discussing with the company commanders, he made his decision to resign. Winston accepted with equanimity.

Ultimately it was all down to Winston's more enlightened attitude to discipline but McDavid was placed in a very difficult situation. Technically, of course, he had acted correctly throughout. But I found out later from the MP who escorted me back that when he initially spoke to Jock he advised him to quietly send me back to my billet, not make a fuss and deal with it after consulting a senior officer before deciding whether to bring the matter to the colonel's attention. Jock was uneasy about this and said that as adjutant he had no choice. The MP said, alright, whatever; but he didn't have to, and walked away.

Thankfully for everyone's sake concerned (especially mine), the whole incident was quietly laid to rest. Hardly anyone knew (I told none of the lads, not even Davie Thom, that I planned to leave) apart from the officers concerned and they of course were relieved that there would be no official action taken. The MPs didn't want to know, either.

As for Mr Churchill, I now looked at him very differently. I was young and impressionable and admit to developing a hero-worship for him. I knew of him of course from my time in the Gorgie Library. He was at Omdurman. His famous escape from the Boers in South Africa. I had read *The River War* and *Malakand Field Force* and been thrilled by descriptions of his escapades. But I found it difficult to reconcile the hero to the man who was our colonel. It was because at first he seemed so remote. Well, I was just a wee lad, and the great affairs of statesmen like Winston Churchill were way beyond me. But as I lay there I remembered a conversation I overheard concerning him back at Ayr Barracks.

'Sir?'

'Yes, my boy?'

'They were really cruel to you about Gallipoli.'

By this time he was back at his desk, writing. I had gone back to lie on the bunk as I was feeling woozy again. But he looked up.

'What was that you said?'

'When I was at Ayr, one of the corporals told me that Gallipoli was not your fault but the stupid generals'. It was a good plan but they made a mess of the whole thing.' I stopped. I felt like an idiot: I mean, here's me from a tenement in Gorgie discussing strategy with Mr Churchill. I immediately cowered into the bed.

'Did he really say that?' Then I sensed a change in his manner. You can think me daft but he seemed to go all misty-eyed. I could not believe it but he looked like he was going to cry!

I thought that as I owed him so much I had to continue to try and cheer him up.

'Yes, sir, he said you were a scrap goat.'

His demeanour started to mellow and a spark of humour returned.

'You mean: *scapegoat*.'

'Aye, that's the word. He said you "carried the can for all the bungling idiots who wasted so many men's lives." Those were the exact words he used, sir. I haven't forgotten them.'

'If that is the opinion of your very fine corporal, then I am grateful to know that in Ayr Barracks I do have at least one sure vote at the next general election.'

He looked down, lowered his pencil, took out a hanky and blew his nose but, child that I was, I understood that he was indeed crying. Now, I was always a soft-hearted wee laddie and on many occasions had to console my poor mum for whatever reason, be it when that drunken swine of a father of mine hit her or when she got maudlin drunk; and without thinking I got out of the bunk and walked around the desk to where he was sitting.

I put my hand on his shoulder.

'Och, dinnae worry, sir. I can promise you five votes in Edinburgh. My mum and me and my sisters. That's when we're old enough, of course.'

I realised what I had done and started to back away. 'No! No, my boy,' he said kindly, 'don't be afraid, compassion is what separates us from beasts.'

He then composed himself as I stood before him.

'Now, James, there is something important we must discuss. I am, as you know, a great man. But there is one important element of my life missing at present. I require a batman. This is a terrifying and onerous duty for a young man as it requires great qualities in the individual chosen, for you are to be my very eyes and ears; and also I am advised by Corporal McLeod that you are the best bullshitter in the battalion. This is a vital requirement for a batman as no self-respecting great man can allow his boots to be dirty. Therefore I have chosen you. Can you accept this most holiest of vocations?'

I did not know what he was talking about at first. I admit my chest swelled a little when he spoke of my prowess at bulling boots. Then it dawned on me.

I knew that his previous batman had been injured when a stray shell burst above him whilst he was collecting supplies off wagons. 'Oh yes, sir! I'd love to be your batman, only…'

'Only what?'

'Does it come with extra pay…?'

Chapter Five

I put behind me the events leading up to my appointment as Winston's batman, or *soldier-servant*, as was the official term at the time, and focused all my attention on getting to grips with my new responsibilities. Cleaning and ironing his kit, bulling his boots and having his meals ready were among the more mundane duties bestowed on me. But I like to think I became more than just the colonel's domestic. I was excused some normal batting tasks such as driving and acting as bodyguard, but received training in routine clerical duties at Winston's insistence. In return I was given a nice billet in the rear area in a large farmhouse that was unscathed by shellfire, known as Maison 1875, endless opportunities to pilfer from stores and a regular bath in his own tub (not whilst he was in it, I may say, and another of my jobs was fighting off batmen of officers who always wanted use of it when Winston wasn't around).

I also received first-class grub and was introduced to wine. Before you get the wrong idea at this, remember we were in France and if truth be told the wine was a safer bet than the water. But I never drank to excess, nor was I allowed to. Apart from whisky, whose taste I acquired later, I have never been much of a drinker.

There was no school for frontline batmen; it was the ultimate in on-the-job training. I brought with me my housekeeping skills but if I were to rely solely on them I wouldn't have lasted a week. Fortunately our relationship was not of the normal master/servant variety and consequently I got away with much. At least, you'll never hear me agreeing with the old maxim about no man being a hero to his valet.

But early on in my tenure I was able to prove myself by using native Edinburgh wits to cement my place as the trusty and resourceful batman Winston envisaged when appointing me.

One morning Winston was at Laurence Farm, writing away at his desk. A bombardment broke out and true to form he went outside to have a look. A shell came crashing down near him, dust and dirt blew everywhere and when everything settled down, on returning to his desk he discovered he had lost a very important piece of paper.

For nearly two bloody days he drove me daft, trying to locate this precious document. He would not tell me what it had written on it and truth be told it was the first time I ever saw the colonel worried. On the morning of the day after the incident I brought him his breakfast and again he asked me if I had found it.

'I don't know what I'm looking for, you won't tell me what it says so how do I know what to search for? There's paper and mess all over the place! My mum would go mad if she knew I was living like this!'

'Jamie.' I learned that when he called me that instead of his usual 'James' it was an indication that he was emotional or worried. 'That piece of paper contains highly sensitive information and if it were to fall into the hands of the enemy, you would at best be looking for a new colonel and at worse being asked to form part of my firing squad!'

My hair stood on end at this and I stepped up my efforts to look for something of which I had no idea what that 'something' looked like.

That same morning we received word that a general was paying us a surprise visit. Now, this individual shall remain nameless because he was absolutely detested one and all by the officers and men of the battalion. When word got out that he was coming you could hear seven hundred voices cursing: Oh no, not *that* bastard!

The great man turned up in his red tabs and jodhpurs with

his entourage, and Mr Hakewill-Smith showed him into the Farm where the general immediately started giving Mr Churchill a dressing-down for the state of the place (bear in mind we had just received this direct hit).

'Well, Churchill, what have you to say for yourself? I have looked at your trench work and it is a positive disgrace. The sentries appear to be exposed to the enemy, and *this!* This command post is a shambles! How is a commanding officer to lead by example when he lives like a pig? There are no defence works round your post! It is a danger, an absolute danger, sir!'

The real danger was the look on Winston's face. I have come to know it well over the years. Up to that point he appeared to me the most even-tempered and amiable of men but I saw for the first time Winston Churchill's temper flaring. I cringed.

'Sir, danger is a factor inherent to warfare and this is a very dangerous war!' he responded furiously.

The general went on and muttered that it just wouldn't do and it was not good enough.

I never did have much time for bullies. There was my dad, of course, and the odd joker I came across at school and usually gave them what for, but I wasn't going to tolerate my colonel being treated like dirt by this buffoon. I decided to extract revenge.

Tea had not yet been served.

'Mr Churchill, do you want me to make the general a nice cup of tea?'

Still flustered, Winston turned to me.

'Why yes, my boy!' the general butted in. 'I would love some.'

'Coming up now, sir,' and I went off to the mess area to work my vengeance.

As you may have read, trenches in the Great War were not exactly like the North British; and they had a nasty habit of attracting unwanted guests, namely mucking great rats. The Farm attracted its fair share of rodents also and we had a cat called Jack, a large tom and the finest rat-catcher you ever saw, to deal with our resident vermin. He was a big black beauty with a wee white spot on his chest and he caught those buggers lovely but he never ate them, just dumped them proudly at your feet and then got some nice milk or a pat as a reward. He was the battalion mascot, all the lads loved him and later on an officer who was returning home took him and he ended his days nice and quiet in a home he deserved.

I knew he had caught a rat that day and went and got a hold of it by the tail. I proceeded to make the general's tea and then dunked the rat in the cup and left it to stew for a few seconds. I then returned through to Winston and the general.

'Sorry, sir, all our best crockery got smashed when the shell hit but I have a nice mug here for you. Do you take milk and sugar?' I asked innocently.

Oh yes, he says. Lots of both, my boy.

I went back to the tea and proceeded to pick up some of the endless amounts of rat turds that lay about and added a few lumps. Once I had given the cup a good stir, I fished them out and adding milk and sugar brought the drink through.

'There you are, sir, hope you like it strong!'

After the general left (hopefully with a touch of bubonic plague to add to his other reasons to whinge and greet), Winston stormed off on his rounds to visit the lads. I started to clean up the room but gave up and stopped and had my lunch. I sat in his chair, eating a sandwich when I happened to put my hand down the side as you do looking for any loose change that may have slipped out. Strike me! I found a piece of folded paper. I opened it up and read it.

I have decided not to tell you what it said because I quickly realised that this was the important document that Winston was going spare trying to find. All I will reveal was that it was from the War Office and it was signed by a very famous person of the time. I'll give you a clue as to his identity: he had a very large moustache.

My immediate concern now I had read it was: how do I get this to Winston and at the same time convince him that I had not looked at the contents? Who knows, I may be in trouble because if I get captured by the enemy they may torture it out of me. The more I thought about it the more of a sweat I got myself into. I wracked my brains over what to do. As I sat there, unexpectedly I heard Mr Churchill's voice. Oh God! He was coming back early! What will I do with the note?

Then the spark of genius entered my Scottish head. His service jacket was hanging up on the peg! That's why he's coming back! He was so flustered by the general's visit he stormed out on his rounds, forgetting his coat! I dashed over and with no time to spare, grabbed a brush and his jacket and slipped the note into the top pocket.

'James, where the devil is my coat?' he roared.

'I'm just giving it a clean, sir,' and made to brushing it down. 'Hello, what's this?' I put on what I hoped was not too great a show. 'There's something in the pocket here, Colonel Churchill.'

'What's that?'

Suddenly he dashed over and grasped the note.

'Hail Caledonia!' he exclaimed as he unfolded the sheet of paper and looked over it.

'My boy, you have saved England!'

I was about to say that that was Scotland's prerogative. But why state the obvious?

A few days earlier a parcel had come for him that had remained unopened. That evening he stood before me and held a large round tin in both hands.

'James, I am not normally a suspicious man but before I hand over your reward I have to ask you two questions: First, did you have anything to do with that note being found in my pocket and did you at any time look over its contents?'

'No and no, sir!' I answered.

'Good. Second, I have been advised that General ------- took very ill with an extremely nasty bout of sickness and vomiting shortly after his inspection of our command post. Do you know anything about this?'

'Certainly not, sir!'

He reached out the tin to me.

'Enjoy Messrs Fortnum and Mason's bounty.'

Not long after being appointed batman I was moved permanently into Laurence Farm whilst the colonel did his stint in the line, as a result of a mishap when returning back to Maison 1875 one moonless night after Winston dismissed me. Losing my way whilst walking along the edge of the burn, I fell headfirst into the Warnave and after making a racket fit to awake the dead in nearby Plugstreet churchyard, managed to make my way back to the billet. On my entering the building there was a momentary silence and then laughter broke out when my so-called pals realised that the *tattie-bogle* standing in the doorway dripping river effluent was not some local Belgian ghoul but their own dear Jamie. Winston heard about it and forbade me from any further nocturnal fishing expeditions by arranging for a foldaway cot to be kept in the kitchen at the Farm which I used. As well as removing the risk of twilight drowning this arrangement had the added bonus that when I woke during the night feeling peckish, finding something to alleviate my hunger was never far away.

Plugstreet remained a peaceful sector except for sporadic gunfire and now and then a stray missile causing damage. One salvo crashed into a trench which luckily was unoccupied at the time. When the repair crew went in they found that the parado which had been demolished contained the bodies of two Frenchmen killed when their army occupied the area long before us. For some inexplicable reason known only to them, our allies used the bodies of their dead to shore up trench works.

I stupidly went over to have a look and when I got there a few other lads had congregated. The bodies were decomposing, skeletal and emanated a ghastly slaughterhouse stench that reminded me of the rear of the butcher shop in Gorgie Road during warm summer afternoons, when discarded meat and offal were dumped in bins. My pals and I used to dare each other to remove the lids and stick our noses in and see who could bear the smell the longest.

Two blokes were trying to put the remains into bags but in between pulling and shovelling were retching and spewing and not making a very good job of it. I had seen enough and scarpered. But the stink clung to my nostrils for the rest of that day. And remained with me long after.

Colonel Churchill started painting, which amazed everyone. One bright but crisp late February afternoon in the forecourt of the new reserve command post at Soyer Farm, I sat and watched him, fascinated to observe the process of how with a piece of canvas and some paints he could create something from nothing. While he painted he asked me endless questions about myself, my family and my life. Strangely, when he painted he did not speak about himself, which was just about the only time he never did. I told him everything.

There really was not much to tell. But I felt easy talking to him. I held nothing back. I told him about my parents, how they drank, my father's accident at work and his death, and my brothers being taken away, and disclosed every detail of how I lied my way into the army. I told him about Hearts and my old job on the milk cart and what books I liked.

'What are your hopes and dreams for the future, James?' He had his brush in his mouth at this point, as he was mixing paint with his fingers.

I answered truthfully, 'I want to look after my mum and sisters and want to know what my brothers are doing. I want to get a good-paying job somewhere where I can use my brains, not labour my guts out. I wish I could do something where I could be a writer like on a newspaper or something.'

'Those are all fine hopes, James. I have friends in the press; maybe I could recommend you to them.' He started back on the canvas. 'I believe your mother is a truly good woman. One of the more insidious aspects of our age is the notion that class and upbringing are everything, and the perception that the so-called "ordinary people" or lower classes – how I despise that term! – have nothing to offer but their sweated labour, is something I have battled against all my political life. The amount of raw talent that is sadly wasted and never realised due to circumstances of poverty and ignorance is a terrible indictment of any society.

'But if any good can come out of this terrible war, it is that the "classes" are seeing each other in very different ways than they were previously. The well-heeled young officer serving alongside the young labourer finding that each must depend on the other and that in so many ways each young man is no different from his comrade, that they have the same hopes and dreams, is the one beacon that this war has ignited. Do you understand what I am saying?'

He always explained things to me in such easily understood ways. 'Yes, I think I do. Mr McDavid and Mr Hakewill-Smith and I were talking about books when they were at dinner and they have read the same ones as me! They both like football, too.'

'Yes! You can see the common ground that being all

together here in the mud has thrown up. I do not say it will usher in a new world order, but I do believe a better understanding can be borne from it.'

He was an unusual man, this Winston Churchill. It would normally be unheard of, given the conventions of the times, for the son of a lord to take the time to listen to someone like me; and more, to offer up the deeper recesses of his mind. Yet I did not feel anything other than liking for him. It was impossible not to and I felt safe as he radiated such confidence.

I was stirred by mention of his newspaper friends. Knowing him as I was getting to, he never made promises he could not keep. So I began to daydream to myself of working on Edinburgh papers like the *News* or *Evening Dispatch*, reporting on matches at Tynecastle and Easter Road, bringing home good money and living in a nice house.

They were a young man's dreams. But Colonel Churchill's words somehow made me feel they were dreams that could come true.

There were the usual patrols, which Winston stepped up in frequency. This made him even more popular amongst the men because he started going out on them himself. One night he went out with his bloody great knee-length boots, long trench coat and daft Frog helmet, and a big torch strapped to his side. He was with another officer and got spotted and they both dived into a shell-hole which happened to be full of other blokes.

All of a sudden a great light comes on and all of them were lit up like flares and he shouts, 'put that fucking light out!' only to realise it was the torch he was carrying, which somehow got turned on when he jumped into the crater. That got a laugh later but was certainly not considered amusing at the time.

Now that I was no longer required for trench duty I started to feel guilty about not sharing the same hardships with my pals. Davie told me I should think myself lucky but I badgered Mr Hakewill-Smith for days to be allowed to go out on a patrol though I had to be careful because if Winston found out I might get into trouble. On the one hand I was his batman and excused these kinds of hazardous duties and on the other, though there was no longer any mention made of my real age, there was an understanding that I was not to be allowed to do anything dangerous. That was a bit incongruous when you consider that my predecessor as Winston's batman, Watt, was badly injured by a stray shell whilst lifting bottles of rum off a supply wagon.

Mr Hakewill-Smith was a kind-hearted soul and we became fairly friendly, if only as much as a fifteen-year-old batman and a nineteen-year-old subaltern could in those days. When I asked to be included in his patrols he would fob me off with remarks like, 'Oh, Jamie, tonight will be an utter bore. I only have to lie and observe for a short time, you'd fall asleep with the dullness of it all,' and other rejoinders in a similar vein.

Then a sap was partly blown out when the Germans blew up a mine. A sap was a trench that was dug out forward of the firing line. From the air they stuck out like a sore thumb and were used for observation purposes.

The blokes in the sap were nearly buried alive but men ran forward to assist and pull them out. They were in an understandably traumatised state, physically and mentally, plastered with mud and shivering uncontrollably from shock, but at least they were breathing.

The sap was left as it was but a few nights later Winston ordered that it be reoccupied. My pal Jackie Lawson was due to go out with Hakewill-Smith and another bloke but I collared Jackie and said for five bob I would go in his place. Jackie was glad of the offer but baulked at the price and got it down to two shillings and then cried off going out, stating he was ill.

When I arrived at the parapet at the given time, helmeted and carrying a pistol, Hakewill-Smith was standing with the other lad and asked me what I was doing there.

'Jackie is sick, sir! I volunteered to go in his place!'

Bomber (as he was known) gave me what can only be described as a look of sheer malevolence, unusual on such a cheery young face. 'Jamie, if you're pulling a dodge…?'

I assured him I wasn't and accepting the *fait accompli,* Mr Hakewill-Smith led us out into the night along the trench line to the sap. We made our way quietly as it would be expected that we would reoccupy it. When we got there it had of course been left as it was, and as we tried to make some room for ourselves by chucking out dollops of mud and debris we must have attracted too much attention, for suddenly we heard a THUD and, looking up, saw to our horror the sparks from a trench mortar as it came spinning down towards us.

We could only crouch down low as possible and pray when it exploded, fortunately to the side of us but the blast blew my helmet off and I felt like I had been hit on the side of the head with a mallet. The next moment Hakewill-Smith was dragging me backwards towards the firing line. The other bloke, who was unharmed, was left to watch over.

Bomber and I were sent to the aid station. His face was scorched and I was floating in and out of consciousness. The doctor was sent for and I started vomiting through the concussion and Hakewill-Smith had cream rubbed into his burns. Two more men were sent forward to assist at the sap, where on the following day work began on repairs.

I was carried back to my bunk. I remember nothing after the mortar exploded, and was given a full account of events later by Duncan, the mess orderly, who looked after me and took over my duties. Winston said little about the matter though he could have blown his stack at me and Mr Hakewell-Smith.

The next few days were hazy but in between throwing up and feeling awful, I do remember being given a lovely hot bath in the colonel's tub.

There was nowhere safe when we were in the line. The Farm was less than a thousand yards from the German positions and did not escape the odd shell. It was heavily reinforced as Winston insisted that he would not move from it.

One day a shell hit whilst Winston and a few others were inside. Lieutenant Kemp, who was responsible for signals within the battalion, received serious shrapnel wounds and had to be evacuated and Mr McDavid suffered a hand injury. Duncan and I were making our way back from unloading wagons and saw him sitting outside, having his wound seen to. Colonel Churchill never received as much as a scratch.

Duncan and I became fast friends. In his mid-forties, craggy-faced and repository of a remarkably varied and imaginative vocabulary of foul language, he was consistently incapable of holding down promotion through the drink he consumed and the trouble it got him into. He had been made mess orderly, where he was able to utilise undoubted talents and expertise picked up over a lifetime of service in the regiment: cooking, washing, sewing, first aid, and general odd jobs. Duncan could turn his skilled hands to anything with quiet efficiency as long as he kept away from the bottle.

He told me about his life, that he had been orphaned and brought up in a home in Ayr and joined the regiment as a twelve-year-old band-boy. He served in South Africa as part of the mounted infantry raised whilst the regiment was stationed in Krugersdorp under a certain Captain Trenchard, later the founding father of the Royal Air Force. Duncan had taken part in operations against Boer commandos and on one famous occasion had tracked down their great leader,

Christiaan de Wet, who had been laying low in the Northern Free State, looking for an isolated British force to attack.

The commando then advanced into the Transvaal where a British force lay at Frederikstad. The Boers attacked but the British were prepared and held down de Wet until reinforcements arrived, including Duncan's mounted fusiliers. This time the tables were turned and after heavy losses the Boers made off.

I was enthralled to hear such tales. Duncan knew all the lore of the regiment and as he worked away at his tasks was always singing or whistling old tunes. He told me of the Battle of Dettingen which was the last battle where the British monarch was present. The regiment was there, then known as the 21st.

Their colonel was one of the great characters of our history, Sir Andrew Agnew, who is reputed to have been the author of the famous saying: '*Dinnae shoot till ye see the whites o' their eyes!*' There was a song written about the fusiliers at the battle and Duncan taught me it. The words I recall best are:

The Frenchmen did not care to face old Scotia's Fusiliers;
So, on the field of Dettingen, they launched their Cuirassiers,
To charge the stubborn phalanx of the sturdy Twenty-First,
And drive forever from the earth the corps by them accurst.

Chapter Six

Winston's arrival resulted in a stepping-up from our line of trenches being known as a 'quiet area' to a fairly noisy one on occasion. The Germans thought nothing of lobbing shells over and spraying us with bullets whenever they felt like it. One day a particularly accurate 'stonk' of shell fire came over and four or five blokes all got hit. None died, thankfully, but Colonel Churchill on being informed was furious and demanded 'retribution for this outrage'.

He called in the company commanders, Mr Gibb and Captains Harvey and Ramsay, and ordered that a trench raid be planned for the next few days. This was a type of patrol where the object is to grab a prisoner for information purposes. They were pretty hairy and no one liked going on them.

Fortunately Captain Ramsay was able to persuade him that it might be better if we did the same thing back, with bells on, and allowed the lads to let loose at them during a ten-minute 'hate', as it was known that the boys were not happy at what happened and someone had been heard to say, 'Why does this *Sassenach* colonel no' let us get tore in tae these fuckers?'

We would get our opportunity a day later when Winston ordered up a nasty surprise for our Teutonic neighbours.

We were ordered to stand to at the parapets. There was huge excitement all around and even lads in the reserve positions asked if they could take part. Major Sinclair told me to grab my rifle and join in the fun. The new soup-plate helmets had just been issued and many did not bother to wear them but Duncan advised me to put mine on. I told him it did not fit.

The fact was it was too big for me and kept slipping off. Winston asked me where my helmet was and told me to bloody well put it on or else he would boot me up the arse. Duncan then gave me a cap-comforter to wear, which helped to keep it on straight, but it still tended to slip over.

I stood on a box on the fire step because I was so small, and next to me were Winston and Duncan, when exactly on schedule the barrage erupted with a tremendous din, officers' whistles blew and all around our boys were yelling, 'Yip-pee!' 'Yah-hoo!' 'Here it comes, Huns!' and 'Duck, ya buggers!' as we all opened up, cracking shots off at a furious rate at the German lines as eighteen-pound shells sailed over our heads. Winston, in between shots with his revolver, was working his way through a box of grenades.

We were too far from the German trenches for any to land, but he turned to me, saying, 'James! Give them one of these with love from Gorgie Road!' and handed me a bomb which I chucked over the parapet as far as I could and was thrilled to hear the blast from it as I then picked up the rifle again and fired clip after clip from my Lee Enfield.

I must admit I enjoyed it thoroughly as all the lads did. Winston would stop and offer me his revolver, which I used but found too large for my small hands and handed back after only two shots fired.

Then the Germans opened up themselves, sending bullets and whiz-bangs our way. Some lads ducked but others kept on firing. Winston took no notice of incoming, and continued shooting and chucking pineapples. Following his example I too kept blasting away and he turned to me, his face joyful like a small child being bounced up in the air. 'Is this not the life, James! Is this not the life!' he cried. I just laughed, 'It sure is, Colonel! Brilliant!' and he punched me lightly on the arm and I felt myself swell with pride.

The 'hate' came to an end and the men were laughing and joking with each other and some shouted over to the Germans, 'Ye'll 'no mess wi' the Killie boys!' 'Hope it hurts, ya bastards!'

and 'Mak' a sausage oot a' that, ya cunts!'

The last was Duncan's contribution.

Winston then went round shaking hands, congratulating everyone, and ordered a double ration of whisky for the battalion that evening. Duncan and I had to lug these boxes over from the supply area as the colonel had arranged an urgent requisition. It meant a fair number of bottles for each company.

Winston gave me and Duncan the night off and we spent it at Maison 1875 with Sergeant Douglas, Tommy Reid, Davie Thom, Jock Paterson and a few others as the bottles were passed around. Wisely I had given half my share to Duncan and the other to Davie. Jock did not like whisky and was slugging beer I had nicked for him from the stores. I stuck to cherryade which I was acquiring a serious taste for. I loved these evenings: laughing, joking and having sing-songs with my pals. It was what soldiering was all about: comradeship.

Unfortunately, Tommy Reid was what you would call a 'One-Can-Dan'. This alongside the fact he was only five feet two (another one who slipped by the recruiting sergeant) meant that he suffered in drink from 'wee man syndrome', which often had amusing results.

'Ah kin sojer better than ony man in this here battalion!' he declared after another swig from his bottle. He had now reached the point where all sense had departed; thankfully the rest of us were too busy chatting or drinking away ourselves to pay much attention.

'Ah'm better than that yon Sassenach colonel and *far* better than that Glesgae arsehole, Black Boab *effin'* Douglas!'

Unfortunately for Tommy as he had no doubt forgotten, the said Black Boab, namely Sergeant Douglas himself, was sitting in the corner of the room getting quietly pissed, and on hearing this leaped up from his formerly passive state of intoxication as if stung on the bum by a bee, and making his presence known, roared:

'WHAE SAID THAT?'

'*AH* fuckin' said it!' boasted Tommy, his thumb pumping his chest.

There was a momentary pause of chat all around. Tommy then grabbed the nearest weapon to hand, namely, a broom that had been leaning against a bunk.

'Here, you!' I bawled. 'Pit that doon, that's ma' best besom!' It had been removed on loan from the Farm and I wanted it back.

'Ach, away back tae Edinburgh, ye wee Hearts poof!'

There were moans of 'Steady now,' 'Is he drunk?' and 'Git him tae his bed!' when Tommy added further insults to yours truly:

'Suckhole; that's whit you are an 'a!'

'Whae are ye callin' a "suckhole", ya wee prick?' I roared back. My temper was up now and I was about to advance to the front when Davie and Jock rose from their chairs and shoved me to the side. The sight of the two smallest men in the battalion squaring up must have been the last straw for these two serious drinkers whose only desire was peace and quiet in order to get *bluitered*.

'Come on, Tommy, gie it a rest, eh? Yer spoilin' oor night with yer slaverin's!' Jock tried to reason.

Tommy then adopted what is described in law as 'a threatening attitude' with my besom towards Jock, and Davie caught hold and pulled it from his hands. Tommy then made to swing at Jock, missed, slipped and fell forward as Jock caught him under each armpit and lowered him gently onto his backside.

Then as he tried to sit up straight, he began to moan, 'Oh, Goad! Oh, Mum!' and proceeded to vomit all the colonel's good Scotch over his shirt and onto the floor.

'Och, in the name o' Christ'!'
'Whit a waste ay guid whisky!'
'Get him tae his *bunk*!'
'Ah'm no cleanin' *that* up!' roared Duncan angrily.
The Scots at war.

Unlike my comrades, I had no concerns with hangovers the morning after. But that following evening a cool, clear head would be an essential requisite. For I was about to volunteer for a task that would place me in grave danger and if I failed, history would have changed.

That night I was pottering about in the colonel's room in Laurence Farm. He had lots of books sent from home and encouraged me to look them over. I never needed a prod to read and as I was sitting at his desk flicking through *Twenty Years After* with a nice cup of cocoa and a biscuit to hand, I heard a commotion outside. I went to have a look and saw two officers talking away together but not looking happy. It was Captain Gibb and Mr McDavid. I stopped to listen.

'Bloody man has had it this time!' Gibb sputtered furiously.

'Do you think they know it's him?' McDavid asked, clearly tense.

I stepped outside, the book in my hand. Gibb looked over at me.

He turned to McDavid. 'Who knows? He's stuck fast and no one can reach him. Christ, what a mess!' I just knew they were talking about Winston.

'What's happened? Where's Colonel Churchill?'

'Jamie, get back to bed!' said McDavid testily, turning to me.

'Is he alright? Can I do anything?' I slowly moved towards them.

They started talking quietly together, Gibb clearly trying to suggest something but McDavid appeared reluctant. I hovered around, trying to listen.

'…We have to bloody well try!' Gibb raised his voice and turned towards me. 'Jamie, Mr Churchill has got himself caught under the wire. We need someone very small with a low profile to crawl up and cut him loose.'

'I'll do it!' The words were out before I could think.

Winston had gone out on patrol with another soldier. He went first as usual but forgot to take wire cutters with him. These were with the other man. He had been making a real racket but inexplicably the Huns had not fired. This was because a strong rumour had been going around for weeks that the Germans knew Winston was with us and they meant to capture him. He was known to wear a French helmet and he had it on tonight.

In trying to reach him the other soldier had been hit but managed to make it back to the parapet. He was at the casualty station but Winston was still out, caught on the wire. Neither side dared make a move. If Jerry went out we would fire and they would do the same. It was a bloody nightmare. Especially for Winston.

I went back into the Farm to grab my jacket and then followed McDavid and Gibb to the trench immediately behind where Winston was positioned. Using a trench mirror I could just make out in the murk what looked like a body lying prone underneath the second line of wire.

Captain Gibb handed me the wire cutters, which were as long as my arm. 'Now Jamie, here's what you do. You keep low, so low you're chewing on mud, d'you hear? You slowly crawl to where Mr Churchill is and you snip the wire and free him, alright?'

'Aye, sir, I'm only wee and they won't see me, I promise.'

Gibb visibly bit his lip and put his hand on my shoulder. 'Now look, son, we think they know who it is and that's why they won't fire. But if they spot you they'll aim for you, so keep right behind him at all times. That way they won't see you to shoot at.'

I have to admit, at that moment I was not scared. I was confident I would not be seen. I remained bareheaded as the clumsy helmet would impede me, but the wire cutters were too big to stick in my belt so I held on to them.

It was a moonless night, and bitter cold. Leaving Gibb behind with a 'see you later' I made my way over the parapet and through the gap our scouts had mapped, and saw that Winston was only about twenty-five yards away. I snaked along, feeling my way vigilantly, ignoring the freezing wet, cloying earth and mud that soaked into me. The putrid stench where I edged near or into contact with something organic made me gag, and my worst moments were trying not to vomit or cough but force myself to swallow down the bile that rose in my throat. The wire cutters were a menace, too; but I held them across my arms as though a rifle, as we had been taught at Etaples.

I remembered the area of wire Winston was lying under was a known position that was not covered by the Germans. It may have been a lucky couple of shots from elsewhere that got the other soldier. I had another thought: maybe they did see him and thought he had bought it. Captain Gibb may have been wrong in his summing-up of the situation. I grew increasingly confident.

I reached where the colonel's feet lay and stopped. I dared not whisper but tapped three times on the calf as it was the soft part of his boot and would not make a sound. I was slow and deliberate in my taps, but knew he would get the message. I laid down the cutters and felt my way along the wire to where he was snagged. As it was so dark I had to rely on touch and ran my fingertips along the metal, careful not to cut myself as it was razor-edged. I remember thinking that I should have worn gloves. My fingers then found the two large buttons on the back of the coat and here the tension was tight where the wire had caught and held him fast. I tugged but it would not release, and risked slicing my hands to pieces. Hands that were beginning to numb in the freezing night air.

I would have to use the cutters. I pulled them apart and pushed the points in around the buttons and snipped. One broke immediately. I moved to the other but because the tension was less the wire around it would not break. All this time Winston did not move. I focused on the task and remained cool, taking my lead from him as I could do nothing about the sound I was making. Then after a sequence of determined gouging, twisting and wrenching, his coat at last dropped free and he appeared to push himself ever so slowly backwards. He was released.

We both bobbed and weaved our way back. It was only when we both fell into the trench that he turned and saw who it was that had saved him.

'Thank heaven for the young man from *Auld Reekie*!'

I know it's corny but that is absolutely what he said. Then again, it was Winston and he had a way with words.

'That was fucking marvellous, Jamie!' congratulated Mr McDavid, grabbing me by the shoulders. Captain Gibb, clearly relieved, and others gathered round to acclaim me also, shaking my hand and ruffling my hair.

'Indeed,' agreed Winston, still breathing heavily and encrusted from head to toe with congealed and freezing mud. 'We will have to decide on a suitable reward for such a daring exploit. But first, if you could *temporarily* return to your normal duties and run my bath I would be most grateful, my dear James.'

I did not get a medal or mention in dispatches, the simple reason being that it would not have looked good if it came out in the press that the hero who saved the colonel was only fifteen years of age.

I mean, what would the Germans have thought? They read our papers too. Letting underage boys into the British army, and worse, the boys doing what the grown-ups couldn't? No, it was better to hush it up.

Not that I was bothered. Soon after, I was presented with a very big box of goodies from Fortnum & Mason from the colonel. I gave away the drink to my pals, but as the battalion hero, I was left to keep all the jars of delights to myself to enjoy in full.

Which, I can assure you, I most certainly did.

Chapter Seven

Some days were pretty awful, as when shells came over and copped a few lads, and the odd patrol that went wrong. Winston shared the same dangers and was everywhere, checking on the men's welfare. He was able to deal with this and battalion administration effectively at all times.

He had a mania for ensuring the men's health was monitored along with his obsession with hygiene and would personally inspect their feet to ensure they were well looked after. This was correct and was only unusual in that a senior officer was taking such close and personal interest. Down on his knees scrutinising Dod Lindean's tootsies he declared, 'Lindean, you have the finest left foot I have ever seen. It was made for running down the wing at Parkhead.' From somewhere a voice piped up, 'It would'nae be the first!' Dod was a Blue-nose, and got stick for days after.

He instituted concert parties for the first time in the battalion. The officers were kicking themselves when he announced this because none of them had thought of the idea. This was all unheard of previously and it went down like a house on fire with the lads.

An old barn behind the trench line was gutted (there was no shortage of volunteers for the work) and a stage of sorts was built and benches knocked up. On opening night Colonel Churchill took part in sing-songs and though he had the most awful voice did a very creditable turn on *Charlie is My Darling* which had the boys roaring back '*the young Chevalier!*' in reply.

When our best singer, wee Jimmy Aird, got up and sang '*My love is like a red, red, rose*' the colonel unashamedly started blubbering into his hanky and handed Jimmy half a crown. There were sniffles and greetin' faces in the audience after that one, too. The Scots as well as being notoriously cynical can be remarkably sentimental and we were no exception. Next, Davie Thom, the battalion comic, got up and told such stories that if my mum had heard, she would have dragged me home and washed my ears out.

The highlight of the evening came at the finale when Winston returned to the stage to recite a poem about a corpulent duchess. The officers tried to sit poker-faced, pretending they were somewhere else as this masterpiece was performed but as Mr Churchill moved on to the stanza about the duchess, a sailor and a coconut, their stony faces cracked and like the rest of us they joined in the uproarious laughter followed by riotous applause and vociferous demands for an encore.

For all this and more the lads began to worship him.

One lunchtime I was at a loose end, as the colonel was out inspecting the men in the trenches. I always made him sandwiches to take with him when doing his rounds and was left mooching around when Drew Pirie, one of the lads roped in to help with cookhouse, saw me through the doorway of the Farm staring back at him.

'Here, Jamie, stop standin' like a fart in a trance! Help me oot wi' these containers!'

He was taking up lunch to the boys in the saps including the one where I had almost headed a mortar a while back. I grabbed a handle in each hand and we made our way forward.

We had only gone a few yards when Drew stopped. He looked around him, then upwards.

He then glanced at me. 'Dae ye hear that'?'

Before I had the opportunity to respond, Drew roared out, 'FUCK'S SAKE! Jamie, git doon!'

Needing no second invitation I dived down, letting loose

the canisters when there was a crashing explosion from a shell landing in front of us. Trenches were built with traverses which meant that blasts and bullets did not sweep down through them, wiping everyone out. Apart from ringing ears and the crap scared out of me, I was unhurt.

Rising to his feet, Drew asked me if I was alright. I said yes. 'Oh, Christ!' he swore. 'The saps!'

We dashed forward, zigzagging round the trench line, and came across a scene I relive in my nightmares. We were at what was left of the sap where I and Mr Hakewill-Smith were almost killed on that memorable night. I looked over the edge of what was left of the parapet and as God is my witness I asked Drew, 'What's a side of beef doing in here?' I had in my capacity as Duncan's assistant to carry large sides of meat off wagons to the kitchens and on viewing the sight this was the first thing that came into my head.

'Eh? Whit did ye say?' Drew looked at me, and ordered calmly, 'Jamie, go back and tell Captain Harvey what's happened.'

I looked around again and registered that the 'side of beef' was in fact a man's bare leg attached to his lower abdomen and nothing else, and his private parts were hanging against the thigh.

My eyes focused on another strange, creamy-white object that was in fact a severed hand lying beside what was left of an ammunition box, and a foot in an army boot resting on top of the parapet. There was what could only be described as a reddish, spaghetti-like substance running down the sandbags that were still intact, and an arm lay across a smashed rifle butt lying amongst the debris. The rest of the three inhabitants of the sap had either been blown out into no-man's-land or had disintegrated.

There were no dramatics. I did not scream out loud in horror or faint or remain transfixed in shock. All this took a bare few seconds from reaching what was left of the sap to my turning around and running as fast as I could back to the forward trench.

When I arrived back, breathless, I ran into Captain Harvey, the homely features of his young face fused with a blend of worry and relief.

'Jamie, are you alright? What the hell were you doing there! You're wounded!'

Still blowing hard from my exertions, I could only gape at him. 'I'm wounded?'

He knelt down and gingerly lifted my lower trouser. The putty had come loose and looking down I noticed that my leg was soaked and started to feel a dull ache in my calf.

'No, it's not a wound, it's a burn; you've been scalded. Jamie, get to the aid station now.'

When the shell came over, I had let go of the food canisters and one of them, containing hot soup, had spilled over my lower leg, burning me severely.

I had not noticed anything until Captain Harvey spoke to me.

Chapter Eight

A few nights later, Colonel Churchill invited Archie Sinclair, the second in command, Captain Shaw, who had temporarily been attached to battalion to assist with signals until Lieutenant Kemp recovered from his injuries and Mr Hakewill-Smith to Soyer Farm for dinner.

The youngest of the officers (and the only regular left) was Mr Hakewill-Smith, nicknamed 'Bomber' because one of his duties was grenade-throwing training and keeping an eye on stocks of that weapon and other ordnance. He was a short, cheery lad who I got on well with as we liked to talk about books and football. It was strange having to address him as 'sir' but we had many chats together where formality dropped away and I think he was just lonely for someone his own age or near enough to talk to.

I looked forward to these 'mess' nights as I liked arranging them with the colonel and Duncan. I particularly enjoyed serving the officers and, occasionally, generals who popped in. One of the latter was the colonel's good friend, General Tudor, an artilleryman and an absolute gent, who gave me a nice tip which he was under no obligation to do after I had served him his dinner. Listening to their banter was an education, too.

Like everything else, Winston planned these evenings with precision but explained them to me in the simplest and most easily understood fashion:

'Now, James, just remember, the most important thing about a mess night: keep the drink flowing!' That was the only advice he gave and I stuck to it.

Amongst the regular packages sent to Winston was a large, heavily packed crate that arrived the day before. When he saw it he clasped his hands in delight, mumbling happily about someone called 'Roger'.

I always saved some of the contents of the parcels Winston received from home. Along with Duncan I prepared a dinner starting with my mum's recipe for potato soup (my home-made soups would become legend, particularly tomato, but I was always quick to give Mum the credit) followed by a main course of fillet of chicken in a wine sauce with veggies, spuds and gravy. A dessert of treacle sponge with syrup would round it off.

'Thank you, Jamie,' said Archie as I served the soup. 'Is this the famous *tattie a' la Gorgie*?'

'Aye, Major, and there's plenty more if you want it!'

'It is my certain belief that Mrs Melville's soups help make the distresses of war much less insufferable!' slurped Winston over a huge spoonful of potato and onion. That man was the messiest eater I ever saw.

'Wait till you try her egg and bacon pie!' I cried, struggling with a wine bottle.

'Give it here, Jamie,' said Mr Shaw. I had not yet quite mastered the knack of using a corkscrew.

I stood over him and watched. 'See?' he said, as the cork popped, and handed back the bottle.

I could never remember whether to serve to the left or right but went round filling each glass before returning to assist Duncan, busily preparing the rest of the meal.

The bottle did not last long, of course.

'James!' roared Winston.

I rushed back through to the dining area.

'James,' declared Winston, 'there is something missing from my life at the moment and when I go without it, life becomes appalling and unbearable! Can you think what it might be?'

I'm sometimes slow on the uptake and for the life of me did not know what he was on about.

'Ehmm… Mrs Churchill, Colonel?'

The others guffawed and then inspiration came to me.

'More to drink!'

'Eureka! Yes! Now bring us one of the bottles of champagne.'

I went through the back and found the crate that had recently been delivered to the colonel from England, and slipped out a bottle.

I returned with it, certain that this time I would not require assistance. It had wiring round the cork and I began to unwind it where it had been twisted off.

'Ah, Pol Roger 1895!' exclaimed Winston. He looked like a small boy in a sweet shop eagerly waiting, being handed over his favourite treat. 'Can you manage to open it yourself?'

I had never seen a bottle of champagne before and did not know much about them. 'Yes, I can. This looks a lot easier to open than the wine bottle.' I removed the wire and began to dig into the cork with my thumbnail…

Winston turned to Bomber. 'Such a fine bottle, Edmund, have you ever… JESUS CHRIST!' At that moment I turned directly to where Winston was sitting and as I dug away at the cork it edged out more and I was now in front of him as the cork popped and crashed into the ceiling. Winston ducked to his left and just managed to get his head under the level of the table as the cork came down, bounced off the table and settled on the floor. Luckily the bottle had been pointing more in the vertical than the horizontal at the (near) fatal moment.

I did not know where to look; I stood, mouth open, looking at the bottle as its contents seeped out all bubbly over my fingers.

'The bottle's faulty, sir!' I wailed. 'It's no' me tae blame!' At moments of stress I was sometimes careless of my mother's entreaties to speak the King's English. It was no use turning for help from Archie and Mr Hakewill-Smith because they were almost on the floor themselves, not exactly ducking for cover, but because they were nearly crying with laughter.

By now Winston was back sitting upright. 'Why, I have been shot at by insurrectionists in Cuba,' he declared, 'I have been ambushed by native tribes in the North West Frontier of India, attacked by savage Fuzzie-Wuzzies in the Sudan, charged with the 21st Lancers at thousands of hostiles at Omdurman and been chased by Boers all over the High Veld. I have been lambasted, scourged and browbeaten across the floor of the House of Commons and on election campaigning and never been as much as scratched or suffered a broken nail! Far worse than all that I have described in being hazardous and injurious to my person, were my experiences as part of the English public school system; that I survived *relatively* unscathed!

'But I could never have imagined that my life would end sitting in a farmhouse in Belgium at the hands of James Melville of Edinburgh, armed with a bottle of Pol Roger 1895! Executed not by a bullet but by a cork! But if I am to expire in such a manner then I am grateful that as the instrument of my death hits me full in the nose, my last ever sensation will be catching a sniff at my moment of expiration of the world's finest champagne!' Everyone including me roared with laughter.

They settled down and Archie slapped me on the back as I filled his glass.

Winston took a huge gulp after I poured and handed me back the glass to refill. 'Ah! Pol Roger 1895!' he declared after smacking his lips. 'When I became President of the Board of Trade in 1908, my very first senior cabinet posting, in order to celebrate I ordered some very fine champagne of which this has always been my favourite. I worked my way through it lovingly and with devotion. Recently, I ordered a case to be sent to me here as I missed it so very much. James! You are my most trustworthy young friend, bring over a glass!'

I brought over a whisky tumbler and he took the bottle and filled it. 'Gentlemen, I ask you all to partake with me. I order you to raise your glasses to the King, Scotland and the Royal Scots Fusiliers!'

We did and I had my first taste of champagne. I had no idea what it would be like, so I just took a small sip and found it sweet and bubbly, which I suppose is the best description there is of that drink.

'What do you think, Jamie?' Archie asked.

'It's gone right up my nose!' I replied, which naturally aroused further hilarity.

I went through the back and left them to gas and guzzle together as Duncan and I sat and had our own dinners on our knees and yarned away for a while. I have to say, that night I had never felt happier in my young life. I believed I was being looked after and also, somehow, I was growing within myself.

I was evolving from a lad who spent much of his life worrying too much about circumstances that I should not have had to concern myself with, namely, being responsible for looking after drunken parents and young children: my sisters. In Wardlaw Place I used to sit up at night waiting for the door to open and Dad to come in, wondering as to the extent of his drunkenness and how violent a mood he may be in. I was fed up with being punched and kicked, trying to drag him off my mother and getting backhanded slaps. I once had to slam the door on him, when he was in one particularly bad mood, and just managed to get it locked. I peed myself in fear when he burst it open, and managed to dive under the bed whilst he tried to pull me out and my mother screamed at him to leave me alone.

In truth, sometimes I was glad he was dead. How would my life have developed living with that? If he had lived I am convinced that sooner or later he would have killed one of us in his drink-induced rage. Filial love, the ties of 'blood': they can only go so far. Fond memories of my father, indeed.

But now, in this frequently bombed farmhouse in Belgium a few thousand yards from the German lines, I was for the first time *alive* and enjoying life. I felt valued. Of course, I knew my mother valued me but that was in a different way. That was as the son of a woman who had deep feelings of inferiority about herself and her upbringing, or why else would she have married a man like my father? I tried to be her protector; I *was* her protector, because I understood her. Though I was a child, I knew her secrets.

I was the only person in her life who could see no wrong in her; I would always defend her, but in all that I had placed a burden on myself because I was trapped; I was trapped against her bruised body and battered soul. I would only escape from that by doing what orphans and children of broken homes have done all through the ages: run away to join the army. I was no different from the sons of workhouses and the street. I would go on to follow the drum to find a place for myself, to *become* myself just as all the others had.

'James! The plates!' Winston's roar broke into my reverie.

I went through and started clearing the table in order to serve dessert.

'Your escape, sir, tell us about it.' I heard South Africa being mentioned and my ears pricked up as I was aware of Winston's famous adventures in the Boer War. Mr Hakewill-Smith was keen to hear as he himself was South African born.

'Oh, sir,' I asked, 'if you're going to tell about that, can I listen too?'

'Of course, my boy,' Winston replied, 'but first you must serve our dessert because I cannot finish as delicious a meal as this without something sweet to round it off! What is it to be?'

'Treacle pud and syrup!' I announced.

'Bravo!' roared Archie. 'More of Mum's magic?'

'No, Fortmans and Massons, I think, Major.'

'That is Fortnum and Mason, my dear James, and they are purveyors to the King, you know,' Winston corrected.

'Well, if it's good enough for them, I suppose; but I bet it's not as good as my mum's,' and I headed through the back quickly in order to serve them and return to sit down and listen to the colonel.

The story is well known. They made a film of it too; I saw it years ago. The young bloke who played Winston was pretty good in it, I thought. But I have actually heard the man himself describe it and he made events seem so real that it made you feel as if you were there with him. He was boastful of course, but he was also humble in explaining the times when he was at his lowest.

There had always been question marks about Winston's conduct. In this, his most famous exploit, he was originally to be part of a group of three who were escaping together but on jumping the wire at the state-school-cum-officers'-prison in Pretoria, where he was held as prisoner of war by the Boers, Winston had taken off on his own without the other two. He explained to us his reasons after telling us the full story.

He relit his cigar and took a few puffs. 'I am sometimes asked whether I acted dishonourably by making off myself instead of waiting for my fellow escapee comrades. But to those who say that I say this: *you were not there*. The exigency of the moment told me that now was the time! That when such opportunities arise the best-laid plans, as our fellow Ayrshire man himself has said, *gang agly*! You may know that moment one day, Edmund!' and he looked at Mr Hakewill-Smith. 'You may have to get up from the position you have been ordered to hold because you have spotted an opportunity to *take*! Initiative is a quality that is discouraged by the old but there are times when spirited men of action and thrust must stake their all and strike while the iron is hot! For he who hesitates may have lost the moment, the impetus and thus, the day!'

I understood what he meant by this, and a fascinating discussion ensued as I sat cross-legged on the floor, looking up with a bottle of pop in my hand.

'But sir, it is a true military maxim that no plan survives the first sting of battle. That officers must use initiative in order to adapt to changing circumstances,' Mr Hakewill-Smith pointed out.

'Yes, but how many *do* act so?' retorted Winston. 'The navy has for a hundred years now been an effective weapon because it relies, teaches, *and invokes* initiative in its captains. I will let you all into a secret, even you, James. In 1914 the fleet was ready to sail *before the war had actually been declared!* I, as First Lord of the Admiralty and acting under my own initiative, had, after careful calculation of the threat, ordered the navy on full standby and at the very *instant* of war's declaration I sent my signal to the fleet: *"Commence hostilities against the German navy!"* But the army? No, it is the moribund service sadly, I must admit, and it has always been the case. It is a melancholy fact that our army has only flourished under those mavericks that fortunately, England,' he quickly realised his error, '*Britain* has been blessed with at her greatest hours of need: Marlborough, Wolfe, Moore and Wellington, to name but four.

'All these men were mocked, despised, ridiculed and blackguarded because they were different. Whether it was due to them coming from lowly or undistinguished backgrounds or had histories less than pure, they inspired jealousy through their brilliance: Wellington had more to fear at Whitehall than he ever did in the Peninsula; John Moore was forever defending his actions against men who knew nothing of war; Wolfe, admittedly a loathsome man as his conduct at Culloden testifies, nevertheless was a wholly original thinker in the art of war. Only a genius could conceive his plan of men scaling great heights at Quebec with ropes and having the nerve and luck, yes luck! to see them though to success. My great ancestor, John Churchill, Duke of Marlborough, was laid low by the jealousies of little men.'

'Was it not said that Moore and Nelson were enemies?' interjected Captain Shaw.

'Whilst attempting to wrest Corsica from the French, where Nelson lost his eye, they did quarrel,' answered Winston. He was warming up now and would soon be in full flow. I loved it all, listening to him speak of all these famous men as if he had personally known them.

'They disagreed over strategy,' Winston went on. 'It all began when Admiral Hood, the naval commander, wrongfully requested Moore to accept the recommendation of the then *Captain* Nelson that a vigorous attack on Bastia would be a success, if they would strike immediately, rather than accept his own commander General Dundas's belief that it could not be done, and to make it known of his acceptance to the general as leverage. In his heart, Colonel Moore, as was his rank at the time, knew that it could succeed but felt honour-bound to side with his own general. This would cause a wholly unnecessary rupture in relations then and later between these two officers of genius and humanity.'

'Wasn't Moore an MP for a while?' Archie asked.

'Indeed, he was Member for Lanark when he was a very young man for a short time under the patronage of the Duke of Hamilton, his close friend. He stood as an independent and would brook no interference and accepted the position on the proviso that he would only vote on actions that his conscience was clear on.'

'Yes, admirable,' Archie drawled. 'Then again, as an independent he could afford such scruples!'

'His father was only a simple doctor but by his abilities the young John rose to prominence,' Winston continued. 'Moore was a man of great honour; this was the main reason he found so much trouble in his life. In Corsica he clashed with the

British Governor, Sir Gilbert Elliot, when he wrongfully raised a brigand to be successor to the great General Paoli as leader of the Corsican people against the advice of Moore and threatened to have him removed from the island.

'In Ireland he was asked to investigate Lord Westmeath, who was accused of illegally and fraudulently withholding pay from his regiment. He was indeed found guilty and another powerful enemy was made. When he commanded an army sent to Sweden to reinforce that land, which at the time was Britain's sole remaining ally against invasion by the Russians, Moore clashed with the insane Swedish King Gustavus, who asked him to perform duties that were in excess of his written orders. Moore refused and was threatened with arrest! His Majesty King George's emissary threatened war if General Moore was not released from this threat immediately, and the Swedes capitulated.

'In Spain he suffered by the fact that false reports were being made to Castlereagh and Canning in England as to the strengths of the Spanish armies. These reports were also emanating from the British representative in Spain, John Frere, whom Moore distrusted. He was left fatally short of funds with which to equip and feed his army. Then the worst news imaginable reached his ears: Napoleon himself was in Spain at the head of an enormous army and was determined to annihilate the small British force in his midst.

'General Moore's great strategy in Spain was to lure the French after him, thereby drawing its strength north, in order that Lisbon and Portugal would remain safe for British forces to land there later, and away from southern Spain where the patriot armies were undefeated. He had to keep his plan secret and this had a serious effect on the morale of the army, who believed that they were retreating ignominiously; and thus discipline came close to breaking completely, abetted by the terrible conditions and lack of supplies getting to the men and, it has to be said, the poor performance of many officers.

'Yet this great man suffered through the jealousies and incompetence of those who did not understand war. He clashed continually with Frere, who sent scurrilous reports back to Castlereagh, who believed them. He was not helped either by the very low calibre of many of his officers, who would later be quick to lay blame at the feet of a dead man. They scoffed at his humane methods though his army was made up in large numbers by scum from prisons, pulled in by notorious "crimps", that were in many cases uncontrollable. In all this he still kept to his principles; only in extreme circumstances did he resort to hanging looters and pillagers who were stealing from good men in the army.

'This great soldier was indeed a man of honour in all matters. It is said that he had never personally killed an enemy in battle and deliberately would not in fact do so. His training methods, his creation of Light Infantry and his humanity rightfully earned him the mantle of "true father" of the modern British army,' Winston concluded.

'He died at the battle of Corunna, but he beat the French!' This was my sole, excited contribution to the discussion, for of course I had heard all about Moore at school, the man our teacher labelled 'Scotland's greatest soldier'.

'Yes, James, he did! His army was in full retreat throughout that dreadful winter campaign, harried all the way, but he was able, through his will and genius, to turn that battered and bedraggled band around and strike at their pursuers! In doing so he won glory, but was struck from his horse by a shell. He lay dying, but kept himself alive long enough to be told of the victory.

'Then they buried him in his cloak and the great Marshall Soult himself, whom he had defeated, built a monument over his grave as a mark of the deep respect of one great general for another.'

It was stirring stuff, certainly to me. Archie was sprawled with his leg over the chair with a brandy glass and a knowing look but young Mr Hakewill-Smith and I were truly spellbound by it all. I think both of us were imagining ourselves on that dreadful march through northern Spain, freezing in the Galician winter, and comparing it to the nice warm farmhouse we were in now; and even the trenches we cowered in seemed like luxury compared to that terrible Iberian ordeal. Then Winston rose and began to declaim in a deep and sonorous voice:

> *Not a drum was heard, not a funeral note,*
> *As his corpse to the rampart we hurried;*
> *Not a soldier discharged his farewell shot*
> *O'er the grave where our hero we buried.*

> *Slowly and sadly we laid him down,*
> *From the field of his fame fresh and gory;*
> *We carved not a line, and we raised not a stone,*
> *But we left him alone with his glory.*

Once finished, he sat down and took out a handkerchief to rub his eyes.

'Colonel,' asked Mr Hakewill-Smith in an attempt to lighten the mood, 'in your opinion was the Duke of Marlborough a greater soldier than the Duke of Wellington?'

This was a subject as close to the heart of Winston Churchill as you could get. He blew his nose and poured more brandy.

'That, though an excellent question, is an unfair one to ask of a Churchill,' he replied. 'Whichever way I answer I could be said to be accused of bias; or worse, being accused of appearing *not* to be biased! It is like being asked to choose between one's children! My answer is that both had such great qualities, each was the equal of the other.'

'But Robert the Bruce would have clobbered both at the same time! Eh, Jamie?' Archie winked over at me.

'Both dukes, certainly,' Winston responded, 'would have met their match in the Bruce. Great generals are great generals regardless of the age they live in or their armoury, be that of the Schiltrom, the Flintlock or the Baker rifle!'

'The Bruce liked the axe, Winston, just ask Henry de Bohun!' joked Archie.

Winston then went on at length about the achievements of Marlborough in detail. The battles of Blenheim, Malplaquet, Ramillies and Oudenarde, in all of which our regiment played a role, were each explained and described as if he himself had been there to view them. It was enthralling, but the impish Captain Shaw, at the end of Winston's monologue, leaning back in his seat, declared:

'Corporal John was a fine general, yes, but I wouldn't have trusted him with my grandmother!'

'Yes, indeed,' admitted Winston, 'he was known as a rake in his youth but his marriage to Sarah, his beloved wife, was one of history's great romances.'

'He was thrown in the Tower of London too, I believe,' Shaw continued in his mischief-making.

Winston, unaware as always when he was being ragged (or was he?), dived into another discourse. Meanwhile I could see Archie was slowly losing the will to live at this point and I whispered a question to him:

'What's a "rake"?'

'A man who likes chasing after the lassies,' he whispered back.

Wondering how on earth the word 'rake' could be used to describe such a pursuit, my mind started to veer off the subject being presently discussed. It became far less interesting to me as Winston and Shaw discussed matters like James II's bleeding nose and something called 'interest'. Shaw would mention 'duplicity' and 'rapaciousness' and the duke's double dealings with the Jacobites, and his wife's political interference, and Winston would respond with tales of the duke's great reforms of medical procedures for the wounded and injured, pensions for soldiers and their dependants and instances of his ordinary humanity, of how when his army was on the march in Germany under heavy rain he passed by a group of men who were too exhausted to carry on and invited the men to get into the coach he was travelling in whilst he got outside and walked.

I knew that some of the officers deliberately took advantage of Winston on occasion. I have no doubt that Winston used underhanded, emotionally devious methods in order to win their approval himself. The tears that flowed from time to time such as at the concert when he heard a song sung by one of the lads would have appeared genuine to the lower ranks but the demonstration of the same with sophisticates like Shaw might not cut it.

Young as I was, I was starting to grow more aware of human nuances and I found that with certain types, Captain Gibb included, they were laughing *at* him. I liked Captain Gibb despite that tendency of his, as he had the saving grace that his manner was not sneering or cynical, but more one of wry amusement mixed with genuine admiration. It seemed to me that Shaw wanted to hurt; that I could not forgive. I was glad he was going to be with us only temporarily.

At the time I myself was too young to comprehend the hidden meaning behind the colonel's passionate championing of these two men Moore and Marlborough, other than plain and simple admiration for them both as military greats. Of course I understood it later. He saw himself to be a visionary just like Sir John and the duke; an innovator and a genius laid low, as they were, by pettiness and jealousy. Moore and Marlborough would, despite their struggles with the powers of the day, prevail and have their genius laid bare for all the ages to see and admire. I believe Winston felt he was of the same mettle, but at this point in his life truly despaired that he would ever be allowed to prove it.

I got up to refill glasses and remove plates, and while through the back, washed up.

'...then we will accept your judgment, Winston,' I heard Archie conclude as I came back through a short time later. 'But when these men cannot be found, what then? How do we win our wars if we have no Bruces or Moores to hand?' he asked, stretching back in his seat.

'Why, we have Tommy, and Jock, and Taffy and Paddy, of course!' hailed Winston.

On hearing this, I stood and recited without pause:

For it's Tommy this an' Tommy that, an' "Chuck him out, the brute!"
But it's "Saviour of 'is country" when the guns begin to shoot;
An' it's Tommy this, an' Tommy that, an' anything you please;
An' Tommy ain't a bloomin' fool – you bet that Tommy sees!

'Well said, Jamie! Bravo!' Archie cried, putting down his glass to clap his approval.

'That was well remembered, James! It is right that you should know your Kipling!' Winston stood and shook my hand. The truth was I only ever remembered those lines because of the swear words.

Winston then turned to Bomber. 'Now, Edmund, have you something in your repertoire to add to the evening? Remember, it must be martial!'

'Oh, I just can't think, sir!' Mr Hakewill-Smith replied. Then, composing himself, he stood and began to recite:

The loyal Stewarts with Montrose,
So boldly set upon their foes,

> *And brought them down with Highland blows,*
> *Upon the haughs of Cromdale.*
> *Of twenty thousand Cromwell's men,*
> *Five hundred fled to Aberdeen*
> *The rest of them lie on the plain,*
> *Upon the haughs of Cromdale.*

'Bravo, indeed!' Winston exclaimed. 'However, there is much of what we would term "poetic licence" in that dirge, Edmund!'

I tapped on Archie's shoulder. 'What does that mean?'

'It means whoever wrote that song, Jamie, was just making it up as he went along.'

'Shaw! Are you not to take your turn in the harmony?' asked Winston.

'Oh, I wondered when you would get round to me!' laughed Captain Shaw, a handsome and moustachioed paragon, reputedly a ladies' man. I wondered what he would recite.

'Let me see.' He stood, cleared his throat, and started to sing:

> *Maxwelton braes are bonnie, where early fa's the dew,*
> *Where me and Annie Laurie made up the promise true;*
> *Made up the promise true, and ne'er forget will I;*
> *And for bonnie Annie Laurie I'd lay doun my head and die.*

His voice was fine and clear. As he sang there was total silence and others outside the Farmhouse stopped to listen to the sweet sound.

Winston, tears pouring from his eyes, congratulated the singer with a hearty shake of his hand and then spoke after blowing his nose.

'My friends, let us all now raise our glasses to the immortal memories of the great warriors of genius we have discussed this evening. Let their stirring deeds forever encourage us to do our best to act with courage, humanity and magnanimity as all warriors should! Let us also drink to all our Annie Lauries, wherever they are now!'

We stood, Mr Hakewill-Smith self-consciously, Archie and Shaw knowingly, myself solemnly, and together drank the toast. We all settled back down and then I came out with what I had deduced from the evening's conversation:

'So what you are you saying, Colonel, is that unless you are considered to be different, are a genius and disobey orders, you can never be a success in the British army and win our wars?'

There was silence. 'James.' Winston uttered. He puffed on his cigar and looked over at me.

'James Melville, it is not the place of batmen, even those as eminent as yourself, to tell British officers the truth about their army. Now I do believe that biscuits have yet to be served and I am aware that my last parcel from home contained some small supply of Roquefort.'

'Is… that the really stinky cheese, Colonel?'

'Indeed! Now remove our dessert plates and proceed with the cheese and biscuits.'

I went off, brought the cheeseboard through and then nipped back in to start on the dishes. There was some treacle pudding left and I had a few spoonsful whilst I washed up.

I had just finished, when I heard Winston order, 'James! Another bottle of champagne!' I brought it through and this time handed it to Archie, who winked at me.

'…mostly farmers and miners, really. I'm the only regular left!' They were discussing the peace-time occupations of the officers and Mr Hakewill-Smith was describing them to the colonel. 'What did your father do, Jamie?' Archie said as he worked on the cork.

I had feared this sort of thing. I really did not want to

discuss it with anyone. But at the same time I knew how kind these men had been to me and it would not have been right to clam up. 'He... he was a fitter. In a factory that builds machines for paper mills.'

'A fine trade!' Winston declared. 'Where would we be without paper?'

Archie opened the bottle and went round each man and poured. Whilst on his feet he asked, 'Jamie, could you relate to us the circumstances of your home life?' Archibald Sinclair would one day be the leader of the Liberal Party. He was also a baronet and Winston also was a Liberal at the time. I had been taught from an early age to despise Tories and that at least Liberals had social consciences of a sort.

'Pull a seat over to the table, James. I believe it is always a good thing to listen to the experiences of the young and to value their opinions,' said Winston.

I sat down. I really did not know what to say. The evening, which had been so thrilling, had suddenly died on me.

'It's alright, Jamie, we're not prying. I will try to make you understand why we're interested,' said Archie, kindly. 'Colonel Churchill and I are very much interested in social reform. Do you know what that means?' I nodded but was not too sure.

'What he would like to see is that ordinary people get a better deal in life. Whilst in government, Mr Churchill brought into legislation new laws on working practices and pensions in order to improve the lives of the poor. He is always looking for ways to further improve things; that is one of the main reasons why he is in politics.'

'James,' Winston asked, 'tell us about your home.'

I looked around the faces in the room and began, 'We live in a house in Wardlaw Place. I've three sisters and two brothers. Two of my brothers were taken away by the Corporation. They were twins. They were taken away to be adopted and we've not seen them in years. We don't know where they went. We've not had a letter from them. My dad...' I stopped. I was starting to feel light-headed, akin to the sensation I experienced moments before I passed out when I was first brought to the attention of the colonel.

'Go on, Jamie, you are among friends here, there is no reason to feel shame for anything that you tell us,' said Archie.

Winston, aware of my discomfort, got up and came over to rescue me. He understood my awkwardness, and recognising my distress announced, 'I think this young man no longer desires to say more, Archibald.' Winston then went through to his own room and returned with a slab of chocolate which he handed to me.

He then put a hand on my shoulder, 'Never feel shame, my boy. You are as good as any man here and have lived your young life with honour and integrity.'

He returned to his seat. 'Now, gentlemen, I am going to pour another glass of champagne as I feel it always tastes better after a brandy. I will then relate my fascinating adventures in America where I was invited to visit to lecture shortly after my exploits in South Africa.'

I perked up; like all youngsters I was beguiled by the United States.

'You've been to the *Wild West*, Colonel?'

'Yes; and all America rejoiced at it!'

Word got out, as these things always do in small communities, about my exploits with the champagne bottle. For a few days after, wherever I went the lads would pretend to duck and start whistling the tune *Champagne Charlie is my Name*. Some changed the words and sang out loud whenever I appeared:

> *Champagne Jamie is his name,*
> *Killing colonels is his game!*

Chapter Nine

In early March the colonel was due for a week's home leave. Being his batman, I overheard (and listened in to) any number of conversations he had; the usual ones regarding battalion business but also a lot of political discussions. Most of it was over my head but even I could not help noticing how frustrated and downright angry he was at his treatment by the government. In particular he said a lot of nasty things about the prime minister, Mr Asquith.

I am older and wiser now, and understand that his frustrations were those of any unfortunate man who finds himself made scapegoat for the actions of others. But I was shocked to hear him lambasting Lord Kitchener also for his 'tardiness and ineffectualness in preparing the army for the campaign'. The campaign being Gallipoli, of course. Back in those days Kitchener was regarded as having almost godlike powers and even my mum had a wee picture of him on the wall at home. He was omniscient, not just because of the famous poster of him, but because he was deemed to be, like the King, beyond criticism and as a child I read of his achievements in avenging the saintly General Gordon and overcoming the Boers.

The truth was more complicated, and many young writers today have attempted to paint a different picture of him, but back then he was untouchable and hearing Winston criticise him was for me a jolt indeed.

In view of his up-and-coming leave, I heard him discussing a speech he intended to make in the House of Commons. I assumed that leave would have meant him spending time with his wife and family but he had different ideas on how he would pass his furlough back in England. The speech in question became notorious as the one where he would call for the reinstatement of Admiral Fisher to the War Cabinet and would go down like a lead balloon, damaging further his already battered reputation. He'd have been better off staying at home with his family. But he was no ordinary officer on leave; and no ordinary Member of Parliament.

I was clearing away the plates after lunch at Soyer and Archie, in between chatting to Winston, was asking me if I wanted to head back home, too. I had not really thought about it. Winston had told me I could as I was due leave but he also said that I would have the run of the rear command post if I decided against it and he would leave me some goodies from his last parcel from home and also some books, which he insisted I read. This all sounded very nice to me, the thought of taking it easy for a week with nice tins of Fortnum & Mason's best and some pleasant reading. I was tempted to forego, leave which would have involved a lot of train travel and the ghastly thought of two sea voyages. I still had not forgotten the horrors of being sick on the way over.

It was not that I did not want to see my mum. I wrote all the time, but the truth was that I just wanted some time to myself. Archie said don't worry; I would be left in peace, off duty, and could take it that my week out of the line could be regarded officially as leave.

The 6th was a well-run battalion with very high morale, for in many units men in so-called rest areas were made to work on trench repairs and other labouring duties. This was an outrage, considering that in some places they spent nearly six days up to their knees in water in the front line trenches and were exhausted when relieved, only to be turned into mules during their so-called quiet period. Winston would have none of that nonsense.

I had come to like and respect Major Archie Sinclair. He was a good-natured type who took a genuine interest in people.

He shared a lot of similarities with Winston in that he had a rich American mother but by the time he was five both his parents were dead and he was brought up by his grandfather, who was a bit of an old bugger. Though suffering an unhappy childhood like Winston he was exceptionally positive and showed a kind and caring attitude towards everyone regardless of rank and would be a great mainstay of Winston's in the next war. As you have probably gathered the 6th was a lucky battalion: all the officers without exception were top class. They were all civilians in uniform, and learning as they went along, but they all pulled together and I have no complaints about any of them.

In the end Winston was away ten days, having requested another three days leave on parliamentary business. He spent them trying to patch up his already bruised standing after the unfortunate speech received almost universal condemnation. When he returned, he showed up at his office at Soyer Farm, sat himself down in his chair and did not speak.

Knowing nothing, of course, of what occurred, and glad to see him back, I greeted him with a hearty cry. 'Welcome hame, Colonel!'

He stirred in his seat. 'Yes, Jamie, I understand that I am at least *home.*'

'We missed you, ye know!' I continued, cheerily. 'Nothing much has happened, though George Allan got a splinter in the side when a shell fell short! Me, I finished *The Pickwick Papers!*'

He perked up. 'Ah, Mr Pickwick! I am glad to hear that, Jamie. My life has taken a downturn. Oh, for the optimism of Mr Micawber!'

I knew that character. 'Aye, he always thought things would get better! But what's wrong, Colonel? Just wish you were still home, eh? I ken!'

'James, bring me some tea and let me see my mail.'

I went through the back and prepared a brew and grabbed

the bundle of mail that was kept in a drawer awaiting his return.

'Here ye are, Colonel!' I handed him the mail and left the teapot on his desk.

'Is that not from Brigade?' I asked.

'Hmm,' he murmured as he sliced open the letter on top of the pile.

He read through the communication slip, put it back down on the desk, stood up and began to laugh.

'James! We have an informer in our midst!'

'What? What do you mean, Colonel?'

He picked the slip back up and read out the communication from Brigade to me. It was marked for the personal attention of the Commanding Officer, 6th Battalion, Royal Scots Fusiliers, and stated that there were concerns being raised over 'undue leniency' being shown by Lieutenant-Colonel Churchill in regards to disciplinary issues, in particular towards the lower ranks. The brigadier felt he must make it clear that it was an essential part of his duties to ensure that at all times Lieutenant-Colonel Churchill set an example expected of him in order to maintain good order and morale.

'So, who has "grassed me up"?'

I looked at him but did not know what to say. He then picked up the flimsy, tore it into pieces and threw all the bits into the wastebin at the side of his desk.

He was back in business.

Chapter Ten

In early April occurred a minor incident which escalated to involve courts martial and death sentences being handed out. In view of how I have described the leadership structure of the battalion and the character of its colonel and his officers, it seems improbable that matters could have reached such a grave condition. That they did was all down to one barrack-room lawyer, an inexperienced young subaltern and a large bottle of rum.

It all began when about half a dozen blokes who served in Captain Ramsay's company were at Maison 1875 soaking up the contents of their rum ration the night before they were due to return to the line.

Two of them were fit and able to get out of their bunks next morning, and head off with the rest of the reserve to replace us. But the other four were too sick drunk to make it and lay where they were, in a state of hangover, which must have been pretty bad indeed because they were all good lads with flawless records.

When it was discovered that they were missing from the roll, a young officer of the company panicked. Instead of speaking quietly to Mr Ramsay and sorting it out in a less formal manner, he acted independently and had them arrested; they were left to sleep off their hangovers on the orderly room floor.

Later, one of the four men, who I will call 'Smith' as I do not want his real name revealed because he was a major player in the trouble that followed due to his cussedness, demanded that he speak to his company commander and have immediate representation.

From my own experience I knew that the subaltern had

messed up and Winston nearly blew a gasket when Captain Ramsay reported the matter to him. Smith had demanded a full court martial in order that he and the three others could have their names cleared. The young officer had lost his head and swore at the men, at one point accusing them of cowardice. Smith had not forgiven him this and got it into his skull that a guilty plea would prove that the men accepted their culpability, but when evidence came out about the lieutenant's conduct it would sway the court in their favour and they would therefore act leniently.

The papers went through and a field general court martial was to be conducted. The night before the tribunal, I was witness to a secret meeting arranged by the colonel with the ringleader, Smith, in an attempt to induce him to reconsider his guilty plea.

It was late at the Farm and Winston was with Archie and Captain Ramsay, who by now was at his wits' end as he began to contemplate the very real prospect of carrying out a death sentence via a firing squad. It should not be forgotten that all our officers were civilians in uniform who would go back to their day jobs once hostilities ended. None of them envisioned such a scenario as conducting an actual execution.

I was hanging around the mess serving area, basically a small room that had been turned into a kitchen which was close to Winston's makeshift office, when I heard voices murmuring about someone being ready to be brought inside.

'Absolutely no one must know,' I heard Winston say.

'Aye, but will he remain quiet?' Captain Ramsay moaned. 'He absolutely insists on pleading guilty and has convinced the others to do the same! There's no getting through to him! He's never been any trouble before, none of them has. Until this! It's so… middling! It's not enough to shoot a cat over!'

I heard other voices and peeked round to see Smith, a short, greying, almost waif-like and heavily pockmarked man in his late thirties, standing before Winston, who sat at his desk. The other two officers stood to the side of the colonel as the crackling sounds and glow from the fireplace, along with the dull light from an oil lamp, provided the backdrop to the furtive scene.

'Smith, I have brought you here to have a little discussion,' Winston began. 'Please sit down.' Archie brought a chair round. Smith looked awkwardly at it as if unsure of what to do but then slowly sat.

'Would you like a drink?' Winston asked.

'Sir, drink is partly the cause o' the trouble I am in and I huv nae wish tae get in tae any mair. No thank ye, but thanks for askin'.'

'Well, I am going to have one.' He poured from the decanter on his desk as Smith looked over at it.

'Are you quite sure now?'

I have to admit that though I was as exasperated with Smith as everyone else, I admired his manner in front of the colonel and was pleased to hear him say: 'Alright sir, I would be honoured tae drink wi' ye.'

Winston poured a generous tot, rose from his seat and walked round the desk to hand the glass to Smith.

'Where were you employed before you joined our battalion?' asked Winston, back at his desk after taking a sip of his drink.

'In the yairds, sir!' Meaning the Greenock shipyards.

'You were a union convenor, I believe. That is a very important position. It would mean you not being liable for conscription in a 'starred' position like that. Yet you volunteered. Why?'

'It wiz my duty, sir, tae ma country. There wid be enough guid men tae fill ma boots back there, them as being too auld to join up. I wid be returned to ma post at the end o' the war.'

'I sincerely hope that you do and that is why we are having

this meeting. Mr Smith, I think you may, understandably, misconstrue the ethos I am instilling into this battalion. My belief from long years of service is that there are very few bad privates but very many bad officers. But amongst those good privates there is sometimes a belief that all officers are institutionally bad, and amongst the bad officers the reciprocal belief that all privates are recalcitrant and non-compliant. Do you share my view?'

'I dinnae quite folla, sir.' Neither did I at first.

'Would you ever expect me or Captain Ramsay to accuse you of cowardice?'

'No sur, niver! You'se ur gentlemen!'

'Then it follows that Lieutenant ------- is not a gentleman. Or is he merely an inexperienced *young* gentleman that over time will learn never again to use such a term as "coward" to describe good, reliable, honest men like yourself and your three comrades?'

Smith, trying to comprehend the gist of what Winston was saying, mumbled that he hoped it would be the case.

'Therefore it follows, if you follow the logic, that not *every* officer and *every* court martial desires to shoot men and if there is a way around that to the satisfaction of good order and discipline then that way should be found?'

Smith, glass in hand, declared: 'Sir, ah ken whit ye're saying but oan ma honour I ken I did wrang in gettin' sick drunk and no appearin' fir duty. If a boy acted like that in the yairds he wid get his erse kicked! Pardon ma language, sir. *There it follows* that I must plead ma guilt and hope fir leniency when it is seen that I and ma comrades were provoked by the false accusation o' cowardice and shirking which nae guid, honest sojer should be allowed tae endure fae ony man alive!'

Winston drained his glass. I could see that even he was admitting defeat in the place of such obstinacy, but knowing my man I knew he would be secretly admiring of Smith. That gave me confidence.

'As for that matter, and your case has been put most eloquently, I must leave it to the president of the court to decide the outcome. I will only ask this of you: consider pleading *not guilty*. I wish you the best.' He then opened a drawer and lifted out a half-bottle which he placed in front of him.

'There appears to be a bottle of whisky on my desk, Major?'

'So there is, Colonel.' Archie lifted it and went round to Smith and slipped it into his jacket pocket.

Smith saluted and was led off by Captain Ramsay.

Winston then rose from his desk and, picking up the decanter, hurled it in anger against the wall where it smashed into pieces. I rushed through with a brush and shovel as Winston pounded around the room exclaiming: '*Bloody* man!'

Only Archie was now left with him.

'Calm down, Winston!'

'Calm? How can I be calm when those fools are going to shoot four good men of mine! For what? All because a silly boy accuses grown men of cowardice! *Cowards*! If any man called me that I should strike him on his arse!'

'General Furse! You have to see him. The commander in chief will automatically sign any death warrant unless he hears personally from the area commander.'

'The commander in chief would sign his *own* death warrant if handed to him!'

I had finished sweeping up the glass. It was a pity as I had always thought that decanter a lovely object. I then stood and looked at Winston.

'Those *people* must try and understand that this is a *citizen* army! A new *kind* of army made up of butchers, tailors, foundry workers and lawyers, bankers and baronets! It is an army of independent men, of *thinkers*! Of men who will return to their professions, their offices, their farms! The entire King's Regulations require to be rewritten! It must take cognisance of the fact that men are not to be treated as automatons any longer and that the wars of the modern age cannot be won by such!'

Archie sat down, a concerned look on his handsome young face. 'Winston, we have to think. They will be found guilty of desertion. They will be sentenced to death. The order needs to be confirmed.'

'Yes, yes, yes!'

'That gives us time to get Furse and fill him in on the case. You and Ramsay will write a letter, each stating that the sentence is unjust and must not be carried out. Furse will of course defer to your findings and he will force the commander-in chief's hand. He *has* to.'

'I will telephone Dai,' mused Winston, meaning Mr Lloyd George. 'I will not allow these deaths.'

'Do it through normal military channels first, Winston; don't make any more enemies. You won't help the lads or yourself.'

I knew that General Furse was a friend of Winston's and a proper gentleman. He had kidded me on when he came for a visit, saying that he should have brought his tin helmet with him as he heard I was deadly with a champagne bottle. I felt confident that if he were involved, the accused men would get a fair crack of the whip.

'Alright, it will be done as you have said. It makes sense but it will mean a lot of apprehension and anxiety for those unfortunate men.'

'Colonel, you can do it! You'll tell them as you always do!' I declared, breathlessly.

Turning to me, Winston responded, 'Jamie, that beautiful decanter was a wedding present. I must ask you on your honour that should you ever meet my wife you will never mention to her the cause of its destruction.'

I thought for a moment. 'It was smashed when a shell hit the farm!'

'Yes. A brilliant solution and most logical, given our present circumstances. But please don't tell her I was there when it happened.'

The court martial went ahead and was held with officers from a nearby regiment back at the farmhouse at Moolenacker. Mr Hakewill-Smith was sent as counsel for our men. At first this seemed a strange choice, bearing in mind his youth and inexperience. Captain Gibb was a solicitor in civilian life, but the thinking was that as 'Bomber' was the only regular officer and this case was going to be a foregone conclusion thanks to the men's decision to plead guilty, then it would be good experience for him to be there at least to gain experience of court martial procedures.

The men entered their pleas, then the president of the court, a senior officer of the Gordons, in an unprecedented break with procedure asked the men to reconsider. He told them if they made such a plea when the charge was desertion, the court would be unable to come to any other conclusion but to find them guilty and sentence them to death.

Then, in an even more unusual step, the president halted proceedings and told Mr Hakewill-Smith to go outside the courtroom with the men and have a 'chat'. Bomber did as advised and asked Smith one more time to reconsider. The other three were wavering, understandably, and then Smith dived in and told them to stick with him as he would 'see them through'.

After some talk among themselves, all four declared that they were standing by their original decision. By this time Bomber had given up and led them back in, where, inevitably, the expected sentence was passed. One can only imagine how the other three were feeling.

The letters from Winston and Mr Ramsay were read out in court for the record. Then the ball started rolling as Winston embarked on a frantic dash to see the area commander,

General Furse, who was himself shocked to hear of the whole sorry affair. By this time the sentence had been confirmed by the commander in chief, General Haig, by rubber stamp. I would doubt he even bothered to read the charge before signing it.

The date was set a few days later for the sentence to be carried out at the churchyard in Ploegsteert. No one could take it in. It was beyond belief that such a thing could happen in our battalion.

The dreaded day arrived. A select number of men from every battalion in the division had to 'attend'. I am glad to say I was not one who was chosen but Duncan was and he told me later what happened.

A hollow square was formed around the yard as the four men were led in. They were in their shirt order only and were made to stand against the wall of the church. Duncan said that blokes around him were angry and the mood was tense; he said the slightest spark could have started off a riot. Captain Ramsay was chain-smoking and Duncan thought Mr Hakewill-Smith looked like he may pass out at any moment.

All of a sudden a motorcyclist rode into the churchyard with a piece of paper in one hand, screaming, 'Stop! Stop! For fuck's sake, stop everything!' The Provost Marshal and Major Sinclair went over to the rider and he passed them the paper. They both looked over it and Duncan saw Archie look up at the sky and laugh and hundreds of men seeing the same all breathed in again and then started chatting and milling around. One could only imagine how Smith and the others were feeling.

The Provost Marshal called for silence and read aloud from the note:

'As a result of fresh evidence being presented for the attention of the Provost Marshal, in the matter concerning

Privates...' and he read out the four names, 'it is the decision of the commander-in-chief to rescind sentence due to be carried out on said date and that in further consultation with the area commander, General Furse, delegation of suitable punishment is to be passed to the commanding officer, 6th Battalion Royal Scots Fusiliers where the recommendation is that the aforementioned private soldiers receive light, non-custodial sentences in view of past exemplary conduct.'

There were huge cheers, hats flung into the air, whistles and shouts. Archie and Captain Ramsay made their way over to the four men, one of whom had collapsed, and escorted them back to our rest area.

It was later rumoured that the Provost Marshal knew all along what was happening but once the system was set in motion it carried a momentum that no one was able to stop. No one except Winston.

When he got back from his mad dash across France, which included visiting General Haig himself, he expected a telegram to the Provost Marshal's office to have been received but it appears to either have gone astray for a while or it was not considered official enough to halt proceedings at first. Thankfully, someone in the office took responsibility and ensured the message made it to Plugstreet just in time.

Winston was absolutely furious when he discovered that the firing squad had been prepared and the men were forced to endure such an ordeal. His ire was raised to such an extent he had a blazing row with the Provost Marshal and threatened to have him flogged! This was all hushed up but Archie told me about it later.

As for Smith and the others, as far as Winston was concerned they had been punished enough and he put it on record that they were given labour and latrine duties for a fixed period but quietly they were told to go back to normal routine but stay off the rum for a while. The slaggings and piss-takings they would inevitably receive from their mates would have been punishment enough.

Towards the end of the same month we started hearing rumours that the battalion was going to amalgamate with another, due to Scots regiments being unable to find enough replacements for all the casualties they were chalking up. This caused a wave of speculation throughout until the colonel addressed us and told us it was indeed true.

We all wandered off, pretty depressed at this news. The thought that we would lose a lot of well-liked officers and worse, the colonel himself, dampened everyone's spirits.

Many felt that Colonel Churchill had been very lucky for us and the thought that he may soon be gone was unsettling. For the officers it was worse because some would end up without a regiment and from that moment Winston worked tirelessly for a few days, trying to find places for those who would be left out of the new battalion, which would be known as the 6th/7th.

In regards to the colonel's position, I knew from conversations I had overheard with Archie that he was in two minds about what to do. I heard him say he believed that he could do more to help the men if he was back in government; but if he was offered the colonelcy of the new battalion he would consider it. He wanted back to politics but was wavering because he loved soldiering. In the end the decision was made for him, as the colonel with the most experience between the two was chosen and it was not Winston.

I was making some sandwiches for him to take out on his rounds when I heard. A telegram arrived and he and Archie discussed it as I stopped to listen; and I must confess to becoming quite upset. I was young and idolised Winston and could not imagine a world without him. Mr Churchill then rushed off in his endeavours to assist the officers who had not found a place in the new battalion.

Later on that day Archie asked me if I wanted to replace his batman, Martin, when Winston left. Mr Sinclair was being sent back to his own regiment, the Life Guards. He said he would be able to organise my transfer to his regiment without difficulty.

This was a major consolation to me, if you will pardon the pun, and I said yes and thanked him profusely. But the downside of transferring was leaving my pals behind at the 6th. All in all I was pretty miserable at this time.

The next day, May 1st 1916, was to be the last day in the line for the colonel of the 6th Battalion Royal Scots Fusiliers. It was also the day in which my own life would be changed forever.

Chapter Eleven

That morning, Winston and Archie were out on their final rounds of the men in the outlying trenches, saying their goodbyes. I was busy clearing up Laurence Farm for our departure later on in the day.

Winston's spare boots were outside to air off and I returned to pick them up. I stood at the door of the Farm with a boot in each hand, banging them together to remove lumps of dried mud, when I felt myself being picked up and thrown to the floor. A shell which had fallen short had crashed through the roof of the Farm, exploded and nearly carried me off.

I was badly hurt. The explosion had loosened the lintel above me which fell away, giving me a glancing clout across the head which knocked me down dazed; a loose beam collapsed and banged off me, cracking four ribs, and a large chunk of shrapnel lodged in my right leg, the force from which had fractured it in three or four places.

There was a small ditch full of thick mud at the door of the Farm. This was caused by subsidence and one foot was in this and the other resting on the step when the blast spun me around one way whilst my foot was wedged the other. This would snap something deep inside my knee.

I lay looking up, unable to comprehend what was happening. I was told that Winston and Archie coming back from their rounds were only yards away when the shell hit and after the dust settled they saw see me lying in the doorway.

I then remember Archie looking down at me and felt something being tightened round my leg. Archie kept asking me, 'Jamie, tell me about the Hearts! Who plays for the Hearts?' Later I realised he was trying to get me to talk in

order to ward off shock. Then I saw Winston taking off his
trench coat and recall thinking: *don't do that, Colonel, it'll get
dirty and I'll have to brush it off,* but then he came and laid the
coat over me and said, 'It's alright, Jamie; we'll have you in
hospital very soon.' After that I passed out.

I woke groggily in the courtyard at the Farm. Normally,
injured men would be taken to the Advanced Dressing
Station, which was down at the end of the communications
trenches known as 'Charing Cross'. In my case there was no
need for this as it was easier to get a wagon into the courtyard
and thus I could be evacuated away quicker to the Casualty
Clearing Station.

I lay on a stretcher with Archie looking down anxiously,
holding my hand. Duncan and the battalion doctor were busy
working on my leg.

'Oh sir, what happened?' I managed to croak.

He rubbed my hand. 'A shell fell short and hit the Farm but
you're alright now; you're going to the Clearing Station.
You've been given morphine. Just let yourself fall asleep, son.'

It was a lot more serious than he was letting on. They were
able to patch me up before forwarding me on to the Casualty
Clearing Station at Bailleul with not a moment to lose. Once I
got there a South African doctor took charge. I looked up at
him in anguish and pain as the morphine was wearing off but
I have never forgotten his kindness as he said to me, 'Don't
worry, *kerel,* you'll be alright now, I'll make sure you're
kicking a football again pretty quick. You just relax now, *hey*?'
His accent was thick but strangely comforting, as he exuded
confidence, but all the time the main thoughts going through
my mind were for my mum and how she would react when
the telegram came to the door informing her what had
happened to me.

I visualised some kind of mistake being made by the War
Office, and instead of the message telling her I had been

wounded it would instead say I had been killed. I had heard of instances of this, and I imagined her terrible resulting grief; grief I had caused her by my selfish actions in joining the army illegally in the first place.

I tried to remain calm. A nurse appeared at the other side of my bed and took my pulse but I could not help but wail like the pitiful child I was, 'Please tell my mother, please tell my mummy I'm alright.' And the nurse put her cool hand on my forehead and squeezed my hand and said, 'It's alright, darling, we'll tell her, we'll tell her you're safe and well and will be coming home very soon.' They then proceeded to put a mask over my face and operate. The wound was serious and I was told later that the South African doctor's skill saved my leg.

It was still touch and go. I woke up in a huge tent, which is what the clearing station was. My leg was well wrapped and I was told I was being evacuated to England as soon as possible.

I was being sent to the Queen Alexandra Hospital in London. I asked why not home to Edinburgh and the orderly told me they could not risk further travel because he told me baldly there was a chance the leg may have to come off. This news left me devastated and I lay for the rest of the day in dread of what may become of me.

The next day, half-awake, I was put in an ambulance along with some other blokes to be sent to the base hospital at Boulogne. I remember lying back with an immense feeling of peace and calm; of course this was caused by a healthy dose of morphine. In reality I was away with the fairies and after I got to the hospital a doctor read my notes, looked at my leg and put me on a boat that afternoon to be evacuated back to the UK. I must say that was probably the most pleasant sea voyage I ever experienced, mainly because I cannot remember much about it.

A splinter had made a six-inch gash around my thigh just above the knee. It had to be sewn up and the leg set, as it was broken in three places with the impact. The force of the blast had twisted me around with the result that something deep inside my right knee called the interior cruciate ligament tore apart, which was inoperable. This meant that, with all that, I would feel a lot of pain for the rest of my days and I would not be able to walk or run as I had before without discomfort.

The bones would set fine, though, the doctors believed. They didn't. My army days were over because I would need a walking stick when the pain got too bad (which it did). It also would lead to a nasty side effect in that sometimes when walking up or down stairs it would just all of a sudden go on me and I would have to hold on to the rail or bannister or I would fall over.

I don't remember much about the boat trip but I recall waking to a repetitive, clacking sound and movement and realised I was on a train which was heading for London, having been taken off at Folkestone. I wonder how many soldiers left on the thoroughfare now known as Remembrance Road marching and were carried back up it later, like me.

It had all been very efficient. Two days after I received my injuries I would be lying in a hospital bed in London. Only a few months later those efficient systems would be tested to the hilt by the attack on the Somme.

I would wonder to myself what all those orderlies, nurses and doctors must have thought when a stretcher was brought before them and they saw someone in uniform barely out of childhood, lying on it with a leg almost blown away. What must they have been thinking? How did it make them feel to see me like that? They may have just hidden their feelings behind the mask of dedication; that being their main barricade of defence against the horrors they saw daily. Did the sight of me make them blanch, even with all that they had grown used to witnessing? I would have feelings of guilt for long afterwards for the trouble I felt I had caused many.

I only know that I owe those unthinkingly kind people everything. From Winston and Major Sinclair, to old Duncan at the aid station, to that wonderful nurse who comforted me, and that marvellous doctor. They would say they were only doing their jobs but I suspect that they all made a singular effort on my behalf for the reason that I was just a boy. As for that doctor, I was able to trace him later. His name was Kobus Van Heerden, from Paarl in the Cape Province, and I wrote him a letter of thanks.

Up till the blast I have to admit I had a good time. I enjoyed being a soldier, but mainly I enjoyed being spoiled by just about everyone I came into contact with. I suppose I had a winning way also, which helps, but from the basic training onwards I felt I had been taken care of and had no complaints. I had had tricks played on me at times but I got on with it and none were malicious.

It was my first time overseas and was exciting to me like reliving my favourite book, *Kidnapped*, or reading the adventures of Allan Quatermain and Richard Hannay. I had read those penny-dreadfuls, *Union Jack*, *Magnet* and *Boy's Own Paper* avidly and soaked up the exciting adventures in far-flung outposts of the empire where sturdy Britons surrounded by bloodthirsty heathens relied on plucky young lads to carry messages to relief columns and thus save the day.

I fantasised about being a mounted warrior with my racy bush hat, riding with my mates across the veld, chasing Boers to their extinction. Being like David Balfour, hunted by redcoats across the moors, having my own rifle; it was what any boy would have wanted. Being Mr Churchill's batman was tremendous fun at times. I was well fed, too. He and Archie had tried to educate me and had valued my opinions and I had learned so much from everyone.

When in the line, I felt no fear because I had no idea of my own death. It was unimaginable. The battalion had suffered grievously at Loos and in some horrific fighting around Ypres and the old salts talked about it but I believed I would escape because I had a mother and sisters and a football team, Hearts, back home and how could I get hurt? I went on patrol and was excited at the danger even when I got hurt on that one occasion at the sap. As for when I helped the colonel at the wire, even now I shudder when I remember my state of mind that night. I was completely devoid of fear.

But now, with this wound, everything changed. I was not impervious. The hand of war had reached out and smitten me. It could have been much worse but when I lay in those stretchers, bunks, ambulances and berths, vulnerable and helpless, it came to me how reliant it had left me on others and worst of all how my previously inviolable flesh had been torn and my bones fractured by something loathsome and repugnant.

I wanted no more war. I was glad I was out of it. I would badly miss everyone especially the colonel, but I believed that if I returned I would not make it back a second time. My first loyalty had to be to my mum. As I lay there in Bailleul on that bed before the operation, I wanted her there more than anything. I kept seeing her face and could not but imagine her pain and solitude should she learn of my death.

Now she would no longer have that worry. I understood that the leg was the price I would pay for that, and the loss of the colonel, Archie and the others.

How differently things would turn out from what I expected.

My recuperation began in London at the famous Queen Alexandra Hospital, where I remained for four months. I underwent further operations as my leg did not set correctly at first as a bit of bone was actually grafting over another.

I underwent a strict course of therapy to get me back on my feet. It was tough at times because it was constantly painful. The nurses did not mess about and wanted me up as quickly as possible. They were right, I believe, and I wanted the same because I did not want to be a cripple and worked hard at my therapy and they were all very pleased with me but as for returning to the 6th as a soldier, that was that for 027 Private James Melville.

I have to admit that by and large I enjoyed my time in the hospital. Whilst I lay on the stretcher with Archie after I was hit, Mr Churchill was making frenzied calls to the medical authorities on my behalf to ensure I received the best care possible including being sent to the Queen Alexandra Hospital, which was fairly new back then. He had always shown particular concern for the wounded in the battalion, but for me he certainly went all out in making use of his contacts, which was to my benefit.

I wrote to my mum and told her everything that had happened and explained why the medical staff had insisted that I remain in London. I gave her the news that I was being discharged medically from the army as I knew this would please her greatly, and would be back home when released from hospital.

She responded, telling me how relieved she was as she had received a telegram informing her that I had been wounded but no details as to the extent. But a letter arrived from Colonel Churchill himself, advising her fully of my condition. Naturally all this had caused a lot of heartache and I envisioned her having many sleepless nights until she received my letter, which, to be fair, I wrote as soon as I could and in fact arrived only a few days after the telegram.

I was also given a promotion! Yes, I was now *Lance Corporal* James Melville and I sewed on my stripe and felt like a king.

Winston had arranged this to ensure my pension would be more generous. Later, I discovered that, due to War Office regulations, as I was underage I was in fact not legally entitled to receive a pension! Winston had intervened personally on my behalf by informing them of my exemplary conduct. I still don't know how he managed to wangle it all for me, knowing army bureaucracy, but I heard that my actions on the night when Winston was caught under the wire were mentioned and rather than awarding a belated medal, which would have been controversial in light of my true age, a compromise was reached in rewarding me with a full invalidity pension augmented through my promotion.

I received letters from pals, keeping me informed of events at the new amalgamated battalion. I was pleased to hear that Duncan had been made mess orderly for the new colonel. He was a lonely old soul, having no one back home; the battalion was both his family and his life.

Winston wrote me and sent parcels from his suppliers. Normally a colonel writing to his former batman would have been unheard of, but Winston was no ordinary colonel (and I like to think I was no ordinary batman). The letters were chatty and stated that he was now back permanently in London and would try to visit me and I was to inform him of my progress, which I did.

Despite the generally painful time I had at the hospital physically, there was major compensation emotionally for me in the lovely form of a young Voluntary Aid Detachment Nurse or VAD as they were known, named Gemma. She was not much older than I and before long we become close.

It was very a big risk to her personally, this friendship we had. The young, Red Cross-trained VADS were watched like hawks for even the most minor infraction of the legion of rules that governed their lives and we had to meet alone secretively and never for very long. We dared not be seen holding hands, never mind kissing, and when we were able to it was a very quick squeeze of fingers and a brushing of lips on a cheek whilst nervously looking around on the off-chance that we might be seen.

I found these secret liaisons exciting, naturally, and they added to my experiences whilst in the hospital. When I was well enough, I was encouraged to go out for walks and as the hospital was centrally located in Millbank, I was able to view some famous landmarks within a short distance of the hospital. The Houses of Parliament and Westminster Abbey were very near to hand and I would sit in Parliament Square and enjoy watching the bustle of London life with a bottle of pop and a cake from the hospital canteen.

During my time there the great Battle of the Somme began on the 1st July, as is well known. The hospital soon became inundated with men brought back and my girl Gemma, though very inexperienced, was whisked off to help deal with these cases. Every nurse was required, due to the huge crises caused by the sheer volume of casualties brought in daily. I never saw her for days on end and when I did I noted how her demeanour had changed markedly from the way she had been formerly when we first met.

I was due for release by the middle of September. On the day of my discharge I was surprised to receive a visit from my old colonel, Winston himself.

I said my goodbyes to all the staff. I shook hands with the orderlies and one of the doctors came round and sat me down and gave me the prognosis, which is pretty much as I have described. I kissed goodbye a couple of nurses (on the quiet, of course) who were crying and in truth I was a bit tearful myself in saying my farewells. Once again, I had been well looked after and had no complaints.

I was getting my kit together after all this and planning to have a nice wee tea with Gemma before the train to Waverley when I received a tap on my shoulder and turned round and saw it was him.

'So the warrior has survived intact, I see!'

'Colonel!' I was truly pleased to see him as I missed him so very much.

He grabbed my hand and shook it and sat me down on the bed beside him. It was strange to see him in civilian clothes.

'I hear the dashing knight has found himself a damsel!'

'Aye! Gemma! She's my girlfriend! We're going out for tea in a wee while,' I declared, proudly.

'Then back to *Auld Reekie...*?' He left the last two words hanging but I did not notice at first.

'The train to Waverley and then home. I don't know what I'll do there at first, just look after the girls for a wee while and get myself a job. I'm really glad to see you, Colonel. I miss everyone, Archie... oh excuse me, Major Sinclair, Duncan, Davie. All of them. I miss the life I had there.' I looked down. I was only just coming to terms with the fact that I might never see any of these kind friends again.

'You are missed too, James! Especially by me! Employment is also a very important subject and one I must broach with you. I think you may be aware I am, like you, no longer a warrior of the working day and must return to my true love, politics. My aim is to be given a new post in government but I must work very hard towards that end. When that day arrives I will require the services of trusted assistants. I would like you to become one. How does that sound to you?'

For Winston, the amalgamation and his failure to become the new colonel of the enlarged battalion had come as a blessing, because all the time he had been with us he had been hostage to secret fears about the future direction of his life. Even though we all adored him and saw his true value he felt he could do more, not just for us but for the entire war effort, if he could get back into government. He was determined to get into the frame.

'You mean you want me to be a *servant*?' My voice rose in indignation, having misunderstood his offer. 'No, sir, I am no man's butler!' I had become a bit of what would later be called a Bolshie, and did not like the idea of being a flunkey, with a dickie collar and white gloves and yes-me-lording. It was demeaning. That's what it was, *demeaning*.

'But you were my *batman*!' he retorted, barely containing his amusement.

'Aye, but I was a *soldier*, that's different!'

'Now, James,' he began, 'you will not be a "butler" or a "servant" though I know of those who would give their eye teeth to be employed as such by me.' Still full of himself, you'll note. 'I want you to remain as my batman, of a sort,' he continued, 'only you will be swapping the trenches and patrols and mess evenings and pilfering goodies for the equally deadly dangers of politics! As my assistant you will watch over me as you did in France. You will keep an eye on what is going on around me and tip me off if you hear anything that may be useful. I have a very good job lined up for you already if you will accept it.'

'A spy!' I exclaimed in horror.

'No, no, no!' He had his head in his hands at this point, but through his fingers I could see the humour in his eyes and knew he was having me on. The colonel always had the patience of a saint with me even when I was cheeky towards him back at the Farm, where I often complained about his messy habits. But usually what Winston wanted, he got.

Anyway, the more I thought about it the better it sounded. In Edinburgh I would be back to square one. But I wanted something better. I had seen something of the world and mixed with all these distinct people, distinct *classes* of people, and discovered that they were not too different from me. I had been fortunate in those I met but I always believed fortune favoured Jamie Melville. And I really missed *him.* His company, his kindness, generosity and humour. I was tempted by the world he came from and wanted to see more of it for myself.

Jamie Melville of Gorgie could make it there. I remember when I told Winston about wanting to work on a newspaper and he said he knew people who could put the word out for me. Young as I was I realised this was my one true chance in life. I could go back home to Edinburgh and miss it; or grab it right now. From this moment my life could really begin.

He told me to have my tea with Gemma and then catch the train home. I was to stay there for a short break and think it over and then when I was ready return to London if that was to be my decision.

'But where will I sleep?' I asked.

'Sleep? Why, you will have a very nice room here in my London residence. And before you mention it, though I note with some surprise that you have not, I will ensure that you receive an appropriate salary for your service.'

'Mm, well.' I rubbed my chin. I was standing before him as he looked up slightly from the bed. 'I'll have to talk it over with my mum. She expects me home you know, Colonel Churchill. I mean, I'm a man now, and I'm a lance corporal! I've a man's responsibilities. I've three wee sisters to support. I've not seen the Hearts for a while and I want to know how they've been doing. It's a big decision. I have to be very careful that I make the right choice.'

Archie Sinclair would tell me that Winston had discussions concerning me whilst back at the Farm. Winston wanted to take me back to England with him when he left the battalion, to offer me a better life. I often wondered why I had not been sent home after my true age had been discovered. The legal procedures for under-age soldiers at the time were that if a soldier was discovered to have lied about his age and was under nineteen and serving overseas as I was, the decision as to whether he should be discharged and returned to the United Kingdom had to be decided by the commander-in chief of the army.

By any standards this was morally reprehensible and a complete washing of the hands in trying to deal with the issue of so many young lads being where they should not. Winston knew of this rule, of course, but knowing him, if he'd wanted me sent home he would have arranged it. I was glad, of course, that I had not been returned. Archie asked me to become his batman because he saw how upset and unhappy I had become at the thought of Winston's leaving the battalion. But this was just to keep my chin up whilst Winston arranged everything. He was extremely busy at that time trying to find suitable places for officers left out after the amalgamation.

Then that shell hit the Farmhouse. Winston told Archie that it had been the worst moment of his time at the battalion when he saw me lying injured and he decided that should I survive he was determined to try and help me make something of my life.

A cynic may say Winston felt guilty at not sending me home sooner and wanted to make it up to me. I do not believe that. He genuinely cared for people, *all* people, regardless of class or rank. I believe that in me he saw someone of potential; and something of himself.

He was speaking again and as always was being very persuasive in order to get his way.

'I might add as an extra incentive to aid you in your decision-making, if you come to London to be my assistant you shall have the opportunity to mix with many illustrious figures! I shall take you to the House of Commons! Great men shall have the opportunity to meet the *remarkable* James Melville! Would you deny them the chance of that? How can you!

'Oh, and by the way, if you *are* living in London you will be able to have tea with the beautiful Gemma any time you like.'

I was persuaded. 'I'll do it. Now, about the salary…'

Chapter Twelve

I had some thinking to do on the train home to Edinburgh. Before that I had discussed my new set of circumstances with Gemma at a wee tea shop near King's Cross. She was naturally delighted at the prospect of me returning back to London so soon, for up till then we had both quietly assumed that we were never going to see each other again.

But things had worked out alright for me once again through Mr Churchill's intervention. Gemma and I had our tea and then she kissed me full on the mouth in front of everyone on the platform. I boarded the train in a very pleasant daze, completely love-struck.

Nowadays the journey between London and Edinburgh only takes a few hours but back then, and with the war on, it was slow, crowded and uncomfortable as hell. Worst of all my leg was absolutely walloping and I had to stand for long periods leaning on the walking stick, now a permanent feature of my life.

I finally found a seat after leaving York, and only then because a conductor, seeing me in uniform with a stick, took pity and allowed me to sit in his wee alcove in the guard's car. He was a real decent chap as he let me have some tea from his flask while he was away doing his rounds. Most importantly I was able to stretch my leg out for a bit, as standing was excruciating.

Eventually, after what seemed a hundred stops and starts, the train arrived into Waverley very late; too late for a cable-car or taxi. I walked home to Wardlaw Place.

It was nice to be back and the stroll was not too bad. I enjoyed the sights and smells of Edinburgh again, namely the Castle, Princes Street and on into Gorgie past Tynecastle Park with that particular aroma from the breweries at nearby Fountainbridge. I always associate them with my home town; they are part of me, and it was good to be around them again.

Finally arriving at the tenement that was my home, and still having my key, I let myself in and making as little noise as possible, stuck my head in the room and saw them all snuggled together in Mum's bed. That was the best moment because everything was as it had been and nothing had changed.

So I thought.

Next morning, I popped out early for some rolls and made up breakfast for everyone. On awakening and seeing me they were overjoyed and the girls clung to me, especially Maggie. My mum cried and held me, uttering over and over, 'My wee boy, my wee boy.'

I had lots of sweeties in my pack for the girls and a nice wee brooch for Mum that Gemma picked out for me. The girls were then packed off to school and Mum and I were able to sit down and have a chat.

She liked her new job at the ministry office and it paid well, and had fully recovered from her injuries from the blast. She then told me outright that she had stopped drinking completely. This was pretty unexpected as she would never acknowledge her drinking before. It slowly dawned on me that she was now talking to me as a grown-up and not as a child.

Mum then said that there was something I needed to know. A man at the office whom she had been seeing for a time had asked her to marry him. He was a widower with grown-up children and lived in a nice house in Murrayfield. She had yet to make up her mind on the matter.

I sat back in my seat. This was big news. And I was secretly very glad to hear it, not only for Mum's and the girl's sake but for my own, as I realised it could solve a lot of problems at one stroke.

'Do you want to marry him?' I asked.

'He would be a good provider. He's a bit older than me but he's well-mannered and has an important position at the ministry.'

'Well, Mum, it's up to you to decide. I mean, I can meet him and let you know what I think.'

At that she seemed satisfied. 'That's a good idea.'

I sensed that she had already made up her mind but wanted me to have a look, just to be sure. I felt flattered but equally, somewhat disconcerted. She saw that I was no longer the wee lad who had left a year before and with all I had seen and done in Belgium I was now to all intents and purposes an adult and therefore my opinion would be valued as such. On the other hand I was perturbed a little, and felt uneasy.

She left for work and I hung around the house for the day as my leg was still throbbing. I read the papers and focused on how Hearts were doing. I found myself drawn to some of the advertisements for military items: Thresher & Glenny trench coats and field service uniforms, leggings and puttees at prices that no ordinary Tom could afford, with a drawing of a sturdy, pipe-smoking officer wrapped warmly against the chill. An Onoto Pen, that *'fits the uniform pocket'* and Malloch & Armstrong ear defenders *'for the prevention of deafness'* at the price of 4s 1d. The latter had competition in the form of an advert for fibrous plasticine *'guaranteed to defend against gun deafness.'*

I got by sticking bits of cloth in my lugs during 'hates' and when the Huns let rip.

I noticed a small article that mentioned Winston and his return to politics. I thought about what he told me at the hospital and recalled a conversation I had had with Archie Sinclair. We were at the Farm and I was ironing Winston's kit at the time. Archie appeared and asked me if I could darn a pair of his socks.

He slumped down in a chair and picked up a newspaper.

'Well, sir, what's happening back in the old country?' I asked as I created my usual razor-sharp crease in a pair of the old boy's trousers.

Archie stared at the paper. 'Stay out of politics, Jamie, that's my advice to you.'

'I heard one of the lads say that Mr Churchill will never get a job in the government again. Is that true?' I had heard this one night when Sergeant Douglas had been yarning away and declared that Winston had more enemies than friends. Gallipoli had finished him and he would never get any further because too many in the House, both Tory and Liberal, hated him.

'The lad may be right, sadly, Jamie. Winston has more enemies than you and I have had hot porridge for breakfast.'

'But *why*, sir? He's so nice to everyone and all the lads like him. How can *he* have enemies?' I was a child, remember, and everything was still black and white. When I saw Winston Churchill, I saw a man who cared for his soldiers and people in general; he cared for my mum and had never met her. The men felt safe around him and trusted him never to risk their lives unnecessarily. He was also great company, amusing and extremely generous. What was there to hate?

'Oh, mainly because people are jealous of him,' Archie replied. 'He was once seen as a real go-getter, Jamie. He's ambitious also. Very. He does have a tendency to rub some people up the wrong way. He's also quite brilliant and in brilliant I mean the way Mozart and Napoleon were brilliant. A remarkable man in so many ways and others simply either pretend to be unimpressed or believe him a cad.' He laughed. 'But please don't tell him I compared him with Napoleon or it will make him insufferable!'

I thought back to when Winston came to see me in hospital and appeared very upbeat and excited about his return to politics. Of course he was not going to tell me how he really felt. And anyway, I was so convinced of his genius I assumed that he would step back into where he left off before he joined the 6th. But remembering now Archie's words, it began to dawn on me that Winston was not infallible and that he had to struggle just like the rest of us.

I was angry and saddened by this. Angry because I thought back to people like General ------- who did what they liked and showed no concern at all for people like me and the lads and my mum. He who sat in a nice chateau way behind the lines drinking champagne and pig-sticking and such and turned up once in a blue moon for an inspection and had the cheek to slag off Mr Churchill, yes, *my* Mr Churchill, and then buggering off back to his cosy billet. Well, it made me mad. I was saddened too, because it seemed to me that the same type of men had stopped Winston from getting what he wanted because they were jealous of him and not as talented.

I was just a young lad, naive and innocent, but I had no end of self-belief and confidence. I would leave for London to be at his side and keep an eye on him just as he had said that day at the hospital. I always felt safe around Winston but now, Winston would be safe around me, Jamie Melville. I would sort *them* out.

The Saturday after I got back I went to meet the man who wanted to marry my mum. His name was George and he turned out to be quite a decent sort. He must have been about forty-five (Mum was barely thirty-five at the time) and as far as I was concerned he was getting the best woman on earth. Unfortunately I made a bit of a fool of myself when he took me out alone to look at his garden.

You'll remember me saying that I had a blind spot when it

came to Mum and the girls. Well, when we were alone I told George that if he married my mother and treated her badly I would be back up like a shot to beat the daylights out of him. I had killed men in Belgium, I said, and I would think nothing of battering him if he as much as touched a hair of any of their heads.

He said nothing. What could he say? But he was warned, as far as I was concerned. Later I would have cause to regret my threat as he turned out to be a real nice man and the girls were very happy and he paid for them to go to a small private school. We laughed it off years later, of course. Most importantly, he did not bear a grudge and I think he always respected me.

I had sewn up all loose ends in Edinburgh. I told Mum about Winston's offer, naturally. She seemed very pleased that I had made a good impression on such an important man. Mum then told me that she had decided to marry George. The date would be set for early the following year but she thought it best for probity's sake that she stayed at Wardlaw until the wedding date was announced. That is the way it was, back in those days. I think she was hinting that I take off sharpish.

I wasn't stupid and knew I was in the way. This saddened me and I felt a little let down. I was no longer of financial use to her, nor was I required to bring up the kids whilst she slept off drunken binges. The times were unforgiving. You had to pay your parents back for being born. But I adored her. I still do. She had a hard life and was finally getting a lucky break. But looking back now, I know that the only tangible thing she ever left me was the desire never to be such a parent myself.

Now that I knew I was not wanted at home it was easier to reconcile the fact that I was doing the right thing in returning to London. But I had been reflecting a lot and in doing so, came to terms with leaving behind everything I had known.

I thought of my dad and the life he led. Married at eighteen, did he think his life would end at thirty-three years old, lying dead on the pavement a few yards from home? What did *he* want from life? He was so kind when he was sober, before the accident. He would do anything for anyone. But he became maniacal in drink and tried to savage three little boys in his pain and misery. He also beat his pretty wife to pulp and drove her to the refuge of alcohol herself.

I remembered before the accident good times, like being taken along with my brothers Tom and Arthur to Tynecastle regularly, which I loved. He would hoist me over the turnstiles as we went to cheer the likes of Charlie Thomson, the man who 'played in every position except goalkeeper', Percy Dawson, whose transfer fee of £2,500 when he was moved to Blackburn Rovers was a then world record and the celebrated Bobby Walker, our hero, who was known as the 'the greatest natural footballer who ever played'.

Dad somehow arranged for us to meet the great man one day after a match. Bobby bent down and shook my wee hand and I felt like I had met God himself. And there were newer heroes, like Paddy Crossan and Tom Gracie, to roar on. Poor Tom, he was one of the brave Hearts players who signed up in 1914 but died of leukaemia whilst doing basic training. He was still playing football at the time and never even made it to France.

And Paddy, golden Paddy, the one all the lassies chased after who also joined up at the start; at least he survived but was badly gassed and never the same player again. I had a few whiskies in his pub whenever I was back in Edinburgh. But he gave away too many free drinks and the stress of the business collapsing added to his bad memories and his ruined lungs. He died young, barely forty.

This was all part of me. Who I *was*. But now I was taking the momentous step of leaving my home and family. But somehow I knew my dad would approve of what I was doing. He would have been filled with pride. And when I thought of Winston I did not feel concern. I felt safe. I believed I was walking with someone who was special and would see me through.

I had saved his life in an act of childish innocence and was someone whom he believed was worthy and had potential. I have to say, even then I saw him as a father figure. Did he see me as the type of son he wanted? Whatever it was, I could not wait to return to London. Edinburgh had nothing for me now.

It was time to leave home.

Chapter Thirteen

Until recently Winston had been living at his brother Jack's home on Cromwell Road. I would learn that his family were always moving from house to house for whatever reason. This seemed strange to me, being born and raised in the same wee room and kitchen all my life, but I expect they got used to it.

He now lived with his wife, Clementine, and his three children in Eccleston Square in central London. I sent off a telegram to inform him when I would be leaving Edinburgh and I received a response advising me to just turn up at the door. I have to say this greatly excited me when I read it. I showed it to Mum and the girls and they squealed with delight, thrilled that their brother moved in such exalted company.

I had pangs of real regret at the thought of leaving these three wee angels. They would not leave me alone most of the time I was back I and was forever playing daft games with them and walking to the sweetie shop and buying them their favourites from the jars displayed in the window (and helping myself to the odd one or three). They kept asking about Belgium and I told them stories at bedtime about my adventures and was tearful when alone when I thought that soon I would be leaving them behind.

When I originally left for the army, I believed it to be only temporary; until the war ended and then I would be back. But this was different. I was truly leaving home this time and knew that I would never be back again except for short visits on holidays and such. But I was consoled by reminding myself that soon my family would be living in a nice big house and would want for nothing.

I took stock of my kit and decided that the uniform could

now go into mothballs. Though I had a right to wear it a bit longer, the rather lonesome stripe on each arm was to my mind not enough leverage when I turned up on Winston's doorstep. Any servant opening the door to a tiny wee kilted laddie would have slammed it in his face. So I thought.

I headed off to a well-known tailors in Leith Street and bought myself the best suit I could afford. Mum chipped in also and bought new shoes, shirts and ties. I skinted myself doing all this purchasing and only had enough left for the train down, plus a few bob set aside for emergencies.

I said goodbye to the girls from the door (I hate farewells at railway stations; Gemma's was different as I was heading back shortly anyway). Maggie was crying again and it set off the other two. They would miss the big brother who bought them sweets and played with them and was such fun. I was down and a bit apprehensive, to tell the truth. But Mum told me I was doing the right thing as I had been given a real opportunity that few lads from my background would ever experience. I had to take it and make a success of it. She knew I would and said she was proud of me.

Leaving Maggie to look after the little ones, Mum waited with me at the stop, regaling me with anecdotes about the deplorable state the city's transport system had been reduced to through shortages of materials and essential workers. A car then turned up and she made me promise I'd sit inside and not head up to the uncovered top deck. Forcing the fare into my hand, she then waved me off.

I felt completely alone for the first time in my life, as I looked out at the familiar shops and buildings, as the car headed for Princes Street and Waverley.

The journey down was just as bad as the one coming up but this time I ensured I got a seat with a bit of space to stretch my leg out. I held it in for hours but finally gave up and had to go to the toilet but when I got back some swine had taken my place. I had a row with him but he would not budge and at one point I threatened to brain him with my stick, until a fat guard squeezed through and said I would be chucked off at the next stop unless I calmed down.

As a parting shot I called the bugger a hell of a name and then moved away up the cars. I ended up leaning against the toilet door, which was handy because I could pop in for a seat when my knee got too bad for a short while.

I arrived at King's Cross in the early evening and caught a taxi, which dropped me off outside a terraced house in an early Victorian residential area built around elegant gardens which reminded me of Charlotte Square in Edinburgh. I hovered around nervously for a short while.

The truth was that I was scared. I hoped in my innocence that Winston might walk by and see me or if he were in the house that he would spot me at a window. After a short while I screwed myself up and went to the door and knocked with my stick. It opened and a maid stuck her head around.

'I have to see Colonel Churchill. I'm Jamie Melville.' I usually addressed him as Colonel. I always wondered in my own mind the most suitable term to call him. In Plugstreet when we were yarning away at night it seemed daft to keep saying 'sir' and 'Mr Churchill' all the time so Colonel stuck because it was pretty simple.

Later, Mrs Churchill told me that he loved being called that and he regretted that I was the only one who did. It appealed to him because deep down he loved being a soldier and my calling him that reminded him of it and of the happy times he had spent in uniform. So Colonel it was. When I was older I did call him Winston but that was only in private or when he was being an old swine.

The maid was not much older than me. 'Oh yes, sir. You're expected.'

Well, 'sir'! To be addressed as that nearly floored me and she let me in and asked me to wait a second as she went off to get Mrs Churchill.

I stood in the hallway with my bag and tried to straighten myself up. There was a long mirror and I looked at it and grabbed my tie.

'Dinnae worry, Jamie, the colonel doesnae' have to inspect you any more, ye know!'

I turned in surprise to see a tall, extremely beautiful young woman of about thirty beaming down at me, holding out her hand. I took her fingers and squeezed them slightly and said, 'Hello, Mrs Churchill!'

I always liked that lady. Photographs of the time never did her justice; she was a real beauty. She was called a lot of things by some very snobbish and ignorant buggers and I chinned one for making a nasty comment about her once. But she was top drawer as far as I was concerned. She took in a wee laddie from Scotland and made him feel very welcome.

Those days were different from now (thank God); the so-called class system would receive a serious blow from the Great War but you still had to know your 'place' especially if you came from Gorgie, and that woman could have behaved as a perfect snoot to me as per the times. But the fact was she made me feel very easy and as she led me through the house I instantly relaxed and felt a whole lot better than I had only minutes before.

I was glad to find a seat because my knee was louping. I must have looked peely-wally, too, and did not want to cause any kind of scene by falling asleep or worse in my exhaustion. But I was tired with the long journey.

She came into the room and sat down opposite me.

'Jamie, Winston is still at the House and sometimes doesn't get home till late. Why don't I show you your room and you can get unpacked? I must say it's lovely having another Scots voice around the place!'

'Oh? Who else is Scottish here, miss?'

'Why, me! My maiden name is Hozier, don't ye know! I was looking forward to seeing you in your kilt but it's alright, you can't be a soldier forever, thank the Lord!' and I noticed for the first time her affecting a Scottish accent.

She was very English in her everyday speech but when she was with me she relaxed and rolled her r's. She was born and bred in England but like the good old Queen Mum today, considered herself a true Scot. God bless her.

I followed her out the room up the stairs. The house was, to my mind, huge. I was brought up in a room and kitchen in Gorgie, and anything was big after that. There seemed to be doors and stairs everywhere until we came to a particular door, which she opened, and I was led into a lovely big bedroom with a chest of drawers and built-in cupboards and a nice big window. There was a chair also and an empty bookcase.

'What do you think?'

I just gaped and said the first daft thing that came into my head. 'Oh, Mrs Churchill, this room's bigger than my mum's house!'

Tactfully she did not answer that but instead told me that dinner would be ready shortly and that I should unpack my stuff and come downstairs. She then left me and I went and sat on the bed and just stared into space.

Why were these people being so kind to me? I was nobody. I admit I had a pretty high opinion of myself when I was young. But I was still a child of my times and this was all very difficult to absorb: maids calling me 'sir', being given a room to live in; a room to *myself* for the first time in my life. It was like one of those fairy tales I read out to the girls.

I got off the bed and took my kit out of the bags and put it away tidily. I then tried to find my way downstairs but walked down one floor too many and ended up in the basement where the servants usually stayed. I walked up one floor and looked left and thankfully saw the front door and found my bearings again. I wandered through to the sitting room and Mrs Churchill was there and she then led me through to the dining area.

I made my next introductions to three wee kiddies planted down at the table. A boy and two girls.

'Jamie, I'll introduce you to Randolph,' she pointed to the lad, 'Diana and Sarah.' Randolph was five, Sarah, the youngest, was barely a year and a half and Diana, the oldest, was nearly seven. The wee girl was propped up in a baby chair and Randolph and Diana were moaning about not wanting to eat their dinner.

'This is Jamie, everyone, Daddy's very good friend from the army who has come to live with us. Say "hello, Jamie".'

The two who could mumbled their hellos.

Diana looked at me and asked, 'Did you kill Germans too?'

I was skilled in the art of dealing with wee bairns and answered, 'Only the ones that didnae eat their suppers.'

They both looked at me and decided to focus on the contents of their plates. Mrs Churchill chuckled and I then tucked in to my grub, which was very nice indeed, but it felt strange having the maid bring it out to me. We ended the meal with a glass of wine.

I was worried that Mrs Churchill had got the wrong idea of me being the typical Jock soldier, that is, a piss-head, but it was only a wee glass and I took little sips. It was sweet and not that bad and I realised that it was in fact cherryade, my favourite!

'Surprised you there, eh!' Mrs Churchill laughed and from that moment I was her slave for life. 'Winston told me you like cherryade, and I'm glad to hear that you gave him tellings off about his drinking and other faults.'

'Oh aye, Mrs Churchill, I had to tell that man off a few

times, you know. But he listened to me in the end always. I had to look after him, which was my job when I was his batman. But he looked after me, too.'

'And I'm very grateful on both accounts and I'm sure your mother is also. He speaks very highly of you and at one point he never stopped talking about you! This is unusual, as you know, because normally the only person he speaks about is himself!'

'Aye, he's a right blether! Many's a night I could'nae get to my bed because of his yapping. But you know he's real interesting and I only fell asleep a few times.'

The conversation, as you can see, was going along nice and relaxed. We were enjoying ourselves talking about Winston and Belgium. She then asked about me and my family and I told her about my mum and the girls and also about George and Mum's plans.

'That's wonderful news, Jamie! I'm sure she'll be very happy and the girls will be taken care of. It must make you feel a lot better to know she's found someone nice.'

'Aye, George's alright and it's a load off my mind. It's a hard thing being the man of the house, you know.' I was falling into deep Edinburgh-ese at this point, as you will have noticed, and she loved it. 'Now I know they'll all be taken care of I feel a whole lot better.'

'And I believe you have a young lady-friend, too.'

'Aye, Gemma. She's a smasher! She's a nurse and I think I might marry her one day.' I don't know why I was revealing these intimate thoughts to someone I'd just met.

'We'll have to have this important lady round for dinner soon then, eh?'

I was lapping all this up but I must confess I was stone-tired. I sensed that she was having a good time too because we talked on till late, mainly about Winston. She told me about his desire to get back into the government and of the many obstacles he had to overcome in order to achieve that goal.

It was dark outside now and I was really failing but a thought kept coming into my mind as we spoke, until I could hold it in no longer.

'Miss, why do you really think the colonel wanted me to come down to London and leave my home?'

She sat back in her chair. 'Jamie, Winston is probably the most selfish but at the same time the kindest and most generous man I have ever known. It's difficult to reconcile that fault with those qualities but in Belgium, he told me, you saved his life with an act of amazing courage.

'He told me also that he thought you had many of the same qualities he has, namely, that you are loyal and honest, and those that he lacked: consideration for others first before yourself. He felt you deserved a better life. Please don't think we're being patronising.'

I did not know what that meant. She went on, 'But he wanted to; he said he needed to give something back to you by offering you an opportunity that would in probability always be denied by circumstances out of your control. Does that help you?'

I have to say I was near tears when I heard this. 'I don't want to disappoint him. Or you, that's all. You've been put to all this bother with having a stranger in your nice home and I just hope I don't let you down.'

'We both know you won't and its nae bother, dinnae worry.' And she winked at me.

Then she saw I was knackered and I was led up to my bed. I got into my jammies and went out like a light. My last thought was that I really wanted to see the colonel again.

And I could not wait to see Gemma.

When I awoke that morning and got up I had forgotten which floor the loo was on. I eventually found it without disturbing anyone in their beds by knocking on the wrong door and returned to my room and lay back on the bed. I expected the colonel got home late and was in his kip. He was an early riser in Belgium but I was not sure how he would be in civilian life.

I dressed and left the room, heading downstairs for my breakfast. I walked into the dining room and there he was at the table wearing a horrible silk robe that looked like it had been pinched from a Chinese knocking-shop.

'Colonel!'

'James, my boy, how are you!' He stood up, grabbed me by the arm and gave me a big shake. 'Sit down and help yourself, laddie. This time there is no need for you to wait on me, hand or foot!'

'Och, it was never any trouble, colonel! You know that!'

I tucked in to bacon and eggs. It was like old times, because I always ate with him at Laurence Farm as he hated dining alone. He hated being alone at any time, that I knew.

'And how is your room?'

'It's lovely! I can't wait to get books to fill the bookcase. It looks daft being empty like that!'

He chuckled. 'Don't worry, I have a few of my own that you may borrow, as today begins the third stage of your education!'

'What do you mean, Colonel?' I asked, mouth full of toast.

'Your education in Edinburgh was the first stage and then life with the 6th was the second, now here in London will be your finishing school!'

What was he on about? Never mind, he had it all planned out, which was fine by me.

We chatted about Edinburgh. I told him about Mum and he exclaimed that it was remarkably good news. I filled him in about Hearts and told him about the train down and that swine who took my seat.

'Outrageous!' he roared with a mouth full of mushrooms.

'I should have clouted him but I showed great *restraint*,' I lied. I had heard this word recently and wanted to try it out.

'Temptation resisted is the true sign of character, James.'

'Naw, I still wanted to do him.'

He pushed his plate back. 'Now we must come to business matters. As I told you at the hospital I intend to regain a place in Cabinet. However, it appears that this is going to take time and effort. James, I will tell you now, I have many enemies. Men who are unforgiving and have long memories. At the moment I am heavily involved in the Dardanelles inquiry. I must clear my name first before anything else can be achieved; therefore I believe I have a year until I can rightfully regain that which was lost.

'I want you in time to become my personal assistant. Remember when I asked you to become my batman?' I nodded. 'That was a very difficult position to undertake for one so young. But you proved yourself and became in my opinion the finest batman in the British army. But you had to learn the ropes first, so to speak, and to become my personal assistant you must learn new ropes, and ropes that, though more difficult to get a grip on than those of the batman, I am sure you have the ability to grab a hold of and deal with, with great aplomb.'

There he goes again, I thought. Blethering away. What's with all these ropes? I had visions of myself swinging through trees like Tarzan of the apes.

'Colonel, does this mean I have to go to school to learn to be an assistant?'

'A *type* of school, yes. This is through no fault of your own. Your education in Edinburgh was not designed for such a role. Nevertheless, this is what is required. I have through my friend Mr Lloyd George found you a position at the Ministry of Munitions head office at Whitehall Place. There you will learn the skills of typing, note-taking, economics and other interesting areas. It pays well also. And in the meantime I will take you along to the House on occasion so that you may observe its doings, and allow you to meet many important men so that you get yourself known. How does that proposition sound to you?'

I was gobsmacked. Sitting in a nice warm office? Well paid? It sounded like the very idea. I knew that my own education was basic. I was a great reader but understood that there were so many areas of life of which I was ignorant. There were things that I read in some books I just did not comprehend. It was not ideal but I understood the reasoning.

'What you are saying, Colonel, is that I need to serve an apprenticeship.'

He jumped up in his seat. 'Precisely! How marvellously put and I could not do better myself! An apprentice, yes, but an experienced one with a wise old head.' My chest swelled and I beamed my delight at this description of myself. 'And it is only but for a year, whereas I believe normal apprenticeships can take up to five,' he added.

'In this new environment you will come across many unfamiliar things,' he counselled. 'Open your mind to them! Embrace the new! But I must warn you. You will undoubtedly come up against pedantry, small-mindedness and office politics. There may be those who are jealous of you. There will be those who will appear snobbish. My strong advice to you is to demonstrate, at all times, that restraint you so admirably showed to that son of a bitch who took your seat on the train.'

'You mean...'

'I mean, pound the shit out of anyone who upsets you, *after* office hours only.'

Chapter Fourteen

That same day I went to visit my girlfriend, Gemma, at the hospital. She was seventeen, slightly more than a year older than me but I was her first boyfriend and we were completely in love. She was taller than me but I would soon grow and catch up, if only just overtake. She had wavy blond hair that maddeningly was usually covered by her uniform cap, brown eyes and the prettiest face I ever saw. She was fairly new and a probationer when I came to the hospital and given only basic tasks to begin with.

She told me that one of the first things she was taught as a nurse was never to fall in love with any of her patients. Now, for a young girl surrounded by sturdy but wounded young men this advice would have been akin to me getting a job in a sweet shop (you know how I like sugar) and being told not to handle the goods. So, when I came along with my bad leg, looking so young, recipient of parcels from Fortnum & Mason's and letters from eminent politicians, added to that a Scottish accent, well, Cupid did not have to take an especially difficult aim regarding this wee girl when this fascinating young Caledonian was within easy reach.

Soon we were chatting, then we were laughing and finally we were kissing. She could have been thrown out of her job for this but the other lads in the ward were good sports and kept quiet.

I sensed that though Gemma was bright and intelligent, she was a lonely girl. As she was the daughter and, I suspect, the forgotten one of the family nothing great was expected of her. Her parents seemed to be typical of their class in that they were forever buggering off on weekends shooting and having soirées and such. She could not debut because of the war; she wanted to become a nurse in an army hospital but was underage at the time.

She told me her parents only seemed to acknowledge her existence in their lives the day she told them that she wanted to become a nurse. Naturally her father, a wealthy solicitor, forbade the idea. Daughters of that class were for marrying off as respectably as possible. In those days a girl could not be allowed near any boy unless they were heavily chaperoned. She told me that if we were to meet up together for something as innocent as a walk in the park, a relative would have to be there to keep an eye on us.

The stultifying prudery of the age seems beyond belief now. It was beyond belief back then. The life expected of her was go to school, debut and marry the first chinless inbreed that caught her fancy. The thought of any young girl of her class working in a hospital surrounded by males was beyond comprehension to her parents and completely unthinkable to allow.

She had an ally, fortunately. A powerful one. Her grandmother, who was a supporter of the suffragette movement and women's rights and as radical in her thinking as her son was archaic. She was an acquaintance of the famous Emmeline Pankhurst, herself. Mind you, after meeting her I did not think it unusual that her son, Gemma's father, should turn the other way as the old girl was an absolute harridan.

Her husband, Gemma's grandfather, had passed away years before (a lucky escape, possibly) and she had plenty cash of her own with which to ease her widowhood. Her father had been wealthy and in her own marriage she held the purse strings. She still did. Her late husband was also a solicitor and not seen as a suitable catch at the time, but her own father saw something in him (probably his tolerance, as she was a handful even then), relented and allowed them to marry.

She was the biggest influence in young Gemma's life, that was obvious, and my girl also inherited the old dear's feistiness (she could sort my hash out too, I noticed). She stood her ground with her dear auld *faither* and when he said no, she ran off to Granma who set about getting her number one grandchild what she wanted.

Gemma packed her bags and moved in with the old woman, and her grandmother set about using her connections to get Gemma signed up through the Red Cross to the Voluntary Aid Detachment, and Gemma became a VAD. This organisation was made up of mainly upper-class women who gave up their time to assist in hospitals, and on the outbreak of war they were needed badly. They were treated like second-class citizens by the professional nursing system as they were seen as untrained amateurs, and as they were often highly educated people, they were critical at times of the rigid and at times unnecessarily strict discipline and often stifling lack of flexibility allowed in the working lives of nurses in those days.

Though Gemma was underage at the time, her grandmother made a quiet donation to the organisation's coffers, told Gemma's father in no certain terms to keep his mouth shut, and her granddaughter was accepted.

I was taken to meet the old woman and thought she was terrific. I had never met such an opinionated powerhouse in my young life. Gemma insisted I wear my kilt (the Royal Scots Fusiliers wore trousers on active service, something my mum was glad of as she envisioned me getting pneumonia wearing a drafty kilt) and when we got to the plush Kensington home she was all over me, describing me as 'her wee Bonnie Prince Charlie fae the Hielands!' in a very good Scottish accent. Young or old, rich or poor, it never fails: they all love a kiltie. She also laid out a spread of cake which I had never seen the likes of in my life, and in order not to insult her hospitality, I ensured few remained to clear away.

I had yet to meet the parents and frankly, I was in no hurry to. Little did I know at the time that the pleasure of meeting that lot would be far ahead in the future.

Gemma and I met up in the hospital canteen. I was desperate to give her a kiss but we couldn't as there were too many folk around; we held hands under the table, as she was not allowed to be seen doing that in public. I dared her to kiss me as I was ready to blast the ear off any old bag around who objected, but acceded to her request not to on the proviso that the next time we saw each other she owed me a huge smacker on the lips.

'Is it what you want?' she asked after I told her about the job at the ministry.

'It's not what I expected but it does make sense. There's so much I don't know, Gem, and this is a good way to learn. It's only for a year and hopefully by that time the colonel will be back in business. The main thing is I'll be living in London! I can see you anytime I want!'

'Oh, I'm so glad to hear it! As long as I'm the only girl you want to see! It's really exciting! Mixing with people from the government! I just knew you were the boy for me when I first saw you!'

'So it's my money you're after, my lady,' I said as I leaned closer to her.

'Mm, that and everything else!'

At that moment I just could not contain myself. I had thought about it for some time. I think she had a right to know and really it was about time I told her.

I was never exactly the sort to get tongue-tied, but when that wee girl smiled and looked into my eyes my insides turned quite mushy and my mouth would dry up. I had to overcome this on this occasion so I screwed myself up and said what had to be said.

'Miss Gemma Rebecca Ashby, I have something to tell you.'

She looked directly into my eyes.

'Gemma, I love you.'

Whether there were people around or not she did not care but leaned over very slowly and kissed me on the lips. It tasted like heaven and I had up till that moment never felt such a sweet sensation in all my life.

'I love you too, Jamie Melville,' she whispered as she slowly pulled away from me.

All this *and* I supported Hearts. Things could not be better.

Chapter Fifteen

For Winston, the year ahead would be frustrating and at times his mood would be very down. He would pass the time making speeches during debates at the House and become heavily involved in the Dardanelles inquiry. He started writing articles for newspapers and had his portrait painted. Briefly, there was excitement in July when his friend Mister Lloyd George was promoted to Secretary of State for War, leaving his post at Munitions, and Winston hoped that he would be his replacement. Unfortunately, it went to someone else.

A few days after I returned to London, Winston accompanied me to the office in Whitehall Place to meet my new employers. I was extremely excited at the thought of going in and out of such a building; it was near Downing Street and he took a detour to show me the prime minister's residence. As we walked past he glanced at it; I could only wonder what he was thinking.

We entered the ministry building and went up a few floors and I was sat down in an outer office whilst Winston went in. He came out a short time later with a man in his early fifties who was only slightly taller than me and rather squat; he had a very large head covered in a mop of still-blondish hair and a fresh, clean shaven face. With a ready smile he shook my hand and told me his name was Mr Laird, a fellow Scot, and that he would be supervising me in my new role. Winston then left us.

I was ushered into his office where he sat me down at his desk. He asked me to wait a few moments and left the room to return carrying a typewriter, which he plumped down in front of me. I was no stranger to this machine. Back at the Farm the company clerk, Willie Reilly, would sometimes let me use his if I was at a loose end to do some minor tasks and I enjoyed playing with it and on one occasion he let me type out a letter for the colonel. I remember handing it to Winston and him reading it over and without a word signing it and I went off with a triumphant smirk on my face. I was no inept.

I soon discovered that life in this office would be far different from what I had experienced in the 6th. Mr Laird asked me how proficient I was and I truthfully told him what I had done previously. He seemed satisfied and informed me that for a couple of hours each morning a Miss Paget would tutor me to bring me up to speed.

This sounded good and on hearing the 'Miss' I immediately envisioned some pretty little schoolmarm type who would be putty in my hands.

He let me bang away at a short letter he had prepared by hand. When I completed the task he looked at it and just 'hummed' and then said he would now show me to my workplace. We went along a corridor and into a room that had about a dozen desks with bods plodding away. This was where I would work. It was the requisitions department which dealt with orders from front-line areas. These had to be passed on to works departments in order to ensure the correct amount of ammunition and shells reached the right places. He made it sound very interesting.

We then returned to his office and had tea sent up and we chatted about the job, Scotland and football. I took a liking to Mr Laird and when he told me just to knock off home but he would see me bright and early ready for action the next morning, I felt that things could be a lot worse.

I started out the following day to begin my new job. The walk from Eccleston Square to the office was not too far and I looked forward to passing by all the famous sights each day on my way to work.

I made my way up to the office and just stood around. No one spoke to me as staff came in and chatted to each other before beginning their day. Mr Laird then entered, showed me to my new desk and introduced Miss Paget to me. That was the first disappointment. Instead of a pretty young school-teacher she turned out to be reasonably young, in her late twenties but with a wizened, narky wee face and a pair of front teeth that would have put a chipmunk to shame. She shook my hand and pulled a chair up beside me and began my typing tutorial.

She was not very helpful and was what we call in Scotland a *nippy sweetie*. She kept disappearing and leaving me alone with my task but if I got stuck and went to ask for assistance she would say she was too busy with her own work and would come and see me later. 'Later' never transpired. I ended up having to seek help elsewhere by approaching a fellow with spectacles called Albert, who turned out to be a very decent type who was happy to assist.

If it was not for him and another chap called Stan I don't know what I would have done. Stan told me that Miss Paget was a well-known pain in the neck and the rest of the staff detested her. The problem was, she had been there that long she knew everything and was tolerated for this reason alone.

The daily 'tutorial' became shorter and shorter until by Friday she did not even bother to come over. I had to seek work and Albert and Stan would pass over some of the simpler tasks to ease me in. Albert was an older bloke in his late thirties who was married and Stan was younger, in his early twenties. He would later be conscripted though his job was protected (or 'starred' as it was known) due to some mix-up, but he served and thankfully survived the war. He was a real nice lad from the north and along with Albert was my only friend there.

I received my first pay packet at the end of the second week and it was quite a tidy wee sum. I now no longer sent money home and Winston refused to take digs off me, insisting that I open a bank account and save a fixed amount each week. This was the pot crying the kettle black because Mr Churchill was the worst spendthrift I ever knew. But I had been thinking along those lines myself.

For the first time in my life I walked into the offices of the Bank of Scotland in Bishopsgate and opened an account in the name of James Melville Esq., c/o Eccleston Square, the City of Westminster, London. Winston signed for me as I was underage and I regularly put my wee bit away each week, for as my old granny used to say, your best friend in life is a pound in the bank.

I saw very little of Winston for weeks on end as he was involved in the inquiry to clear his name over Gallipoli. I followed the hearings in the press and it seemed there were plenty of guilty men around as the prime minister, Mr Asquith, did not want the findings of the inquiry to be made public as some very eminent people would be implicated. Winston insisted that it should be out in the open and he had a real fight on his hands.

Then, in early December, there was great excitement. Three senior members of the government resigned, including Mr Lloyd George. They were unhappy with Mr Asquith's running of the war and had had enough. A plot was afoot to unseat him.

That very day for the first time in my life I was invited by Winston to visit a Turkish bath at the Royal Automobile Club buildings in Pall Mall. He had with him his great friend, Fred Smith, later known as Lord Birkenhead, whom I first came upon in Belgium when he visited Winston at Laurence Farm.

The ambience of the baths was ornate and luxurious and their healing powers had worked wonders on my leg as I relished the sensation of a completely painless existence, if only fleeting; and hoped there would be further visits.

I mused on this whilst sipping at a bottle of pop and listening to Winston and Fred gassing away about horses, a subject that has always been the most crashing bore to me. Happily they veered off that topic and started on politics, which was more interesting. After a short while Fred (or 'F.E.' as he was known) announced that he had to leave momentarily in order to receive an expected telephone call.

'Well, James, what do you think of the baths?' Winston asked after Fred took off. He looked like a sweaty, red-faced Buddha with his towels wrapped round his waist.

'Aren't these places supposed to be for people with gout?'

'They do attract all sorts, including the gout-ridden. But the ancient Romans swore by them and the great men of the time conducted much of their business there.'

'But that doesn't happen now?'

'No, not so much now, but you never know.' He leaned back and chewed on his cigar. The last remark was enigmatic, even to me, as I sat and drank my cherryade.

Fred returned and resumed his seat. 'I'm to meet David and Max at home now.'

Immediately Winston perked up. 'Am I invited?'

I knew that Winston had promised his wife that he would be home to dine that night and I was surprised to hear him ask this.

Fred's face was expressionless. 'Dai says come along if you want to.'

I thought this sounded strange but Winston stood up and gathered his towels around him.

'James, I have to leave now with F.E. I need you to go home and advise Mrs Churchill that I will unfortunately have to forego dinner this evening as I have an extremely pressing engagement.'

After that he was off to get changed. Fred sat down and appeared in no hurry.

'Mrs Churchill is going to go daft!' I thought out loud. 'He hasn't been home this week for tea!'

'Jamie, that's Winston for you.' F.E. drawled. 'That poor woman is a veritable saint and puts up with God knows what from him but at least she has the consolation of knowing that Winston *too* knows that!'

I decided to take a stroll home rather than catch a taxi; Fred had offered to drop me off but I thought it best for Winston's sake that he should not run the risk of Mrs Churchill seeing me coming out of the cab whilst spotting him being whisked off elsewhere.

I let myself in, as they had given me a key, and steeled myself to tell Mrs Churchill the bad news. Once again.

That evening I sat in the dining room till quite late, chatting away to Mrs Churchill. By this time I was calling her Clemmie and she was the most informal of people when she was alone. She was only a young woman after all, barely thirty, ten years younger than her husband. She told me she felt silly when I kept calling her 'Miss' or 'Mrs Churchill' and insisted that I call her by her first name. She was an interesting person because she had ideas and views that were very modern for the times she lived in.

She told me in some detail about her life. Her parents were divorced and, if the truth be told from how she alluded to them and what I would find out for myself years later, they were both upper-class trash. Her mother was a well-known courtesan (or *'hoor'* as we would say in Gorgie) and her father was a rogue and womaniser who himself was previously divorced.

No surprise that these two divorced also and Clementine, her sisters and brother had a pretty unsettled childhood. She went to school for a while in Edinburgh but hated it. They ended up living in Dieppe in France for a time and there, Clemmie's beloved sister Kitty died of typhus aged only seventeen.

From how she described her childhood, and again, these are my own feelings on the matter, they had a pretty easy and luxurious life compared to my own upbringing and also that of about ninety per cent of the country.

They moved around, living in London or on the south coast; a holiday home in Scotland and for a while residing in France, as I said. She claimed they were 'relatively poor' and a major concern was never having enough white gloves to change during the day. Her mother's favourite had been quite openly known to be the sister who died and Clementine was somewhat forgotten.

She was rescued by a relative and went to live with her for a while, which she recalled fondly. She said that she had wanted to go to university, which was unusual but not unheard of for women of that time, but her mother was against it and wanted her to be the usual wallflower and debut instead of using her brain at a seat of learning.

For a period she taught French to children to earn money and by this time she had blossomed, as is well known, into one of the great beauties of the age.

I listened to her, enchanted to hear of such a life. It was so far removed from that of my mother, she might as well have come from another planet. My mum was only about five years older than this woman but in all her life could only dream of debuting and living in France and meeting society beaus; if she ever did that, though I know she *would* have had her dreams. I pondered the meaning and the reason for it all and remembered Winston's words to me whilst he was painting at Laurence Farm, when he spoke about wasted talent and unfulfilled lives.

In the end all it boiled down to was whether you had enough food to feed your children. My mother had to rely on our school feeding us free malt every day; Clementine worried about dirty white gloves.

After that conversation I confess I became unsettled and whilst not exactly having feelings of inferiority about myself, I did feel that the gulf between people like Clemmie, her class and the real world I knew were insurmountable. Clemmie meant well but meaning well does not feed six children and return two of them who were taken away from their mother, and all this was happening in the richest nation on earth at the time, with an empire that was pouring wealth back into the mother country.

She left me quite late and went upstairs and I remained in the dining room. I had recently started to read Shakespeare and the play that would become my favourite was *Julius Caesar*. Winston had made a bet with me about learning Mark Antony's speech. I had started to memorise it, though much of the language was still above my head. I would read it, scribble it down on a sheet of paper, then hold my hands in front of my eyes and recite two or three lines.

Soon two or three became nine or ten and after that I was confident I could pull the whole thing off. It was a way of focusing the mind on a problem and working out ways of my own to overcome it. Winston had what they call a 'photographic memory' to aid him, as it was well known that he could recite great passages of anything he turned his remarkable mind to, but my trick was to read it, then write it down and then somehow it seemed to stick.

I was on my feet, reciting, when I heard the main door being unlocked. I thought it odd; usually a cab dropped him off at night and I had not heard one. I knew that Fred lived in Grosvenor Gardens, which wasn't that far away. I would have walked it even with my leg, but Winston never walked home at night so late.

He saw the light on in the dining room and must have thought the last person in had not bothered to put it out and came through to see me standing there with *Julius Caesar* in one hand and the other over my eyes.

'I've nearly cracked it, Colonel!' I announced.

He said nothing. Removing his overcoat, he threw it over the table and sat down.

I could sense unhappiness in him as I knew him well by now, and expected hours of brooding silence. I had seen a few instances of this over the last months and hated it when he was like that because it was utterly heartbreaking to observe in someone so kind such depths of desolation and loneliness. Well, that's why Jamie Melville was around. As I did at the 6th I would do here: look after him.

'Colonel, what's wrong? What happened?' I stood next to him. 'I think I'm going to win the bet. I know the whole speech. *Mark Antony*. Do you want me to recite it?'

'They are all, all dishonourable men,' he mumbled, inaudibly.

'Colonel? No, they are all *honourable* men:

> *Come I to speak in Caesar's funeral.*
> *He was my friend, faithful and just to me*
> *But Brutus says he was ambitious,*
> *And Brutus is an honourable man,*

I declaimed. I stopped and looked at him.

'Colonel, do you want a nice glass of brandy?'

There was the tiniest twitch of a smile around the lips.

'James Melville, I cannot help but wonder what life would be like without your good sense. Yes, bring us both a drink and join me in the sitting room.'

I got the drinks and we went through and sat down.

'Is it alright I if I ask what happened?'

He took a large gulp of brandy. I was already on my feet to grab the bottle but he waved me away, gently. 'No, James, it's quite alright, I'll do the pouring. It's enough that I have kept you up so late. Your mother would be most unhappy.

'What has happened?' he continued, 'Mr Asquith has resigned.'

'Really? But that's good news!' it was; the prime minister had been Winston's implacable foe in government and whilst he was at Number 10 Winston believed he would never get back into the Cabinet.

'Yes, yes it is. It very much looks like Mr Lloyd George and not Mr Bonar Law, as expected, will replace him.'

'That's even better! He's your good friend!' I sat back, 'Oh, it's all going fine now, Colonel!' Then I stopped. I was not sure I should be gloating over such momentous news.

'No, it is not. Mr Lloyd George has advised me through our friend Max Aitken that he does not at this time feel constrained to invite me back into the Cabinet.'

I was shocked to hear this. 'But why invite you to dine with him tonight? To tell you bad news like that! The bloody swine!'

'The invitation was an error on Dai's part. An understandable one, though my ire is not directed at him but at others.'

I could not think what to say. Remember, I was sixteen years old. All this *chicanery* was far above me.

I learned later that Lloyd George was unable to offer Winston a position in Cabinet as part of the price for his being made prime minister. Once again, Winston's enemies had denied him a place at the seat of power and Lloyd George in a moment of non-thinking exuberance had said yes to Winston being at the meeting but had dived away in order to ensure he was not around when Mr Churchill turned up. He sent his lapdog, Max Aitken, to deliver the news to Winston. In my innocence, I spoke from the heart.

'I just don't believe they'll keep you out for long. Once Mr Lloyd George is in place for a wee while you'll be back, you'll see!'

He now only sipped his brandy.

'Yes, I will have to wait. Meanwhile, thousands more of our brave comrades will die needlessly. I will have no part to play in trying to win this war quickly and with as little loss of life as possible. That is my frustration, Jamie. *That I will not be allowed to make a difference in order to save life.* I try not to hate. James, you must help me try not to *hate.*'

It was a long night and the brandy bottle was empty by its end.

Christmas arrived and Winston and his family headed off to Blenheim Palace. Before we all broke up to go our various ways I invited Gemma around for dinner. Mrs Churchill and she got on together like old pals and Winston made the effort to be there and regaled us with wonderful stories; about him, of course.

I went up on the train and stayed at Mum's and visited her future new home in Murrayfield. It went very well and I regaled the girls with stories about London and all I had seen there. George and I got on better and the last conversation we'd had was never mentioned.

It seemed that things were alright now for Mum; she looked less tired, which was a good thing, and I just hoped in my heart that it was not all a show for me. I always was a natural born worrier; I suppose I can't help it, it's the way I am.

I left Edinburgh after New Year, feeling a lot more settled. There appeared to me to be an easy relationship between Mum and George, and the girls were used to him now and I felt a lot more relaxed on that account. I have always been over-protective of my loved ones and have had difficulty knowing when to pull back, on occasion. But now I felt that I should try and accept that I no longer was responsible, they were doing fine and I must get on with my own life and to try and not worry about them.

Things at work were not going as well as I had hoped. Hamster-features herself, Miss Paget's immediate superior was a man called Mr Hammond, a tall, dry-looking cove with spectacles, who had about him as much charisma as a toilet brush. They both worked in tandem and originally I was to be the third member of their section in the office.

I began to feel nothing but loathing for this man. He was an arrogant swine who virtually ignored me from day one. He never spoke to me or ever greeted me with a 'hello' in the morning and when I left (on time) each night I could feel daggers in my back from him as I reached for my jacket and stick. When his phone rang he would rarely bother to answer it so I would have to and if the voice asked for him, when I passed it over he would flash me a look of such malevolence that if I had not been Jamie Melville but some other wee lad, I might have baulked in absolute terror. Once after such a call, he condescended to speak to me.

'Melville, when the telephone rings and someone asks for me, take a message and tell them I'll call back!'

What was the point of having a phone on your desk if you never answer it? I thought. That was his job, was it not? The juniors were not supposed to answer the telephone. I did not like the 'Melville' bit either. I decided if he called me that again, I would have it out with him. No one called me that; not even eminent officers and true gentlemen like Archie Sinclair or Colonel Churchill.

I kept away from them both from then on. Stan and Albert gave me work to keep me busy and together they helped me develop into the job. One day, Mr Hammond did not come into work and Miss Paget was out in another office and I had to sort through their mail. I dealt with various letters addressed to them and found one that was opened but marked 'return to sender'.

It contained a cheque for four hundred and eighty pounds, ten shillings and eightpence issued by accounts to pay a contractor for work supplying shell casings by a firm in east Dechmont in Lothian in Scotland. Now, I knew that area as I was from the west of Edinburgh. As far as I was aware, I knew of no munitions manufacturer or engineering firm who could take on that size of work in east Dechmont. It was a tiny wee place with a pub, a church, a post office and a few houses and nothing else.

Why was an invoice from Accounts being returned to Requisitions? Then I saw that the cheque was signed on behalf of the Ministry of Munitions by none other than Norman Hammond Esquire.

The mailroom were forever trying to work out which area each letter received was to be assigned to because many were just addressed to the Ministry, Whitehall Place, London, and had to be opened so the mailroom could sort out where each letter should end up in the building. On opening this one, the sorting room saw Hammond's name and thought it should go to him. The senior mailroom assistant who dealt with all the mail was off sick that day. The junior had to cover for him in his absence.

I thought it odd but when I considered those two, Mr Hammond and Miss Paget, I never suspected anything other than it was just a mix-up. As they were both such snoots and jobsworths I just thought that there was an easy answer somewhere and then let it go and moved on to something else.

Chapter Sixteen

Time seemed to pass by very slow that year. I got on with learning the job and seeing Gemma, though it was not easy as she worked very long hours. She did get a weekend off now and then and I looked forward to these, as she did.

I made a few journeys north to my home to see the family and took in a game at Tynecastle if I could whilst there. But I could not stay long, with the long journey back, and after a while I no longer made the effort. I did make it up for the wedding of Mum and George at St Giles, which went well. The sight of my wee sisters dressed as maids and squealing when they received their favours was one for the cameras.

My relationship with Gemma developed and became my anchor in London and I would soon appreciate the depths of her emotional attachment to me. As a nurse she was worldlier than most girls her age and would discuss some of the things she had to contend with on a daily basis, including dealing with the more intimate bodily functions of her male patients.

She described them in such a humorous manner that I could only laugh but at times I was secretly horrified that this young girl was doing what she was. I do not think it makes a difference whether it was back in those less permissive times or the more enlightened era of today; if your girlfriend is a nurse you will be shocked at what she tells you from time to time.

But I never forgot that nurse who held my hand in Bailleul and from that moment on regarded all who followed that profession as veritable angels, and did not grudge any poor, wounded soldier in delirium the comfort of my girl telling them that she was their mummy and loved them dearly, to help ease their pain and troubles. I was proud of her. We spoke of these intimate matters when I stayed the odd weekend at her granma's, in separate rooms of course (her grandmother was not *that* modern in her views), but we would sneak into each other's rooms late on and lie near-naked together in each other's arms.

We smooched heavily and felt each other intimately but that was as far as we went. We were lovers in all but consummation as we lay there talking, kissing and caressing and I loved those few nights we spent together if only for an hour or two before I sneaked off back to my room; they are a cherished memory and will be to my dying day.

She spoke of the first time she had seen the wounded men come back from the Somme. They were brought in caked with mud, bloodied and with filthy bandages hanging off them and Gemma along with a more experienced nurse had to pitch in the best they could.

We lay together as she recalled, 'The first man we came to must have been asleep with exhaustion or through morphine but I remembered how old and worn-out he looked, though he could not have been more than thirty. He had his leg blown away below the knee. The bandage was saturated and needed changing and I hung back, letting Sister remove it. I remember that all the time I was watching her, to concentrate on the task and try not to pass out. All the girls fainted at one time. It was accepted but only the once; if you did it again you had to report to Matron for a "talk."

'I remember I was feeling alright, then the bandage was removed, the stump swollen and raw and I could see the white gristle and congratulated myself that I had passed the test, only I hadn't because there were sutures inside the wound and Sister pulled on one and when it came out the blood started to spray all around. The next thing I remember was waking up.' I knew how she felt as I recalled my own memories of fainting, and the experience at the Casualty Clearing Station, as she continued, 'I was helped to my feet by a soldier who had seen me pass out and had climbed off his stretcher to assist me because Sister was too intent on trying to stem the flow of blood and everyone else was too busy. The soldier who helped me put his arm under my head to pillow me and I remember looking up at him and thinking, how strange, this man who had come here to be helped is in turn looking after *me*, and I felt ashamed that I had let him down.'

I listened and imagined the scene. 'The soldier was a good bloke; he *understood*. You had nothing to be ashamed of.'

'I got back to my feet and he asked, are you alright now, dear? I said yes and he went back to the stretcher; well, he almost fell back onto it. I then noticed he only had one arm. One arm, and he used it to pillow my head with. After that I never fainted again.'

Day after day during July she dealt with similar cases and worked twelve-, sometimes fourteen-hour shifts seven days a week. She had the odd night off during that time and would come and see me for a short while.

I did not mention that I saw in her the change the experience had made; she seemed so tired and it had been difficult to talk to her at times as she appeared distracted and distant. But I did my best to be cheerful and kind to her though I could see she was far away, her mind elsewhere.

She lay across me, her face close to mine. 'The only thing that sustained me was the thought of getting away to see you, even if only for a short while. I *had* to see you, I needed your sweetness and little kisses! To hear your lovely Scottish voice!' Her fingers caressed my face. 'Just holding your hand meant so much. To know that there was someone nice and homely to spend a short time with away from bandages and smells and screams and nurses and rules, that's what got me through it all.'

We clung tight together. 'It tested me. Before, being a nurse was an abstract, it also meant being a rebel; that was something that was attractive to me. My grandmama would tell me that I must always be my own woman with my own mind and be true to myself. I saw myself flaunting conventions, being a nonconformist like her; she has always been my heroine. I wanted to be like her, like Florence Nightingale or Mary Seacole. But soon, in being like her, like *them*, I was not being myself any more. I had forgotten who *I* really was.'

She began to cry and I was not sure what to say. I know now that a lot of it was down to the appalling shock and stress affecting her over those last few months and it now came pouring out. As I knew, she had no loving parents to run back to or any real close friends to confide in. At the hospital the regime was such that they had to show no feelings, no weakness, or they were kicked out. Being a VAD and subject to close scrutiny, she did not want to let the others down. She would have been terrified most of all of disappointing her grandmother.

Her one outlet for relief from it all was me. But through all that time we barely saw each other, due to the punishing hours she worked. When we did meet I noted the change in her but even though I was young and understood from my own experience to some extent how she felt, I knew from what she described now that in the ordeal she had suffered, for it was an ordeal, she did not have what I had to sustain me through my own trauma.

I had great friendships and trusts built up in the 6th; it was always there for me and when I was hurt that network, Winston, Archie, Duncan and the others aided me and sent letters and gifts. Together with meeting this girl they helped me through the worst of the physically painful and mentally tough challenge of trying to overcome my injury. My acceptance of the fact that I would never be the same, at least bodily, was eased by that group I was part of because I knew they all understood what I had gone through.

Gemma had no such luxuries. She was on her own; except for a wee lad she had just met but clung to as the only tangible thing in her life to look forward to. I was someone who offered a little unconditional kindness and affection to help her through her unhappiness. I was deeply moved to feel wanted and needed by this girl. I felt I had purpose in my life. To be needed and to be loved by someone is never to be alone.

'I love you, Gemma.' I kissed her hair. 'You're *you*, my girl. You can do anything, you're so clever! The smartest wee girl around! And the most beautiful, too!' I babied her with endearments and caresses and she started giggling again amongst the sniffles and told me she loved me.

'Has it been worth it in any way?' I asked after a short while.

'Yes, because I met you and I know I can last the course now. But I have to confess to being disillusioned by it all. Not the ideals of my grandmama, I still champion all of that, but I know now that I could never throw myself in front of any of the King's horses for my causes or beliefs, as I'm not true enough to myself and realise now what I am. I'm not in the mould of the great heroine. The war has proven that to me.'

'Gemma, the same happened to me. I thought being a soldier was like a dream. I had all these new friends like Duncan and Davie, who looked after me. I had a rifle, I was made batman for Mr Churchill and I absolutely loved it. All the officers spoiled me, especially the colonel, and then when I kept telling myself what a lovely time I was having, a shell came over and nearly blew my leg off and the result of it all is that I'm a cripple for life.'

'You're not a "*cripple*".'

'As long as this war lasts I'll be a *wounded* hero. But as soon as it ends I'll be seen as a cripple.'

That we were both so young and filled with the pain of disillusionment and broken dreams was not unusual as those feelings were shared by millions of others during that ghastly war. The tragedy for us was that we had not been legally old enough to have served in our chosen fields to begin with. Both of us were running away from unhappy homes as a result of being badly misguided by the various adults who should have shown due care and responsibility towards us.

Neither of us had ever been drunk; we were both below the then legal age of consent for much of what the world had to offer; the sum of our life experience of naughtiness was lying bare-chested together for a short time underneath the covers in her bedroom in her grandmother's house. Yet we had both seen and experienced horrors that should have been unimaginable to us as the youths we in fact were, and when I think back to those days I realise that at the age I was then I had become all the man I ever would be and she the woman.

I do not believe either of us was uniquely wilful or headstrong or would have been beyond the control of any responsible guardian and run off regardless, either. With the proper care and circumstances, both of us should have been back in our respective homes living normal lives.

We discussed other matters, including my problems in the office. I told of my unease at finding the returned cheque. If I suspected fraud, I must tread carefully. She insisted I speak to Winston and no one else.

I decided to act on Gemma's advice and broach the subject of the mysterious cheque signed by Hammond with Winston. It troubled me, the thought that I had been a soldier in the front line and had friends there whilst people back home were profiting from their sacrifice. The great Battle of the Somme had been fought with no sizeable gains worth mentioning and had been brought to an end. Arras and Messines were on-going and Passchendaele was the next slaughter being prepared.

The casualty lists printed in the daily press were a reminder of what was really happening. At Martinpuich in August, whilst the Somme battle was being fought, my old battalion, now known as the 6th/7th, formed part of an assault group that distinguished itself, but as the months went by I sadly noted names of lost friends in the papers and would constantly hear Winston banging on about the men being betrayed by inefficiency and poor practice back home.

This rang true to my own thinking. A large part of the way I was feeling was influenced by a feeling of guilt about being at home whilst these men were bearing the brunt of the real pain in France. I felt pretty useless and hungered like Winston to do something meaningful with my life.

I explained to Winston what I had seen in the office and my views one evening after he had returned home early for once from the House. After scrutiny and questioning he sat back in his chair.

'Do you know anything about the man you replaced when he left the office?'

'He's supposed to have had a terrible row with Mr Hammond over something. I'm not sure what happened but I heard he was given another job elsewhere in the ministry.'

He asked me his name and wrote it down.

'I want you to say nothing of this to Mr Laird. It may well be nothing. It may be something else entirely but I want you to make a note of everything you see from now on that comes across these two individuals' desks that you feel uncomfortable with. Under no circumstances question them about anything and carry on as normal.

'James, I sense your unhappiness and frustrations with working at that office. We are both going through an unhappy period at the moment and I believe we may have to wait a little longer before there is change in our circumstances. But never fear that circumstances will not change. They *will*. When they do, things will become a great deal better.'

This failed to mollify me and I allowed my frustrations to show. 'I don't like being here whilst my friends are in France, Colonel. I'm living an easy life whilst they're suffering. Damn this bloody leg! I'm fed up with it!'

I was indeed fed up. I was young and when the doctors had initially told me the prognosis I just nodded my head but did not believe them. I could not accept that I would not get 'better'. I still believed that in time my leg would mend and I would be back to my old energetic self. I missed playing football, running and simple things like sprinting up and down stairs. I used to do everything at a hurry because I *could.* But months had passed and the pain and discomfort had not gone away.

'It is an honourable wound, James, the most honourable kind of wound there is,' Winston soothed. 'I feel that you must accept it and resign yourself to that acceptance and carry on with your life. As you say, you worry about our friends in the battalion; remember many are now passed away and in light of that you should always remember that in comparison with them and your own circumstances, I am sure you would prefer your own.'

'Of course, I always think of that but it doesn't change the fact that I feel useless! Colonel, how long will it be before you're recalled? How on earth can the government leave someone like you out of the Cabinet? It defies belief!'

He beamed his delight. 'Ah, James, how far you have travelled since that day you disgraced yourself on parade by grinning like a monkey at your commanding officer! I am humbled that you have such a high estimation of my abilities! Indeed I do wish your confidence in me was shared by certain members of the House of Commons! However, until such time I must be patient; therefore it must follow that even the army's finest batman must too remain patient.'

I did not feel any better, but as time passed by it did seem that Winston was slowly working his way back into favour. The prime minister, Mr Lloyd George, desperately wanted Winston back but he had to play Liberals and Tories off against each other and also hope that Winston would not shoot himself in the foot, which he was prone to do.

He took me on occasion to the House and introduced me to a number of famous people like Mr Balfour, Mr Asquith and this odd short-arse with a face like a burst tomato, Max Aitken. I have to say they were all very nice to me. I did not meet the prime minister as he was always busy, but I lived in hope.

I sat in the viewing gallery whilst debates were going on but in truth I found them utterly boring, particularly if Winston was not there to speak. I moaned about this to him but he told me that this was part of my education to watch and study parliamentary procedure, as I would be able to see for myself how the House operated.

Chapter Seventeen

One day in mid-April, Winston came into my office at the ministry. Mr Laird was all over him and I was delighted when, in front of that pair of horrors, Miss Paget and Mr Hammond, he approached me and told me out loud that I must accompany him to the Commons as he was to take part in an important debate and I must be there to 'support' him!

You can imagine how I felt to clear away my desk, grab my coat and head out of the office along with Winston Churchill whilst that bunch of pedants sat there with their great, gaping gobs wide open. It was wonderful.

The day would be tarnished somewhat, but would end fine. All of what followed would be blamed on my famous temper.

We left the office and strolled towards the Commons. I loved walking with him, though he always set such a brisk pace and I had to tell him to slow down, which he did with profuse apologies.

Winston filled me in on the debate which surrounded the government's recent suppression of a newspaper called *The Nation*, which was Liberal in its leanings. He considered the grounds for its suppression spurious and that the influence of the notorious Lord Northcliffe was involved through his Tory connections in the coalition government. Winston believed the government's hand had been forced by 'evil' counsel and in all probability a harmless newspaper was being closed down just to score a few points.

We entered the House and he left me to take his seat. I made my way to the gallery where only a few were in attendance, and sat at the front where I could get plenty of room for my leg, and a good view. I had brought a newspaper with me and slipped a couple of biscuits into my pocket for a snack as I knew from past experience that it might be a long haul.

After a short while the chamber started to fill and I stood to see if the prime minister had entered. He had not yet arrived and Mr Andrew Bonar Law, leader of the Conservatives and Chancellor of the Exchequer in the coalition government was standing in for him.

The debate began when Sir William Pringle, Liberal MP for North Lanarkshire, asked on what grounds circulation of the newspaper *The Nation* had been stopped.

Mr Bonar Law stood to reply, 'This course was taken because articles in this journal were of a nature that may help the enemy as they have been widely used for propaganda purposes.'

I looked at Winston but he was looking down.

'Is the right honourable gentleman aware,' responded Mr Pringle, 'that articles on the same subject, of the same character, and to the same effect have appeared in other newspapers and have been used in identically the same way; and is it the case that *The Nation* has been selected for this treatment because it is one of the main organs of Liberal opinion in this country?'

Mr Bonar Law replied that if indeed any other newspaper printed similar articles they would be treated in the same manner.

Winston then rose to speak. 'Was the matter considered by the government before or after the action was taken?'

There was a rumble from the House, and a few hisses. I tried to ascertain who and where it was coming from but it was hard to say.

'I have already explained it was taken after consultation with the government and in that respect precisely the same course has been adopted as has been followed for over a year,' the Tory leader retorted. I knew there was history between him and Winston. Mr Bonar Law had been vociferous in demanding Winston's resignation over the Dardanelles.

Then Bonar Law tripped himself up and Winston dived in when another Member stood and asked a question of whether the suppression was in regards just to the one issue of the paper or whether the paper itself was to be banned outright.

'I am told said action was taken after consultation with the government,' Bonar Law replied, still looking over to Winston. 'My answer is the reverse of that.'

'Then it was taken before consultation with the government?' Winston fired back, seeing his chance.

Bonar Law ignored him, as the Member pressed again his point on whether the suppression was total or just for one issue. Bonar Law replied but he did not seem sure himself, or claimed he wasn't.

Winston then responded, 'Might my right honourable friend supply the House with some of the articles to which exception is taken in order that every newspaper may be able to avoid such errors in the future?'

More hisses were heard and this time some cries of 'Gallipoli' and 'Go back to France!' I still could not quite make out where they came from as there was more chat and one Irish MP continually interjected about Irish newspapers being treated similarly, asking why this was not discussed.

Watching all this banter going back and forth and observing how MPs behaved, I could not help thinking that if I had acted like that back in my old school, cutting in when the teacher spoke, raising my voice, booing, hissing and such in Gorgie Primary, I would have been leathered. Yet here were the custodians of our nation acting like a bunch of neds! I'm told it has always been the case and it still is today.

Winston again asked for examples and there were more angry retorts from the Tory benches. By this time I was starting to become exasperated myself because I understood from what Winston told me that this small newspaper was either being made an example of or there was something more to it. I had read it myself from time to time and in all fairness I could not say that it was 'helpful to the enemy' in any way. That to me was nonsense.

The Liberal Members were giving back as good as they got. Fellows were pointing their fingers at each other and standing up and being pulled down by their neighbours.

After things had settled, Bonar Law condescended to reply to Winston's second request for an example of how the paper was aiding and abetting the enemy.

'In my opinion, it is quite unnecessary to provide a specific example. Some of the articles referred to have appeared in other newspapers. What my right honourable friend suggests is that we are making an exception because of the character of this paper.'

'No. I am suggesting to my right honourable friend that we have a right to know on what grounds there has been an objection taken,' Winston replied.

Then a notorious Tory Member, a crony of Lord Northcliffe's and well known to despise Winston, rose to speak. He was former admiral Sir Lionel Hunter-Baines, who had previously taken umbrage during the infamous debate that Winston took part in when he was on leave from the trenches, where he called for the reinstatement of Lord Jackie Fisher to the Admiralty.

That had been a disastrous speech and had been very damaging to Winston and was not amongst his finest moments. It had called once again into question his judgment to many people but knowing Winston I believe, and this belief was shared also by Mrs Churchill, that it was done out of loyalty to the old man; mistaken loyalty in this case, sadly, though I know that Clemmie despised Fisher and once actually told the former colleague of Winston to his face that he had nearly ruined her husband.

Hunter-Baines stood, enjoying his moment to the full, and

began, 'I had not intended to interpose in this debate until I experienced the pain of listening to the comments of the late First Lord of the Admiralty, also lately "Colonel" Churchill.' There were loud and sarcastic laughs from the Tory benches at that. 'I believe most strongly that if the government of the day, that is waging a terrible war, believes that there are elements within our country that act to succour the enemy then it is the duty of that government to remove by all possible methods that aid, and ensure that it has no longer the means to continue. If the honourable Member for Dundee,' and by this he was still referring to Winston, 'wishes to see an example of such conduct he merely has to go and have a look at the bottom of the birdcage he keeps at home to see one, for that is where such trash usually ends up in Liberal households, I am led to believe!'

There was a huge outburst of laughter; and it has to be said, from all around the chamber. I was becoming more agitated as Members stood and leaned over and laughed and pointed to Winston. He just sat there with a mild look on his face. I could feel myself shaking, I sensed the build-up of rage within me and blood pounding in my ears; the red mist came over.

Then Hunter-Baines, who was holding some notepaper in his hands, scrunched it up into a ball and threw it over at Winston where it hit him and fell to the floor.

That was it.

Before I knew what I was doing I had jumped up and, leaning over the rail where I would only be yards above where Hunter-Baines was standing, I yelled:

'YOU! AYE, YOU! BISCUIT-ARSE! If you chuck wan mair piece a' paper at the colonel I'll come doon there and smack yer teeth that far doon yer throat, ye'll be eatin' yer supper through yer arsehole!'

I had heard this disgusting remark being made one night at Maison 1875 when Davie Thom and Tommy Reid were cheating each other at three-card brag. Sergeant Douglas told me that if he ever heard me make such a comment he would personally write to my mother. Though strangely, he did not seem to mind me playing cards for money. It's a strange and mysterious thing, the Presbyterian mind. But in that moment for some inexplicable reason I replayed the whole remark out loud. Verbatim as they say.

It caused a sensation. Members looked up, some shouting, 'Who is that young scoundrel?' 'One of Churchill's foul mouthed Jocks!' 'Call the Messengers!' Others more sympathetic (Hunter-Baines was despised on the Liberal benches) exclaimed, 'I'll hold his coat and be his second!' 'Bravo, young man, come and sit with us!' 'You sure can pick 'em, Winston!' and other witticisms.

Breathing in deeply and still shaking, I felt my anger begin to subside. I looked around at the few people in attendance alongside; some were laughing and others were trying not to look at me. But I was defiant and unrepentant; no one spoke to the colonel like that! No one!

'Whit the fuck are ye lookin' at?' I shouted at one fellow near me who was smirking, and I left the gallery and went down to the lobby.

I hung around for a few minutes then went outside to get some air. It dawned on me then that I might have embarrassed Winston severely at a time when he was trying hard and with some success to get back into the Cabinet. But I decided that I would go back into the lobby and wait because when I watched all those buggers baying at him, he looked so forlorn and I felt sorry for him.

As I sat waiting with my paper, I was surprised to see the prime minister himself, Mr Lloyd George, striding through the lobby with another gent. He seemed agitated and annoyed and I caught him just as he disappeared down towards what I would expect to be the chamber, fulminating about 'a nuisance' and 'bloody Bonar Law' and waving his arms in the air.

Winston told me afterwards that the prime minister had been called away from preparing for an another engagement and as he rose to speak in the House on the debate moments after I saw him pass by, he announced his annoyance at the fact he had been summoned to attend at the very last minute this debate and was going to be late for an important dinner engagement at the United States Embassy. The infringement of democratic liberties that the suppression of *The Nation* involved appeared less important than a slap-up meal courtesy of the Yanks, mused Winston.

The prime minister then made a short statement supporting the action and left the House, presumably to head off for his nosh at the embassy. The debate continued and Winston got in a good few points without the assistance of me shouting down hecklers, and democracy was seen to be served.

The House broke up and the lobby soon filled. I stood up, looking for Winston. It had been quite an afternoon; I had calmed down and the truth be told, was proud of myself for dealing with that rogue the way I had. The only cloud was the effect it may have had on Winston's future.

Then, to my utter astonishment, amidst the gathering crowd of Members who were congregating together, I saw Winston standing chatting to Hunter-Baines and they seemed to be positively laughing and joking together! I could not fathom this at all; only a short while ago this man had humiliated Winston and now they were behaving like best pals!

Just as I was trying to come to terms with this, someone appeared where I was standing, looked at me and said, 'Jamie, you sure are a lion, kid!' I tried to remember who this man was. He spoke with a Scots-Canadian accent, and I then recognised his big head, ugly face and shortness of height.

'I don't like people who talk like that to the colonel, Mr Aitken!' I said defiantly.

'Sure, I believe you, but Winston is more than a match for the Hunter-Baineses of this world. But gee! That was one funny thing you said! Where did you learn that? On the terraces at Tynecastle?' At that I laughed along with him. I should have asked how he knew about my team but then William Maxwell Aitken, or Lord Beaverbrook as he was better known, did have a special talent at finding out information useful to him.

'I'm gonna buy you and Winston dinner tonight!' declared the exuberant Canuck. 'You're coming to Claridge's with me! I believe you have a swell little girl too? Is it possible you could bring her with ya?'

I said that I would find out what shift she was working that day and see if she was free.

'I'd love to have you all over. Winston says you're a real fine fella and any pal of Winston's is a pal of mine!' He winked and then thankfully Winston came over to join us.

'Ah, James! Scotland is renowned as a land that has produced such beauteous poetry, and Edinburgh is London's only true rival as the capital of great literature. But today I have come to the conclusion that if one wishes to learn how the English language must be spoken, one must make one's way to Gorgie Road!'

Even I could not but smile at this. 'Sorry, Colonel, but I've no regrets, that man deserved it!'

'Indeed, and he has spoken to me to enquire whether it is safe for him to walk the streets, fearing that an assailant might waylay him and deal with him the way you so colourfully described!'

'You can tell him he's safe unless he ever does it again in front of me!'

'Winston, I was just telling Jamie here that you, he and his gal are coming to dinner with me at Claridge's tonight,' butted in Aitken. 'I mean that. I wanna hear more from this guy!'

I did wonder later how Aitken had heard my outburst for he'd given up his seat in the House months before to take up his new one in the Lords. I was certain he wasn't sitting in the gallery either. But I might have been wrong.

'Claridge's will be splendid, Max,' Winston replied. 'Now, if you will permit me, James and I must head home to prepare for this evening.' We went outside and hailed a taxi and stopped at the hospital and I went in and spoke to Gemma. After mentioning Winston's name to her charge sister, she was allowed to finish her shift early.

'Colonel,' I asked after getting back in the cab, 'how can it be that one minute that man Hunter-Baines was embarrassing you and the next you were joking with him in the lobby?'

He laughed out loud. 'Politics! Politics, James! Hunter-Baines is a nobody. But he is a nobody who, due to a certain number of assured votes in his constituency, has been given the opportunity every now and again through parliamentary privilege to be permitted to humiliate his betters and perceived enemies and thus try to weaken them before his peers. He is nothing. The moderate wing of his party despises such types and longs to be rid of them. But do not concern yourself with today. It will not be reported but it will be long remembered!' He then said in a quieter voice, 'Were there any ladies present at the time?'

In those days, women had to sit separately from men but from where I sat I had noted a few viewing from their own gallery. I think I nearly died with shame at that moment. 'Oh, God, yes, there were one or two.' I had my head in my hands. 'My mum must never hear of this!'

'Indeed not,' Winston agreed. 'But I for one shall never think of teeth and arseholes and suppertime quite the same way ever again.'

Chapter Eighteen

From April 1917, my old battalion took part in battles around Arras whilst being part of the 15th Division. I scanned the newspapers for days and noted that they suffered losses whilst being held at a place called Orange Hill, but went on to take the village of Monchy. They also took part in an attack on Guemappe where they seized and held a trench against furious German counter-attacks. It was in this action that my good friend Jock Paterson was killed. He was shot whilst fighting off one such assault.

I noted with great sadness my wee pal Tommy Reid's name also listed among the dead. This left me desolate for days afterwards when I thought of the good times I had shared with Jock and Tommy, and my feelings of guilt resurfaced once again; guilt that I was alive and well and out of it all.

Since my release from hospital I had made regular out-patient visits to see specialists, who advised certain exercises I should undertake in order to try and alleviate the sometimes constant pain in my leg. Younger doctors with new ideas were developing new courses of therapy continually as the war progressed, as medical science tried to keep pace with the challenges faced by horrific wounds and injuries to the men coming back from France.

They wanted me to be a sort of guinea pig and I was happy to do so. I was allowed time off one morning a week to go to the hospital and try out various stretching exercises. It was all experimental but medicine had come on in leaps and bounds. Some days the exercises made my leg worse but the doctors were much attuned to that and would let me judge when to stop. I had to answer questions on how it went and I enjoyed those mornings, mainly because I got out of that office and away from some of the ghastly people I had to work beside.

By that time Gemma had been moved into a post-trauma ward. Her workload lessened, thankfully, and she started to spend more time in the administration block, helping with paperwork. I strongly suspected the hand of Grandmama in all this. I would visit the old girl now and again (not just for her cakes) and we would chat about Gemma. I felt it incumbent on me to tell Granma how tough a time her granddaughter was having and that I worried about her. But the old dear was not daft, and resolute as ever, she heard me out and with another quiet word in the right ear, eased Gemma's circumstances.

As for the young lady in question, my girlfriend began to talk about a new Australian doctor whose arrival at the hospital had shaken everything up with his new ideas and colonial brashness. At first I liked the sound of this bloke, Peter Sullivan; he sounded like he did not give a toss for convention and that reminded me of someone else I knew.

But Gemma began to talk about him all the time.

I began to get to grips with my job a lot better, though I now barely spoke to Hammond and Paget. I was convinced that they were up to something. Alongside my natural suspicions, when both of them disappeared from the office on the same day, I started carrying out secret investigations of my own. On finding hotel reservation vouchers and rail tickets in their wastebins I would phone the hotel in question, asking for details of their stay, pretending I was Hammond claiming I had lost a watch or something.

Sometimes the hotel would just slam the phone down on me but I did find talkative receptionists who would be more co-operative. I would feign to be a policeman and ask if Mr Hammond had brought a young lady-friend with him.

All this passed the time. The sheer arrogance of the two of them thinking I was not important or relevant enough to notice any of this outraged me. I am not naturally conspiratorial and I confided in my friend Stan my concerns. He said I had to provide evidence and that would mean asking questions, screening their work and opening their mail, which would have been impossible. Finding the cheque regarding the East Dechmont fantasy munitions factory was a fluke. But I longed to find something that I could use to nail them definitively.

With this in mind I decided to track down the man who had left the office after the reputed argument with Hammond. My fellow workers were a pretty close-mouthed lot and when I asked Albert, one of the blokes I was friendly with, about the incident in an offhand way in order not to rouse suspicion, he gave me a faraway look and just said, 'Oh, that was Eric Drake,' and nothing more. Albert was less forthcoming than Stan and I never discussed Hammond with him again.

Stan, who by now was in the army, had been more revealing when I had first started there and had told me that the three worked together but Eric did not get on with Hammond and Paget, and one day it came to a head and they started arguing. It must have been quite a scene for that place; a show of emotion of any kind by that lot must have been as rare as seeing snowflakes in August. Yet no one appeared to know anything.

I knew I would get nothing out of anyone there and of course, I was not going to ask Mr Laird. Although I did like him, he was tainted in that he was *of* that place. I decided it best to trust no one.

I discovered that Eric Drake had been transferred to the Kingsway office by speaking to the doorman at reception, who I became friendly with. I then seized the chance to meet him when I was sent round to Kingsway one morning to deliver some documents. Handing over the papers at the front desk, I asked where Eric worked.

I was directed and made my way into the office. I stopped at a desk and asked which was Drake and I was pointed to a bald-headed man in his forties, bent over his desk at a typewriter.

'Are you Eric Drake?'

'Yes?'

'I'm Jamie Melville. I've got your old desk at Whitehall. Do you have a minute to talk about Norman Hammond?'

At the mention of that name his face dropped.

'That bastard. I can spare a few minutes.'

'I think it's better that we speak somewhere private.'

He agreed and we left the office together and made our way to the entrance of the building and stopped a few yards outside. He lit a cigarette after offering me one, which I declined.

'I've been there a few months now and I'm having problems,' I began. 'One thing I don't understand is why I was given your job, as you're senior to me. Do you mind if I ask you why you left?'

'Are you having trouble with those two?'

I hadn't mentioned Miss Paget, which intrigued me.

'Eric, are you able to tell me why you left?'

He didn't know me from Adam, but he would have known of me being his replacement in his old job. But for whatever reason he opened up and told me his story.

'I'm not a violent man, Jamie; I want you to know that right from the start. I began working with them about six months before I left. They were pretty close, the two of them, and always worked together but the workload was increasing, another body was needed and senior staff sent for me. From the start, both of them told me nothing about the job.

'I'm senior in grade to Paget but Hammond deferred a lot to

her and gave her jobs I should have got. The result was that I didn't have much to do and went looking for work elsewhere. I spoke to Laird about it but he was either useless or in with them. He's probably both. I ended up at a loose end most of the time and just answered the telephone or covered for them when they were out of the office.'

'How often was that?'

'Oh, at least once a month. He would be off one day and they were both away the next. Usually Fridays through to Mondays.'

'Where to?'

'Helping out up north, Manchester or Brum, so I'm told. Scotland once or twice.'

'Why those two: Paget and Hammond?'

'Paget knows the job inside out. Hammond is her stooge. I'm sure they're screwing each other though the very idea of the two of them at it is utterly repulsive.'

I agreed. The very thought was indeed quite distressing.

'Eric, what was the argument about, the one you had the day you walked out?'

He reached over and stubbed his cigarette out against the building wall. 'Jamie, something is going on in that office. I *know* it is. I found a cheque signed in Hammond's name.' I nodded. 'It was made out to an armaments factory in Derbyshire. Only, this factory doesn't exist. I collared Hammond when he came back and asked him about it; he said he signed a lot of cheques, this was just one more. I said, you don't look at what you're signing your name to? He said I was to mind my own business. I then said outright, why did you sign a cheque for a firm that doesn't exist? He walked away from me and went straight to Laird's office. Everyone had stopped what they were doing and were looking over at us. I followed him through the door.

'I went straight in and Laird asked what this was all about. I said I thought there was fraud being committed. Laird said sit down. Hammond walked out. I said where the hell are you going? Laird said, "Calm down."'

He stopped and glanced around.

'There are only us here,' I noted. 'Do you want to tell me what happened? What did Laird say?'

But his manner had changed. 'Does it matter now? I'm out of there and got a better-paid job. These people do what they like; I should never have mentioned any of this. I have to go.'

'But you have and you did. Tell me how it ended.' I put my hand on his arm. He looked at it.

'I've heard about you; you're the friend of Winston Churchill. He's a strange pal, giving you a job in that place. Are you sure he *is* your friend?'

'Never mind that,' I snapped. 'Alright, you've told me. Now I'll tell you what I can. I think they *are* at it. I found a cheque, just like you. And Winston Churchill *is* my friend. Don't you ever forget that. You've told me all I need to know. Don't worry; your name will be left out of it. For now, anyway.'

I left him and made my way back to the office, pondering on his reasons for not telling me the gist of the conversation he'd had with Mr Laird. But I could guess at it. Laird was in on it or did not want the fuss of raising a stramash over the issue.

He may have gone to his superior and discussed cutting a deal with Drake, and got rid of him by giving him a better-paid job on the condition he kept quiet. I had no way of knowing. I was given the job as replacement, being junior and therefore of no consequence.

They all disgusted me.

Chapter Nineteen

I understood much later why it was important for me to take that job. I came from a manual work background and had absolutely no conception of life working in an office. I used to walk along George Street in Edinburgh and look through office windows at people typing and talking into telephones and thought it a magical world. Paper, pens, typing and telephones were the tools of those who worked with their minds.

My dad would come home in his overalls covered in oil and sweat, carrying his tool box, and wash up in the sink and slump down in his chair, sometimes too exhausted to even eat his supper. He spent his day working in a factory that made heavy machinery for the paper industry. An accident would occur there that changed all our lives.

One day he caught his arm in a lathe. Another fitter had to strip the whole machine down and then as gently as possible remove the shredded limb out from it. He was sent to the Royal Infirmary as the injury was so severe, and underwent two operations to try and reset torn muscles. Neither was a success and from then onward to mask the almost constant pain he started drinking. It might have worked out better for him had the arm come off but I will never know. From my own experience I would always rather have the injured limb attached, regardless of the discomfort.

Dad was a very slight man with weak lungs and after the accident I don't believe his constitution was up to the heavy labour. But he had to get on with it. He drank, that was his escape, and his manner changed completely towards us from his normal good-natured self to that of a violent inebriate. He came home to this tiny house full of kids and a wife trying to keep it all together and whatever was eating away at his soul made him take out his unhappiness on us. I was naïve and thought that kind of existence never existed for office workers, for people who used their brains. They earned better money and lived in nicer houses and had nicer lives.

Now I could see that there was just as much avarice and nastiness in this new environment I had entered as any other. Whereas in my dad's world a shout, a row and then a cleared atmosphere normally prevailed after any dispute involving working men, you could not do that in an office. I thought of the 6th and the raucous way we all acted at times, but it was out in the open. There was never any fear or shame in revealing your feelings or your emotions.

The culture here in this very different, this *middle-class* world, was to me cold, sterile, far more hypocritical, more deceitful. A look, an unexpected note on your desk, was the way discord was dealt with. Nothing was ever direct. The public exposure of any kind of sentiment was the ultimate anathema to a caste of people I was starting to suspect were devoid of emotional adequacy.

I began to hate it all.

I longed for the mythical year to end, the year Winston said he needed to get back into cabinet, when he would employ me. But it was now July 1917 and nearly ten months since we'd had that talk and I had received a jolt back in November when Winston was left out when Lloyd George became prime minister.

Winston did have a few successes. The Gallipoli inquiry findings were made public by the new premier and went a long way to exonerate Winston of all blame and he was heavily immersed in the new phenomenon of tank design for the army. It's long forgotten, like so many things about Winston Churchill, that he practically invented the tank himself.

As for me, not only was I was convinced that there were serious wrongdoings at my work but even worse than that I now strongly suspected my girlfriend was seeing someone else behind my back.

We were both very young but in those days sweethearts invariably mated for life and, as for the fact that we were so young, for someone of my background it was not unusual to think of marriage even at sixteen years of age. As Gemma was my first real girlfriend and I was in love with her I fully expected that love to be reciprocated unconditionally. But I was immature in many ways though mature in others, and was uncertain in my own mind about the extent of the feelings (I imagined) Gemma had for this young Australian doctor.

With this to deal with and the situation at work, I faced two serious problems:

I strongly suspected Paget and Hammond of fraud. I believed they were issuing cheques to non-existent companies and pocketing the cash. I had worked it out. They had a contact in accounts who sent out the cheques and a pal in the mailroom to screen the inward post, and it was a four-way split. I found another letter returned in such a manner and noted that I always found them when they were both out of the office at the same time, which was bad luck for them. Or maybe they just accepted there was no risk: who knows the criminal mind? This was how they were receiving the cheques. As for the latest letter found, I stuck it in my pocket. It had been returned unopened (obviously their chum in the mailroom had been off that day) and I took the chance, opened it and was proven right.

They had cold-shouldered me from the start, having been forced to accept another worker in their section, and carried on with me in the same manner they had dealt with the previous occupant of my desk. Only, that man had been a far more experienced member of staff and more difficult to control. But they had got through that one unscathed and believed that with me they could relax as I would be deemed easier to handle.

The second problem was that all Gemma talked about when we were together was Peter Sullivan this and Peter Sullivan that. He was from Melbourne. He liked Australian rules football and supported Carlton, who played at the Carlton Oval in Melbourne. They were nicknamed the *Blues* but known as the *Butchers*. If I was to ask Gemma who Heart of Midlothian were, the name of their ground, their nickname, the colour of their jerseys and who Bobby Walker was, she would just look at me and say, 'What was that?' Suddenly she had become an expert on a so-called sport that had *no* rules and was played by colonial louts.

The truth of it all, of course, was that she was just a young girl of eighteen years of age. She was in love with me but this swaggering Aussie was flirting with her no end, and I am quite sure now that that was all it was. She was attracted to him but had no real designs and was just mixed up but she had absolutely no idea that it was driving me nuts.

I had deliberately sidestepped the issue every time she said that I should meet him. On my visits once a week for therapy, I was well away from where he worked so there was thankfully no chance I would bump into him in such a big hospital.

But in the frame of mind I was in with everything else going on in my life I was reaching the point where I wanted to confront this paragon of male virtue and have it out.

And have it out with everything else that was getting to me.

One day in the middle of July I decided to tell the specialists at the hospital I would no longer be attending out-patient appointments. The therapy they were trying on me was more often than not causing increased pain and discomfort. These decent people meant well and I was quite pally with some of them, but I was now disenchanted with everything in London, and the constant pain I would be in for the rest of the day after recent sessions was adding to my unhappiness. They took it well. We shook hands and a couple of them arranged a drink with me later.

I decided that same day to collar this Peter Sullivan character. I made my way to Gemma's ward and saw her leaning against the wall with a file clasped in both hands against her chest and this character in a white coat reaching over her with an arm stretched high up on the wall.

I walked over to them. 'Gemma?'

'Oh, Jamie, how are you, how's your leg? This is Dr Sullivan! You've finally met!'

'Oh hello, Pete. Busy, are you?' My back was up.

The man in question was over six feet tall with a nose that was almost touching his chin, which I have noted is a peculiarity of Australians. Here I was, about five feet four inches; but five feet four inches of jealous and angry Scotsman. I do not believe there is a match anywhere on earth.

'Hi, Jamie! How are you, mate! I was just telling *Gem* about the weather back home this time of the year.'

'Yes, Jamie. Did you know that it's actually very cold in Melbourne in July! Who'd have thought it? He says the climate there is so changeable that they describe it as being like having "four seasons in one day".'

'They must do a roaring trade in umbrellas,' I sneered.

Peter laughed out loud, a very happy, infectious kind of laugh.

Innocent that I was I believed that that was all they were on about (they probably were) but could not resist making a joke. Turning to my girlfriend I announced, 'Gemma, I've told my doctors I'm not coming back. I'm fed up with them and this hospital.' (I did not like him calling her 'Gem', which was grating on me.) 'I'll hang around till you knock off for lunch, if it's okay with your boss here.'

Peter turned to me. 'Ah, don't worry, mate. Gem can knock off early if she wants. See you around sometime, Jamie, and we'll go for a few middies, eh? Or should I say "pint"?'

I have to admit on meeting him, loath as I am to say it, I instantly took a liking to him. But my suspicions would not go away. I was convinced he was after my girl.

Then everything, the office, Gemma and Winston's situation, all resolved itself one Friday morning a few days later.

I kept the latest cheque that I discovered and hoped it would cause a reaction when Hammond returned from his latest dirty weekend and found that it had gone missing. This could result in a couple of scenarios. He may suspect that his partners were cheating on him or that someone in the office had taken it. Naturally the latter would have focused the suspicion onto me. But if he did, what in reality could he do about it? He may start sweating, thinking I had reported it to Mr Laird. Or maybe he thought I would come to him and ask to be dealt into their little syndicate. There would be no harm in letting the son of a bitch fret for a while before I decided on the next move. I was in the cat-bird seat, as the Yanks say.

In truth, I did not know what to do and now trusted no one in the office. Not Mr Laird, whom I had liked. Stan had recently gone off to the war and Albert was just too square and timid to be of any use. The obvious choice was the colonel but I was still undecided. I felt bad about having to own up to the fact that I had made sneaky phone calls to hotels at ministry expense, masquerading as a bobby. I should have known that nothing would have thrilled Winston more than me telling him about that but I was loathing doing so. Then events caught up with me and once again my temper was arbiter.

That Friday at the office I had to deliver some forms to the top floor of the building. As it was first thing in the morning my leg did not feel too bad and I headed up without the stick. Unthinkingly I ran up the stairs two at a time and missed, tripped and an explosion of pain that was almost electric in its intensity shot through my leg and I almost yelped out loud from the shock.

I began to feel nauseous and sat to catch my breath on the stair and take it slow and easy and pray that the pain eased off. Then I heard someone climbing the stairs behind me. It was Hammond. He stopped to look at me and said, 'Melville, get off your behind and get those forms up to where they should be!' Then he started up the stairs.

I snapped. I was so angry and filled with loathing for this man, this thief, that I gripped his ankle and tripped him. He went crashing down, his spectacles flying off, and I rolled over him, forgetting my pain, and had my right hand around his throat.

'Listen, bastard. My name is James, or Jamie or *Mr Melville* to you. I've seen men killed and maimed and I'm not taking any more of your shite! You're just a thief and a liar to me. Men are dying every day and you're stealing from them!' and then I eased off his throat with my right and smacked him full in the face with my fist. Twice.

I got to my feet. Hammond lay gasping, his nose starting to bleed profusely; I suspect I had broken it for him and felt a tinge of remorse at that, but it passed. There was one issue I had now resolved in my mind: I was not going back to that office ever again. Not Hammond, Mr Laird or Winston bloody Churchill could drag me back. I decided that I would end it all that day and limped back downstairs to my desk to grab my coat. No one looked up or took notice.

I went outside and looked for a cab to take me to Gemma's hospital. I stopped one, climbed inside and after advising the driver my destination, sat and looked out of the window. London could go to hell. The cab arrived at the gates of the hospital and I got out. I made my way to the ward where I knew Gemma was working and found her in the admin room with two other nurses.

'I need to speak to you. Now!' I declared, speaking far more assertively than was necessary. She had never seen me like this before and her face reddened almost immediately. Noting this but feeling no weakening in my anger towards her, I did an about turn and left the office and stood outside. Moments later she slipped out, closing the door behind her.

'Jamie…'

'I want to tell you that I'm leaving London. I'm not going back to that horrible office as I can't stand it there, it's full of crooks. I'm going back home to Edinburgh right away. You can marry Peter Sullivan for all I care. I know you don't love me any more because you love him. You can tell the colonel I'm sorry I let him down but I just want to go home now!' I burst into tears. She just looked at me with her mouth gaping and her eyes wide open.

I turned around and held my hands in front of my face so no one could see me crying. 'Jamie, Jamie!' I heard, but kept walking.

I made my way to King's Cross after popping into the bank to withdraw some cash and checked departures for Edinburgh and noted the train left at midday. I bought my ticket and a paper and sat in the waiting room, my mind racing in all directions at a hundred miles an hour. I kept reliving two scenes: my fist in Hammond's face and the look on Gemma's when I shouted at her. I thought of Winston and felt such shame that I had blown everything. Did I really want to go home? I was not sure. What I did want to do, what I *needed* to do, was just to see people that I knew, that I trusted.

My mum, the girls. It was a comfort to me to know they were just a train ride away. I would stay with them and get a job. George and I got on fine now. But did I really want to do that? I loved Gemma. She was so sweet, and what if I was wrong? I wanted to see her to say sorry and let her cuddle me. And I wanted Winston to sort it all out as he always did.

But it was too late. I had bought my ticket and did not know how to resolve it all. Yes, for once the great Jamie Melville was stuck for an answer. I realised I was just a wee boy still in lots of ways and had a lot to learn. But I would think on the long train journey north. I would go to Mum's and re-plan my life and write to Winston and Gemma explaining myself.

It was just about the time when I usually had my morning tea at the office. I bought a cup and a wee bun from the girl in the waiting room, drank it down and ate and then went for a wander to look at the bookstall. I always take comfort in books. I bought *Kidnapped* and thought back and remembered the night at the Farm when Winston told us about his escape in South Africa. I recalled that he mentioned that he had carried a book with him throughout his adventure. It was *Kidnapped*.

It was always one of my favourites. It had comforted me in the past at home. I loved the story and knew it so well. My dad would take us to South Queensferry during summer and we would walk past the Hawes Inn where David Balfour stayed and he would buy us an ice-cream. I missed my dad. When sober he was such an easy-going soul, when he was not tired of the pain and fed up and got drunk. What did he do to deserve such an unhappy life? Did he love us all? Did he feel remorse in the morning? Or could he just not remember his outrages? I retreated to fantasy to escape this privation and ran away to the library. The old spinster who worked there approached me one day and asked about my bruised face. I said I got into a fight with other boys. She became used to seeing me there; it was my refuge.

I thought about David Balfour and realised he was like me

and Winston was like Alan Breck. David was strong and sensible and had bad moments but always made it in the end. Alan would always appear when most unexpected and retrieve the situation. This time, unfortunately, Winston would not sort the problem. He was away in his life. What were my problems compared to his? I was arrogant in the extreme to think a man like that would bother about me.

I sat down and started reading and became engrossed. I read up to where David was washed ashore on Mull and then I stopped and got up to look for the WC.

I returned to my bench and the book. I always loved the 'Flight in the Heather' chapter, in particular the part where they were holed up in Cluny MacPherson's cave and David and Alan argued over the card game. It was so funny and I equated it with the relationship between me and Winston and felt better but at the same time I missed him. And I wanted Gemma, despite everything; I wanted her back.

The clock ticked slowly by until 12pm.

I noted the platform where the train was due to pull in and made my way over. I needed the stick as my leg had almost seized up. I thought I may have actually damaged it with that fall on the stairs. It added to my misery, the dull, constant, nagging pain of the damned thing, along with everything else.

I stood waiting and leant on the stick as the benches around the platform were taken, as it was busy. The main thought in my mind was ensuring I got a decent seat on the train.

Suddenly I heard a commotion and an absolutely titanic roar of:

'JAMES MELVILLE!'

I turned and through the crush of people saw Winston in his top hat and Gemma together, fighting their way through the crowd standing at the edge of the platform.

'Jamie, please come back! Don't go!' Gemma, out of breath, cried out as she ran up to me.

'James, do not board that train! There is nothing that cannot be sorted out between us!' Winston pleaded, blowing hard.

I was startled to see them both and at the same time completely torn in two. Gemma must have got to the House and grabbed Winston. And the fact that she and Winston went to all that trouble...

'I can't, Colonel. I've let you down! I won't go back to that office and that man Hammond! Please understand, they're criminals!' I turned to Gemma. 'I'm so sorry, Gemma, and I understand that Dr Sullivan's a better catch than me, a wee boy from Edinburgh, a nothing. I hope you're happy with him.' And I choked on that, and broke down in tears.

'Oh, Jamie, it's *you* I love! Not him! I'm so sorry if I led you to believe otherwise. Please come home to us. *Please.*'

'Yes, Jamie.' Winston said, now breathing normally. 'Come with us, we have wonderful news for you; this is a very special day and I must share the news with my two most *special* young friends!' Then he grabbed both my arms and looked directly into my eyes and said, 'Come *home.*' I just crumpled and walked off with them each at either side of me.

They led me away to a taxi. I got in the middle, Gemma holding both my hands in hers.

'Does your leg hurt, sweetheart?'

I nodded but I had more to worry about.

Winston turned to me. 'When we get home we will sort everything out. There is nothing on this earth that myself, Colonel Winston Churchill, and James Melville, lance corporal, cannot achieve between us! We are a perfect combination, I with my genius and you with your inherent Edinburgh good sense to see us through any difficulties! Now the news, and it is good news. I have been recalled to Cabinet! Yes! And can you guess what is to be my remit? Minister of Munitions! I shall officially be your commanding officer again! And remember, all commanding officers require a batman and in this case, as minister, I will require a special assistant.

'My old chum, Eddie Marsh, whom you have not yet met but I can guarantee you will like, shall become my private secretary once more but will require an assistant. That shall be you, my boy! You!'

He was positively bouncing and I had not seen him so happy since we returned from Belgium.

'Is that not wonderful, Jamie!' Gemma said, holding my hands tighter. 'You'll be an important young man!'

'He *is* an important young man!' exclaimed Winston. '*He* is James Melville, who has uncovered a dastardly plot to defraud the government and has personally struck down the villain involved!'

I was amazed to hear this but I should not have been surprised. 'How did you know that?'

'Ah well, that is for another time. So now, my boy, back to Eccleston Square?'

'Well, Jamie?' Gemma kissed me on the cheek and Winston grinned.

I did not really have to think about it. Winston had done it again. But this time with a little help from Gemma. And she was my true love. I knew that now. 'Yes, I want to go home.' Winston looked at me. 'Home to *Eccleston*.'

'Wonderful!' he declared.

'Only...' I began.

'Only what, my boy?'

'Can we return to King's Cross so I can get the money back from my train fare?'

Chapter Twenty

We dropped off at Eccleston Square and piled into the sitting room, where we were joined by Clemmie. Tea was sent for and Winston told me to stretch out my leg on a settee. He wanted to call for a doctor but I said a hot bath was the only remedy for soothing away the aches. Winston then relayed in detail the morning's events.

On being summoned to see the prime minister he was informed he was back in the Cabinet. He was so happy he headed home to break the news to Mrs Churchill. He said she was entitled to be the first to hear it, bearing in mind she had borne the brunt of his behaviour for over a year whilst he was champing at the bit to get back.

Clemmie and I looked at each other. I would have thought his wife should hear first but that was Winston.

Then Gemma spoke up. 'It was a good thing too! I made for the Commons first and was told you weren't there but I took the chance and headed for Eccleston and luckily Mr Churchill answered the door!'

'Yes!' Winston said excitedly, 'Your messenger, James, played her part with military precision as we planned our campaign to bring our errant Caledonian friend back to the fold! I deduced that you had made for King's Cross and immediately telephoned the stationmaster and enquired of the time the next train to Edinburgh departed. I determined that you could not have made the earlier one as it had left prior to your, shall we call it, your *confrontation*, with fraudsters and lovely young ladies who are very much in love with you! So together we rushed for a cab and made our way to the station!'

'And we found you! Oh, I'm so glad, Jamie!' Gemma gushed.

'I'm glad too! Colonel Churchill, I'm so sorry to spoil your great day!' I was indeed remorseful and feeling a bit daft. I had put these two nice people who cared for me to such trouble because of my stupidity.

'No, no! There is more!' Winston continued. 'And might I say that nothing on this earth could spoil my day! Indeed it added to it, as earlier I received startling information and the mission that Gemma and I undertook was like being in action! It required planning and forethought and daring! And the mission was a success!'

I settled back. He was going to tell us something...

'I must let you both into a great secret. It has been suspected for long now that fraud is being committed at the Ministry of Munitions office in Whitehall. Special operatives whom I am not at liberty to discuss have infiltrated various departments of the ministry disguised as workers in order to root out this corruption.'

My eyes widened. 'Really?'

'And today they apprehended their main suspects with a little help from a certain lance corporal who is known to us.'

I can be thick at times. 'A lance corporal! Who was that?' I mentally tried to run through all the people in the office.

'Is there another lance corporal among us now?' Winston asked, looking at the ceiling.

'You, Jamie, you silly!' laughed Gemma.

'Oh! Me? But I never told anyone, Colonel! I had no proof! I suspected but I wasn't sure. It's only when I thumped that swine, Hammond...' I caught myself. That had been assault; a police matter...

'Ah, yes! The famous James Melville method of settling difficult situations! But he would not have known that there was a witness to this scene.' I cringed even more and could feel the blood draining from my face.

'Our operative!' Winston jumped out of his seat. 'He

observed all this and claims that it was Hammond who struck the first blow! And the reason was that the same James Melville confronted him with his crimes and demanded justice! And that the young man James Melville merely defended himself from this vicious and dastardly attack on his person.'

'But Colonel, it didn't...'

'Jamie, shut up and go and have your bath now!' I was startled to hear this from Gemma; it was her ward voice which she used when dealing with lip from stroppy patients.

Winston, by now enjoying himself immensely, was grinning from ear to ear.

'I see what you mean, Colonel,' I said, and slink off the settee. I turned to Gemma, sulkily. 'I'll away and have my bath now.'

'Good, and don't forget you're not just having one to soothe your leg. I want your neck and face washed too, my lad!'

Women.

Winston later gave a full rundown on what was going on in the office. Paget and Hammond and a clerk in Accounts called Whitmore had concocted an elaborate system of defrauding the ministry along with, as I suspected, a contact in the mailroom. Miss Paget opened up an account in a false name and cheques which should have been going to (fictitious) contractors were making their way into those four's pockets. So far over £8,000 had been defrauded that officials could trace.

Hammond and Paget had spent the money on away days and staying in fancy hotels where they were having it off, apparently. Hammond was married too; with children, the filthy brute. Whitmore was a gambler so you can imagine where his share was going. Their mail was being opened along with everyone else's in the building, including mine, as part of the secret investigation. I was correct about east

Dechmont; the only connection with the military there was the army hospital at Bangour Hospital, a mile or so away.

I was pleased with myself, spotting that. Winston congratulated me and declared that local knowledge was a priceless asset of war. The four culprits would get hard labour and I thought, good luck; I hoped they would all rot.

As for Mr Laird; not proven. He left for another position so I suspect a deal was cut somewhere. But I will never know for certain as Winston said no more on the matter.

He then regaled us with his vision for the ministry now that he was in charge. A lot of fat needed trimming off and good men must replace the failures who had let the soldiers in the trenches down. I was all for this, of course. Industrial relations needed a hard look at also as there were too many strikes causing stoppages and costing men's lives.

'Who's Eddie Marsh, Colonel?' I asked as he finished his discourse.

'Eddie is my very good friend and he will be yours too! A brilliant man in many ways! He will assist me in my new duties as he has in the past at the Admiralty.'

'What'll I do now?'

'We shall find something for you, fear not. But now we shall leave you two young people alone to talk.' Clemmie rose with him and he turned to grin at Gemma. 'But first I will order some more cake because I see that James has gone without for about thirty minutes! I do believe that is a record for this district!' He chuckled and left the room.

I ran out after him and caught him as he was climbing the stairs.

'Colonel?'

'Yes?'

I looked down, shamefaced. 'Once again, I'm sorry. I have to grow up, I know, but I promise never to be so daft again.'

He leaned on the rail. 'That is love, James! It makes the most stoic, the most brilliant of us behave like fools! It is the curse and it is the very source of life! I too have behaved as such over one girl. Oh, she was such a vision as dreams are made of in her loveliness! It was long ago now but I regret it not, nor should you of your dear sweet lassie! Now go and speak with Gemma and make things good again between you as they should be. Goodnight, my boy.'

'Good night, Colonel.'

I returned to the sitting room and sat across from Gemma.

'We have to talk,' I said.

'Yes, we do.'

I ran my hand through my hair. 'I don't know where to start.'

'Start by telling me that you still love me.'

I searched for the words that summed up all my fears as I believed at that moment I had to tell her everything.

'I do love you, more than ever. When I was waiting at the station I wanted you to appear and just hold me. That would have been enough. But I feel so stupid at times. There's so much I'm ignorant of and I'm scared that people are laughing at me. They see me with this damned stick and think I'm a cripple. And they see me with Winston and laugh at him for being seen with a wee cripple. And yet I didn't really want to go home, though it is my home. But now I think my home is wherever you are. But when you spoke about Peter it was like a knife in me. He seemed everything that I was not.

'What can I offer you? Your parents are well off but would see me as a peasant. That's why I keep avoiding them. Because it would hurt you and I can't stand the thought of you being hurt. Can you understand why I felt like I did? It was not just jealousy, it was more. It was like the dream was over. I thought that I could better myself but was kidding myself on all the time. I'm amazed every day that someone like you wants to be with someone like me, the way you look, the way you speak; you're what I dreamed about and now you're really here I can't believe it and expect it to end.'

All my inner thoughts and worries flooded out. She never said a word, just listened. I felt empty and just leaned back on the settee.

She came over to me and knelt down. 'I never thought to meet someone like you. But I've been selfish because I forgot how dear you were to me when we first met, when I first went into the wards and dealt with all those casualties. How I *needed* you then. I've tried to forget how miserable and unhappy I was and though you meant so much to me you were part of it all and a reminder. I admit I've taken you for granted, Jamie. I've been so unfair to you.'

'Do you still love me?'

'I love you and always will. Do you believe me?'

'Yes.' And I did.

'I knew I truly loved you and could not bear you to be gone when I saw how unhappy you were when you came to the hospital and shouted at me. When I saw you at the station alone all I wanted was you in my arms.'

She held both my hands and looked into my eyes.

'Do you still love me?'

'Yes, of course.' I was so choked I could hardly get the words out.

She leaned over and kissed me.

And everything was right in the world.

Chapter Twenty-One

Winston brought his usual dynamism to the ministry. Everything was shaken up. The departmental system was replaced with a Munitions Council consisting of eleven members, each responsible for a specific area of armament production. There had been scandals in the past of near-catastrophic shortages and the drive was now on to get sufficient quantities of the shells, ammunition and all else to where they should go: to the men who needed them in the front line.

Winston brought in old hands from his Admiralty days and I was given an official post amongst the junior assistants reporting to his private secretary, Edward Marsh, who was just about the most cosmopolitan individual I had ever met up to that time. He was a couple of years older than Winston and very soft-spoken, to the extent that at first I could barely understand what he was saying.

He was the great grandson of Spencer Percival, the only prime minister of Great Britain to suffer assassination when a disgruntled merchant with a grudge against the government burst into the Commons and shot him dead. As part of a legacy bequeathed his family by the State each of his descendants inherited a sum of money. This came in useful for Eddie's artistic pursuits and he called it his 'murder money'.

A patron of the arts, he assisted struggling new artists with handouts, advice and recommendations. It was his idea (and his money) that set up the famous Georgian poetry group.

He was a friend of Rupert Brooke, Ivor Novello, Lawrence of Arabia, Paul Nash, W.B. Yeats and D.H. Lawrence, to name but a few. Through him I would meet many famous people in time or those who would go on to be well known. He knew

Lady Constance Lytton, who was a major figure in the suffragette movement and a friend of Gemma's grandmother. Lady Constance was the sister-in-law of Pamela Plowden, Winston's former love and one of the most beautiful women of the age. It was she who made the famous remark, 'The first time you see Winston Churchill, you see all his faults and the rest of your life you spend discovering his virtues.'

Eddie was exotic in many of his personal tastes and would today be described as 'gay' but at no time did he behave towards me in any manner other than that which was appropriate as my immediate boss should, and always with extreme kindness and understanding. He was very patient with me. I had been foisted on him by Winston and he just got on with it.

Eddie would in time introduce me to the artistic side of life and educate me a little in that world. Some of the things he introduced me to I will describe later and you can judge for yourself the merit in them.

My duties were at once secretarial, gophering, valeting and pouring oil on troubled waters when matters became stressful. I worked in a small office with a couple of older female secretaries who acted as my mentors and also in time became friends. In return I was able to observe first-hand how a large government ministry operated and witness genius in action, that being the Rt Hon. Winston Churchill, Member for Dundee.

Not at all bad for a wee lad from Gorgie who left school to all intents at the age of fourteen. I was paid quite a nice sum, more than I had earned in my previous job. I would try and forget that place; it was a useful learning ground. That's all it was.

I accompanied Winston and Eddie on tours of factories and regional offices and got to see a bit of the country and really enjoyed it. On these trips I was Winston's batman again, washing and ironing his kit. I did the same for Eddie; it was no bother and I felt I was earning my keep. But all the time I was learning how things worked. I may not have been at the meetings where Winston tore strips off factory managers who were not producing the goods, but I sure heard about it later from both of them discussing things together.

There was a change of lodgings for yours truly. When Winston became minister he moved into the offices, which were based in the old Hotel Metropole, near my old job in Whitehall Place. As for his family, they found a nice place in Sussex and Winston packed them off there as he was worried about raids from Zeppelins. They stayed there more often than not and Winston would head down there on weekends.

I was found a wee room in the Metropole. It wasn't bad and I moved my bookcase in. I would go up to see Eddie, who was a terrific boss, if he was working late at night and have a cup of tea and gas away as he regaled me with stories of his many colourful acquaintances.

I was able to bring Gemma round when she could get time off. There, we had for the first time in our relationship the opportunity to have some genuine privacy together without having to resort to subterfuge. Eddie caught us once together; not quite *in flagrante*, but almost at the point of. He was the sole of tact and understanding and was not in the least judgmental and I never felt any awkwardness around him regarding the subject. It may have helped that Eddie's father was a doctor and his mother a nurse, as he often displayed an interest in how Gemma was faring. Sometimes Winston would drop by my room but that man was a workaholic and these visits were rare on his part.

He worked very long hours and expected the same of all his staff. The female secretaries and Eddie would watch over me to ensure I never stayed up too late and would quietly tip me the wink to disappear, particularly on the one evening a week I was due to meet Gemma. These nights were very important to us as she worked long stretches and sometimes it would be two or three weeks before we saw each other on a weekend, particularly if there was anything going on at the hospital to keep her there. The night we met, Eddie knew that I brought her to my room but he was an absolute brick about it.

Shortly after moving into the hotel, we were working late one evening when Winston surprised me by laying down his papers and announcing, 'Lads; enough. Eddie, get the drinks in. James, order some snacks sent up.'

I would grow to love these rare occasions as they reminded me of mess nights at the 6th with all the great chat, jokes and sing-songs. Eddie was not quite up to singing but he was happy to reminisce and relate fascinating stories of his time with Winston and also regale us with funny stories of his own.

We would sit back in our chairs with Winston puffing away at his cigar and Eddie wearing that daft monocle and an elegant cigarette holder held between his fingers.

'I recall a party where I was waylaid by certain beautiful young ladies,' Eddie ruminated. This immediately got my attention. I knew of Eddie's true proclivities and was not judgmental but was keen to hear of anything that concerned beautiful women and Eddie knew a fair few in his time, if only as friends and acquaintances.

'It was at Lady Cunard's ball. I had heard that a group of young sirens had a new game; one would be chosen to approach an interesting but unsuspecting man. The trick was to find one either of a certain maturity in years, that is, middle age, or one viewed as an enigma, and immediately propose marriage. Unfortunately I was to be the next victim of this form of assault on one's dignity, although happily I was regarded as belonging to the mysterious variety.'

'And was she beautiful?' Winston asked as I listened avidly.

'Yes, quite a pearl. I have no doubt that Jamie would have been destroyed by her.' She sounded my type of girl. 'She sat herself down next to me and drew me into a conversation about Renoir. I gave my views, she hers, to the effect that the painting *Diana the Huntress* had made her nearly swoon on viewing it whilst I retorted that the light in *Dance at Le Moulin de la Galette* made me positively salivate. She then openly asked me to marry her.'

'What?' I said in disbelief. 'What was your answer?'

'"When?"'

For a moment there was silence then Winston burst out laughing as it dawned on me; as usual getting the joke only after everyone else.

'Then there is my chum, Tommy Hulme,' Eddie went on, 'That evening after the ball we were caught short in Soho Square. I moved off to a quiet spot whereas Hulme as was his character merely stood where he was and let nature take its course. A policeman seeing this approached him and said, "Sir, you cannot do what you are doing here," to which Tommy replied, "How dare you! Do you know you are addressing a member of the middle classes?" The policeman merely said carry on, and moved away.'

'Shocking!' declared Winston through his brandy glass.

I sat back sipping my drink, basking in the marvellous repartee. In many ways Eddie was the equal of Winston in his wit and cleverness and shared my old colonel's qualities of humanity, kindness and good nature. When I thought how unhappy I had been in Whitehall Place in comparison to now, I thanked God I had not got on the train at King's Cross that day.

Winston then went on to reminisce about the time he and Eddie first met and how they went off to Africa together in Winston's official capacity as Under-Secretary for the Colonies.

'I recall on our safari to Uganda in 1907,' Winston drawled, 'the incident in which the private secretary to the Under-Secretary for the Colonies was in deadly peril of his life. I had that very day requested of my secretary,' Eddie tipped me a wink, having removed his monocle, 'not to go armed into the bush for as it is well known there is no more dangerous beast than a pacifist carrying a shotgun.

'Suddenly there was a cry as it was announced that a rhinoceros was seen in the area. Coming upon this terrifying creature I aimed and fired, knowing not whether I had hit it, when it took it upon itself to charge in the direction of Mr Edward Marsh.'

Eddie took up the tale. 'This creature that I had never intended harm hurtled towards and I could only stare in a hypnotic fascination as I viewed the agent of my imminent death plummeting on towards me.'

Winston: 'It was then that the noble private secretary, though *unarmed*, made the decisive move that undoubtedly saved his life. I described him as defenceless but he had in fact in his possession the mightiest weapon ever brandished by an Englishman. He released the catch, grabbed it in both hands, the weapon billowed, opened up wide and as the animal, confused by what it saw, veered sideways to avoid it, I shot from my weapon, hitting it full-on as it crashed to a halt and writhed before us in its death throes.'

There was silence; I looked over at Eddie in admiration.

'But what did you use, Eddie, *what* weapon?'

He looked over at me, the cigarette holder clenched high in his teeth. 'An umbrella. A pink umbrella.'

I was curious about Eddie. I had taken an instant liking to him but he would never discuss much other than work or art. It wasn't my place to pry, but I caught a glimpse of the private man one day after he asked me to head round to his flat as he had left some papers there. He lived in Gray's Inn, was unmarried and had an old housekeeper named Mrs Elgy, who was from the north and wholly spoiled him.

I arrived at number 5 Raymond Buildings and rang the bell.

The door opened.

'Mrs Elgy? I'm from Mr Marsh's office. He sent me to pick up some papers he left.'

A dumpy little woman in her fifties with wispy white hair stood before me. 'Oh yes, luv, the silly man left 'em and I *knew* e'd send someone over,' she said with a glint in her eyes. 'Should 'a come 'imself, the lazy booger!'

She let me in and led me through the house. I was immediately struck by the fact that just about every inch of wall space was taken up with pictures. There were bookcases everywhere and each little table or sideboard was cluttered with exquisite objects. I then saw a young man coming out of a room and turn towards us.

'Mr Davis, 'ere's young lad from office! What did you say yer name was, doll?'

I told her.

'*You're* Jamie Melville?' The young man's eyes opened wide. I might have said I was King George V.

Having no idea who this bloke was, I said yes, I was.

'I have to see Eddie tonight,' he insisted. 'He must not allow *that* man to keep him late at work tonight!' He spoke with a Welsh accent and I thought; who on earth is this?

'He works late most nights as Mr Churchill requires his assistance. Do you want me to pass a message to him?' I asked.

'Tell him I won't be here when he gets back if he stays out late again, that's all.'

I said I would relay it and then Mrs Elgy, good woman, shuffled me through to the kitchen.

'There they are, luv,' she said, pointing to a manila folder lying on the kitchen table. 'You just wait 'fore you go. I've summit to give him fer 'is lunch and there's enough fer you an' all.'

She opened a cupboard door and brought out a plate of

small but exquisitely baked homemade pies, three in number, and placed them in a brown bag.

'An' these as well.' She handed me a white paper bag, which through a powerful show of resolve I was able not to open up and look into.

'Don't you 'ave 'em till you get back to t' office now! I'm watching you, Jamie Melville! I *know* who you are! You've been dyin' to get one my pies! Don't think I don't know!' She laughed out loud and shooed me out the door.

Later at lunch we sat around Winston's desk devouring Mrs Elgy's wonderful cooking. 'That bloke in your house says you better not be late tonight,' I informed Eddie, mouth full.

'Really, James, try not to eat like a pig!' Eddie replied in mock horror whilst delicately cutting a slice off his pie.

'The pig is one of the finest animals God ever breathed life into,' Winston declared, chewing away. 'I adore them; a dog will look up to you, a cat looks down on you but the noble pig will treat you as his equal.'

'As for my young friend, he may do as he pleases,' Eddie added.

'Who is he? I mean, what does he do?' I asked, munching away.

'Oh, a musician. An airman, too. He suffered an accident and is convalescing. Just another stray I picked up along the way.'

That afternoon the young chap came into the building, looking for Eddie. I let him into his office and five minutes later he left it with a smile on his face. I later discovered that the young 'Mr Davis' was in fact none other than the famous singer and impresario, Ivor Novello.

Chapter Twenty-Two

Just as I had moved into the hotel, the third great battle of Ypres began. It is now known by its more familiar title as the Battle of Passchendaele. The 6th/7th was still part of the 15th Division and took part in the assault on the Frezenberg Ridge. The initial attacks had gone well and it was believed the German second defence line had been breached. My old battalion's objective was to pass through and make for the third line of trench works.

It soon transpired as the fusiliers advanced that the second line of German lines was still intact in places and as the men advanced they were scythed down by machine gun fire. The lads were still able to advance as far as a position known as the Bremen Redoubt but most of the officers had copped it and the battalion was effectively down to about 150 men. All three companies had separated in the confusion and what was left were ordered to pull back to form up for an attack on another part of the German line later on in the day.

Frezenberg Ridge was eventually taken but later in the month the battalion took part in unsuccessful attacks on positions known as Beek House and the Potsdam Redoubt. Though theirs was a support role, they suffered huge casualties to shellfire and in noting the losses I was distressed to see two names: Davie Thom and Duncan.

I was in the office at my desk, reading the reports in the paper, when I stopped on viewing the casualty lists and kept uttering, *no, no, no* to myself as I saw the names of my friends under the heading of 'Killed'. I could not contain the well of tears within me as they flooded down and my head sunk onto the desk, the moisture dropping from my face onto the newsprint.

I thought of them both. Davie, such a larger-than-life character, who went through basic with me and always had a joke, sometimes *too* many jokes but always offered to help carry my kit on route marches. And Duncan, poor Duncan, he who was my journeyman at the battalion, who taught me how to cook and serve meals, the lore of the regiment, the songs and the history, the tricks of the trade. I remembered walking with him on our daily hikes to collect supplies and the rows he had with the drivers, which were at once profane and humorous. Now I could only envision their still, blasted bodies, the spark of their lives removed, as decomposing meat lying in the Flanders mud.

I saw Davie in life, on the stage at the concert telling his jokes, and me nicking bottles of beer from the battalion stores. 'Cheers, wee man!' he would say as he raised the bottle to his lips and drank as I sipped on my cherryade, pleased with my craftiness. Stealing a half-bottle from Captain Shaw's dugout in revenge for his ragging of Winston and handing it to Duncan, receiving a hearty pat on the back from him and a Madeira cake in a tin he had swiped from an officer's food parcel in return. These were the thoughts that sustained me in those terrible moments.

As I sat in my distress, Eddie walked in, saw me and asked how I was. I attempted to compose myself and showed him the paper.

'Jamie, I'm so sorry, do you want to leave for the day?' Eddie himself had suffered the loss of numerous friends in action, including Rupert Brooke, Billy Denis Browne and Patrick Shaw Stewart. Before the war ended he would lose more.

I decided it was best that I did leave. I would be unable to concentrate and thought that going for a long walk would help me as I could try and reconcile things in my own mind and would do that best if I was allowed fresh air to breathe and most necessary of all, space.

I grabbed my coat and stick, Eddie shook my hand and said take care, and I went downstairs to the main entrance where I came upon Winston who was heading up to the office.

'What is the matter, James? Are you unwell?' he enquired.

If anyone could understand how I was feeling at that moment, it was that man. I tearfully informed him about our former comrades and he put an arm around me as we went for a walk to St James' Park.

It was a warm day. We sat down on a bench in a favourite spot of mine, used regularly when I would go out on my lunch hour where I would take my sandwiches or a pie and a book and while away the time.

'I vaguely remember Thom for his awful jokes!' Winston recalled. 'Of course, Duncan one could not forget. Those two were particularly close to you, were they not?'

'Yes, I knew Davie from Ayr. He was useless at ironing!' I laughed but was masking tears, not altogether successfully. 'I offered to go over his kit and in return he carried parts of mine on marches because my pack was just too heavy to carry all the way.'

'True comradeship!' Winston pronounced. 'There is nothing like it elsewhere in any other form of endeavour. Complete strangers, all thrown together from various different walks of life but forming bonds of friendship that last lifetimes.'

I could see them both in my mind; hear their voices, clear as though they sat with me on that bench. I heard Duncan whistling *Ae Fond Kiss* and, as I looked across the park, I saw Davie lighting up a fag and grinning back at me.

I felt the familiar birth pangs of a blacking-out attack develop within me. Since that day in Winston's presence when we first met, I had experienced these feelings a number of times: sweating, heavy-eyed, racing pulse. It was a consequence of all the new kinds of stresses I had encountered over the last few years. My body just wanted to close down and forget; in sleep. I had learned to control it as much as I could but I usually needed to lie down for it to fade completely. Invariably I was left with a very bad headache.

'Are you alright, Jamie?'

'No... I don't know.' My voice was a whisper. The tears had stopped but I was bent low with my hand spread over my eyes as the bright, late-summer light was now painful to me. I breathed in and out deeper than normal in a manner I had adopted previously through past experience, to alleviate the symptoms and to try to avoid passing out. But my physical distress was far simpler to alleviate than my soul's torment.

Winston rested a hand on my shoulder. 'They will always be part of you. Always remember them for they walk with you forever through life. The dead are only truly gone if we fail to summon them back to us from time to time. You will find yourself talking to them, not only in your dreams but in your waking moments. You will see them in every place you wander and you will stop and smile at their call to mind. But carry on your own life you must, for the dead will not rest if they know you are unable to bear their loss, for you owe life to the *living*.'

That night I awoke from a strange dream. Seconds after I was awakened, as was my norm, I had forgotten the contents of it. But somehow, I felt this dream had been different from any other before. Deeply unsettled I got up, put on my nightgown and, wanting company, went to see if Eddie or Winston were still around. Winston was a demanding boss and Eddie frequently stayed late at the hotel offices.

I did not know much about his private life except that he was always name-dropping; not in a boastful way, but I would hear him talking about Lawrence's, Forster's and Shaw's and overhear conversations with Winston where he mentioned people like Oscar Wilde, Robert Ross and Henry James. It appeared to me that he knew everyone of consequence in the artistic world and I thought it odd that a man who spent so much time with these famous people was, to all intents and purposes, Winston's pen pusher.

I popped my head round Eddie's office door and saw him sitting at his desk with papers propped on his knee. He was bent over them with a pen. It was well past midnight.

'Hello, old man! Can't sleep?'

'I had a funny dream but when I woke, I forgot what it was about!'

'Those are the best kind of dreams then, eh? You're very pale, Jamie, are you well?'

I pulled a chair up and sat alongside him.

'Like me to send for some cocoa?'

'No, I'm fine. The colonel shouldn't be keeping you up this late!'

'It's not Winston; it's my poets that keep me from my slumbers. I'm just correcting; the joy of my life!'

'Who's the poet?'

'Oh, a *poor* little chap. His name's Isaac. Tiny, *tiny* little fellow in a bantam regiment. I'm worried about him. Reading this has quite upset me.'

He was a literary agent for many aspiring poets, painters and writers and spent so much time and money on them and, more, emotional energy, for many of them were in France. Sometimes I forgot the impact it had on him when one of them died.

'Can I see it?' He passed the page over. I looked at it; the handwriting was barely legible and there were spelling corrections, obviously Eddie's. It was entitled *Dead Man's Dump*. I read through it then came to the following stanza:

A man's brains splattered on
A stretcher-bearer's face;

His shook shoulders slipped their load,
But when they bent to look again
The drowning soul was sunk too deep
For human tenderness.

I gave it back to him.

'Does it upset you?' he asked gently.

'It reminds me. I believe my dream may have been about such a thing, I don't know.' I needed to change the subject suddenly. 'Are more of your friends out there?'

'Yes, Sassoon and Graves amongst others. Two young fellows I have high hopes for; hopes dashed for others, I fear. I hope there are none dashed this night.' He got up and made himself a drink.

I reached over the desk for the paper, leant back in my seat and looked at the poem again.

'Is this "Isaac" an officer?'

'No, just a common little Jewish private. He's on leave at the moment; I expect to see him in a day or two.' There were times when Eddie's innate snobbery grated on me. Often I would wonder what he said about *me* to others. I don't think he realised how these remarks bit into my soul. I was a common little private too, at one time.

Like Clementine's white gloves, whenever I thought I was just *me* and as good as anyone, the cold reality of the difficulties I had to overcome through my background reminded me that my brains and innate abilities were never really enough. Winston was a snob in his own way but his snobbery never felt personal to me. In his life he had overcome hurdles even as someone of his lofty birth, and I always believed that he valued me as an individual first and foremost, as Archie Sinclair, Gemma and her grandmother did, all born far higher up the social strata than I. Eddie's condescension reminded me of the daily struggle I faced in the new life I was living. I still flinched at such reminders; and was insecure enough for them to hit home.

Strangely, back at the 6th such comments I would have been oblivious to. It was a marker of how much I had changed; my ambitions had risen whilst my confidence and self-belief had diminished. I wondered if it was all worth it.

Returning to the subject of the author, I responded, 'Common or not he describes how *I* feel. He also sounds like he expects death at any moment.'

'Do you not all think that?'

'I didn't. But after I got hurt I knew that if I ever went back, I would.'

'That makes you feel guilty?'

'All the time.'

'And how do you live with it?'

How did I live with it? I was seventeen and had lived for a century. I had more dead friends than living. I walked like a cripple and fell over if I ran upstairs. I was physically shot and the inner recesses of my mind were changing. A certain sound or smell awakened dreadful sensations in me, sensations that I had yet to understand or acquire defence mechanisms to assuage. But all of it would be for nothing if I gave in, if I did not continue as I was.

'Winston told me my duty was to the living but to never forget the dead. I know that it'll always be with me. It's like my leg. I only now understand how to adapt. I used to think the best way to deal with it was to ignore it and try to behave as I did before. I can't. I never will. When the bad moments come I deal with them as I can. I live with it by just *existing*.'

The following day at the office I was filing for Eddie after sending out invites for the Munitions Council heads' weekly meeting.

It was a hard-working but happy office. I had built up a

strong relationship with my colleagues; my typing skills were improving greatly and I was taking shorthand lessons in the evenings. My best friend was a woman in her late fifties named Helen, who was the senior secretary. She was another one of these formidable, battleaxe types and everyone else called her Mrs Wilson. I didn't. She was Scots and taught me everything about the job and I was virtually her apprentice, comparing her with old Duncan in that respect.

She had a tongue like sulphuric acid and took no nonsense from Winston either and I'm sure he was frightened of her. I thought she was marvellous and I owe her a tremendous debt for toughening me up to office politics and teaching me to be more assertive rather than just losing my temper and threatening to do anyone who crossed me.

Eddie told me he had a meeting that day with one of his artistic friends. He expected him to turn up at the office but was not sure what time so he asked me to keep him company when he arrived as Eddie had a meeting with Winston that could not wait and did not know how long it would last.

Lunchtime came and I headed out to buy my grub. I usually went over to the park but had to hurry back in case this bloke turned up. Thinking that the fellow might have a long wait for Eddie's meeting to end and have no lunch with him, I bought an extra pie as I did not want to see anyone go hungry.

When I got to reception, Janet at the desk called me over.

'Jamie, there's a… *gentleman* who says he has an appointment with Mr Marsh.'

She was used to unusual individuals popping in, but from her tone I gathered this one was more than just a bit different from Eddie's normal eccentrics.

'Mr Rosenberg?' she called over to a man sitting at a bench who stood up and walked over to us. 'This gentleman will show you up to Mr Marsh's office.'

Before me stood one of the tiniest men I had ever seen. He

was not a dwarf but must have been barely above five feet and would have weighed only around seven or eight stone. In his mid-twenties, he wore a very tight-fitting suit jacket, whose trousers *may* have had a crease in them at one time, a shirt with the top button unfastened and a stained, paisley-patterned tie that was squint. On his head he wore a bowler hat.

'Hello! My name's Jamie. I'll take you up.' I offered him my hand.

He took it as I looked into his swarthy and curious, elfin-like face and as he mumbled his hellos he glanced at my stick.

'It's alright; I'm not too good with stairs!'

We made our way up and entered the office. The ladies were out to lunch and we were alone. I pointed to a chair.

'Eddie's at a meeting. It'll be over soon. Would you like a brew?'

He sat down and said yes. I picked up the telephone and ordered tea.

'Have you had lunch yet?'

'No. Do you think he'll be long?' He spoke in a very deep voice and had a thick cockney accent.

'I've got my lunch with me but I bought an extra pie, they're pretty good. Do you want one?'

I handed it over to him and he took a bite out of it and chewed.

'These are alright. Thanks, mate.'

We munched together for a short time and then he spoke.

'Are you Jamie Melville?' I nodded. 'I thought so when I saw your walking stick. I heard you were hit at Plugstreet.'

'Aye, it was bloody murder for a few months but I'm getting used to it now. Are you Isaac?'

'Yeah, do you know me?'

'Eddie read me a poem you wrote. It was pretty realistic, I thought.'

'Did you *like* it?'

No I didn't, but I understood it. He was a poet who, I expect, craved recognition so I sidestepped.

'I wouldn't show it to my girl! But it had relevance to me. I understood the meaning of it but to tell you the truth it brought back memories.'

'Bad?'

'Are there any other kind?'

He just bit into the pie and said nothing. The tea arrived and I opened my drawer and took out a packet of biscuits. I handed them to him and he took out a couple.

'What mob are you in?'

'The King's Own Royal Lancasters, but the bleedin' idiots have stuck me with an engineer battalion. All day long I slog my guts out, repairing this and that. I've asked for a transfer but they won't listen. Typical.'

It was typical; however, putting a slight character like this in a pioneer battalion told me one thing about him: he was probably a screw-up as a soldier.

'Bloody army. Useless,' I commiserated. 'My Gemma's glad I'm out of it.'

'I heard your girl is a VAD and really beautiful. Eddie told me.'

'I met her in the Queen Alexandra. Have you got a girl?'

'Yeah, but she lives in South Africa.' I found out later that he had an actress girlfriend whilst living in that country but that it had ended before he left.

We continued to chat away. He loosened up, as he was a bit stiff to begin with, but I found that, though I was unsure whether he was someone I'd like to become friends with, I did feel sympathy for him, though he seemed pretty odd. But as he was a painter as well as a poet I just put it down to the artistic temperament.

Just then the phone went. It was Eddie, who said he would be there shortly.

'Eddie's just coming. When are you heading back to France?'

'Couple of days.'

I opened my drawer. I had a stash of goodies including chocolate.

'Here mate, take these. Share them with the lads.' I stuck them in the bag the pies came in.

'Thanks, Jamie.' He stood awkwardly and looked at me as if unsure what to do next. 'Have you got a piece of paper?'

I handed him a sheet from my notepad, and a pencil. Just then Eddie came through the door. Rosenberg crouched over the desk and started writing.

'Ah, Isaac! I hope Jamie has shown good Scots hospitality!' But the poet did not lift his head and continued to scribble away.

Eddie turned to me. 'Have you completed the invites, Jamie?'

'Aye. How did the meeting with Winston go?'

'Oh, just fine. He wants me to buzz over to France with him; you too.' I must have pulled a face. 'It's alright! I told him you had not seen Gemma in an age and were entitled to time off.'

'Phew! Thanks, Ed!' I was glad to hear this. Gemma was off that weekend and we planned a trip to Brighton and had booked a hotel room together. Once again I thanked God for Edward Marsh.

'Jamie.' Isaac had finished his writing. He folded the paper and handed it to me. 'Thanks for lunch. Here's something to give Gemma. Say you wrote it for her. You're a lucky boy.' I took it from him.

'We'll head for Gray's Inn. Is that alright with you, Isaac?' Eddie asked.

The little man nodded. He then shook my hand as they both left the office.

I have that piece of paper now, here at my desk sixty years later and it is one of my most treasured possessions. I know the words written on it by heart:

> *If you are fire and I am fire,*
> *Who blows the flame apart*
> *So that desire eludes desire*
> *Around one central heart?*
> *A single root and separate bough,*
> *And what blind hands between*
> *That make our longing's mutual glow*
> *As if it had not been?*

I never saw Isaac Rosenberg again. In April 1918, though he hated being in the army and had few friends there, he volunteered to stay in the rearguard during the German spring offensive and was killed when a force of Germans attacked his trench. His body lay in no-man's-land for weeks, before it was dumped in a mass grave.

Chapter Twenty-Three

Winston was slowly becoming frustrated at the ministry. It was a vital part of the war effort and there was a dramatic improvement in output, but he felt he was missing out by not having a more war-like role similar to that of the Admiralty.

To compensate he would occasionally visit the front line in France. Eddie accompanied him but told me he intensely disliked these trips as Winston insisted on getting as near the gunfire as possible and each time vowed on returning, never again. I would offer to go in his place but Eddie as my immediate boss forbade the idea.

'Jamie, you made it back alive, don't dice with fate a second time. You just stay safe, that's my advice.' He was looking out for me and he was right, of course. I got back in one piece; why tempt fate?

Winston was not the only one feeling dissatisfaction with his lot. I was beginning to feel a sense of discontent with my life at the hotel. Though I was learning a lot and Eddie gave me some interesting things to do from time to time, I felt I was not really getting anywhere. I had a few quid saved up but would soon be turning eighteen and wondering where I was heading in life.

Gemma and I would discuss our plans after the war ended. We wanted a little home and her to work less strenuously so we could see more of each other, but were missing out on so much we could do as a couple. We were young and both of us were prey to fears not unusual in young lovers who are apart far more than together.

I would experience one of these dangers unexpectedly one lunchtime as Eddie and I went over an itinerary for a visit of

Winston's to some factories. He had drawn it up and I was hammering away on the typewriter when he sighed and said, 'I've had enough of this. Let's go for lunch and meet a chum of mine.'

We went to a little restaurant in the Strand. By that stage of the war, food shortages were hitting the home front hard with the U-boat campaign being waged that was sinking so many ships. The fare at restaurants was not what it was pre-war but we managed to dine reasonably well. Eddie never talked shop when we were out of the office, which suited me fine, and he always showed an interest in me, Gemma and my family.

We would chat about his artistic pursuits. I was aware of the various personalities he dealt with and their demands on his time, which I thought were often unbelievably selfish. I quietly marvelled at this man's dedication in being able to serve such a demanding boss as Winston in his day job whilst dealing with what I considered a bunch of prima donnas every other waking hour of his life.

'I must see the manager for a moment, if you'll excuse me.' Eddie rose from the table and shortly afterwards returned carrying a small basket with what looked like a dish towel spread over it.

'Grab a hold of that, Jamie, my boy.' He passed it over to me and we left the restaurant after paying the bill.

I thought we might be headed for the National Gallery. He had taken me there a few times and shown me around the various halls as we viewed the paintings and would describe to me in wonderful detail aspects of each particular picture and anecdotes of the painters' lives, which I found interesting, due to my love of history. But we carried on up Charing Cross Road and turned into Denmark Street and he led us to a main door which was open and we walked up a dingy set of stairs.

Curious, I asked, 'Are you sure this is the right place, Eddie?'

'Of course!

We reached the top landing and he knocked on the door, which was opened by a bearded individual of about forty. To my astonishment, they leaned over each other and gave each other a small kiss on the lips! Then Eddie put his arm around the man and they both walked through into the flat.

I stood outside with the basket, unsure what to do next.

I heard Eddie's voice. 'Come on in, Jamie!'

I entered an artist's studio for the first time in my life. The living room was large and light and an easel was propped up in the middle. There was furniture with cups, plates, books and paints, flowerpots and other paraphernalia arranged haphazardly and the place looked like it had not been cleaned this century. Smells of turps, paint, unwashed clothes and God knows what else mingled in the fetid air. A cat was lying on the windowsill staring out at pigeons flapping away on the ledge.

Eddie and his friend both stood chatting and the artist went back to his paints and then I noticed there was someone else with us and nearly dropped the basket in shock.

A completely naked young female of between twenty and twenty-five years old was lying sprawled on a couch. I have to say she was just about the most beautiful woman I had ever seen. She had very long blond hair and equally long limbs and she then got up quite naturally and walked over to Eddie, put her arms around his neck and planted a huge smacker on his lips.

'How are you, my darling Imogene!' greeted Eddie. 'This is my assistant, the famous Jamie Melville! Jamie, Imogene.'

'Oh, he's just an absolute sweetie!' she said, and walked over and kissed me on the cheek.

'*You*'re Jamie, then! The little war hero! I hear you have a beautiful nurse for a lady-friend!' She then stepped back, mother-naked, and looked *me* over! 'Lucky her!' she pronounced.

'Jamie, give Imogene *her* basket,' Eddie commanded.

Speechless, I did as ordered. She took off the towel and squealed as we both looked at what it contained. Bread rolls, cheeses, hams and fruit.

'Eddie Marsh, you are the most beautiful man!'

'Imogene, get some clothes on and go through to the kitchen with Jamie and have your snack and let me and Charles have a chat, will you?'

I went through as ordered, the girl showing me where, then slipping away. I sat down on a stool at a small deal table, looked around and gathered my thoughts. Trying to get the image of that incredible body out of my mind was a major struggle.

Imogene came through moments later, opened a cupboard and brought out a bottle of wine, which was uncorked.

'Would you like a glass?'

'Yes,' I answered.

She poured one for us both.

She had put on what looked like a man's shirt and nothing else. Her long legs were crossed as she sat on her stool as I tried not to look at them.

'I thought you were one of Eddie's chickens! But when he told me your name I realised I was wrong. Silly me! You're definitely not one of *those*! I can tell that!'

Wondering what on earth she meant by 'chicken' but deciding it best not to show my ignorance, I mouthed the only thing I could think of. 'Are you an artist's model, then?'

She laughed over her roll. 'Very observant, Jamie! I only do this for Charles and one or two others that Eddie introduces me to. But nothing else, you understand?'

I tried my best not to look like the moon-faced boy that I was as she smiled at me. She was utterly ravishing and had that striking, flawless beauty of face that draws men's stares like a magnet, and I was no different from anyone else.

'It must have been terrible for you, in France?'

'It was Belgium,' I corrected. 'But I'm glad I'm back now.'

'I lost a dear boy over there and I don't want to think about it. I'm so glad you're alright.' She did not mention my leg, which endeared me to her more.

'Thanks. I'm sorry to hear about your friend. How long have you known Eddie?'

'Oh, only all my life! He knows my daddy very well. He must be a very sweet boss to you.'

'Aye! Eddie and Winston are great! They've taught me so much.'

'Mr Churchill,' she chewed on a piece of ham, 'I have not met! His wife's a great beauty, and he's such a plain looking pug! Oh well, love is blind they say, but the neighbours are not!'

Besotted as I was, I was prepared to overlook this unflattering description of my old colonel, which was unusual for me, as you will have noted. I found myself looking more directly at her as she ate away from the basket and felt myself drifting off in a daydream.

I believe that at that moment had she asked me to go off and jump into the Thames I would have done it singing and dancing all the way.

'Jamie!'

Eddie's voice coming though the doorway at that moment probably saved my relationship with Gemma and I went back through to the studio.

'Well, let me know, Charles, and I will see what I can do for you!' said Eddie jovially to the artist as we prepared to leave.

Imogene came through and I lingered over my last glimpses of her with the shirtsleeves hanging over her hands and her long legs.

'Bye, Eddie!' she said.

She then wandered over to me. 'It's alright, Jamie, I won't let your little nurse know our secret!' She brushed her lips against my cheek and I could smell the fragrance she had on and nearly fell to my knees as they seemed about to buckle beneath me.

As we walked back to the office I could not speak, my mind a whirl of emotions. Gemma. Imogene. I saw them both. I felt altogether both bad and good.

'Ah! Imogene becomes more outrageous!' Eddie lamented. 'She nearly had you there, Jamie! You can blame me for that; let's keep this our secret, eh?'

'Who is she?' I asked, my voice husky.

'Who is she? Oh, just another little minx. The Duke of ------'s youngest, actually. Due to marry soon, I believe.'

I was unable to concentrate much on work when we returned to the office but was able to complete Winston's itinerary. Eddie looked it over; I had been caught out once already that day.

Chapter Twenty-Four

In March 1918 the Germans launched their great spring offensive. Winston journeyed to Edinburgh for a committee meeting with Scottish area representatives to coordinate an increase in production, particularly shells, to ensure that hard-pressed front-line areas received as many supplies as possible in order to grind down the advance. Eddie would not accompany him on this trip as he was required in London but I could tag along to ensure the boss didn't get lost. He told me to head home for the two days and relax.

I was doing a lot of deep thinking about my family at this time. The situation with my brothers was gnawing at me. I had lost friends in the war but before that I lost Thomas and Arthur. But unlike Davie, Jock and the rest, my brothers were still living and I was young and brave enough to believe that things could be changed. If you were around Winston it was natural to hear the same belief voiced regularly. He was the most optimistic and positive individual I have ever known. I was no slouch but the dynamism in Winston was rubbing off on me, increasing awareness of my own abilities and the conviction that I had to use every advantage I had acquired since meeting him.

On the train to Edinburgh, Winston had his head buried as usual in papers but on these journeys we usually found time for chat. Lately, opportunities to talk like we used to were becoming rare due to the frenetic pace at which he worked and the increasing number of visits to France. I had to grasp opportunities when available and now was the time whilst we were alone together.

I have a habit of adopting an expression when deep in thought that can be wrongly interpreted as looking sorrowful or despondent. He was starting to recognise this in me.

'James,' he asked, peering through his reading glasses, 'what are you thinking? You are heading homewards to see your family and to be near your beloved Tynecastle. What can be playing so heavily on your mind?'

He was always busy, manically so, in his endeavours but when he was able to stop and focus outwardly, as in all things he immediately brought to bear his full attention. There were no half-measures with Winston.

I spoke in a measured tone. 'Colonel, how would you feel if one day two men knocked on your door, barged their way into your home and took young Randolph and Diana away? You're never allowed to know what's happened to them or where they've gone and you never receive as much as a letter telling you of their whereabouts.'

'Your brothers. My answer would be that I would feel as your mother feels: utter devastation.'

'I don't know the rights or wrongs regarding what happened and why. I suppose if you were told that a pair of children were removed from a drunken, violent home you would say, "Quite right, too."'

'I can only assume that the decision by the authorities was taken after careful consideration of the matter.'

'It may well have been. But the manner in which it was done and the treatment my mother received when she went round to find out where they had gone was inexcusable. There was nothing done to help my parents. There never is.

'If we'd lived in a bigger house and my dad had earned a bit more and hadn't had the accident he might never have become a drunkard. There are so many 'ifs.' There were worse cases living beside us, I can tell you. We think my mum was dobbed in, which is laughable really, when you think how hypocritical people can be.'

He put down papers he was reading and sat back. 'James, I

marvel at how you have grown over the last two years. I saw something in you the moment I cast a glowering eye over you on parade that day. You have become an extremely well-balanced and mature young man and are able to dissect an issue from both sides, which is an admirable quality.

'Indeed,' he continued, 'the authorities *could* have made some enquiries about assisting your parents directly before taking action but alas they may not have. Until we are in full possession of the facts we cannot come to a firm conclusion. However, it is not too late for your mother to do that herself now.'

'Yes I know, but I believe she's decided to *let go of them* in her own mind as being the best way to come to terms with the pain. I understand her reasoning even if I don't agree with it. She was a beaten down soul, Colonel; my dad died soon afterwards, I left home and then her accident. George coming into her life has made a difference and has been her sole stroke of fortune recently.'

I now came to my decision. 'Colonel, *I'm* not going to let it go. I want to know. I *have* to know. I'm going to speak to her about it, but in order to try and trace their whereabouts I may require your assistance.'

'You shall have it; without equivocation.'

The train pulled into Waverley. It was the same smoky, dark and unwelcoming arrival point as it is now. A porter assisted us with our cases up the Waverley Steps and we turned right into the North British. Normally I would have delighted in the irony of a boy from a room and kitchen in Gorgie staying in one of the Capital's premier hotels but my mind was focused solely on one topic.

I unpacked our bags. I had a wee room on the same floor but it was still luxurious, facing over the glass roof of the railway station onto the High Street. We then went to dinner.

'Your mother received the telegram?' Winston asked as he munched away.

'Yes, I'll go round tomorrow. Do you want to tour the sights this evening?'

'A stroll after dinner would be fine. Let us walk down the Canongate and view Holyrood Palace and then I would like to take a walk back up the Royal Mile, past St Giles and on to the Esplanade and view the fine scene from there.'

After dinner we started our walk and for once he strolled. It was all up and down inclines and cobbled stones but I was unable to decide if his forbearance was on account of my leg or his desire to enjoy the sights at a leisurely pace.

We stopped for a drink after leaving the Castle Esplanade at the Eagle pub later known as the Ensign Ewart. He regaled me with the story of the Kilmarnock soldier who snatched the eagle from the French at Waterloo. I knew the tale of course, but let him go on.

When we left I pointed over to Victoria Street, just yards away.

'That's where my dad's lodge is, Lodge Roman Eagle No. CVX on the Roll of the Grand Lodge of Scotland.' I always remembered those words, as Dad's Masonic certificate was framed on a wall at our home.

Winston looked over and then turned to me and recited:

We meet upon the Level, and we part upon the Square,
What words sublimely beautiful those words Masonic are.
Come, let us contemplate them, they are worthy of a thought;
On the very walls of Masonry the sentiment is wrought

I found out later that he was himself a Brother in the Craft.

We made our way back to the hotel, via Castle Terrace and then into Princes Street. We cut into Rose Street and had one last drink in the Auld Hundred and he asked me my plans.

'I'll take Mum out for lunch tomorrow and then advise her of my intentions,' I replied.

'Tread gently, James. It is a bitter subject, one that cuts all women the closest. I rely on your discretion, good sense and understanding. So must she.'

The following morning, after seeing Winston off in a cab to his meeting, I took a car to Murrayfield from Princes Street. I made my way to Mum's and after some tea and chat she asked me out for lunch and we headed out together up the town. Winston had told me to make myself scarce but be back in time to meet him for the train returning south.

Mum wanted to buy me something and asked what I would like. Normally I would have been horrified at the thought of her wasting money on me but I was sensible enough to appreciate that it would mean a lot to her to indulge me.

I had a cheap watch which was always stopping and as time-keeping was important to me when keeping an eye on Eddie and Winston's coming and goings, we went into Princes Street together to look for one. We ended up in Jenner's and went up to the tearoom for a cuppa and a cake after we had chosen a suitable but at my insistence inexpensive wristwatch.

'Do you miss home?' Mum asked over her cup.

'I miss you and the girls and Hearts, but no, I don't miss Edinburgh any more. I don't know why that is.'

'When are we going to meet Gemma?'

I didn't know the answer to that. When I first started seeing her, all I wanted was for my mum to meet her. It never happened through circumstances but now, I had known her so long Mum's approval no longer mattered as much.

'We'll try and come up for Christmas.' I had thought that the easy answer. I was worried about my mum. I felt guilty, too. Life had been very good to me but I felt sorry for her.

She had experienced the agony of having two of her children

taken from her because of her drinking which then became progressively worse. Only when I became a parent myself could I truly understand the pain of that and of being powerless to prevent it happening. But if not for the fact that the school we went to gave us kids a spoonful of malt every day we may have ended up malnourished, because many a night we came home to no dinner. She had failed the rest of her children as she had those who were removed. But young as I was I understood the emptiness inside her that loss had left.

I thought of all this as Mum and I chatted. I accepted that financially she and the girls were secure. I had to accept, though she would never admit it, that she did not love George. But there was something I could do that would alleviate a major part of her pain. I had been given an opportunity and could not live with myself any longer if I did not grasp it.

Our conversation had dried up momentarily. 'Mum, do you ever wonder about Arthur and Tom?' I then asked outright.

She looked at me. 'Only every day.'

'Do you want me to find them?'

It was too much for her and she took out a hanky and started to cry.

'Oh, I'm so sorry, Mum!' Raking up painful memories added to my guilt but I had to be ruthless. They were my brothers and I wanted to know. Most of all I wanted her to know.

'No, no. Please find them and tell me how they are.' She put away the hanky. 'You haven't told Mr Churchill or Gemma, have you?' I knew for her this was a great shame to be hidden away and never spoken of.

I took her hand. 'Mum, you have to trust me because I may need Winston's assistance to find them. If I ever needed help I would go to him whatever the problem and I know he would never tell a soul. Leave this with me!' She perked up greatly and we left the tearoom for more shopping in Princes Street.

I stayed for dinner at Murrayfield. Afterwards, having said

my goodbyes, Mum walked me to the stop. I told her not to worry and expect good news soon. I knew a man who could fix things.

I collared him in his room that evening.

'My boy! Come in! I must say I look forward to you telling me of how your visit went!'

He was genuine in his interest in people, loved to talk. I knew him of old and could tell he was in the mood for relaxation and chat that was anything but shop.

'Now, settle down and tell me everything. But first allow me to pour myself a very large brandy and light this cigar and I shall order some cherryade from the bar.'

I told him about the conversation with Mum. He looked at me intently at all times, interjecting here or there. He then asked for the boys' full names and dates of birth and the date they were removed from our home. I had brought all these details with me, taken down in meticulous detail at Mum's that afternoon.

When it was all over he leaned back and sucked on his cigar.

'I will make immediate enquiries. These boys' whereabouts shall be located. You, your mother and sisters will learn of the boys again, that I promise. I will make no judgment; I will only do what is right.'

'Colonel, that's all I want for my mum's sake.'

For my own, too.

Chapter Twenty-Five

I met Gemma after returning from Scotland and we sat together in St James's Park. I liked sitting there with all the great buildings and landmarks only a short stroll away. I have to say I had begun to finally like London. So many good things had happened to me there, the best of all beside me on the bench we shared. I was content to leave Edinburgh, where only sad memories remained.

After the Peter Sullivan saga, Gemma and I became closer and began to reveal more intimate and deeply hidden things about ourselves to each other as young lovers do. Back then people were less open than they are now, even to their nearest and dearest, but I had seen how brooding lives away left those around damaged and mystified as to why, and determined that I would not go down that path.

She told me that her mother and father had affairs. Her father was a successful solicitor in the City and her mother was rarely at home, pursuing her own interests. It was a way of life to the children. Gemma had been forgotten and the only time she felt noticed was when she told her mother she wanted to become a nurse.

I told her how much it pained me that I could not see the wee girls who were my sisters and how I missed watching them grow up. I would understand years later that this was more of a paternal feeling than brotherly. It exemplified the unnatural way I was brought up: the child who was the oldest bringing up the wee ones, parents elsewhere. The youngest, Annie, would have forgotten her real father and seen George as the replacement. Thankfully the oldest girl, Margaret, no longer had my old job.

My own schooling effectively ended at fourteen years of age

when my dad died and I had to go out and work on the carts. I would give over every penny I earned to Mum and she handed me back a bob or two to buy a sweetie or a second-hand book. But all the time I had a brain that was of use. I remembered Winston's words about wasted talent. Those kept passing through my mind like a refrain. If he had not taken me in I would be back in Edinburgh doing God knows what. Labouring, in all likelihood, and with my leg I would not have lasted long; for what employer in those days would have given a job in an office to a wee laddie with a stick from Wardlaw Place?

Many men who were wounded or incapacitated in some way coming back to their old jobs after the war died young because they were no longer fit and there was no other choice open to them. From my own battalion, George Allan, who lost half a lung, went back to the railways and died only a few years later; and he was barely thirty years of age. Sergeant Douglas was gassed and had a leg nearly shot away at Arras, went to work in a foundry but ended up being invalided out and lived on handouts until old comrades found a place for him in a veterans' home.

I have already spoken of Paddy Crossan. Of the other Hearts players who served, Jimmy Duckworth died after being weakened from pneumonia and Bob Mercer dropped down dead after playing in a friendly match. All these were young men in the prime of life. I did not want to go down that route. I saw all those men from Heart of Midlothian Football Club go off to the war and those that returned were shadows. I felt stuck in time in 1914 with my team. It took years for me to renew my interest in Hearts as I could not feel the same way as previously about them for long periods.

I did not want to return to a life that someone of my class was expected to. But I was starting to feel uncomfortable about my new one in ways I was yet unable fully to comprehend. It all started in the Munitions office in Whitehall. I had such optimism about working there in the beginning but slowly my confidence in myself, which had always been very high, took a severe dent at the treatment I received. It may well have simply been just my bad luck to meet a group of unpleasant workmates and of course this happens everywhere. But they had no right to look down on me. I had been a serving soldier who received an honourable wound but human nature being what it is they may have decided that I was malingering and being favoured by high-ups.

But weighing up both sides of the coin, as is my nature, when I started to work with Winston and Eddie my life changed for the better. Eddie treated me as well as Winston did and was also incredibly patient with me. I would find out years later that Eddie was very pleased to have me as I acted as a sort of outlet for them both during stressful periods, with my good nature and humour. I could tell them off when it was needed in my own idiosyncratic style and act as peacemaker when Winston became difficult.

In return Eddie showed endless patience with a half-educated but eager young man and between the two of them they moulded me into an effective assistant in the work they were doing. Once, Eddie paid me the huge compliment of telling me that he was glad I had not gone to a public school as I would have learned nothing there and what I did have would have been thrashed out of me, and my talent for self-education was worth more to him and Winston than any stuttering, pimple-ridden product of Eton or Winchester. But the truth was I felt out of place and out of my depth.

I unloaded all this onto Gemma that day in the park and she recognised something in what I said that reflected her own life.

'I feel like that too. But not when I'm at the hospital. I feel inferior when I go *home*.'

'Yes, in some ways our lives are similar. In your case you were sent away as soon as they could get rid of you to school and barely saw them after that. I was thrown out of the house to work before my education ended and handed over every penny earned.'

'When I came home they were always away and I had Nanny. I...' She became tearful. 'I never received a kiss or a cuddle or hug from anyone but her. I was scared to approach my mother and father. They were distant and it just wasn't done.'

I was upset that my inner thoughts spoken aloud had awakened painful ones in her as she was usually a sunny and cheerful-natured soul.

'My mum gave me plenty of kisses and cuddles. The problem was she was usually drunk at the time. Does that count?' I joked, to lighten the mood.

'All I know is, I'll never be like that to my children. *Never*!'

I hugged her. 'I'll kiss and cuddle you anytime, that's what I'm here for!' and gave her a kiss on the cheek to prove it.

I told her about Tom and Arthur and my plans to find them. She held my hand at one point because I got quite upset and agitated when I voiced my innermost thoughts over painful recollections.

'Winston will help you, I'm sure of it,' she insisted, after I had finished.

'I know he will. But I feel bad about it because right now things are very serious in France and that must take up all his attention. I know that man so well and how he works. I'm being selfish, I suppose, in saying this but I feel I'm using him because I know how soft-hearted he is. He'll get me the information on the boys pretty quickly, I've no doubt.'

'You're not using him. He understands perfectly. It'll all be worth it when you see them again, I'm sure it will.' I don't think she could possibly imagine a world where children were there one minute and gone, removed, the next. It exemplified the gulf between us which she was trying to bridge and understand.

'When this is all over we have to talk, Gemma.'

She was now looking into my eyes.

'I know.'

'Talk about us.'

'Yes.'

'For that I don't need Winston's assistance. If I ever need any help for that, I'll just look into your eyes.'

We did not need to kiss. The look we shared was enough. A cold spring breeze suddenly blew and we got up and she put her arm through mine. But neither of us felt the chill.

When Winston returned from Edinburgh he planned further trips to France. He was now being sent there to act as official emissary to the High Command to review the situation himself and report back to the prime minister. He went there either by boat and stayed a few days or flew over in the morning, returning at night. He asked me if I would like to accompany him but I loathed sailing and was terrified at the thought of flying, so shied off these invitations. Before, Eddie would head off such requests at the pass himself but the visits now were sometimes daily and it was harder for Eddie to find excuses for himself, never mind me. I felt bad about this as Winston's face would drop when I refused but he never forced the issue.

At this time, early April 1918, the Germans had already launched their infamous *Kaiserschlacht* ('Kaiser Battle'), the major offensive that nearly won them the war. It was a terrible time as the British armies, particularly the 5th under General Gough, were driven back at huge loss, as ground taken at huge expense a couple of years before yielded within a few days to the German stormtrooper tactics.

Marshal Foch, the great French general who would soon be appointed Generalissimo of the Allied Armies, believed that if the men in the field could hold on, the German offensive would run out of steam, and overrun its supplies, and if properly organised an Allied counter-offensive could sweep them all the way back and may even crush them. Winston told me all this when he got back from France.

Chapter Twenty-Six

One Friday morning at the end of the month, Eddie handed me a sealed envelope with my name on the front. It contained an official letter, a rail ticket, a telegram and a folded over office memo note from the Ministry of Munitions with a paper clip attached to something inside. The letter informed me that my brothers, Thomas and Arthur Melville, were now residing in Scarborough, north Yorkshire, and had been legally adopted by a Mr Arnold and Mrs Ida Humphries. It stated their address in the town's north shore.

The rail ticket was an open return to Scarborough via York from King's Cross leaving the next day and the telegram was confirmation of a paid reservation at the Grand Hotel. I opened the memo, which had some handwriting on it, and a banknote fell out. The memo said: *'Stay away from boats but give my regards to the donkeys!'* Winston knew well my horror of the sea.

Eddie gave me the rest of the day off to pack and make my plans. I knew Winston was leaving for France shortly and wrote him a thank-you letter and gave it to Eddie to pass on. I noted that the telegram from the Grand confirmed up to a week's stay there so I had plenty of time and opportunity (and money) to conduct my family business.

Next morning, I boarded the train in a second class carriage and just watched the countryside go by, my mind in a swirl. I noted the letter mentioned a Mr & Mrs Humphries. Would that now be Tom and Arthur's names? It had been four years since I saw them. What would they be like now? They were just over twelve months younger than me and would both now be nearly seventeen. At that age they would not yet be in the army but would have been registered as part of the conscription process.

The twins were identical neither in looks nor in character. Tom was the likeable of the pair; Arthur, a watcher and deep thinker. When my dad used to come home drunk and violent and lashing out, Arthur would never make a move but I or Tom would always rush to help the other. Arthur would hang back and only get involved if the old man was ready to pass out, when it was nice and safe. He never helped Mum at home with anything much, whereas I was always washing and ironing whilst Tom got on with a lot of the other work.

No, I did not have many fond memories of Arthur, but Tom was my favoured brother as he was a kind-hearted and generous wee laddie, similar in nature to myself. But they were young men now so I resolved to try and keep an open mind.

I changed trains at York after a short wait and got on a smaller one, which took about an hour to reach the seaside resort and arrived early afternoon. I turned right at the exit of the station (I had asked a guard for directions on the train; he just laughed and said, 'Turn right out't door and you can't miss it, lad!') and came to what was once the biggest hotel in Europe and it was as impressive a sight then as it still is now.

The weather was warm, bright and pleasant and I fell in love with Scarborough instantly. Despite my stomach I always liked being near the seaside and have always felt that the sound of the ocean at night had a quality that was somehow reassuring.

Scarborough had its wartime misfortunes. In December 1914 a squadron of Jerry battleships bombarded the town out of the blue, killing nearly twenty people and causing a lot of damage. The Grand Hotel was hit by two shells at its main restaurant and a couple of rooms above it got whacked also. A bloke in the hotel later told me that there had been no one injured but a waiter who had recently been given a warning for always turning up for work late had that morning heeded his caution and got up in time. If he had stuck to his previous watch-keeping standards, he would have been a goner.

Bag in hand I walked in through the main entrance. There was a very grand staircase in the lobby which was built extremely wide so that toff ladies could walk down it without their long dresses catching. I presented myself to reception and booked in.

As I was doing this I heard a commotion at the main door and turned to see what it was. A little bellboy, who must only have been about eleven or twelve years of age, was struggling with a bunch of large suitcases. He had hold of one but the others were the problem and he tried to put another under his arm and grab a third with his free hand.

Some joker in a suit with his back to me was hurrying the lad on, saying, 'You're keeping the gentleman waiting, hurry up!' whilst this wee soul was trying his best and getting no help at all from his boss. People were starting to look round and the bellboy got in a worse jam when one of the cases burst open.

'Oh, for God's sake, what now!' his boss snarled. At this I had seen enough and, leaving the bloke at reception, strode over and, bending down, grabbed a handful of clothing and started dumping them back in the burst case. The bellboy looked down at me and wailed, 'Oh no, sir, please!' I looked into his red, tearful face and thought: if your chief says something, I'll belt him.

The 'boss', changing his tone, turned to me. 'That's quite alright, sir. Quite alright!'

I got up and stuck my face in his. 'It's not "quite alright"! If you were any kind of a *real* manager you would have helped this wee laddie and not made things worse!' I was raging and quite uncaring of how it looked.

He stepped back and then I stopped and looked at him again.

'Arthur!' I exclaimed. It was my brother!

He looked at me blankly. 'It's me, Jamie!'

'Jamie? Jamie!' The light dawned on him and we shook hands and wandered back to reception.

He asked what my room number was and told me to head up and unpack and he would be up in a few minutes.

My room was on the third floor and had a lovely view of the sea and the town. It was a premier room with all amenities and for its day was the height of luxury. A second-class train ticket but a first-class suite: thanks, Winston.

I unpacked and then there was a knock and Arthur came in.

'I see you've still got a bad temper,' he laughed.

'I see you now speak like a bloody *Sassenach*!' I guffawed back. His accent was distinctly watered down and he spoke like he had 'bools in his mooth', as we say in Scotland.

'Oh well, I can't blast out Gorgie slang now, you know!'

We yarned away for a short while. I told him about Mum and the girls. As I spoke it suddenly dawned on me that he knew nothing about our father.

'I take it you don't know, then.'

'Know what?'

I told him Dad had died and how it had happened. He did not speak or show any emotion. He got up and stood over me.

'Well, thanks for telling me.'

I tried to get things back on a positive beat and spoke a little about Winston and my job. He pretended not to be impressed and probably thought I was boasting. Being in his company for a short while made me realise that my feelings towards the boy had not changed now that he had become almost a man. I still did not feel much liking for him. That scene in the lobby exemplified him as I remembered him, and he had not really changed. I asked him why he had never written to our mother.

He shrugged his shoulders.

I asked about Tom. He said that he worked the boats for Mr Humphries, who owned a small fishery business. They were not rich but were well off and had a nice house.

I did not want to go any further. I knew Tom would be more forthcoming. Arthur was a closed-mouth little shit. At one point I wanted to smack his teeth when he shrugged his shoulders at me.

He told me that it happened to be one of Tom's days off and he would be at home lying up or doing the garden. I enquired what time Arthur knocked off. He said he was on the back shift till ten. I then asked what his position was at the hotel.

'Trainee manager. The pay isn't good but I get a yearly increment until I'm full manager. It's not bad. I may stick it but the truth is I can't stand fish! You'll never get me near a fishing boat either! Not like Tom!' I could understand that and mentioned my experiences on troopships.

His eyes widened. 'You mean *you* were in the army? Is that what happened to your leg?'

'All will be revealed later,' I said enigmatically. I did not want to go into details as I'd had enough of his company.

'Alright then, later. What I'll do is telephone Mum and let her know you're heading her way.' At first I wondered what on earth he was talking about but thought it best not to say anything. We left the room and went downstairs in the lift.

We walked to the main door and he pointed me in the direction of the North Bay and gave a rough idea where the Humphries family lived. I had their address and was happy to take a stroll. Agreeing that we would see each other later, we parted.

I liked Scarborough but it had taken a dislike to me. Scarborough is all sheer inclines and the way to the North Bay involved a steep walk. I did not know at the time that there was a funicular railway lift at the side of the hotel (it's still there today) right down to the road at the bottom of the cliff and I could have taken that and had a nice walk along the beach. For some reason Arthur failed to mention this. I wondered why but thought it typical of his lack of empathy or interest in other people.

I wandered down through the town, looking into a few bookshops and found my way to the old harbour where fishing boats lay moored. I bought myself cod and chips and a bottle of cherryade from one of the many establishments and sat on a bench and ate. Seagulls prowled around me and I threw them a chip or two but no way were the buggers getting a bit of my lovely piece of fish.

The view was very scenic with the small lighthouse, the ruined castle high on the hill and on my right as always the Grand itself, majestic on its cliff. I thought there could be far worse places to live.

I finished my lunch and got up and tried to find my way back though the winding streets of Merchants Row and Eastborough and took a few wrong turns but eventually after asking for directions I came to the north end.

I passed by the cricket ground and had to double back on myself at one point as I have always had a terrible sense of direction. All along the sea front were houses which are mostly bed & breakfast hotels now. I walked on past lovely gardens with a small lake, called Peasholm Park, and found the street off Burniston Road where the Humphries family lived. I was glad because by now I was struggling. I had walked from one end of the town to the other.

It was a detached house with a nice big garden with trees and hedges and lovely roses laid out. I opened the gate and walked down the path to the door and gave it a rattle with my stick.

The door was opened by a pleasant-faced lady of about fifty.

'Yes, dear?'

'Are you Mrs Humphries? I'm Jamie Melville. Arthur telephoned about me.'

'Of course! Do come in.'

I wiped my feet and followed her into the sitting room.

'Nice today!' she said.

'Yes,' I replied. 'Nice and sunny!'

'Sit down, love, I'll just bring in tea now. I don't have a girl, never have. I prefer to look after my own house,' she smiled.

I took a liking to Mrs Humphries. I was impressed by her saying she did her own housework, which explained her opening the door and not some maid. She brought through tea and cakes.

'Well, what do you think of Scarborough?'

I had a mouthful of Eccles cake but managed to say, 'I like it alright but there are a lot of hills to climb!'

'Yes, it keeps you active!'

I finished my cake. 'Mrs Humphries, I came here to see Tom and Arthur for my mum's sake. For my own, too. I just wanted to know how they are. Arthur looks well. How is Tom?'

'He's out in't garden! He's always doing summat, is our Tom!'

I managed to remain calm. 'Oh, that's nice, how about I go out and say hello?'

She said it would be lovely and showed me to the back door. She told me that I had to tell him tea was ready and to come in and wash his hands.

I went out the back. The garden was even bigger than the front and had a couple of large trees at each end down at the bottom. There was a shed and a bloke bending down with shears in his hands.

I stopped. I did not know what to say. I then walked over slowly and stood about two or three yards behind him.

'Come on, the Hearts!'

He turned round and looked at me.

'Come on, Tom. You know, the Hearts! Remember when we met Bobby Walker?'

'Jamie!'

He stood up, grabbed me and we embraced. He was a big

bloke, I noted, not far off six feet and powerfully built across the chest and arms. It was like being hugged by an over-friendly bear.

'How are you, wee man?'

'Oh, just fine! I see you haven't grown much!'

'That's the sea air!' I remembered he was on the boats.

'I'll never be a sailor, Tom, I get in a bath and I'm seasick!'

'Oh, but it's grand, Jamie, just grand! But let's get in and have tea, eh?'

We returned to the house. Tom washed and we met up in the sitting room. Mrs Humphries was still there.

'I'll leave you lads to talk, eh? And there's more cake. You know where, Tom.'

'We'll need it if Jamie's here!' I was pleased that he remembered my love of goodies. But it made me feel his loss from my life all the harder. Mrs Humphries then got up and left us.

We chatted away easily and soon were on the subject of his and Arthur's experiences after they left. He told me that when they were removed from Mum's it was the most terrifying moment of his life. They were kept in a big house full of kids in Edinburgh and told that they would never see their parents again as they were both drunks and were a danger to them. Then one day they were informed that new parents had been found for them and they had to go and live by the sea in Yorkshire. This frightened them more because it was so far away from home.

But when they arrived at the Humphries they were treated very well and just got on with it. It turned out that the couple had a son who also worked on the boats but had drowned when one foundered in a hellish storm with all hands lost.

It had nearly killed Ida. Her husband feared that she would try something 'silly' in her grief, and as they could not have any more children he decided to adopt in the hope that it would give her something to live for. They were offered twin boys from Edinburgh. Mrs Humphries instantly said yes, without even knowing any details about them.

Tom said that the worst part was going to school as they were targeted, being Scots and adoptees, but they could take care of themselves. I thought he was being kind to Arthur; I couldn't see him being much cop in a fight with a bunch of Yorkies.

Other than that it was fine. Mr Humphries took them down to see the boats and from that moment Tom was hooked, literally for life, to the sea and wanted to go out, and said so. This naturally sent a shudder through Mrs Humphries, but the old man just said, we'll see, son. Arthur took one look and thought, no chance.

Tom had a girl called Irene. She was a nurse in the hospital in Scarborough. I asked him about his army status. He said they were still waiting to be called up, Tom wanting the navy, naturally.

There was not much else for him to tell. He asked about Mum and the girls.

'Tom, Dad is dead. He's been dead four years.'

He just gaped at me.

I was struggling now. It had been easier with Arthur, who I could be matter-of-fact with due to his cold manner. But Tom was a different proposition.

I was able to give him the details and after I had finished he looked at me.

'Those buggers could have told us! They owed us that, those buggers!' he spat out, angrily.

By this he meant the Corporation, but he then asked, 'And Mum?'

I told him how she was, everything. He was pleased she remarried.

We chatted some more and then I left a silence for a few

moments and spoke my piece.

'Tom, you could have written. I never expected Arthur to bother, but why didn't you?'

'I wrote to her, yes, but I never posted the letters. I kept them. Remember, they told me that they were evil, that they were a danger to us. Arthur was happy to believe this. He kind of felt he was better than everyone up there anyway. He told me later he was glad to leave them. Down here in Scarborough he found a better life; can you blame him? He just wanted to forget Gorgie, Edinburgh, everything. You and the girls, the lot. What were the girls to him? They were just babies.'

'I don't really care about what Arthur thinks,' I said, becoming impatient. 'To be honest I'm not surprised to hear this of him. I knew coming down here that you were both now almost grown men but in being men I thought you would have wanted to find out for yourselves.

'You were there, Tom; you know how nice Mum is. Dad wasn't always a drunk. That was only after his accident; remember the good times we had. He took us to Tynie, to Portobello and Queensferry. *That* was the seaside, too. It wasn't his fault, all that pain he was in. It changed him.'

'You were always closest to Mum and Dad, Jamie, it's natural you defend them the most.'

'Look,' I was getting annoyed, 'they're our parents. Mum's doing just fine now. But we've three wee girls that are our sisters. They worship me and they would you and Arthur too, but you know what? Only Maggie knows about you because the other two can't remember, so stories were made up about you both being sailors who went to sea. God, it was not far from the truth. You were sailing all over the world and one day you both would come back and bring them presents from the South Seas.

'That's the stories I invented for them. Now, I know what happened to you and Arthur was awful but as you say, you got on with it and it seems to have worked out fine but you could have at least shown you were now men with your own lives and understood how hard it was for Mum!' I got up now as I was angry.

'Sit down, Jamie, please, just sit down.'

'Another thing,' I continued my harangue, 'I had to lie about my age to join the army to get away. But if you want to know why I joined it was because I wanted to help them. I got out so there would be one less mouth to feed and I sent home all my pay. I don't know if it was the right thing to do.

'But I'm glad I did it now because if I hadn't God knows where I would be today, or them. You and Arthur got away and it was the making of you both but *you* should have been the one to try and make contact again. I expected it of *you*.'

I really wanted to leave. I had found out all I needed to know. It was time to go, but I sat down to try and give him a chance to speak.

'I'll not deny all you've said,' Tom began. 'It's really sad about the girls. Let me think about it. I haven't thought about this in years. One thing: Arthur is just not interested. It's not that he bears them any malice. He just doesn't have any sort of feelings for family like you have. You always were the peacemaker, trying to keep everyone together, but you'll find that sometimes in being the peacemaker you just end up driving people further apart. Let it go for 't' moment eh?' He sounded real Yorkshire. 'Just let me think on it and now, tell me what you've been doing.'

I calmed down. I had let out my frustrations on him probably a bit unfairly, but it passed quickly. As before, our brotherly disputes once aired were soon forgotten. We had picked up from where he had left off and nothing had changed.

I then told him everything about myself. The 6th, Winston, my first office job and the new one in the ministry. And I told him about Gemma.

'A nurse, too!' he cried.

He was impressed to hear it all but was concerned about my leg. I told him it was more of an inconvenience but at least it had got me a pension!

We spoke until late in the afternoon and Mrs Humphries joined us. I stayed for tea and Mr Humphries came home. He was bearded, big and jolly and very amiable and I liked him immediately. We sat around the dinner table as Ida brought us our meal and I have to admit I missed this and envied Tom his life. Mrs Humphries seemed filled with love and affection for these two boys and I knew that their coming here was probably the best thing that could have happened.

Mr Humphries and I chatted about the ministry. He was interested to hear I had experience in accounts and dealing with payments and requisitioning. I told him I was self-taught and had no accountancy qualifications but I could find my way around a profit and loss and a balance sheet. I tried not to sound boastful but also told him about Eddie and Winston and gave him some examples of work thrown my way.

'You're a very talented young man, Jamie! All you Melvilles are the same, eh, Tom?' he laughed and Tom answered, 'Jamie was always the smartest, Dad, he were always reading summat!'

'A great reader, are you, lad? Well, you must come upstairs and have a look at my library and tell me what you think!'

With some people it is drink or food or racing or football but when I hear the word 'library' my antennae always shoot up.

'Show me the way after dinner, Mr H!' and everyone laughed.

I stayed the full week and thoroughly enjoyed myself at the seaside. Tom took me down to the steam trawler he was a crew member of. I got on board but there was no way I was going out in it even just around the bay. I enjoyed the banter with the fishermen, all salty types, and it reminded me of fond times at the 6th with men of my own class and I felt comfortable and relaxed in their company.

We then went to see Mr Humphries's office in Eastborough in the town. I realised that I had probably walked past it already the first day and had not noticed it. The office was small and inside it, an old boy, a young girl to type and a cat. There were boxes all over the place filled with files and invoices and God knows what else and I noted that there was no telephone.

'Bit different from what you're used to, eh, Jamie?' laughed Mr Humphries.

'A lot smaller, yes!'

'I could use any new ideas, lad. Speak up, don't be shy!'

I did not want to state the obvious to this kind-hearted man and was flattered that he valued my opinion. I decided to play it safe. 'I'll have a think about it, Arnold,' (he had told me to call him by his name), 'and I'll let you know!'

We then walked to Peasholm Park and fed the ducks. After that we headed back up to the churchyard where Anne Brontë lay. Then, against my better judgment, I walked with Tom and Arnold up Castle Hill. We reached the top but unfortunately my leg was louping and I had to take a seat but was able to admire the view and Tom handed me a bottle of pop.

'It's really lovely. I could live here.' I was thinking out loud as I sipped on my drink.

'What, and miss all your London pals! I would have thought you would be bored stiff here, Jamie!' joked Tom.

'Don't mock the lad, Tom,' rebuked Arnold. 'London is not the be all and end all, y'know.'

'No, it's not,' I mused. 'It is not that.'

I then got up, as I felt better, and we headed back down. We got on a tram to the Spa near the Grand and had lunch.

The week passed by and I bid my farewells. Arnold took me to one side before I left.

'Send me those ideas you have, lad. I will say summat to you now. There would always be a place for you here. I get the feeling you're a bit confused about what you want to do, what you want to *be*. I'm not telling you how to run your life, I've no right. But just remember, this home is *your* home, too. I've asked the boys till I'm blue in the face to write to their mother. Arthur just won't do it.

'Now I think Tom will. I've also told them they should go up and visit. I think out of the three you are the sensible one, Jamie, though I also think you were dealt the hardest deal. But you've come through fine and your mother should be proud of you; proud of all of you. Now, I want to see you here again lad, on holiday or just to visit, and don't forget you have to return those books as there are plenty more to choose from!'

I thanked him and Ida for everything and promised to be back.

I had done my duty for my mother; and for myself. I had tried to have an open mind on the way up on the train about Tom and Arthur. But I wanted to believe they had been torn away from their home to live in a house where they had been beaten and starved by wicked foster parents, chained up so they could not run away and that all they could think about was their own dear mother and brother and sisters and the thought of returning to them was what sustained them in their misery.

In reality, a very kind woman who had lost her only child had grabbed at the chance of adopting two poor, neglected children and brought them up with as much love and care as if she had borne them herself. They say that one man's rubbish is another man's treasure; I could not help thinking that one poor woman's agony, my mother's, had been another poor woman's salvation. It would be difficult to reconcile and to accept but the main fact was that they had turned out alright. Nevertheless, I could not help wondering how things would have turned out for them if they have stayed in Edinburgh. Or for that matter, how things would have turned out for me.

I spoke of this to Winston when I returned. He came down to my room at the hotel with brandy and a bottle of porter beer and told me it was time I tried a proper drink because he could only trust a man who drank cherryade so far.

I laughed, but was a little sorrowful. I did not want Winston to think of me as grown up; I just wanted him to see me as a wee boy, so he could continue to spoil me rotten. I thought that now I was nearly eighteen his attitude towards me would change. Thankfully, it did not. He treated me like a wee boy for nearly fifty years.

'The most important result of your visit is that you can put your mother's mind at rest, James. Also you have implanted the idea that Arthur and Tom must endeavour to try and visit her.'

I sipped some porter. 'I just hope they do. I think Tom will but I don't have much hope for Arthur. Still, it's answered a lot of questions I had all these years. Fancy them not being told about my dad!'

'Yes, that was most cruel; that you were left to inform them. It is the world we live in, James: survival of the fittest! The weak are consumed! It is not the kind of world I envision and with my many reforms I have tried to change it for the better.' Remember, Winston was the man who created old-age pensions, reduced the working week and created labour exchanges for the poor.

'This porter isn't bad, Colonel. Can I try some brandy?'

His bad habits were rubbing off on me.

Chapter Twenty-Seven

The situation in France began to improve as the German offensive ground to a halt and the Allies were able to go on the attack. By August, the Germans were in full retreat and Winston began to dream of the war ending that year but was making contingency plans for munitions production to go on well into 1919.

I took Gemma up to Scotland to finally meet my mum, who met us at Waverley. She gave Gemma a hug and they both cried and a cab drove us to Murrayfield where all the girls were excitedly waiting because they knew Jamie always brought goodies for them.

George and I went out into the garden. I had taken to Tom Thumbs occasionally after Winston introduced them to me and told George I did not want Mum to see me smoking. He laughed.

'Does Mr Churchill think the war will end soon?' he then asked.

'He's quietly optimistic, but still planning ahead.'

'I can only hope we don't lose anyone else we know. There's been more than enough loss.'

I knew he had lost a nephew at sea and as for my five cousins who joined the Royal Scots early on, two were dead and one was an invalid having suffered in a gas attack. Afterwards he could only get a job labouring on the roads in all weathers, coughing his guts out in the land fit for heroes. Sadly, Cousin Robert turned to drink; and did not live long.

Loss was all around me. But there was gain. If not for the war my life would have been different. Mum would still be in Gorgie as there would have been no munitions factory where she would meet George. I would probably be doing some soulless job with no prospects. The war with all its horror and misery had been good for me in many ways. I had to reconcile that to myself; and live with it. But I could still thank God that both my brothers were safe.

We went back inside. By this time Gemma had Annie on her back and was running through the house with Lizzie following them, shrieking at the top of her voice.

'Gemma's a big hit!' Mum declared. 'She's lovely, Jamie, I'm so proud of you!'

'Ach, the kilt does it every time!' I explained and grabbed a piece of shortbread.

The girls went outside into the garden and carried on their games with Gemma.

'Jamie, you'll never guess but Tom's been here.'

'Wonderful!' I cried.

'Yes, he came up for a weekend and is coming back soon.'

'How did it go?'

'He's a big laddie now! I hardly recognised him when he came to the door! This big, handsome boy lifted me up in the air and said, "Hello Mum!"' She then burst into tears and I went over and sat next to her.

'That's wonderful news, Mum!'

'He wants us all to go down to Scarborough. He told the girls he has his own boat and he'll take them out on it! They never slept all night after he told them! Mr and Mrs Humphries sound very nice people.'

'They are. They're the nicest people you'll ever meet. This is all so good, Mum. I'm so happy for you.'

Tom had sent a telegram advising he was on his way up to Edinburgh. He got off the train at Waverley and made his way to Warriston Cemetery to see Dad's grave and stood by it alone, leaving flowers. Later, at home with Mum, he opened up his suitcase. It was full of seaside treats: rock, candy sticks, seashells and starfish for the girls.

The sailor had finally come home from the sea.

Winston was back in France, where he would stay a week. Again he asked me to go with him but I told him I planned a weekend during the bank holiday to go up to Scarborough with Gemma. I'd got out of it once again but knew sooner or later I would have to accompany him.

I told Gemma all that had happened the last time I went up to Yorkshire. She was excited when I asked her to come with me as we could make a little holiday for ourselves. I telegrammed Tom and we headed up on the Friday as Eddie let me knock off early.

On the Saturday we strolled around with Tom and his girl, Irene. It was the height of summer and the weather was fine. Scarborough was very busy as people flocked to the seaside to try and forget about the war for a while. We did the usual donkey rides, lunch at the Spa, the castle (this time I took it very slowly) and ice-creams at Peasholm Park.

That evening Arnold collared me in the library. I was handing back his books and looking for more from the collection.

'Well, what about your ideas from the last time, then?' He meant his offices, which I had looked over previously.

'I need a good look around first. Preferably when your employees aren't there!' I offered to go the following day, Sunday. Gemma could come with us as she had administrative experience from the hospital.

Next morning after breakfast we walked with Arnold to Eastborough and he unlocked the door and let us in. The office was small but it could have been made bigger if something was done about all the boxes lying around. There was no sign of a telephone.

'Arnold, you have a phone at home but how else can you contact the office other than by walking down here?'

'We don't have one here because Ted just won't use it! He's set in his ways and will have no truck with one.'

Most of the smaller fishing companies kept their offices at the small harbour building but the pre-war Humphries Fishing Company had been able to afford one in the town itself. Tom told me that when the war broke out, the Admiralty had demanded three of Arnold's five-boat fleet for minesweeping and patrol duties with the crews being sworn in as naval reservists. He dug his heels in and allowed only two to go as the business would have folded with any less. Later he got another one back as the Admiralty was forced to accept that the population needed to be fed and would not be if too many fishing vessels were shadowing German patrols rather than catching food.

'Well, that must change. It means you're cut off from the outside world. That's just daft. No business these days should be without a telephone in every office.' I lifted up one of the boxes and put it on a desk. I looked through it and found invoices dated back to the late nineties. 'Surely there's no reason to retain documents this old?'

'He keeps everything.'

'Well, I wouldn't. There's no filing system I can see worthy of the name. How do you know what to look for? It's not difficult to set up. You can get rid of most of these boxes and have a couple of cabinets holding invoices going back from ninety days up to say, three years at most. This place needs gutting. Like your fish.'

'Ted has it all in his head.'

'Not good enough. What happens when Ted is on holiday or off sick? No one around is left who has any detailed knowledge or knows where to find things. No, you need to rip this place apart, get a telephone and bring someone new in with experience, to run it like a modern office.' I thought of Whitehall and the secretive behaviour of Hammond and

Paget. Not that I suspected Arnold's employees of fraud.

'What do you think?' Arnold turned to Gemma.

'It does seem awfully cluttered and it's not like the offices Jamie and I work in. They're a lot bigger of course but the principles should always be the same: efficient filing systems, getting rid of old paperwork and the telephone. Yes, there should be one.'

'Ted is getting on a bit now,' Arnold rubbed his chin, 'but I hear what you're saying. It's no use talking to Tom as he's clueless about this kind of thing.' I had already taken note that he rarely mentioned Arthur for any reason. Arnold turned to me. 'How long do you think it would take to gut this place, then?'

'You'd just have to roll your sleeves up and get on with it, but I don't think it would take long.'

'Well, what about now if it's not asking too much?'

'Now? What about it, Gemma?' I asked.

'On one condition: Mr Humphries has to buy us cod and chips for lunch!'

'No problem, lass and I'll even throw in 't' cherryade! And you just call me Arnold! None o' this "mister" nonsense!'

It was an enjoyable day. For me it was a busman's holiday but Arnold let me be the boss and do things my way. I would ask him certain questions about items I found but he deferred to me, which I thought showed that he was a smart man and flexible in his thinking. He was open to new ideas and had good ones of his own to offer. At lunchtime we went out and got our fish suppers and sat by the harbour. It was hot and I had my sleeves rolled up.

'It's really nice here, eh, Gemma?'

'It's lovely! I want to come back again! Will you have us back, Arnold?'

'Any time, love! Watch out for them seagulls! They'll have

the chips out o' your fingers!'

We finished up and headed back to the office.

Later that evening I was in the library, looking through books. It was becoming a centre of intrigue as Arnold again took the opportunity while we were alone to have a chat with me. He was your typical plain-speaking Yorkshireman, which was refreshing when I compared him to some of the double-dealing scoundrels I had come across in the City.

'So, how's it going in London?'

'Oh, the usual. But I'm going to have to accompany Winston the next time he goes to France. I can't keep ducking out of it forever!'

'Funny you hating boats! Not like Tom, he was born a sailor if there ever was one!'

'I like the seaside but the sea doesn't like me!'

He chuckled. 'I might have to have word with Ted. He won't be happy when he sees state of office, Tuesday morning!'

'I'll leave that painful duty to you!'

'The joys of leadership, eh! Have you thought about when we last spoke? About you and Scarborough?' I had been wondering how the subject would be brought up. Over the period I had considered raising it myself but was now glad I hadn't as Arnold's mentioning it first indicated his intent.

'Arnold, I've thought a lot about what we discussed. It's very tempting to me but the decision, if I have to make it, will probably be the biggest of my life. It doesn't only involve me, there's Gemma and Winston to consider and I have to be sure I'm doing the right thing.'

We shook hands and he told me to take my time and that he would understand either way my final decision.

He left me to look over the books. I only picked out a couple, one of them being *The Tenant of Wildfell Hall* by Anne Brontë.

We left on the Monday. From the connection at Scarborough to York we luckily had a carriage to ourselves, which helped enormously to leave me to think and test the water with Gemma.

Firstly I asked her what she thought of my brothers and the Humphries.

'Well! Tom is an absolute honey! Irene's got a catch there, I can tell you! The Humphries are super! How wonderful to have such loving parents and a house full of laughter and fun! It must be such a relief to you and your mother to know how well things ended up.'

'What do you think of Arthur?'

She paused, 'I'm not sure. He's so different from both of you. There's an atmosphere between him and Mr Humphries but Ida worships both of the boys, so I think Arnold deals with it the best he can. I wonder what the problem is between them?'

I knew. Arthur was homosexual. I had long suspected this. The more I thought about it the more my attitude changed from antagonism towards him and more to acceptance. Seeing him that day at the Grand — even though he had annoyed me — and after at the Humphries home, made me realise that he would always be out of place wherever he went and had to try and fit in as best he could.

Tom had taken to life in Scarborough as easily as I had the army. We had both found a place we were comfortable with but Arthur never would. He would always be an outsider. In those days they jailed you for it. It was regarded as an illness. But they don't usually jail you if you are ill. What an age of hypocrisy it was. His life must have been difficult at the best of times.

Winston told me a few horror stories concerning the subject in regard to the schools he had been at. He had been accused of it at one time. It was proven to be a scurrilous accusation and he received damages as a result. All this I could never discuss with anyone except on the quiet with Winston or Tom, who knew himself, of course. I never mentioned it to Gemma until years later.

'I don't know. Anyway, what do you think of the town?'

'It's very busy but it was a bank holiday. It has everything you need. A railway station, shops.'

'A hospital?'

'Yes, that too. What're you thinking?'

I had been thinking of little else for a while now. This holiday had an ulterior motive behind my planning of it as I needed to get Gemma up there to visit and also to talk to Arnold and subsequently had killed two birds with one stone.

'Arnold has offered me a job in the business. I think he wants me to run the office and Ted will get the heave or retire early.'

'What about us?' I was not expecting that. Arrogantly, I had naturally assumed she would want to come with me.

'You'd come with me of course. Why? What about us?'

'How long have you been considering this?'

'I was asked in a roundabout way the first time I came here in April. I didn't give it too much thought at first and didn't think to bother you. Lately I've thought more and more about it but I can't make up my mind.'

'You told me that Winston said you have a bright future with him.'

'Yes, I did and I might well have. But I'm not sure if that's the future I want for myself. For you either.'

'Remember when we sat in St James's Park and you told me we would soon have to talk?'

'Yes, I remember.'

'Are we having that talk now?'

'I suppose we are. But I didn't know then about Scarborough. The talk was to be about something else but

Scarborough has got in the way and I needed you to see it for yourself before I spoke to you.'

'That's not like you, Jamie. You usually rush in where angels fear to tread. This "talk" must be very important to you.'

'To you, too.'

'Well?' She looked at me and I put my hand on hers.

'Will you marry me?'

Her eyes, which had appeared a little anxious, lit up as she broke into a relieved smile. 'Yes.'

'We'll have to get engaged first and wait a while. Can you wait?'

'Yes.'

'I'll have to ask your old man. I'll have to *meet* your old man.'

'Poor you!'

We both laughed. It was out at last but the elation was tempered by the dilemma that I faced. 'Well, is it to be Scarborough or is it to be Winston?' she asked, reading my thoughts.

I could not answer. She held my hand. 'What does your heart tell you?'

I paused. 'Winston; first and always. But my head says Scarborough. I want a settled life, I want peace. I want to be around people I'm comfortable with. I want nice surroundings, fresh air and to be near the sea.' She laughed and patted my cheek, knowingly. 'I want to be with Tom and Arthur. I don't want to go back to Edinburgh. That's hard for me to reconcile as Mum and the girls are there. But it hurts to remember. Do you realise, when I think of my home I feel *pain?* I *never* want to go back there.'

'And the case for Winston?'

I sighed, 'Only that he made me what I've become. That I owe him everything. He's given me the greatest opportunity I could have dreamed of. He has faith and trust in me. He's my friend. With him, I could go anywhere! We talked about me becoming an MP one day. Can you believe that! He was serious! He said the House needed one or two honest men even if they were hard to find!

'He said I could in time become his private secretary once Eddie moved on. Do you know how difficult that would normally be for someone of my background? The sky's the limit! No, I'll change that. For Winston *there is no limit*. There's nothing that can't be done. To be around that is exhilarating!'

'Are you tempted?'

'Of course! I could do so much. In ten years' time I could be a Member of Parliament! I've learned about procedure and been to the House on many occasions. I've been introduced to everyone. He's let me see it all and it's been tremendous. Most of all he's let me see what's *possible*.'

'Only you can decide, Jamie. I think you could do anything you turn yourself to. You're capable. But all I want is your happiness and I can see the attractions of both choices you have. It doesn't matter to me which one you take. I'll be with you as your fiance, as your wife, whatever you choose to do.'

A very long kiss followed; the other attraction of having a car to ourselves.

Chapter Twenty-Eight

In late October, Winston called me into his office one morning and poured a drink for us both, brandy for him and a whisky for me.

'There is a matter which I wish to discuss, James. Peacefeelers are being sent out from Germany and the war may very soon reach its conclusion. I must go back to France shortly and this time I would like you to accompany me. My young friend, I want you to see the end. You have been with me so long now that I owe you that. I know that Eddie has counselled against it and he may be correct in his advice but I would like us to end our war together: the colonel and the finest batman in the British army.

'When I left the 6th I left it with the heaviest of hearts. On my last day there I addressed the officers and told them that although I am an Englishman, it was in Scotland that I found the three best things in my life: my wife, my constituency and my regiment. I must add a fourth: my true friend, James Melville.'

We left during the last week of the month. The war would end two weeks later but there was still a lot of dying going on.

I was content this time to go with him and I felt this trip may help me find closure for in my mind I was using the trip to say goodbye, not to Winston, but to the war.

Winston's trips *were* vital. They were innovative too, as he was the first senior politician to act as a sort of roving reporter (which of course is what he was when a very young man) who could get a strong feel of the situation and report back his conclusions. He would be no use, however, if he got too close and caught one. Whilst not there to act as bodyguard, I was someone who could tell him off when he was getting a bit *too* near the heat, which is where he invariably ended up.

The boat going over was the usual hell-ship and I retched my way through the entire voyage. I heaved away, swearing 'never again' like most drunks do the morning after; and I had the trip back to look forward to. It never seemed to fail, once out of protected harbour waters I would feel the familiar pain in my gut and it would start. But always as the boat neared its destination and sailed into calmer seas, my stomach would miraculously settle back and by the time we had docked I was right as rain again and usually feeling ravenous.

Winston had set himself up near the British headquarters at Montreuil, at the town of Verchocq about fifteen miles away and requisitioned the chateau there, which was about twenty miles away from the German front line. He had come to some sort of agreement with General Haig and used it most of the time he spent in France towards the war's end.

He persuaded Eddie to come with us, which had been no mean feat. He was not happy being there and told Winston straight that there would be no more joy-driving for him up close to bullets and shells as he had had enough of that on previous occasions. Winston called him an 'ignoble fellow' and said that he must use me as an example of how an Englishman should behave. Eddie had the good grace to say that I was a Scotsman; and Winston could get stuffed.

We hoped to meet up with Archie Sinclair and I looked forward to that as I always had a soft spot for him even before he held my hand outside the Farm when I got hit by that blast. He was second in command of the battalion but took one end of the stretcher that carried me to the ambulance and of course stayed with me for a while. He did not have to do that, but it was another fine example of the calibre of officers of the 6th.

It was not a happy trip and it was all down to a lot of

peculiar behaviour from Winston. I had never seen the Colonel in one of his celebrated difficult moods; where he would behave remarkably like the most spoiled of children and quite beyond reasoning with. But I would see him for the first time in one of his infamous 'black dogs' which is what I believed caused all the trouble.

This particular 'dog' would leave a memory imprinted on my mind that will stay with me until my dying day.

We disembarked from the ship and a motorcar awaited us and we clambered aboard. The driver had sandwiches prepared. I tucked in with relish as by now my much maligned stomach was crying out for sustenance after its recent exertions. A bottle of wine was passed around and I had a glass, being rather dehydrated through all that spewing.

As the car drove away Winston ordered, 'Driver, take us to Fuck and Bugger!' I coughed out my piece of sandwich and nearly fell out of the car laughing as Eddie explained that the chateau was beside the town of Fouquienbergue and this was a fair example of Winston's pronunciation and he had heard worse when in more exalted company.

On the way to our destination we must have hit a nail or something in the road because a tyre burst and we stopped to allow the driver to replace it.

Normally, you sit back and have a smoke and wait for the task to be completed but Winston fumed the whole time and cursed the driver something rotten. I had never heard him speak to someone in that manner before. To me, he always appeared comfortable and relaxed in the company of working people and was usually exceptionally kind to waiters, cabbies and the cleaners at the office, whom he always tipped generously at Christmas.

It was so unexpected that Eddie and I just stared as he harangued this poor man, till I turned on him and told him to leave off the fellow. Winston swung round angrily to me but Eddie put a hand up and said, 'Winston, calm down.' He then sulked off and sat at the edge of the road. I was furious and Eddie had to placate me also.

I got out, assisted the driver and between the two of us the tyre was replaced and then Eddie took the driver away and spoke to him quietly alone. Winston remained at the side of the road, swigging out of his hip flask.

'Are we all ready?' asked Eddie as he returned to the car.

I was back in my seat but Winston remained where he was. 'Colonel! Come on, then!' I shouted.

He screwed the cap back on the flask slowly, rose and made his way back to us. He did not speak.

The motor was started and we headed back on the road. Eddie was chatting to me about some papers we needed working on that evening. Then as we drove along we came to a fork and Winston insisted we turn left when the driver said we needed to turn right. Winston shouted, Do as you are told! and I just wanted to stop the car and get out. So did Eddie.

We motored along and the road seemed to disappear as we drove in to thick bloody hedgerows where we had trouble turning the car round before heading back to the fork and taking the right turn. The language from Winston was frightful.

'Winston, what is the matter with you!' fumed Eddie after another tirade of bile.

'Bloody driver is useless!'

'He's not useless!' I butted in. 'You're confusing him by giving him the wrong directions!'

I was sitting in the middle and Winston to my left. He just growled and childishly turned himself around so he was facing the side and had his back to me.

Eddie and I looked at each other.

The atmosphere was awful from then on until we reached

our destination, where we met up with Archie Sinclair. I was very pleased to see him and we shook hands and he insisted that I address him from now on as 'Archie' and asked how I was.

He was married now and had swapped the cavalry for a machine gun company and for a while had considered transferring to the Royal Flying Corps but he felt loyalty to his regiment and men must come first and he decided to stay. This was typical Archie.

We stayed the night at the Chateau at Verchocq, which was very plush. I had a room to myself and whilst Archie and Winston went off for a chat over drinks after supper, Eddie retired early. Winston asked Archie to become his liaison officer between the ministry and the military, which would mean him spending more time at home, but Archie turned him down as he felt an obligation to his own colonel and did not want to be seen running off to a cushy number thanks to having friends in high places.

Winston was unhappy at this as he was a man who did not like being told no and spent the evening trying to change Archie's mind.

I went out for a wander to get some air and smoke a Tom Thumb as I felt unsettled by the events of the day. I tried to reconcile Winston's abominable behaviour but was left wondering after being in his company now for nearly three years whether I really knew him as well as I thought I did.

I had seen his temper before but not directed at an individual in his presence unable to fight back. It was usually aimed at *them* or *they*: his *enemies*. I knew he was broody and sometimes spent hours seated in a room just staring into space. I had seen that first-hand the night Lloyd George became prime minister and denied Winston a place in his first Cabinet.

Whatever sparked it off had to be something I had no

previous cognizance of, certainly in my dealings with him. But I did not know what.

I would find out soon enough.

We set off early next day and I was grateful for Archie's presence. Though Eddie could normally handle Winston, I sensed something out of the ordinary going on inside him and felt more relaxed with our old comrade around as support.

The motor headed for Arras, where my poor friends Tommy Reid and Jock Paterson died. I thought about asking where the burial area was but decided against it. I knew Winston and the others would be sympathetic but we did not have too much time because Archie could not remain long with us.

We had a humorous moment at the checkpoint before Arras when a Canadian guard stopped us and insisted on seeing all our passes and, enjoying his moment, took his time looking at each one lovingly. Winston was ready to blow his top.

Later on in the morning we arrived at the field of Le Cateau where Archie proceeded to show us around, viewing the ground where in part of that battle, 1st Battalion Royal Scots Fusiliers played a crucial role in stopping a flank attack at Caudry as the army fought a tenacious rearguard action in the fighting retreat of August 1914. Archie reminded us that he had to be back at his command post at a certain time as his commanding officer needed to see him. Winston said balls to that and he was personally overriding the orders of a mere colonel.

This caused a terrible row between them both, which was heightened by their already constant bickering over Archie's refusal of Winston's earlier offer, and I won't repeat what was said. The outcome of the argument was effectively decided when we came to the end of the road where a railway bridge blown by the Germans had fallen across it, barring further access. Archie, who gave as good as he got, was dropped off to see his commanding officer at Brancourt, probably glad to see the back of us. Eddie and Winston then started on each other whilst I tried to pretend I was not there. Winston finished by saying that as far as things went, he would have nothing to do with Archie ever again.

The motor had stopped as all this squabbling was going on and it was very unseemly. Eddie declared he would refuse to go any further with Winston if he continued to behave in such a fashion. Winston then said in reply something unforgivable:

'Then fuck off back to your *pansy* friends in England! James and I are warriors and we shall carry on without you!' Eddie turned pale, did not speak and slowly climbed out of the car.

Thank God I have a good Scotch tongue in my head. I turned to Winston and said coldly, 'Colonel! As far as I'm concerned, I'd rather leave with Eddie than stay around with a bullying swine like you! *You* fuck off!' and I got out of the car in an absolute fury and stood at the side of the road alongside Eddie. I'd had enough of this outrageous behaviour and was not prepared to hang around any longer.

There was a dreadful impasse; when suddenly a car went passed and stopped, turned around and drove back to us. It was the vehicle of Lord Weir, who had served under Winston at the Ministry and was now Secretary of State for Air, travelling around France at the same time, and recognised Winston standing at the side of the road!

'James, I will never forgive you if you leave with that man and let me go on *alone.*' Winston was pleading now.

Eddie turned and told me to go with him as he would get a lift back to the chateau with Lord Weir. He advised me to be very careful and do nothing that I felt may be dangerous. He knew his man Winston and his love of battlefields. Particularly those where the fighting was still on-going.

'Winston, what's going on?' Lord Weir asked from his car. By that time Eddie had climbed in. They spoke and then took off. I felt alone with Eddie gone. I did not want to be near

Winston after my outburst, though I'd meant every word.

But the worst was yet to come. We drove too far forward and got shelled, as we were told later that we were in sight of the German lines, and Winston got it into his head that the Germans knew he was around and were deliberately trying to target him. I was too busy ducking for cover and ended up whacking my knee and it hurt like hell. It was a bad one this time. I knew the sensation as it caused me to feel very sick and nauseous and it would be almost crippling for a while.

I managed to limp off back to the car. The driver had scarpered. He'd had enough; and I don't blame him. Winston was edging further forward towards the shelling and as I rubbed my knee I looked at the idiot and just became more and more angry and frustrated at him.

'Come back! Come back, you bloody fool! Colonel! Winston! Come back here, now!' I roared but had to lean back in the seat as my knee was causing me agony. I wished I could drive so I could start the car up and just bugger off and leave that madman to it.

Eventually he returned. He opened the car door, got in and sat but did not speak.

'I think the driver has done a runner, I don't blame him.' I said. He remained silent.

After a short while he said in a monosyllabic tone, 'We must find him then as I do not wish to remain any longer in this *place*.'

His manner all day had been appalling but this sounded very strange. I could not put my finger on it. But it was odd. What *was* the matter?

'Colonel, are you alright?'

He stared ahead and then slowly his face relaxed. I breathed again as he turned to me. 'Jamie, I have been a perfect *bastard*.'

Here we go, apologies are on the way. I knew my man, you see.

Meanwhile I heard a rustling noise and the driver appeared out of some hedgerows and got in and started the motor up. Winston told him to return us to our base at Verchocq

'Alright now, Colonel?' I asked again after we had driven for a few minutes.

'No, I am not "alright now" but as I have contributed in no small part to making you and others so very unhappy this day, please accept my abject apologies. I note also that your confounded leg is playing up. James, I am so sorry.'

'Are you back to your old self now?' I would say this sort of thing to him when we were alone; I was cheeky to him at times back at the 6th, which he never seemed to mind. I understand now that he was just plain amused by it, more than anything.

'We shall return to the chateau, find a hot bath for your leg and have a good meal. I have seen enough of this *war* and all other wars.'

Chapter Twenty-Nine

Back at Verchocq we met up with Eddie, to whom Winston was 'abject' in his apologies, and over dinner the atmosphere began to return to normal. Afterwards we had drinks with a few senior officers who had joined us.

I sensed that Winston was still not back to his usual self when, unusually, he retired first. Eddie and I stayed up to go over a few papers as he needed them typed up, and we spent a couple of hours working and yarning before he told me to call it a day and get a good night's sleep.

I went to my room, took off my coat and lay on the bed. Eddie reckoned the war only had days to run. It would soon be over. I had survived and thank God my brothers had not been required to serve. We had suffered no tragedies in our family, unlike millions of others.

Why was that, I wondered? I have never been a religious person and whatever spark I may have had was extinguished forever in Belgium. I was fifteen years old and saw human beings that had been shot, blasted, shelled, eviscerated, vaporised and disintegrated. I had seen bodies lying for weeks in open country, rotting away. And the smell, the smell of it! Those who are fortunate in not having had to breathe in such a stench will never understand how lucky they truly are. It clung to you and I spent a lot of time walking around with a broken cigarette end in each nostril or camphor rubbed up inside. Winston insisted on this for me. No one laughed or cared as others did it, too. I hated the sensation and the smell but he made me do it if ever the wind got up and blew that horrible stink over towards us. I remember sicking up a few times and lads holding me as I vomited.

They told me, *Jamie, Jamie, you should not be here, you should be home, this is no place for you.* The older men, missing their own children, were protective, *fatherly,* towards me, as Winston was. Always looking out for me. I should not have been there, yes, but I was…

The wounds are from alien objects blasted into my body from afar, my limbs twisted and broken, until at times I am left writhing in agony at any moment…being left attached to a stick, stairs never ending, relying on this piece of black wood growing out of my hand… doctors, nurses cool, cool, hands, operating on me, sewing up my flesh with thread and ripping out ligament and cartilage to repair what can no longer be repaired or renewed… one nurse, one angel, loving me, my girl, my Gemma, Gemma, Gemma… colonels, officers, corporals, lads visiting me in hospital, looking down at me on the bed, what must they think, looking at this child of war? It could have been me? One day it is them: swallowed whole, by the Leviathan: WAR…they are not coming back, your names will be read out in your parish… HEART OF MIDLOTHIAN FOOTBALL CLUB: my flesh, my blood, men of my streets, of my town, my home: Speedie, Gracie, Currie, Wattie, Boyd, Allan, Ellis… the broken, the sick, the tired and the gassed: Paddy Crossan, my idol, my hero, never again to dash down the turf of Tynecastle… KICK THE BALL, BOYS! SCORE A GOAL FOR THE HEARTS! The maroon, the faces, the colours, the scarves, the wee boys meeting Bobby Walker, shaking his hand: his hand coming away, like they do, like they do… Oh! I want my daddy back… kick no more, sir, I have no legs, my heart has burst; the stench has burned away my lungs and my eyes no longer see… the books have no pages, those that do have no words, I can't see them any more, I never could, I never could… my mummy is drunk and I have to leave her and my daddy has died, pouring his maroon onto the Gorgie road, his body buried, eaten by worms, oh Daddy, please come home to me whilst the wee girls ask about the sea and why it's so big and when Tom comes back will I get a nice shell from the sea and if I put it to my ear will I hear it burst and cover me with dirt and flesh and teeth and eyes and rats and all of it I want all of it to just go away, just go away…

I woke up covered in sweat, breathing heavily. I saw the horrors of my dream clearly and whined quietly to myself. I moaned like a child for Mummy and for Gemma. I kept saying their names as one: *MummyGemma, MummyGemma*, on and on. Mother's softness; her unconditional, perfect love. Gemma, her sweetness, her fragrance and the velvet touch of her skin on mine, kissing my eyes, feeling her breath at night at the hotel when we lay together; here now, the pillow wet through moisture from my mouth and sweat.

Normally my dreams were not vivid, and usually forgotten moments after awakening. This was different. It was what was to come, to remain, and it started that night and sixty years later it is still here. It does not go away; but like watching a film that scares you the first time you see it, after repeat screenings the fear wears off as intimacy with it means knowing what is coming. It does not frighten me now.

I stood up and looked around the room, trying to gather my senses together in an attempt to reacquaint myself with normality. The electric light flickered and through it I noticed that my coat had fallen off the hook on the door and as I knelt down to pick it up, my head spun and I felt myself falling forward, only an outstretched arm reaching the door in time preventing me crashing over.

I went through to the lavatory, splashed my face and looked in the mirror. My eyes had dark rings so deeply ingrained that they resembled two black ridges running down parallel to my nose. The rest of what looked back at me was an unhealthy, clammy shade of greyish pale. I resembled an old actor wearing a bad make-up job that failed him, whilst playing a role far too young.

Drinking a glass of water, I remembered the papers that required Winston's signature. It gave me an excuse to go and talk to him. Talk to anyone. But Winston first. Always Winston.

I knocked on his door, the light shining through the glass above. I opened it and there he was sitting, upright in a chair next to his bed.

'Colonel?' I stood in the doorway. There was no answer.

'I have these papers for you to sign.' I walked over to him.

'Colonel?'

He still had not spoken or moved. I sat down on the edge of the bed.

'Bad day, eh?'

A slight twitch of the lips. 'Yes, very bad.'

His jacket and boots were off and a tumbler in his right hand rested on the arm of the chair. It was empty.

'Colonel? Are you alright?' The man, the room, everything felt strange. It was like another presence was there with us, hanging over our every word and movement. The weak, shadowy lighting and ghostly vapour the chilly air created as we spoke added to the eerie ambience I felt all around me this strange night.

There were no cigar fumes. He must have been sitting like this for hours.

Then I heard him mumble very slightly, *'Kop. Kop, Die Kop.'* He pronounced it 'Dee'.

'Colonel.' I reached over and put my hand on his arm.

'Shoot him, I must shoot him, he is mad, they do not see, see as I do. The Boers have lost, you stay, stay put, you newly promoted brigadier. You, who have stared into death's face this day, who have done as much as any man could do. The Dorsets, the Cameronians, the Rifles, the regiment my father wanted for me, are coming. My boys, my bluejackets are coming, you stay now, or I will shoot you down dead.'

'Winston!' And I slapped his face.

He looked down, closing his eyes.

'It's alright, Jamie. I am better now.' He soothed his face gently where I had struck him.

I took the glass from him, rinsed it and poured some water.

'Drink,' I ordered.

He took a few sips. 'Ghastly!'

'Colonel, I was worried! Ye were awa' wi' the fairies!'

'Bring me my brandy over.'

I fetched the bottle for him, he held out the glass and I poured.

'Sit down, my boy.'

I sat on the edge of the bed. 'Colonel, did you have a nightmare? It sounded strange, like you were remembering something very sad and painful to you.'

He collected himself and began to speak. 'I...I *was* remembering. Or rather, the *remembering* appeared all of a sudden to me. It was in South Africa. In Natal. Spion Kop. The *Look-out* Mountain. I was with the Light Horse and also performing my duties as a correspondent for the *Morning Post*. Our men had taken the hill, the *Kop*, on the evening before but in the morning when the light came up they were shot and shelled to hell by the Boers.'

He was recalling the battle of Spion Kop during the Boer War. It was fought to try to clear the way for British forces to relieve the besieged town of Ladysmith. Winston had been there as a young correspondent during the battle that had become a byword for ineptitude and had caused such a sensation back home. It had been lost, as so many of the early engagements of that bitter conflict were, through spectacular incompetence due to the British army's unpreparedness for fighting a first class opponent.

In this particular struggle, which resulted in appalling casualties, the near-superhuman ability of the ordinary British soldier to endure unbelievable hardship had nearly rescued the situation, only for it to be lost by crass stupidity and bungling from superior officers.

He continued, 'They had not dug the trenches properly for

their protection. The hill was a trap surrounded by artillery and Boer rifles. The commanding officer, Woodgate was killed and Colonel Thorneycroft, one of the finest men that ever lived, assumed command. All day they were blasted and attacked but they held on. Down below no one knew what was happening. I turned up late in the afternoon and decided to find out for myself.' He took a big gulp and shook the glass at me. 'More, James.'

I poured, and listened. 'I made my way up, it was carnage. Shells and bullets were passing over but I remained unscathed. I reached the summit and I, I...' He stopped, breathed in and out hard and then continued, 'I vomited; I vomited like never before in my life.' His eyes closed and he gulped and breathed in and out again. 'All over the plateau were our men. Lying in pieces. *White* men. Boys. Lancashire Fusiliers. Bits of them. Arms. Legs. Heads. Horrors I never dreamed existed.

'Oh, I had seen before dead men in Africa and India. Dead *black* men. Killed by bullet and lance. But never had I witnessed this. What hypocrisy! I was sick, again and again. I finally found Colonel Thorneycroft. He said they were just holding on but needed assistance and supplies. All I wanted to do was to get off that hill, that *acre of massacre* as it became known so I went back down and made my way to the commander's position to see General Warren.

'He charged me to report what I had seen. I told him he had to send orders up to hold on along with reinforcements, water, ammunition, cannon, immediately. He screamed, *"Who are you to tell me my business, you impudent young rogue!"* The fool, the old fool! I said I will take a message up. He shouted: *"Will someone shut up this insolent little shit!"* I nearly punched the old swine!'

He was becoming more animated and had downed most of the brandy. I was beginning to feel my own symptoms of stress increase the more he recounted and my earlier dreams swirled around me vividly as I gripped the top blanket of the bed and felt the sweat from my hand being soaked up.

'But I restrained myself.' His voice now settled into a calmer tone as he continued with the tale. 'He spoke to other officers and later I was sent for. I was told that Colonel Thorneycroft was this day promoted to brigadier, that supplies were on their way first thing in the morning, along with cannon, and fourteen hundred men would be making their way up this night. They must dig in and wait. I said "Sir, I want that message in writing." He cursed and ordered, *"Give this man what he requires."*

'I made my way back up the hill. God knows how I did it because I was in horror of what I would see again; in horror, Jamie! But I made it to Thorneycroft after stumbling over bodies once again and handed him the note. He looked at it but I could tell he was finished. He was far, far away, to some remote and shadowy distance. All he had left was telling him to leave this hill and go. Go! *"It's too hot. Too hot. We need a nice drink of water and a nice chair to sit on in the shade! We are all tired and we have to go now!"*

'The poor man's mind had gone. Twenty-four hours of shelling, bullets and his boys dying had done this to him. He had personally led counter attacks. When some men put up a white flag, he had it torn down and chased Boers running back down the hill but now he had no more to give. Enough. The well was dry. He had ordered withdrawal already and the men were preparing to leave. I said, "No, you cannot do this; here is a direct order from General Warren. You must stay put." *"Get out of my way, damn you!"* he bawled.

'I then removed my pistol from its holster. "Sir, I must warn you, I will shoot you dead if you leave this hill!" He looked at me and I saw the insanity in his eyes. *"Why, I should take a horsewhip to you! You damn fucking bastard!"* He pushed me aside and went off to discuss the note with Hill and Coke and the other colonels. They all agreed except Hill, who said, "We must stay; we cannot go down now, the message is quite clear." But Thorneycroft prevailed, through his rage.

'I walked down the *kop* with him. The colonel of the reserve force was coming up, a force of fourteen hundred men which included those from the Naval Division, for the cannon and he handed Colonel Thorneycroft a note and told him to get his arse back up that hill and redeploy right away but Thorneycroft said, "*I have done all I can, I will not go back up.*"

'So the relief force turned around and headed back, too. And we lost the chance to walk through to Ladysmith because the Boers returned next morning and planted their flag on that hill, that *Spion Kop.*'

He ceased talking and sat back.

'Would you have really shot Colonel Thorneycroft?' It was all I could think of to say as by now I was light-headed. I did not think I would pass out but felt like I was now outside myself, looking down on the individual sitting on the edge of Winston's bed. I felt almost euphoric; as if I had awoken from the peaceful but dream-filled oblivion of a dead faint, or the curious morphine high after I had left the Casualty Clearing Station at Bailleul.

He would not answer. 'It was not his fault. It was that fool, Warren. If he had behaved like a general should he would have gone up that hill himself. It would have taken him less than an hour and he would have seen what had happened and relieved Thorneycroft, who was finished, though what he had achieved that day was as remarkable a feat of military endeavour as you will ever see. No, Warren was to blame. But it will haunt me the rest of my life. For there I looked into the true face of war, Jamie. It was not in the broken bodies, the limbs, or the horrible dead images of the men that I saw its ghastly features. No, I saw its evil countenance in the eyes of

Colonel Thorneycroft!

'Afterwards, I wrote such nonsense in my correspondence about the thrill and excitement of war; but it was all bosh. It was for the readers, for money. *But I know what war really is* and I despise it with all my being.

'But I despise those who prosecute war with incompetence and stupidity even more. I sometimes imagine myself as a great leader who has to make terrible decisions and I *know* that I would make those decisions, however ruthless, however regrettable, in order that war is ended quickly and with as few deaths on *all* sides as possible.'

All I wanted now was my bed and sleep. I could barely keep my eyes open as I stood up to leave. I no longer needed to discuss my own horror; Winston had explained it all to me in his.

'My boy, you look very tired.' He turned from himself to me. 'Your mother and Gemma would be most angry with me for keeping you up so late.'

I made for the door, saying nothing.

'James,' he asked.

'Colonel?' I turned to him.

'Did I hear you address me as "*Winston*"?'

'I did, aye, and I'll probably do it again.'

'Well, there are times when it is appropriate for friends to address each other by their Christian names.'

'Goodnight, Colonel.'

'Goodnight, James.'

He was in better fettle for the final few days of the trip. We drove on to the city of Lille where he was asked onto the saluting stand to view the march-past of the recently liberated city.

The next day we came to a small village that we were advised was safe as it was now behind our lines, but as we got out to wander around it started to receive shellfire and we had to double back sharpish.

The more we saw and experienced, the more nervous, fearful and sick I became. I found myself starting at gunfire and staying close to the motor. Eddie noticed and would remain with me, or at other times, would go off with Winston and then make an excuse and return to the car.

Winston, as usual, was oblivious to my distress. I would see reminders of painful memories all around and feel that if I did not leave soon I would never get home. All I wanted to do was to get back on that boat and return to England. We were voyeurs; and what we were doing was wrong. Everywhere men were still dying and we were like some group of Roman noblemen viewing the gladiatorial games, stuffing our faces with fine food and wines whilst poor men spilled their guts in front of us in order to provide a good show.

It made me feel more that this world I was part of was not for me. It was Winston's world; and he was welcome to it.

In an attempt to control my stress, I would try and focus my mind on something warm and comforting: holding Gemma's hand as we strolled along the beach at Scarborough in the warm August sun. I would think up imaginary conversations between us but they were impossible to sustain because cutting in on these sweet reveries were the horrors of my nightmare, interposing, black and frightening: her darling face fading into that of a corpse and that horrendous smell of death materialising though not physically possible; but the essence of it came to me and all I could see was darkness and ghastly visions fighting a battle with the goodness of my soul.

Chapter Thirty

They called it 'shell shock' back then, 'battle fatigue' in the next war and I believe they call it 'combat stress' these days. Down the ages it has been known about by all soldiers and they have had to deal with it each in his own way. Some, of course, cannot.

As is known, in the Great War they shot you for it in many cases, if you were just a squaddie, whilst the officers were carted off to a nice hospital in Edinburgh where they were encouraged to 'talk' about it. They talked; the lads got shot.

I was now suffering from its effects along with Winston. But he had been through it all a lot longer than I and developed ways to deal with it. I was experiencing it for the first time and the real reason I'd turned down all his past requests to accompany him over to France was that I did not want to be near any reminders of the war.

I just *did not know* how I would react on hearing shellfire or gunshots again. In short, I was jumpy.

It was unfortunate in a way because the trips would have been interesting and given me the chance to see many things and meet a few eminent people. One of those he met was Prime Minister Clemenceau himself who asked him '*Petit ami Jamie écossais?*' My fame had travelled far and wide but I learned that it was because of my infamous outburst at the *Nation* debate in the House that the 'Tiger' had especially wanted to meet me.

If I had gone on those earlier trips I'm sure I would have gone through the same psychosis as I did on the one I have described. No soldier alive is immune to these stresses. Winston certainly was not. But he masked it like we all did. We *had* to. It made him irritable, argumentative and unbearable. In me, it induced stress that resulted in near black-out. Yet men had to remain and deal with it day in day out, whereas I had escaped it. This all added to my guilt. My way of dealing with the dreams and visions was just to put up with them, as I had to with my leg.

I remember when that film *The Battle of the Somme* was being screened around the country. It created a sensation because in those days before television and the mass media people back home had absolutely no conception of what the men were going through on the Western Front. I went to see it and it was fairly graphic, showing British dead and wounded, which had been expected to cause uproar but left many people feeling numbed at the shocking sight.

The scene in the film which stayed with me was not the desolation of the countryside with its flattened and treeless landscape or even the sight of the dead but of two British soldiers returning from the line. They were both dishevelled and neither was carrying his rifle but one of the men gave a nervy glance into the lens and I noted his right hand shaking uncontrollably as if attached to an electric charge as he and his comrade walked together past the camera. I instantly thought: shellfire.

When I saw this my hand went up to my face and I came over all of a sweat. I managed to compose myself and stayed for the film's entirety but for men like that poor soul there were no specialists to go to, no sofa to lie back on and scream away your pain to a 'counsellor'. There was not much assistance after the next war either.

Winston masked his stress in wanting to be near the guns, testing himself. No sane man will deliberately put himself where shot and shell may hit him. At least, that is my view and I have some experience. The man who does that is doing it solely to test himself, *to himself*. I believe that was why he did it and continued to do it into the next war. And his philosophy was formed that terrible night on Spion Kop: war is not for imbeciles and amateurs; certainly not the running of it from the very highest level, not if he had *his* way. One day he would get his way.

We returned to London, and days later it was all over. We were together with Eddie in Winston's office on that day, the eleventh, and that time, eleven o' clock. We looked out of the window along Northumberland Avenue and listened for Big Ben going off.

We shook each other's hands and Winston poured sherry. Crowds were beginning to gather outside and at the Palace, where the King was expected to make an appearance. Eddie left to make a telephone call.

'We have survived our war,' Winston pronounced, 'to return to our loved ones and to endeavour to improve the world that we have inherited. I insist that you have a whisky with me.' I had barely finished my sherry.

He drank whisky during the day with whacking great lumps of ice and soda. I took mine with ice only, because weakened whisky made me feel sick and I was beginning to savour the harsh, thick taste in my throat.

Winston made the drinks and handed me mine.

'If this war has to have a monument, it is to the effect that it has turned James Melville into a whisky drinker!' he joked. 'I have long suspected that my Scotch has not evaporated but in fact fallen victim to the Caledonian in my office!'

'You've caught me, Colonel.' I took a sip. 'I can almost tell the difference between each decanter now.' I looked hard at my glass. 'But I don't know if that's much of an achievement.'

'What is the matter, Jamie?'

I had yet to tell him that Gemma had agreed to marry me. I'd kept that from him since August but the reason was, I wanted to tell him only after I had made my decision about whether to move to Scarborough. I did not want to do that until the war ended.

Back in August it was still uncertain when it would be over. But the truth was, I kept putting the decision off. I was keeping Arnold waiting too, and felt bad about that. It was beginning to drag me down, the weight of the whole thing along with other concerns.

I leaned back in the chair. He settled back, in his listening mode.

'Colonel, I'm just mixed up right now. I don't know what I've done for the last two years. I wouldn't have missed being around you for anything. But my worry is: where am I going now? I've no trade, I've a crippling injury, I've no friends my own age and I only have Gemma, Eddie and you. I've traced my brothers; one I just don't understand but the other I feel close to and I want to be near him again.

'I want to marry Gemma. But what can I give her? I don't even have a home. I live in a hotel, which is very nice of course, but I think about my dad. He was married at eighteen. I'm eighteen now, too.

'But I feel more like I'm *one hundred and eighteen*. I feel like another person. I was a child when it all began. I can hardly imagine now how I survived it all. I think it was because I *was* a child and that I was no harm to anyone and saw no threat that I survived. Now there's no war, there's no purpose for me.'

'My boy, whilst you are here with me there will always be purpose,' Winston stressed. 'You can find a home, you can earn money, and these things are not obstacles. You may only have a small number of friends, as you say, but you can find more! I really think, James, that you are suffering from and please, there is no condescension meant here, but from feelings of inferiority and insecurity.

'These are feelings that I, yes, I, have known! The looks askance at your stick! The feeling that it reflected badly on me, *on me*! that I am seen with you! Nonsense, my boy! I am *proud* to be seen with you, for you are a warrior! Remember when we shot at the German trenches! I saw the light of battle in your eye that only we soldiers share!

'Yes, I know all about that patrol you went on behind my back! You young rascal! It would have been me as your commanding officer who would have had the sad duty of writing to your mother should something have befallen you! I knew of it but could not, would not, cage such a spirit, for that would have been a sin! A sin against the God of youth! For in you I saw myself! Your cheek and impudence, ah, don't think I did not know,' and blow me I absolutely burst out with laughter at this, 'yes, I know what you did to the tea of General -----; your little Ayrshire friend Jackie Lawson told me! It cost me a bottle of wine but I got the truth out of him,' Jackie was one of the lads I told about the rat shit in the general's tea. 'And I knew from then on that you were like me! Indefatigable!

'My boy, marry Gemma in good time. If you are truly in love, and I know you are, do this and let your lives together be happy! I will find you a good job with me. We will find you a home. Fear not. You also, like me, have "survivor's guilt"; yes, all soldiers feel this way. But it is natural.

'Now, we will dine out for lunch today, if we can find somewhere, and then you shall join in with our countrymen the celebration of not just victory, but that at last the pain is at an end and we may all of us strive to make a better world to live in.'

The war for the 6th/7th ended as they were temporarily designated as a Pioneer Battalion. They were involved in counter attacking the German drive at Locre during the great offensive of March and April 1918.

After that the battalion was placed wherever it was needed

but it finally ended up in May at St Omer, reduced to a training unit and eventually absorbed into a battalion of the Cameronians. Thus the 6th/7th Royal Scots Fusiliers faded from history but with a record every man who served in it could be proud of.

I was happy to learn that among the men that survived were my pals Drew Pirie, Jackie Lawson, Corporal MacLeod, Sergeant Douglas and officers Captain Gibb, Mr McDavid and my chum 'Bomber' Hakewill-Smith.

Maroons were going off all over London and people spilled out of offices onto the streets as news spread of the armistice. Already that morning as the bells pealed the eleventh hour, thousands amassed around Buckingham Palace and heard the King address the throng that gathered. Earlier that morning, unbeknownst to me, Winston had telephoned the Queen Alexandra Hospital, pulled rank and arranged for Gemma to come off duty to meet us at the hotel.

Due to the mad scenes it took a while for her to arrive even though it was not far, but turn up she did and we made our way through the crowds to a restaurant off Leicester Square. Mrs Churchill joined us, though heavily pregnant, and I must say that that was one of the great memories of my life, Gemma and I along with Winston and Eddie at the table with wine and good food celebrating the end of the war.

'So, Gemma, what now for you?' asked Winston, after the usual stories about himself.

We were holding hands under the table as she replied, 'Oh well, Colonel.' (I had always told her to address him as this and why. That made two people who called him the name he always wanted to be known by.) 'It all depends on this young man I know.'

'Ah,' said Winston, smelling a plot, 'and is this young gentleman in a position where he has to make a decision on his future regarding a certain young lady?'

'Why, yes, Colonel! However did you know?' she said, eyes flashing at him.

I played along, of course. 'Well,' I said, 'maybe this young bloke should get his finger out, as we say in Scotland.'

'Horrid!' exclaimed Gemma.

'Yes, but apt,' stated Winston. 'One's finger must never be allowed to prevent a decision being made.'

'Well, as you put it like that, Colonel,' I said, 'I was waiting on a special occasion to let you know. Today is that occasion. I have already asked Miss Gemma Rebecca Ashby to marry me.'

'What was her response?'

Giggling now and with a hand to her mouth she said. 'Yes, oh yes!' Eddie and Clemmie came around the table to congratulate us and then the tears flowed, including Winston's.

The subject being brought up did remind me of my concerns again. It was sad as the lunch had gone so well but I was able to mask my worry, as I did not want to spoil the day. In all the two years of knowing Gemma I had still not met her parents. Normally that would have been unthinkable given the conventions of the day but the war was changing all of that.

Gemma had grown in those years. She had a career now in an exacting profession and was no longer willing to accept many precepts of the stringent ethos of the times. The power behind the Ashby family throne was old Granma and of course we got on like a house on fire. But Gemma wanted acceptance from Mum and Dad of her decision on whom she chose to marry. She was under twenty-one and needed consent and, Granma or not, they could still deny her that.

I knew all along I might have to drag Winston into our personal affairs. I was worried about being seen as selfish but knew he would understand. Anyway, he would love the challenge of it because if there was one thing that man loved it was action.

'What is the name of your father and what does he do, Gemma?' Winston asked innocently. He knew all this, of course, as I had told him long before.

We were on the dessert by now and I was on my second piece of cherry pie and cream.

'Roderick Ashby. He's the senior partner at Ashby, Limehouse and Taylor.'

'Jesus Christ!' Winston leaped out of his seat. 'Fart-arse Ashby! As God is my judge, this will be wonderful! Oh! Gemma, my dear, I really must apologise for my language!' I truly admired his performance over my bowl.

'Whatever do you mean?' Gemma asked, struggling to contain her mirth. Sometimes Winston could surprise with his choice of invective, which, to the uneducated, i.e. those who did not know him well enough, could cause quite a stir.

'Oh, forgive me, my dear Gemma! But that man, your father, is an old school chum of mine!'

'Really! What do you know of him? Oh, do tell, Colonel, please!' She was eager to hear as I prepared myself for what was on its way...

'Well... how does one tell a daughter such a story?' Winston pretended to struggle. 'It really is not for the ears of a well-brought-up young lady!'

'Colonel, I'm a nurse, you know! If you don't tell me I shall never speak to you again!'

'Oh, dear!' Eddie theatrically held his hand in front of his eyes. He too had a good idea of what was to follow.

'Winston, don't you dare!' Clemmie, sensing danger, warned half-heartedly.

'A fate worse than very death, Gemma!' the colonel exclaimed, ignoring all the protestations and continued, 'As you have threatened me with such then I must tell you all, and may you forgive me afterwards. Well, here is the tale. You will know that your father went to school with me at Harrow. We were not friends as we had a history of disagreement.

'One day we were playing rugger and he was put in the scrummage at number eight. Now, as you may not know, not being an aficionado of rugby football, the number eight must place his head in such a position that it is fixed between both locks, that is, his head is jammed between two bums! It so happened that I was the owner that day of one of the said posteriors! Your father had a history of beastliness towards me and I had sworn revenge. So, on learning the team sheet that afternoon, for luncheon that day I had consumed strong chillies and beans in order to stir those regions that are gaseous in the lower body.

'And when the time came during the game when a scrummage was called, your father would settle down in his position as number eight. I would await the moment when the chillies and the beans had combined enough to create a truly venomous coagulation then let loose the most powerful and horribly noxious fart, full in the unprotected face of the number eight, your dear daddy!'

Gemma and I were both nearly under the table, crying with laughter. Eddie was snickering into his hands. Clemmie was looking to the side, hand over her mouth, eyes filled with mirth, her body shaking uncontrollably.

'Oh, Winston!' she uttered.

'But little did I know,' he continued, reaching his denouement, 'that I had been too generous in my choice of chilli and that by the second scrummage called I was feeling more than just the normal stirrings; that something way, way more volatile was being created in my bowels.

'The next scrum was called, we took our positions, I felt your father behind me, prepared for action. I could wait no more and suddenly the most cataclysmic, runniest and most diarrhoeic wet fart exploded from my behind and caught the most unfortunate number eight full in the mouth! Oh, you can imagine my horror! But despite such calamities I am pleased to tell you that Harrow prevailed that day. And from then on our number eight acquired a new nickname, that of 'Fart-arse'. Though I was somewhat jealous, as the fart and the arse in question were most definitely mine and not his!'

With that ended the story. What became of Winston's shorts, I thought best not to ask.

Chapter Thirty-One

Eddie said his goodbyes. He was off to a party at the Adelphi being attended by many of his artistic friends including those from the famous 'Bloomsbury' group. Winston and Clemmie left us to prepare for a meal that evening at Number 10 with Lloyd George. They had recently had a row over Winston's future in government; it had been patched up and a sign of that was Winston's being allowed in for the victory dinner. I was happy for him and he left us his farewell:

'James, you must take care of this young lady, it will be very busy soon but you both must stay and be a part of the moment. Join with our countrymen, for it is *you* that have won this victory.' He and Gemma hugged and he shook my hand and ruffled my hair. 'I have booked a table at the Savoy Grill for you both. The bill is paid for.

'This is a momentous day, James. The most terrible war in the history of mankind has ended and you are to be engaged to this lovely young woman! Enjoy the rest of it and I insist that you have a very good meal this evening with some fine wine and worry not about "Fart-Arse!" He winked at Gemma. 'Your wee laddie Jamie and your Uncle Winston, between us, shall take care of all that, Gemma my dear!'

They left us and we wandered into Piccadilly. It was mid-afternoon and we strolled around as the crowds became bigger then wandered back along Whitehall and made our way up to St James's Park for a while, but it was too cold to sit for long. Later we had our meal of which we did Winston proud and left the restaurant and stood in the Strand together.

'Where do you want to go?' I asked.

'Anywhere, as long as it's with you.'

We headed for Trafalgar Square where it seemed all

London had congregated. There were bonfires being lit as advertising hoardings were torn down and fed to the flames as groups of soldiers danced around with girls singing *Keep the Home Fires Burning*, but the atmosphere was pleasant though drink was seen being passed around everywhere. Later, vehicles left around the Square were torched and added to the conflagrations.

We sat for a while, watching the increasing multitude, the numbers of people within the Square now so dense that the entire mass began to sway like a football crowd but all good-natured as I held on tight to Gemma.

But the exuberance of the afternoon had suddenly worn off me. I had been able to forget so much for a short time on a day that was about celebration, but, for many, about reflection and remembrance.

I now seemed unable to focus on the joy around me; I could not comprehend the words of any song, the smoke from the fires brought back to me the acrid cordite, the maroons still being fired were the shells that nearly destroyed me, the cloying mass of rain-soaked clothing mingled with sweat and unwashed bodies became the putrid, fetid stench of corruption built into the trench walls and palisades; the remains of the dead, killed earlier, blasted and exploded into parts and pieces and left where they dropped to earth. I felt the bile rise as one reveller was pushed against me; a choking blast of his body odour hit and, trying to turn to avoid it, I was startled as my eyes focused on a sight set against the flames and glow from the fires of khaki-clad carousers' faces transmuting into ghastly apparitions of maggot-infested corpses.

What I had by now started calling my 'visions' had returned and they were extracting unsolicited payment for this day's merriment and salutation.

'Gemma, let's get away from here,' I was just able to croak.

Mesmerised by what was going on about her, she was

oblivious to my distress.

'Please, let's just walk somewhere and find a seat. Please?' I begged.

Now sensing my discomfort she asked what was wrong but I was short with her and just said that I had to leave.

We wandered off towards the Strand and found a seat outside Charing Cross Station and with relief I sat down.

'Are you alright now, darling?' she asked me, worriedly.

'Aye, it'll pass.' She knew all about the dreams I had been having.

'It must have been all the noise; it upset you and brought those bad feelings back.'

I took her hand. 'I'll be alright in a minute, don't you worry now.'

Though we had a seat, it was cold and I got up.

'It's alright now, I don't want you sitting here, it's too cold.'

'I'm fine really; I want you to just relax. *Sit down* this minute! You've gone very pale.' She took my wrist and checked her watch.

'So, Scarborough?' I asked.

'Is it to be the seaside and cod and chips and not the honourable member for Gorgie Road then?'

'Aye.'

'Have you told him yet?' She edged nearer to me and her lovely face was very close.

'Not in so many words but I think he suspects something is up.'

'*Can* you tell him?'

'Gemma, I love Winston as if he was my father. I can hardly imagine a world now without two people: you and him. But the world he lives in, I'm tired of. In future I may be hungry to be part of such a world again. But the future is just that, the future; and who knows. I'm only interested in *now*.'

We stood up and arm in arm we began to walk back

towards the square.

'Do you want me to be there when you tell him?' she asked.

'No, I'll do it. I have to do it myself, I owe him that.'

'Can you ever completely walk away from Winston, though? Can you do that?'

'It's been the hardest decision I've ever had to make. I hate the thought of upsetting him in any way. But you have to understand, only now I *understand,* we both have given each other equal amounts. We owe each other nothing and we owe each other everything. He owes me his life and I owe him *a life.* He only has two or three real friends in the world. I think I'm one of them because I don't want anything from him and I'll never be a threat. That's not healthy grounds to base a friendship on but in the world he lives in and chooses to live in it's the safest basis of friendship he's going to get.

'I truly believe that one day he'll become prime minister. I do. He's so brilliant! Nothing is beyond him. To know such a man! To call him a friend! That for *me* is enough. But I want to go my own way now. I *know* that one day I'll be back with him. I don't know how, why or when I just know it. Men like Winston don't come around very often.' I stopped and let go her hand looking over the mass of people gathered before us.

'I feel I'm old tonight. I feel like I've lived a hundred lifetimes. I keep thinking of *them. I can't stop thinking of all of them.'*

We were on the edge of the throng, the National Gallery behind us. She looked, as I did, at the scene before us. More and more bonfires lit, revellers arm in arm, uniforms of all the services of the Allied nations, couples together, women with their children in tow, allowing them this chance to stay up late in order to bear witness. There were trumpets blasting out cavalry charges, bugles, a saxophone, violins, drums, cymbals. Flags of all the lands of the empire and others. Waiters coming out of their restaurants with bottles of wine, handing drinks out to anyone passing by. Office workers, labourers arm in arm, drinking from bottles in brown paper bags, shop workers, policemen, the pipes sounding *Scotland the Brave, Scotland the Brave...*

'Can you understand? Do you understand *why*?' I had to speak over the din; the commotion seemed to be getting louder.

She only understood so much. The rest was all my own to reconcile.

'Jamie, I do. I *think* I do. But really, what is London to me anyway? My life is with you. If that's where you want to go, I'll go with you, you know that. I know that you would always think of me. You think more of others than yourself, you always have.

'That's why I trust you. How can I not? I love you. You're my boy.' She squeezed my arm. 'Wherever you go, I'm with you always; you must know that, *always*.'

We stood up together and with an arm around each other's waists we joined with the night, with every one of this night, with those who *were* this night: *Thomas Reid, David Thom, John Paterson, Duncan Davidson; all of them and all of the others.* We made our way through the crowds, past the Column, onwards through the Arch towards the Palace, arm in arm with our people to see the King, who was still waving on the balcony, now lit up with stage lights for all to see; shaking hands, kissing, singing, laughing, drinking; those who stopped to weep, comforted by strangers, *who were not strangers*, for there were none anywhere on this night. We danced and revelled our way along the Mall; in joining with thousands of others, the two of us becoming a small measure of history.

Chapter Thirty-Two

We had set our minds to it. I wrote to Arnold, giving him my answer; though I had business to settle in London first. I didn't mention our engagement or marriage plans as I had yet to resolve this with Gemma's parents. On that score I wasn't accepting no for an answer.

If it meant us moving up to Scarborough against their wishes then so be it. We would marry later and consent could go to blazes. The Humphries home was big enough for all of us anyway. They were understanding people. But I would worry about all that after the actual meeting with the Ashbys. I was not looking forward to it.

But I was unafraid. I was a pretty assertive Jamie Melville these days and had learned so much over the last few years. No one pushed me around (no one ever did) and if the Ashbys didn't like it, they could get knotted.

Gemma was worried, but tried to conceal it. They were still her parents and though she had broken from them by becoming a nurse, marriage was a different kettle of fish. But I needed to make them understand that I was no longer Jamie Melville of Wardlaw Place, Gorgie. I was James Melville, a young man experienced of war, had mixed with the highest in government and was now in line to take up the reigns of part-control in a thriving business.

I was a bit naïve of course, but as far as I was concerned I would always have an ace up my sleeve if things got tight: Winston Spencer Churchill, about to be newly installed Secretary of State for War.

Gemma's parents lived in Kensington. Granma did not live far away and I went to see her first on my own for some moral encouragement.

As always the hospitality was overwhelming. I sat back with some marble cake, which is one of my favourites, and she poured me a whisky. She asked me if I wanted a real drop as she suspected the reason why I had come round alone.

I explained how I was feeling and she laughed. 'That son of mine! You let me deal with him. You must ask him, though; I can't do that for you! I know what his reaction will be but don't concern yourself at first, just remain calm, Jamie. Gemma tells me you have a quick temper!' She laughed again. 'So have I! But on this occasion, restrain yourself and await events! He must understand that you are a good catch. If he cannot see that and just sees a young man trying to marry above himself, he will get the end of my tongue, believe me! I have known you all this time and I cannot think of a more suitable match for my granddaughter! That little girl requires love. She has never had it at home but she has found it now in you, my dear.'

'Thanks, Granma,' I said, for that's what I called her. I only knew my maternal grandmother but very briefly. 'I'll take your advice.'

She knew all about Scarborough. 'I know it'll be hard for you when we're both away from London but we'll visit regular, I mean to. I'll miss London more than I shall ever know; I just hope I'm doing the right thing in all this.'

'You are, Jamie. You've hardly put a foot wrong at any time. I'll miss you both but you must write regularly. Remember, I spent time up there years ago. I stayed at the Grand and can ask for my old room for a few days in order to imbibe the sea air! So do *not* concern yourselves over me; this old harridan has years left in her yet!'

I went over and kissed her. I loved this old woman who had been so kind to me. In many ways she was a terrifying creature, but had always been there for us both unconditionally. I would badly miss visiting her for her advice and support.

I had taken round our Christmas presents and she handed me an envelope in return. I didn't open it till I left; inside was a cheque for £500.

The day arrived and I was invited for 'afternoon tea'. I was dressed in a new suit and looked the best I could. I took the stick as I had nothing to hide as far as I was concerned but I wasn't looking for war-wound kudos either.

Mr Ashby was a tall, thin, cadaverous type. Mrs Ashby was a very good-looking woman, I have to say. But I resolved not to look to her as it very much seemed from my discussions with Gemma that Fart-arse ruled the roost. Or so he thought.

He asked about Winston's new appointment. I said that it would also cover the Air Ministry. This was not widely known as yet but I thought that letting this bit of information out would let him see how close I was to the real action.

'I knew Churchill at school,' he mused. 'A bounder then and a bounder still, by all accounts.'

I kept a lid on my temper, though it was not easy.

He looked directly at me. 'However, I believe he has had some successes despite his failures, and there have been many of them, and I have to accept that the prime minister knows his business.'

'Where will you live now, Jamie?' asked Mrs Ashby.

'Still at the ministry offices until I find a place of my own.'

'You've lived quite a gypsy-like existence, James,' snooted Ashby.

'Yes, and it's all been in the service of my country.' That hit home; he sniffed and said, 'Quite admirable, of course, but I have heard that the life of the gypsy becomes attractive and after a while one finds it less and less desirable to settle.'

'I'm no gypsy and I do wish to settle and that's why I've

come to your home this day. I have something of importance to announce to you all. As you know, your daughter and I have been seeing each other for some time. A strong and enduring love and affection has grown between us; so much so that I have asked her to marry me. Therefore I wish to ask your permission to announce our engagement with a view to marrying when we find a suitable date in time.'

I felt I had handled that well; I was also pleased that I would correctly precipitate the immediate response.

'Marriage? And how would you be able to support my daughter?'

'I have a choice of options. As you are aware, Mr Churchill has now been appointed Secretary of State for War and takes up his post early in the New Year. He insists on retaining his private secretary, Edward Marsh, whom he has brought over from Munitions. Edward desires that I remain his assistant. My salary will rise accordingly. I have also had an opportunity presented to me to become a partner in a successful business run by my brother's foster father in north Yorkshire. So I have a decision to make. However the decision to marry your daughter I've already made. All that I require from you is your blessing.'

'I would have thought you had no decision to make in the matter of your future employment. The government, service to one's king, must come first,' the snobbish bastard snorted.

'That's for me to decide. And now I must leave in order for you to discuss among yourselves what I have proposed. I'm required urgently by the minister.' Winston wanted to know how they took the news and was meeting me for dinner. 'Good day to you all. Gemma, I'll see you this evening?'

I left feeling confident, pleased with my performance. I had looked them in the eye and hadn't blinked. The only reason I suspected for their saying no would have been a snobbish one anyway. They may play the 'age' card. Well, Gretna Green was full of people like us. That did not bother me a jot. I did not concern myself any longer with that particular problem. What I was truly dreading now was what I was about to tell Winston.

We met up at his office in the ministry. I preferred to speak to him there in private behind closed doors prior to going to dinner. I was quaking, I have to say.

He was scribbling away as I knocked and went in. He motioned to the chair and the drinks on a side table. I was glad, as I needed one then, if only to have something to focus on.

I asked how Clemmie was, as their new baby, a girl named Marigold, was born a few days after the Armistice. Sadly, this poor wee soul would not have a long life.

'Thank you, Jamie! Mrs Churchill is fine and sends her regards and I of course will send on yours to her.'

'How are you settling into your new portfolio?'

'The business of war goes on though the actual hostilities have ended! I have to set about reducing an army of millions to less than 400,000! The plan of my predecessor is already causing great concern as men who have served the longest are the last to be demobilised. Scandalous! A shambles, James! It can only take someone like me to sort it out!'

'I'm sure you will, Colonel.' I was feeling morose. Whenever I came into contact with that man it seemed like he had a spell over me. I just loved being around him for the fun, excitement and the unexpected that were always guaranteed. To be at the heart of the running of the country, to see it all happen, *how* it happened, did I really want to give this all up to sell fish in Scarborough?

He leaned back. 'Oh dear, I know that James Melville look; did it not go well at the Ashbys?'

I looked up, 'It was hard to tell, Colonel. I have to say, I think I acquitted myself very well thanks to the good advice of you and Granma. I can't see any logical reason why they would say no. There is none, other than sheer obstinacy and damned snobbery.'

'We shall have to await their decision and plan the next stage of the campaign accordingly. I believe you would have acquitted yourself admirably, James. I know you so well.'

I just did not know how to come out with it, that was the truth. I had played around in my mind various scenarios, practised speeches in my head, anticipated his reactions but even whilst doing this I still knew that when the day came I would struggle.

I was Jamie Melville. I sat up straight in the chair.

'Colonel, there's something I have to tell you.'

'Come into the private rooms then, my boy. We must not be interrupted.'

He led me through the door and down the stairs. We sat down across from each other with our drinks: I knew that Winston always liked to look directly at you when he was in a serious discussion.

I took a breath. 'Colonel, I've been offered a good job by my brother's foster father in Scarborough. As you know he owns a small business that is doing well but he wants me to replace someone who is retiring and become the manager of the office. The view is that the business will be passed on to the three of us: Tom, Arthur and me. It seems I've made a good impression on Mr Humphries when I've been up there. There's a hospital in Scarborough and Gemma wants to remain a nurse and she can be transferred there.

'I'm seriously considering the offer. But the problem will be if the Ashbys refuse to allow me to marry Gemma. We talked about it but we don't want to leave here together under a cloud. We want things done proper. We want an official announcement of our engagement. That'll keep things respectable. I...' I was struggling now. 'I have to do what it right... what is...'

'It *is right* and proper and respectable, but how pompous these words can sound!' Winston cut in as I was clearly struggling. 'You are in love, you are a fine young man and she is a fine young woman! I cannot do much to influence the decision of Roderick Ashby but I can offer to dine with him and provide a reference. Now, that will ask a lot of me, James, for I heartily despised the boy and have no great hopes for the man! But it would not be too disagreeable and if it made all the difference, I should be glad to be of service.

'As for Scarborough, I have long suspected an inner turmoil in you, but it is a credit to you that you have appeared to have suffered the agonies of indecision. This is my response: I simply do not want to lose you. I believe you can achieve great things at my side. Eddie has given me very good reports on the standard of your work and I need no one to give me reports on something far more important: on the standard of your character. It is of the very highest calibre.

'However, the world of politics does have perils and requires certain other abilities. One of them is one that you lack; and it is not a crime to be deficient of it as it demonstrates yet another example of your strength: deceit, and being able to lie. You are incapable of doing these things, my boy, and when you attempt it you make a very poor job. Now, I am a practised liar and deceiver; I have had to be in order to overcome obfuscation, complacency and downright ineptitude in others! I can recognise those faults and happily in you I see no sign of them. I accept that this world that we inhabit makes you feel uncomfortable. I believe it should *not*. But I strongly believe you have particular qualities and abilities and that someday these will be utilised fully in some special way.

'But you are only eighteen years of age and there is plenty of time ahead of you to decide exactly what you want to be in life. That is why I *know* that this is not the end for Colonel Churchill and the finest batman in the British army.

'I believe this present offer you have been made is well within your capabilities. It has more pluses than minuses. I will list them: you will be living in a very nice town; you will be amongst your own flesh and blood, your brothers. You will have security. You will have Gemma with you, who, as you say, can continue her very fine work in the hospital there. You can in time start a family. You are halfway between Edinburgh and London and can visit either with ease anytime and I would feel it remiss of you if you did not visit me when you were down here. In all this remember that you will *always* have a life waiting for you back in London should you so desire. More importantly than all that,' and his eyes twinkled, 'you will quite happily have major distance between you and your charming future in-laws! Though I know you will miss Grandmama Ashby, that fine woman.'

I was unashamedly tearful now and rubbing my eyes. But I never felt ashamed crying in front of him.

He reached over and patted my hand. He had made it so easy, as always. As deep down within me, I knew he would.

'Now Jamie, I believe you have made your decision and I know the pain it has caused you; it will pain me and my wife and Eddie also. But there is something I must demand of you even at this late hour and *I will not accept any other answer than a positive response to this demand*.

'I believe fervently that one day I shall be called upon to undergo a great mission. This duty will not just be to our country but for a cause far higher even than that. What it is, I know not, I only know that it *will* happen. Even as a small boy I believed I walked with my ancestor, John Churchill, the Duke of Marlborough, who saved Europe from tyranny.

'There will be a calling one day and I shall be the one summoned. I know I can only speak of this to very few. You are one of them. When that time arrives, and I know not when, I will require the services of good men, a group of close and trusted confidantes understanding of the danger, who will throw themselves willingly and unthinkingly into the breach to assist me in my mighty task. You shall be one. Will you be at my side?'

It was not flannel, neither was it mystical nonsense. I was under the spell and would always be. It was not said to provide me with a convenient get-out clause. He believed every word of it; and so did I.

I wiped my eyes. 'Of course, I'll be there. Where would you be without me? When the time comes, you won't have to call; I'll already be at your side.'

'Good, then it is settled. Now go and wash your face and let us repair to dinner for we must be ready to hear of Gemma's news. We three friends shall drink to Peace, to Scarborough and to our future endeavours together.'

We met up with Gemma at dinner at a restaurant near the ministry. Winston and I were gassing away as usual when she came in and her place was set.

'Well my dear, tell!' beseeched Winston. 'The tension is killing us both!'

She took a spoonful of soup. 'Oh, it was so very funny!'

'What do you mean, funny?' I said in exasperation as I had been on edge all day. 'Funny? Funny what?'

'My father said that he, Jamie, was just like you, Colonel, and had been "around that scoundrel Churchill too long and I will be damned if I allow my daughter to marry such a common rogue!"'

'Cheeky bastard!' I roared and made to get up.

'Jamie, where are you going?' she asked, agog.

'I have had enough! I'm going round there to belt his bloody jaw, this minute!'

'Sit down, James!' Winston grabbed my arm and swung me back to my seat.

I sat there brooding, outraged. What had this man wanted from me? I was a respectable person with bright prospects. I would love and take care of his daughter and to be called a scoundrel and a rogue was too much. A rogue was someone criminal and I did not take kindly to being described as such. Or common, either for that matter.

'No man alive calls me that!' I thought out loud. 'No one!'

'Calm down, James!' Winston demanded. 'I feel there is more to be added to the story from Gemma if you will please allow her to finish! I implore you to keep your temper under control! Go on, my dear.'

'Please let me finish, Jamie; as the colonel says, keep calm! There is more. Later on, Granma came to the house. Well, you know how unusual that is. She never visits us there. I was very upset with it all and told her what had happened.

'She sat us down in the sitting room and told my father that if he did not allow us to marry, she would alter her will! Yes, you should have seen Daddy's face! He gave in there and then and gave me his consent! Oh Jamie, we're going to be married!'

'Wonderful!' exclaimed Winston. 'I demand to be the first to kiss the prospective bride in congratulations!' and they both leaned over each other and kissed. I felt such a burden falling away from me that it was if I had been pushed back against my seat; my arms and legs felt heavy, I began to sweat and my breathing became difficult.

'Jamie, Jamie are you alright?' Gemma said, concernedly.

'My boy, you have gone very pale, do you require some fresh air?'

'I… I'm alright, Colonel.' Then I became quite light-headed, 'I feel like I'm going to pass out.' They both helped me to the door and once I was outside, the cold air revived me somewhat.

I sat on the edge of the road. Gemma knelt down and took my pulse as Winston rested a hand on my shoulder.

'I have seen this young man like this before. I believe it to be the result of stress,' Winston pronounced.

'His pulse was racing but it seems to be easing down to normal again.' Very handy having a girlfriend who is a nurse, at times.

'I feel better now,' I said. 'It's just that I couldn't breathe and I thought I was going to faint. Can we go back inside now as I still have my dessert waiting for me? It's Bakewell tart.'

They both looked at each other.

'I think, Gemma,' said Winston with a wink, 'your new fiancé has made an immediate and full recovery.'

It all settled into place quickly enough soon after that. Gemma's transfer request was the only thing outstanding but Winston would be able to hurry that along. I sent a telegram to Tom, telling him to have two rooms made up.

Winston took me for a slap-up meal at the Café Royal the night before we left London, and regaled me with more stories. As one tale concluded, he paused to relight his cigar.

I just had to ask him.

'Colonel, would you shoot Thorneycroft on Spion Kop if it happened *now*?'

He puffed away at his cigar. 'Yes, I would shoot him.'

I felt somehow that he was holding something back.

'I would shoot *to wound him.*'

That was what I expected him to say. Though I am still not sure it is what I would have expected him to do.

Finally, I had to know the answer to something more personal.

'Was I really the finest batman in the British army? I was just a wee boy! Surely you've been having me on all this time?'

He blew a smoke ring. 'Unquestionably, yes; you were and are. Remember you were serving the *finest* officer in the British army; do you think *I would settle for second best?*'

After the meal he handed me my references with three signatures attached: Edward Marsh, Winston Leonard Spencer Churchill and David Lloyd George. Yes, the Welsh wizard had appended his name.

I met him once when he came into the ministry for a meeting. He sat with me while waiting for Winston to come downstairs from some other office he was in at the time. He was utterly charming and asked me if I was the famous Jamie Melville.

'I didn't know I was famous, sir!'

'Oh, but you are, boyo! It's common knowledge around these parts that there is only one man who can put Winston in his place and I heard it was you! You must tell me your secret, eh?' I looked into the most sparkling pair of eyes I have ever seen.

'Well, sir, if I told you that it wouldn't be a secret any more would it?'

He roared with laughter and slapped my hand.

'Good one, lad, good one! Now I want to see you at my place for tea next time that boss of yours comes over, eh? Don't forget now, eh?'

The invite never did come but I would get to Number 10 one day by myself.

If you want to find out how, you'll have to wait and hope I last long enough to tell you.

THE END